PENGUIN  CLASSICS

RUTH

ELIZABETH CLEGHORN GASKELL was born in London in 1810, but she spent her formative years in Cheshire, Stratford-upon-Avon and the north of England. In 1832 she married the Reverend William Gaskell, who became well known as the minister of the Unitarian Chapel in Manchester's Cross Street. For sixteen years she bore children, worked among the poor, travelled and, latterly, began to write. In 1848 *Mary Barton* ensured her instant success. Two years later she began writing for Dickens's magazine, *Household Words*, to which she contributed fiction for the next thirteen years; her most notable work being another industrial novel, *North and South* (1855). In 1850 she met Charlotte Brontë, who became a life-long friend. After Charlotte's death she was chosen by Patrick Brontë to write *The Life of Charlotte Brontë* (1857), a probing and sympathetic account of this great Victorian novelist. Elizabeth Gaskell's position as a clergyman's wife and as a successful writer introduced her to a wide circle of friends, both from the professional world of Manchester and from the larger literary world. Her output was substantial and completely professional. Dickens discovered her resilient strength of character when trying to impose his views on her as editor of *Household Words*. She proved that she was not to be bullied, even by a man of such genius as he. Her later works *Sylvia's Lovers* (1863), *Cousin Phillis* (1864) and *Wives and Daughters* (1866) reveal developments in new literary directions. Elizabeth Gaskell died suddenly in November 1865.

ANGUS EASSON is Professor of English at the University of Salford. He has previously lectured at the University of Newcastle-upon-Tyne and at the Royal Holloway College, University of London. His publications include *Elizabeth Gaskell* and *Elizabeth Gaskell: The Critical Heritage* and, as editor, Elizabeth Gaskell's *Mary Barton*, *North and South*, *Wives and Daughters* and *Cousin Phillis and Other Tales*. He has also edited *The Old Curiosity Shop* for Penguin Classics and, as co-editor, volume 7 of Dickens's letters for Clarendon Press.

ELIZABETH GASKELL

RUTH

Edited with an Introduction and Notes by
ANGUS EASSON

PENGUIN BOOKS

PENGUIN BOOKS

Published by the Penguin Group
Penguin Books Ltd, 27 Wrights Lane, London w8 5tz, England
Penguin Books USA Inc., 375 Hudson Street, New York, New York 10014, USA
Penguin Books Australia Ltd, Ringwood, Victoria, Australia
Penguin Books Canada Ltd, 10 Alcorn Avenue, Toronto, Ontario, Canada m4v 3b2
Penguin Books (NZ) Ltd, 182–190 Wairau Road, Auckland 10, New Zealand

Penguin Books Ltd, Registered Offices: Harmondsworth, Middlesex, England

First published in Penguin Books 1997
1 3 5 7 9 10 8 6 4 2

Set in 9.75/12pt Monotype Baskerville
Typeset by Rowland Phototypesetting Ltd, Bury St Edmunds, Suffolk
Printed in England by Clays Ltd, St Ives plc

CONTENTS

I

Ruth, published in January 1853, was Elizabeth Gaskell's second novel. Her first, *Mary Barton*, had been an immediate success on its publication in 1848. Its representation of the human consequences of the Industrial Revolution found its moment in the reading public's imagination, Charles Kingsley declaring that if he had his way, *Mary Barton* would be bill-posted and read from pulpits 'till a nation, calling itself Christian, began to act upon the awful facts contained in it . . . with an united energy of shame and repentance proportionate to the hugeness of the evil'.[1] Widely and favourably reviewed, reprinted three times by the end of 1850, *Mary Barton*, 'A Tale of Manchester Life', as its subtitle insisted, faced the 'Condition-of-England' question. Written intensely and, for many of its readers, devastating in its revelation of conditions in Manchester, it developed, as Thomas Carlyle noted in a letter of congratulation to Gaskell, 'a huge subject, which has lain *dumb* too long'.[2] Publicly successful, *Mary Barton* was a novel written privately, at the suggestion of Gaskell's husband, as a diversion from grief after the death of their infant son. Fame brought Gaskell an awareness that her second novel would be both an object of attention and have attached to it expectations about subject-matter and treatment.[3] It was to be written also for a wider public of which Gaskell was now aware, whether through the enthusiasm and disapprobation aroused by *Mary Barton* among her acquaintance in Manchester,[4] through the general reading public, or through the literary circle of friends and acquaintances the novel's fame had brought her.

With this consciousness upon her, Gaskell set about writing *Ruth* deliberately and slowly. At first, indeed, she had denied to her publishers, Chapman & Hall, that she could write another novel at all (the bother it gave wasn't worth it).[5] But Gaskell was a natural writer. After *Mary Barton*, she became a contributor to Charles Dickens's new weekly magazine, *Household Words*,[6] and clearly was meditating another novel. Yet progress, even when writing began, was difficult. Although by April 1852 Gaskell had sent Charlotte Brontë a complete outline, eliciting her comments,[7] a friend could report as late as 22 November 1852 (the novel was published the following January) that *Ruth* 'is not finished yet', Gaskell being dissatisfied with the last hundred pages, 'and we are going over it very carefully to take out superfluous epithets and sentences'.[8] Apart from helping to date stages of the composition, these responses and reports suggest how Gaskell tested out what she was writing, endeavouring in a collective circle of friends[9] to refine what might on publication be so closely, even severely, scrutinized, however devastating, as she rather wryly admits, such private responses could be. In October 1852 some friends, to whom she had to 'talk aesthetically', even while thinking of 'pickle for pork', 'smashed into Ruth in grand style', frightening her off her nest again (*Letters*, p. 205). The concern with 'superfluous epithets and sentences' was, however genuine, a symptom rather than the real cause of anxiety about *Ruth*, a novel that deeply engaged Gaskell, 'my heart being so full of it', as she declared (*Letters*, p. 205), and one that for Charlotte Brontë combined nobility and a purpose 'as useful in practical result as it is high and just in theoretical tendency' (*Heritage*, p. 200). Style might offer a handle for critics in attacking the book and should be looked to accordingly, but the fear arose out of the subject-matter. Not that Gaskell was in any way deterred by fear from writing *Ruth*, or from publishing it. The book was certainly not ignored, and in April 1853 she acknowledged that in writing it she had known opinion would be divided on whether 'my subject was a fit one for fiction', even while she took 'heart of grace' from the very warmth of people's discussion:

it has made them talk and think a little on a subject which is so painful it requires all one's bravery not to hide one's head like an ostrich and try . . . to forget that the evil exists. (*Letters*, p. 227)

Gaskell, as this process of consultation and delay suggests, was deeply self-conscious in the writing of *Ruth*, and fearful too of what responses to it might be. Those first responses, at a time when Gaskell herself was not well and so the more vulnerable, seemed to realize her worst fears. Unhappy, she compared herself to St Sebastian, stuck full of arrows (*Letters*, pp. 220–21). A number of 'good kind people' (Gaskell's phrase seems unironic) expressed, 'at considerable pains to themselves', their disapproval of *Ruth*, 'rather than allow a "demoralising laxity" to go unchecked' (*Letters*, p. 226). It was claimed by Gaskell herself that *Ruth* had been burnt by outraged readers, while just after publication she 'had a terrible fit of crying all Sat[urda]y night at the unkind things people were saying' (*Letters*, p. 221). But St Sebastian survived his use as archery target and increasingly, as significant numbers of reviews began to come in, Gaskell was cheered by the favourable, thoughtful, and often lengthy notices *Ruth* received.[10]

2

What, then, had Gaskell set about doing in *Ruth* and why was she so confident that what she wrote would be condemned as 'an unfit subject for fiction'? (*Letters*, p. 220.) *Ruth* is about a fallen woman. Seduced and abandoned, Ruth is rescued by Benson, a Dissenting clergyman; bears a child; and resists the temptation to marry her seducer. In placing such a woman not at the margins (where many such women appear in Victorian fiction) but rather at the centre of her story, Gaskell issued a challenge and then further compounded it by her treatment of Ruth's fall and of Ruth's redemption. Such issues provoked attention and, as Gaskell feared, might provoke hostility. And yet to read *Ruth* for the first time, after this account of its author's self-consciousness and of her own sense of its subject's unfitness for fiction, may come as a surprise to the modern reader. It is not – certainly not ostentatiously – about sexuality, though like many Victorian imaginative works it is highly charged with emotion, much of it sexually situated, and finding its expression variously through landscape and weather, dramatic scene and juxtapositions, symbol and allusion and quotation.[11] Nor is *Ruth* about depravity or harsh physical suffering in a sordid environment. Ruth is no sister to Aunt Esther in *Mary Barton*, whose prostitution and alcoholism, bedraggled finery and wretched lodging-house retreat, are unblinkingly reported. In style and treatment, Gaskell, handling what she knew to be a sensational subject, aimed for quietness. Even George Eliot, critically weighing others' fiction in the light of her own developing powers and finding Gaskell 'constantly misled by a love of sharp contrasts', praised *Ruth*'s style ('a great refreshment to me'), singling out the description of Ruth's attic bedroom at Eccleston, so like the Dutch faithfulness of George Eliot's own later fiction (*Heritage*, pp. 231–2).

Gaskell's innovation and the dangerous ground upon which she trod were immediately recognized. Overwhelmingly favourable as the reviews and readers' responses are, welcoming both the novel's subject and the novel itself, they raise important social and critical questions, not least in querying the focus of Gaskell's argument. *Ruth* challenged certain received ideas. While such sexual and moral beliefs were generally undiscussed, they could provoke reactions the more heated for being unarticulated. 'Moral laxity', unchecked, might threaten family sanctity and the very stability of the social fabric. *Ruth* confronted head on the claims that a woman once seduced could only be retrieved (and even then perhaps doubtfully) by marriage with her seducer; or if abandoned, could not return to respectable society, and must remain a humble and excluded penitent. Yet such ideas, so far as they were held (and then largely amongst the middle classes), were under scrutiny by the very people supposedly holding and enforcing them, as the reactions to *Ruth* of most reviewers and of the majority of readers confirm. Those reviewers and readers generally also rejected that double sexual standard, represented in *Ruth*, which exonerated the man and condemned the woman.[12] More difficult, because unresolved by Gaskell herself, were the questions of Ruth's guilt and of Ruth's redemption. Yet here the reviewers are not divided on whether a fallen woman could be retrieved. Rather, they weigh whether Ruth, being guilty, should have Christian forgiveness; or whether, being innocent morally and therefore sexually, it was not forgiveness but understanding that was required. Was Ruth guilty and therefore redeemable? Or was she innocent and therefore not to be cast out? These questions the novel (as the reviews noted) seemed not satisfactorily to distinguish. But either way, despite our perception of what should shock the Victorian reader, Gaskell's representation was held to be right. The real strength of *Ruth*, as recognized then and since, lies not so much in its strength of argument (logically, it is rather weak), but in its moral challenge to received opinion and in its powerful representation of feeling.

Ruth was disturbing because she stood at the centre of the novel, unmarginalized as object of pity or social outcast. Certainly, the fallen woman was no novelty in literature. She had earlier been a familiar and pathetic presence in Wordsworth's 'The Thorn' and, the name with its resonance of pity springing to mind for a poet, in his 'Ruth'. Outside poetry, Gaskell's Aunt Esther is a key if subordinate character in *Mary Barton*, while Charles Dickens's Nancy in *Oliver Twist* (1837–9), never declared or shown to be 'on the game', is proclaimed a prostitute by her red boots. In the novel's Preface, Dickens set out his polemical determination to omit nothing of the 'stern truth', declaring he had abated not 'one scrap of curl-paper in the girl's dishevelled hair', for he had 'no faith in the delicacy which could not bear to look upon them'. This realism, Dickens's 'stern truth', can be seen too in what has been claimed as the *donnée* or seed of Gaskell's novel. In January 1850, Gaskell sought advice from Dickens about a girl she wished to help emigrate. The girl, a dressmaker, had been seduced by a surgeon, then decoyed into crime and imprisoned. While she was ill in prison, the assistant surgeon to Manchester's New Bailey prison was called to attend her. He proved to be her seducer – the girl fainted and the surgeon was overwhelmed by her situation (*Letters*, pp. 98–9). The briefest comparison between Gaskell's account and the story of Ruth demonstrates how essentially remote one narrative is from the other, above all in tone. Rather than the realism aimed at by Dickens or achieved in *Mary Barton*, *Ruth* is permeated by the characteristics of romance. Images of corruption, intensely realized, are certainly there in Ruth's fearful imaginings of her seducer Bellingham's influence upon their son Leonard, yet these are admitted through the interior narrative of dreams and acquire a symbolic force free from any theory of realism. What Gaskell designed in *Ruth* was not another *Mary Barton*. True, *Ruth* is a novel with a purpose, as Gaskell declared and Charlotte Brontë recognized; unlike the earlier novel, though, its concerns are not with the 'Condition-of-England' question. Its style and its story-telling, its very genre, are those of the romance.

Except in the fact of both girls being dressmakers and in the slightest narrative likeness, of seduction and chance meeting again, there is no affinity in tone or setting between the plight of the girl in Manchester's New Bailey and the story of Ruth. The novel is not about prostitution, not about sweated workshops, not in any significant way about industrialized life. Ruth may be a dressmaker and her apprenticeship is hard, but it is short-lived and has none of the attrition represented in Thomas Hood's 'Song of the Shirt' (1843) or Charles Kingsley's swingeing pamphlet *Cheap Clothes and Nasty* (1850). In *Ruth*, Gaskell's heroine is not a pathetic victim of industrial process. Rather, for all its contemporaneity, its rail travel and a chronology that ties the narrative's conclusion closely to the novel's, the setting of *Ruth* seems constantly to recede into a nurturing past that allows the individual space to breathe, free of the evolutionary constraints of the Victorian age.

Naturally, tensions, uneasiness, arise between the 'fallen woman' problem genre and the romance genre of Ruth's heroic development. Gaskell knew she was challenging common conceptions and that sometimes made her nervous. This is felt particularly in Gaskell's indecision, as it seems, over the nature and extent of Ruth's own understanding. She is represented as so ignorant of '*the* subject of a woman's life' (p. 40), if not of its 'depth and power', at least of its social implications, that it takes an angry blow struck by a child to make her realize that cohabiting with Bellingham is wrong. And then, but only then, she seems to take in its full significance all at once. The nature of Ruth's sexual experience so far, we notice, has been largely and deliberately covered by a narrative disjunction after Bellingham sweeps Ruth off to London. We may seek to fill that gap, but with what? That Ruth has fully entered into sexual experience, entered into its 'depth and power', is clear not only in her subsequent pregnancy, but also on her re-introduction, in Wales, where the comic boredom of the 'ark-load' of tourists maximizes their (and the reader's) fascination with Ruth and her compromised situation. Ruth's moment of realization is an episodic intensification, not quite hanging together with what has gone before. In that respect it works like other episodes in the novel associated with the social meaning of Ruth's situation: Thomas Wilkins's despairing flight on discovering his illegitimacy, the memory of which persuades the Bensons to conceal Ruth's situation under the veil of widowhood (pp. 102–3), and Leonard's horrified response on learning he is illegitimate (p. 282).

Such episodes reinforce the gulf between the individual's plight and the world's condemnation, unlikely though it is, for example, that Leonard could understand the full meaning of his birth in social terms. Gaskell, as well perhaps as being 'misled' by that 'love of sharp contrasts' deplored by George Eliot, was emphasizing the innocence of Ruth, emphasizing also the opinion of the world that condemns both what it does not understand and what it should forgive. Ruth is never, strictly speaking, penitent, because she does nothing, herself, that is a sin: her sorrow is for the social stigma she bestows on Leonard, as it is too for the dilemma thrust upon her of how to appear before the world. That dilemma is imposed by the world, not by the gospel, however the world may claim legitimacy for its sanction by quoting the sacred text. The

spirit of the gospel is represented by Benson and his family as surely as
its letter is represented by Mr Bradshaw. Ruth dies. Is this a sign of her
redemption? or an unjust imposition upon the innocent? Charlotte
Brontë protested against this conclusion: 'Why are we to shut up the
book weeping?' (*Heritage*, p. 200). Because, Gaskell might have replied,
the importance of Ruth lies not in any sin, for which a punishment
might be exacted, but rather in the value of what she can achieve after
the world would cast her out as worthless; it lies too in the world's
realization, confronted by the death that crowns Ruth's life, of what
has been lost. Ruth cannot live on in the actuality of 1853, the date of
the action's conclusion and the novel's publication. Death confirms the
pattern of her life's achievement, even while it keeps her within the
imaginative borders of romance.

   In what follows, I want to explore how Gaskell develops that sense
of value, both emotional and moral, that builds up within and around
Ruth, value that offers a culture of feeling and of heroic action, though
if we expect heroism of the epic kind we will be disappointed. Ruth
may resemble a damsel in distress, but the Bensons, even backed by
Sally, are not the paladins of King Arthur or Charlemagne. Heroic they
are, none the less, in a sense that Thomas Carlyle stressed for his age
when he demanded who was the more important in mankind's history,
Hannibal 'or the nameless boor who first hammered out for himself an
iron spade'?[13]

3

Romance is a genre of fiction that emphasizes alternatives to realism's
determinism. Realism stresses a mimetic representation, in content and
style, whereas romance offers representational possibilities, in the shape
of story or in episodes of experience (illness, dreams) or in ways of writing
(symbol, allusion), that extend and explore. While realism is particularly
associated with the development of the novel, novels themselves often
exhibit marked romance elements. Dickens may stress the 'stern truth'
of Nancy's curl-papers, but he delights in the discovery plot that restores
Oliver Twist, the lost heir, to his rightful place and is at ease with Oliver
passing unscathed through experiences that realistically treated would
have produced a criminal monster. Gaskell resists the extremities of

romance: neither Ruth nor Leonard is removed by a sudden turn of fortune from the social and economic (and emotional) sphere in which they have lived out their lives. Instead, though, of Ruth's interaction with the social 'realities' of urban industrialization, Gaskell foregrounds an alternative, as valid as any fictive interpretation of experience through realist conventions. This alternative explores, above all, passional and intellectual development, seeing the two powers as interwoven rather than distinct. Such had been Nathaniel Hawthorne's way in *The Scarlet Letter* (1850) when treating adultery and an illegitimate child, casting his story back to the seventeenth century and infusing his characters' actions with a symbolic world of nature, of sunlight and moonlight, allowing free play to image and to disjunction.

The nature of *Ruth* is clear from its opening, the story being set 'now many years ago', distance in time being a common romance characteristic, while the evocation of the town stresses remoteness and quaintness equally with changes wrought by the modern age; indeed it even gives a sense of the action beginning in the eighteenth century rather than (as the novel's strict chronology would suggest) about 1840. Ruth may cry out under the conditions of the workshop ('how shall I get through five years of these terrible nights'), yet she delights in the flowers painted on the walls and in the beauty of the tumbledown houses covered by snow. The snow is an analogy to the technique of the romance, which transforms not to conceal, but to reveal possibilities previously unperceived by the reader.

In *Ruth*, two obvious features of such romance transformation are the use of dreams and the use of illness. Dreams may express concretely what the characters cannot articulate, or they may represent their deep but unrealized fears. Dreams open ways into psychology and, without breaking the frame of likelihood, into possibilities beyond the ordered bounds of the physical universe.[14] Shortly after Leonard's birth, Ruth suffers a dream of horror: her son, grown up corrupt, repeats like his father the seduction of a girl, who sickeningly 'seemed strangely like herself, only more utterly sad and desolate even than she' (pp. 136–7). For all Leonard's adult prosperity, the girl drags him down to hell where his father is also. It is difficult to imagine Ruth awake committing Bellingham to hell-fire, yet the dream allows she might, as it also admits the terror that Leonard may be his father's son rather than hers, to follow his father in deed and in moral turpitude – all this even while Ruth, awakening, finds Sally 'nodding in an arm-chair by the fire; and . . . her little soft warm babe, nestled up against her breast' (p. 137). The external reality, of Sally and the sleeping infant, has remained suspended while Ruth lives a whole lifetime through the intensity of a momentary dream. Ruth knows she is safe and Leonard is not predestined, yet the dream recognizes her unexpressed fear that Leonard may be not just a replica but a replication of his father. The future course of her actions will show her seeking, by love and nurture, to develop Leonard's emotional and moral nature. Instead of the cycle of repetition, seated in psychic apprehension, that the dream threatens, there are other possible futures. Among them is difference from the father, which proves to be, in Ruth's struggle to create that future for her son, the mother's salvation also.

Fears of separation, triggered by the intertwining of child and father, rise in the shape of dreams at other key moments. When Ruth is first physically parted from Leonard (a night on which the boy also dreams, as though to emphasize the pair's affinity), her dream of terror, though she cannot know it consciously, anticipates Bellingham's return (p. 213) and alerts the reader to the narrative development. Again, after Leonard's illness, Ruth dreams of seeking to save Leonard, even as she is swept back 'into a mysterious something too dreadful to be borne' (p. 256). This dream has a psychological reality in its fear that Leonard might have died, could yet die, and foreshadows in Ruth's dedication to her child that she will die;[15] it 'poetically' prepares us for a death which is the completion of a bargain with God.

Leonard's illness, which provokes this dream, is one of several in the novel. If Gaskell can resort too readily to illness and death (Dickens grumbled that he wished her characters would keep steadier on their feet) and if it has been fashionable to dismiss illness in Victorian fiction as too convenient a resolution of narrative cruces, it yet makes sense to see illness as a marker of crisis not just in the body but also in the mind and the psyche: symptoms and diagnosis are not so important as the significance of sickness, structurally and emotionally. In *Ruth*, the most conventional illness (in the sense of being a fictional convention, illness to produce moral reformation) is Richard Bradshaw's, and that is kept off-stage, the narrative focussing upon his father's crisis of faith and feeling, legalism eventually succumbing to natural love for a child. Both Bellingham and Ruth are crucially ill, twice, their sickness enfolding Leonard's. Leonard's illness, coming as it does after Ruth's confrontation with Bellingham on the sands, seems almost displaced from the illness Ruth's agony ought to have provoked in herself – brain-fever, perhaps – yet it expresses the threat of loss that Bellingham represents. Bellingham's first illness, which mitigates though hardly justifies his abandoning of Ruth,[16] as clearly underlines her emotional commitment to him as it establishes his short-lived interest in her. Illness exposes both emotional deeps and shallows. Ruth's illness, after his mother whisks Bellingham (unprotestingly) off, expresses how close to death the rapidly enforced social and emotional revelations have brought her, and so makes comprehensible her feeling, as she leaves Wales, that in that spot 'so much of her life had passed' (p. 110). Though the temporal space was a few days, the experiential span is reinforced through the body's suffering. At the narrative's conclusion, the successive illnesses of Bellingham and Ruth suggest, first, Ruth's commitment to Bellingham, not by any sexual bond but by the knowledge that she cannot deny the past. Unexpressed though it is by her, their relationship had and must always have meaning for her. Ruth, like all Gaskell's most valued characters, has a sense of history. Bellingham in his delirium demands to know why there are no waterlilies in her hair. He can only (delirious as he is – but the delirium is significant, not casual) recall her as she was, without the changes wrought in her by time and experience. In her final illness, it is true, Ruth gradually sloughs off all her history, but her regression and loss of identity, a 'child-like insanity' without the 'slightest glimpse of memory or intelligence in her face' (p. 366), charts her being laid asleep in the body until she passes, a living soul, into the 'life of things'. Where Bellingham's regression sticks at immaturity, Ruth's illness removes her from individuality, eliding her into the unity of God as her life is completed. At the end Ruth achieves what Bellingham's mother denied her. In nursing Bellingham, she possesses him, even as illness removes the possibility or need of sexuality. She nurses Bellingham as an act of love that is Christian, even dispassionate (if love can be dispassionate). Ruth makes her claim to possess Bellingham, too, without it having to be explicit to her understanding or explicit in the narrative.

These dreams and illnesses, then, emphasize the romance features of *Ruth*. They are not allegorical, they are not prophetic. They do not offer simple interpretation nor do they command a supernatural pattern. From roots in recognizable experience, though, they afford entry into areas of experience and apprehension that the characters could not of themselves plausibly articulate. They work by suggestion, by appropriate structure, to open out and develop alternatives to the overt line of the narrative. Above all, perhaps, they give access to feeling. The power of feeling, including love in its various aspects, expressed through the form of the romance, plays intensely within *Ruth* and, truthful, discriminatory, and tragic, is developed into a system of value in the individual, in the social group, and in divine institutions.[17]

Ruth's susceptibility to feeling, first and foremost, is clear from the novel's opening, as she is juxtaposed with or responds to things beyond the concerns of the workroom, whether the painted flowers or the glory of colour cast on her by the stained glass of the window or the impulse to 'sally forth and enjoy' the snow under the purple heavens (pp. 9, 6–7, 8). Here, Jenny acts as friend and counsellor, clear needs of the orphaned girl whose feelings are so rich and uncontrolled, but Jenny's withdrawal through illness lays Ruth open to danger, since for Gaskell, impulse is not of itself sufficient. Bellingham may argue, at the crisis created by Mrs Mason's dismissal of Ruth, that what is natural is therefore right (p. 50). Gaskell, on the other hand, a believer in revealed religion, is well aware that morality is constructed, though equally clear that the promptings of one's human nature are not therefore to be rejected as the Calvinist would reject them. When Old Tom, on Ruth's Sunday visit to him, seeks to warn Ruth, she can make no connection between her feelings for Bellingham and the biblical text that speaks of the Devil going about as a roaring lion, fitting image though the lion in its strength may be for the passion that Ruth herself is capable of. Feeling is natural, but not therefore necessarily or always right. Bellingham undoubtedly has feelings, but they are selfish and limited, undeveloped by any relationship to sensibility and understanding. His impulses are right, as when he plunges in to rescue the boy from drowning: the moment's heat past, though, Bellingham cannot refrain from complaining about the offensive hovel in which the boy lives. When, late in the novel, we discover that Bellingham took on the boy as a servant, an act of undoubted generosity, it is also apparent that he never bothered to educate him, in marked (and markedly deliberate) contrast to the care Ruth has lavished on Leonard's education, a process productive of her own development not only in book learning, powerfully ignorant as she was before, but also in sexuality, emotion and religion.

The key to Ruth's moral development lies in her sensibility, whereas

Bellingham is constantly constrained by the hobgoblin of self-esteem. When he wreathes waterlilies in Ruth's hair – that act recalled significantly at the novel's end – he treats her as little more than a lay figure that reflects credit on himself: 'Her beauty was all that Mr Bellingham cared for, and it was supreme. It was all he recognised of her, and he was proud of it' (p. 64). Bellingham's diversion lies in cards and he is only willing, even in so slight a thing, to teach Ruth how to play because the boredom it may relieve is his. There is no evidence that, in the elided interval between their flight before Mrs Mason's wrath and their reappearance before the gawping 'ark-load' of tourists in Wales, Bellingham ever offered Ruth any interest by way of books or music or conversation. Wales is only another diversion from the boredoms of egotism. But for Ruth, Wales and nature are a revelation, constituents of a power that, in Wordsworthian fashion, fosters her innate sensibility by beauty and by fear:[18]

It was opening a new sense; vast ideas of beauty and grandeur filled her mind at the sight of the mountains now first beheld in full majesty . . . Even the rain was a pleasure to her . . . she saw the swift fleeting showers come athwart the sunlight like a rush of silver arrows; she watched the purple darkness on the heathery mountain side, and then the pale golden gleam which succeeded. (pp. 56–7)

Later, Ruth rejects not Bellingham (she does not deny their relationship, much less that it had profound significance for her), but his false claim on her and on their child. Her maturity makes this possible. The natural impulse is still there at their meeting on the sands and that is the temptation. She felt it shortly after Leonard's christening ('a strange yearning kind of love for the father of the child': p. 159) and that impulse struggles with her understanding. Ruth believes Bellingham to be bad and yet she loves him. But she can now weigh up what Bellingham has not been to her and his son. Hence, as Ruth acknowledges, her sin would be, not her original relationship with Bellingham but its renewal, even under the spuriously respectable cover of marriage.[19] The storm, as she wrestles with herself, is responsive to her mood (pp. 225–6) and the gargoyle in the church is a mirror of her own self, signifying for Ruth and the reader the agony of her struggle and the rightness of her choice (pp. 232–3).

What has changed Ruth is first the love of nature and then the love of mankind. She is loved and loves in return, but more specifically, it is the love of one man, of Leonard. Leonard is Ruth's jewel, as in Hawthorne's *The Scarlet Letter* the capricious Pearl is Hester Prynne's. By making the child a boy, Gaskell enforces through gender and memory the links with Bellingham. It is Mrs Bradshaw, normally only her husband's obedient shadow, but looking with a mother's eye, who later innocently observes the physical likeness between Bellingham and Leonard (p. 218). Leonard's progress, in his very physical resemblance to his father, challenges hereditary determinism, even while the physical likeness suggests in its overlapping shadowland the possibility of taking after his father. Leonard, in the seeming significance of a physical resemblance, counters the deterministic notions of realism. To Ruth, her dream had suggested that Leonard might become like his father, that he might indeed be worse, but in Gaskell's optimistic – not therefore sentimental – view of the human condition, we are not bound to repeat our mistakes.

This emotional and biological patterning is emphasized by a small detail, typical of Gaskell's delicate subtlety. Leonard's birth is marked by an allusion, comic in its tone, yet deeply significant. Ruth had wished for a girl, not because less likely to remind her of the father, rather 'as being less likely to feel the want of a father – as being what a mother, worse than widowed, could most effectually shelter' (p. 134). Once Leonard is born, though, in the reality of this and not any other imagined child, Ruth 'would not have exchanged [him] for a wilderness of girls' (p. 135). This version of Shylock's lament over the ring, stolen and exchanged by his daughter Jessica for a monkey – 'I would not have given it for a wilderness of monkeys' – sounds a whole world of value, distinct from price. Leonard is precious, like Shylock's ring, not because of intrinsic but because of sentimental value. Shylock recognizes the ring as his turquoise: 'I had it of Leah when a bachelor', a unique and painful tearing open of Shylock's shell of ego that links him in love momentarily but intensely with a wife never before or after mentioned. Such is Gaskell's own power that a jocular allusion illuminates Leonard's significance, stemming back to when, in the knowledge of her pregnancy, Ruth put away further thought of suicide, and roving forward through the future intertwining and developing lives of mother and child.

Ruth stands in marked contrast to other mothers in the novel, whether the deliberately shadowy Mrs Bradshaw, overwhelmed by her husband's personality, from which she escapes imaginatively through the romantic trash of the Minerva Press (not all conformations of romance are valid), or the smothering Mrs Bellingham who (we learn through the comic refraction of Mrs Pearson), confronted by her son's affair with Ruth, 'led him to repentance, and took him to Paris' (p. 264) – her principle presumably being of fire driving out fire. The family is crucial in *Ruth* and yet there are few families that either conform to the supposed Victorian norm or, if they do, remain unchallenged. The family nearest to that norm, almost parodic indeed, is the Bradshaws', and that is challenged by both the elder children. Ruth herself is singularly without family or even guardian, and gives birth to a child without a legal father. Yet when Leonard is born, the iconography is clear. Snow envelops the earth (as at the novel's opening and at Ruth's death), the earth hiding, in words quoted by way of enforcement from Milton's 'Nativity Ode', 'her guilty front with innocent snow' (p. 134). The words are contextually unironic, as the world is guilty but child and mother are innocent. And present at this nativity are the Bensons, Thurstan and Faith, and Sally, Leonard being the incarnation 'in loving whom all hearts and natures should be drawn together' (p. 134). None of the Benson household is married and yet it is in no sense dysfunctional. Gaskell, unafraid of equating a newborn child with Jesus, sees the true family as being not necessarily biological or legal; its shapers are not social or pharisaical enforcement, but rather affinity and spiritual relationship, happiness and love.

The Benson household, living by the spirit and not by the letter, is essentially religious. The modern reader may be uneasy at such a claim, but *Ruth* can scarcely be read, certainly not understood, without an attempt at comprehending it. Perhaps the approach through Ruth's developing sensibility is a way in, since Gaskell draws strongly here upon Wordsworth's conviction of a Universal power that need not be named God. Such is the Romantic glory that Ruth opens herself to in Wales; on the sands at Abermouth it has become more specifically Christian. Overwhelmed by her interview with Bellingham, Ruth becomes aware of the setting sun in a moment of Wordsworthian epiphany:

The clouds had parted away, and the sun was going down in the crimson glory behind the distant purple hills. The whole western sky was one flame of fire.

Ruth forgot herself in looking at the gorgeous sight. She sat up gazing, and, as she gazed . . . all human care and sorrow were swallowed up in the unconscious sense of God's infinity. (p. 250)

Gaskell is of course remarkably undogmatic. Herself a Unitarian who accepted in some measure the divinity of Jesus (in *Ruth* she refers specifically to Jesus as 'the merciful God'),[20] Gaskell approached belief cleansed of the Calvinistic hatred of the human body. It is difficult to be certain what denomination Benson belongs to, though Unitarianism seems most likely, given Gaskell's own allegiance and the Eccleston chapel's history.[21] But the very lack of dogmatic stigmata suggests how Gaskell, like her creation Benson, is unconcerned with sectarian allegiances. She is prepared to laugh, through Sally, at the Evangelical idea of 'travailing in the new birth' (p. 146) instead of labouring to make the beds properly. Indeed, Sally the Anglican, a 'dissenting' presence in a Dissenting household, is witness to the openness of belief of both Gaskell and Benson. The Benson household lives out, not without its occasional jarring or misunderstanding or unhappiness, the Christian life. In their primitive ways, of evening 'reading' and bed by ten o'clock, of Sally's recollection of how she made a neck of mutton pass as seven distinct dishes (p. 138), in prayer and work, a culture is invoked.

These people live by the spirit and are set against Mr Bradshaw, the legalist. Bradshaw is a victim of the letter, but he is not a hypocrite: a distinction sometimes difficult to understand, though crucial for us to grasp when looking back at these Victorian representations of religious-driven behaviour. Bradshaw genuinely believes the Gospel (condemned though he is by the parable of the Pharisee in Luke 18:10−14), yet he makes his son a hypocrite. Bradshaw would never go to the theatre; his strictness makes Richard *pretend* he does not go to the theatre. Bradshaw is tested three times: by the election; by Ruth's history; by his son's accident. Bradshaw is distinctly uncomfortable over the election. Not only does it break his observance of the Sabbath (no hot meals on Sunday, to keep the commandment against servile work), but it raises the likelihood of bribery (packets of money will be needed), even though the agent's man will alone dirty his hands (pp. 207, 215). Bradshaw, brought to the boundary of legalism, sets his foot over it into chicanery. His discomfort is apparent at the dinner-table when Benson declares: 'We are not to do evil that good may come' (p. 210), though Benson too is discomfited, aware of his own false position. That discomfort makes it the more difficult for Benson to confront Bradshaw when Ruth's past becomes known. Yet Benson stands then upon his fundamental conviction that 'it is God's will that the women who have fallen should be numbered among those who have broken hearts to be bound up, not cast aside as lost beyond recall' (p. 288). Bradshaw is not prepared to listen to Benson's witness, any more than to that of his daughter, Jemima.

To Bradshaw, such pleas are not evidence of a need to help human weakness, but of the corruption spread by Ruth. Secure in uprightness, he blinks at his own queasiness over the electioneering 'packets of money', if the agent's man carries the purse, and believes himself impregnable, without need of help. Only with the terrible conviction of his son's fraud must Bradshaw, too honest to deny its fact, then confront a division within himself. Even that he seeks to avoid by taking refuge in a strict legalism, denying kinship, denying his true nature and love, insisting that Benson prosecute Richard.[22] Already forcing himself against the grain yet unable to admit the idea of imperfection, another's or his own, or its need for forgiveness, the love that replaced the letter when Jesus replaced judgement, Bradshaw's tables of the law are shattered by Richard's accident. The man still tries to sustain himself by the known rules: again, he is essentially no hypocrite, even in dealings with his inner self. He becomes a psychic battleground, where the natural love of his son, that should ally itself with the spirit of the Gospel, is pitted instead in fierce struggle against the letter. Gaskell here handles a process of conversion like that attempted in *Mary Barton*, where Carson was reconciled to his son's murderer at John Barton's deathbed, but now with greater technical skill, the representation being part and parcel of Bradshaw's whole nature.

The Gospel, and particularly St Luke's, colours the whole of *Ruth*. The figure of the weeper in the novel's epigraph suggests Mary Magdalen, the sinner who repented and whom Jesus forgave. Ruth is seen as a Magdalen who weeps once awakened to knowledge. She is no sinner beyond the sense in which, being human, we all are, however the world and Bradshaw's legalism may condemn her. She has, though, loved much. Her sins are forgiven her, but she is wakened to a consciousness that cannot efface the past, where she has offended against social and divine precepts, and is the cause of shame to Leonard. She knew, not at the time but in the greater pain of retrospect, that she 'had gone astray'

(p. 127), a phrase repeated at Leonard's christening (p. 150). Such knowledge is part of Ruth's capacity for learning and understanding, in marked contrast to the hermetically sealed complacency of Bellingham, who finding Ruth again, in the guise of the widowed Mrs Hilton, can only, like an exhausted epicure, declare that the 'whole affair was most mysterious and piquant' (p. 234).

Even in death, Ruth is triumphant, while Bellingham fails as he recoils from kissing her dead lips (p. 369) and goes off, despite Benson's rebuke, self-reflective to the end: 'I wish my last remembrance of my beautiful Ruth was not mixed up with all these people' (p. 371). Bellingham is a pretty feeble specimen of a man and it is the feminine that the novel values. Bradshaw's masculinity, perhaps the most conspicuous in the novel, is challenged and found wanting, whether when 'understanding' Hickman over political corruption or in failing to value his child. Such masculinity is of course constructed as an extreme, but throughout *Ruth* there are obvious challenges to masculine assumptions, most of which challenges Gaskell clearly expected the contemporary reader to accept. Benson himself has much of the female in his delicacy not only of body but of feelings also. The claim of men to possess women is denied. *Ruth* makes clear that women are not men's chattels, whether the man is the father who expects Jemima to marry Farquhar because he, Bradshaw, wishes it or the flippant Bellingham who claims 'my' Ruth as he departs to the damnation of his own ennui.

4

In setting out to write *Ruth* Gaskell might be conscious, embarking upon 'an *unfit* subject for fiction', that she was challenging ideologies, a challenge that explains some of her uneasiness in writing and in publishing. More importantly, though, in choosing not the realistic mode of a Condition-of-England novel but the genre of romance Gaskell effects a whole opening out into a world of nineteenth-century experience concerned with women and family, love, value, and religion, conveying that world by a vivid pointillism that captures lives as lived. Gaskell wanted action on behalf of the fallen, including those who, unlike Ruth, are no innocents. *Ruth*, though, represents that action not through female penitentiaries or societies for emigration (though Gaskell did not neglect such means of present help), but rather through the community of feeling and understanding.

NOTES

1 *Fraser's Magazine*, April 1849; quoted in *Elizabeth Gaskell: The Critical Heritage*, ed. Angus Easson (1991) (hereafter cited as *Heritage*), p. 153.

2 8 November 1848; *Heritage*, p. 72.

3 One indication of Gaskell's greater consciousness as a writer in *Ruth* was its publication in three volumes, a standard format, rather than the two volumes of *Mary Barton*.

4 See, for example, *Heritage*, section 11 and p. 82 in particular.

5 *The Letters of Mrs Gaskell*, ed. J. A. V. Chapple and Arthur Pollard (1966) (hereafter cited as *Letters*), p. 72 ('le jeu ne vaut pas la chandelle').

6 *Lizzie Leigh* appeared in the first issue; *Cranford* was sporadically serialized there from 1851 to 1853.

7 Charlotte Brontë to Gaskell, 26 April 1852; *Heritage*, p. 200. The novelists had met in 1850 and, despite their very different backgrounds and personalities, became firm friends until Charlotte's death in 1855; Gaskell paid tribute to Charlotte in *The Life of Charlotte Brontë* (1857).

8 *Letters and Memorials of Catherine Winkworth. Edited by Her Sister*, Clifton (privately printed), 2 vols. (1883, 1886), i, 369.

9 The circle was largely female, though it included John Forster, friend and adviser to many writers – most notably Charles Dickens – while Gaskell's husband, William, gave his usual support both generally and in revising details of grammar and style.

10 For an assessment and a range of the reviews, see *Heritage*, pp. 25–32, 200–329. While a number of reviews had reservations or pointed to weaknesses, the only completely negative one (*Christian Observer*, July 1853) noted that 'We do not pretend to have read through these volumes' (*Heritage*, p. 313). Gaskell said it was a prohibited book in her own house (*Letters*, p. 221), but this because it was on an adult topic – her eldest daughter Marianne was nineteen and Gaskell intended to read it with her sometime. The John Rylands University of Manchester Library copy of the first edition is from the collection of James Prince Lee, first bishop of Manchester, another indication that *Ruth* generally was treated as serious rather than scandalous; corrections in this copy indicate that it was read.

11 Compare the narrative significance of Hetty Sorel's pink ribbon in *Adam Bede*, for example, or the erotic intensity of Tennyson's song from *The Princess*: 'Now lies the Earth all Danaë to the stars, / And all thy heart lies open unto me . . . / Now slides the silent meteor on, and leaves / A shining furrow, as thy thoughts in me'.

12 See, for example, Gaskell's comment in relation to a story of seduction; *The Life of Charlotte Brontë*, ed. Angus Easson (World's Classics, 1996), p. 473.

13 *Selected Writings*, ed. Alan Shelston (Penguin English Library, 1971), p. 53.

14 Compare Emily Brontë's use of Lockwood's dream, early in *Wuthering Heights*, to exhibit the elemental passion that bonds Heathcliff and Cathy even while it devastatingly exposes Lockwood's pathological immaturity.

15 There are several references that acknowledge Ruth's necessary death, though not revealing how or when it must be: for example pp. 110, 166 (suggested by the 'scroll of Fate'); and which place it in an extended time-scale (again, a marker of romance) quite at odds with the surface temporality of the novel that brings the action's conclusion into the 1850s, coterminous with the novel's composition.

16 It also resolves a moral problem in the narrative, by preventing Ruth from having to go to bed with Bellingham again.

17 The point is reinforced by those reviewers who compared Gaskell's work with George Sand's. George Sand was the pseudonym of Amandine-Aurore-Lucile Dupin (1804–76), the author of *Mauprat* (1837), *La Mare au Diable* (1845–6), and *François le Champi* (1848), among other works. What was admired above all in Sand was her 'power of feeling'. For Sand's popularity and influence, see Patricia Thomson, *George Sand and the Victorians* (1977); for the reviews, see *Heritage*, pp. 30–32 and nos. 56, 58, 59. Feeling was claimed by Émile Montégut as the characteristic 'power' of the nineteenth century (*Heritage*, no. 60). Even so fervent a moralist as George Eliot spoke of that 'great power of God', by which Sand delineated 'human passion and its results . . . with such truthfulness, such nicety of discrimination, such tragic power and withal such loving gentle humour' (*Heritage*, p. 31).

18 See *The Prelude*, I, 301–2; Gaskell, always responsive to Wordsworth's poetry, eagerly read *The Prelude* on its publication in 1850.

19 Gaskell rejected the false morality of those of her contemporaries who thought that an offer of marriage from the man, however he had treated the woman, could make all right. See *Heritage*, pp. 281 and 293–4, for responses to the idea that Bellingham could recompense Ruth by offering marriage. Gaskell, though shaken by John Malcolm Ludlow's argument in favour of the marriage, was not convinced by it, delighted though she was by the rest of his review (*Heritage*, pp. 273–86, and J. Miriam Benn, 'Some Unpublished Gaskell Letters', *Notes & Queries*, ccxxv (1980), 508).

20 Page 85; compare *Letters*, pp. 648 ('more . . . what would be called Arian'), 784–5, 860.

21 For the background to Unitarianism, both in general and for Gaskell, see my *Elizabeth Gaskell* (1979), pp. 4–17.

22 While Gaskell properly qualifies the claims of the merely 'natural', the kind advanced by Bellingham, she recognizes the natural call of love, even against the *letter* of Scripture. The rejection of immediate ties of kin and of love when Jesus challenged His mother was painful to her: 'That text [Matthew 12:48; Mark 3:33] always jarred against me, that "Who is my mother and my brethren?" ' (*Letters*, p. 319).

The best current biography is Jenny Uglow, *Elizabeth Gaskell: A Habit of Stories* (1993), which also offers good readings of the work, different though her argument on *Ruth* (see chs. 15 and 16) is from the present edition's. Winifred Gérin, *Elizabeth Gaskell: A Biography* (1976) is sympathetic, if lightweight on detail. *The Letters of Mrs Gaskell*, ed. J. A. V. Chapple and Arthur Pollard (1966), give an exhilarating sense of Gaskell's life and essential if often tantalizing insights into the background and process of composition.

For the contemporary reception of *Ruth*, see *Elizabeth Gaskell: The Critical Heritage*, ed. Angus Easson (1991), pp. 25–32, 200–329. Among the many general studies are Angus Easson, *Elizabeth Gaskell* (1979), which includes much biographical and background information; Margaret Ganz, *Elizabeth Gaskell: The Artist in Conflict* (1969); and, with a particular emphasis on Gaskell as a *woman* writer, Patsy Stoneman, *Elizabeth Gaskell* (1987).

General background on issues such as Victorian sexuality and the fallen woman include Michael Mason's two volumes, *The Making of Victorian Sexuality* (1994) and *The Making of Victorian Sexual Attitudes* (1994). More limited but throwing fascinating light on areas of Victorian sexual behaviour and attitudes (though flawed in its methodology and documentation) is Françoise Barret-Ducrocq, *Love in the Time of Victoria: Sexuality, Class and Gender in Nineteenth-Century London* (1989; English translation, 1991). Studies of women and their representation in the Victorian period include Wanda Neff, *Victorian Working Women: An Historical and Literary Study of Women in British Industries and the Professions, 1832–1850* (1929); Françoise Basch, *Relative Creatures: Victorian Women in Society and the Novel 1837–67* (1974); and Joseph Kestner, *Protest and Reform: The British Social Narrative by Women 1827–1867* (1985), which includes *Ruth*. Specifically on fallen women are Nina Auerbach, *Woman and the Demon: The Life of a Victorian Myth* (1982), and George Watt, *The Fallen Woman in the Nineteenth-Century Novel* (1984), both with a chapter on *Ruth*. More specialized is Monica Correa Fryckstedt, *Elizabeth Gaskell's Mary Barton and Ruth: A Challenge to Christian England* (1982), full on background but defining *Ruth* as a problem novel of an industrialized society. The religious context is explored by Valentine Cunningham, *Everywhere Spoken Against: Dissent in the Victorian Novel* (1975), which includes a chapter on Gaskell. Another crucial influence on Gaskell and within *Ruth* is explored by Donald D. Stone in 'Elizabeth Gaskell, Wordsworth, and the Burden of Reality', in *The Romantic Impulse in Victorian Fiction* (1980). A useful examination that includes comments on *Ruth* is Miriam Bailin, *The Sickroom in Victorian Fiction: The Art of Being Ill* (1994).

Critical discussion specifically on *Ruth* includes the introductions to their respective editions by A. W. Ward (Knutsford Gaskell, Vol. 3, 1906) and Alan Shelston (World's Classics, 1985). Articles include M. D. Wheeler, 'The Sinner as Heroine: A Study of Mrs Gaskell's *Ruth* and the Bible', *Durham University Journal*, n.s. 5 (1976), 148–61; Laura Hepke, 'He Stoops to Conquer: Redeeming the Fallen Woman in the Fiction of Dickens, Gaskell and Their Contemporaries', *Victorian Newsletter*, 69 (1986), 16–22; Peter Stiles, 'Grace, Redemption, and the "Fallen Woman": *Ruth* and *Tess of the D'Urbervilles'*, *Gaskell Society Journal*, 6 (1992), 58–66. Chapters in books (most with useful material beyond the chapter itself) include A. O. J. Cockshut, 'Mrs Gaskell', in *Man and Woman: A Study of Love and the Novel, 1740–1940* (1978); Sally Mitchell, 'The Social Problem', in *The Fallen Angel: Chastity, Class and Women's Reading, 1835–1880* (1981); Loralee MacPike, 'The Fallen Woman's Sexuality: Childbirth and Censure', in *Sexuality and Victorian Literature* (1984); Shirley Foster, 'Elizabeth Gaskell: The Wife's View', in *Victorian Women's Fiction: Marriage, Freedom and the Individual* (1985); Rosemarie Bodenheimer, 'The Maternal Pastoral of *Ruth'*, in *The Politics of Story in Victorian Social Fiction* (1988); Susan Morgan, 'Gaskell's Daughters in Time', in *Sisters in Time: Imagining Gender in Nineteenth-Century British Fiction* (1989); Hilary M. Schor, 'The Plot of the Beautiful Ignoramus: *Ruth* and the Tradition of the Fallen Woman', in *Scheherazade in the Marketplace: Elizabeth Gaskell and the Victorian Novel* (1992); Amanda Anderson, 'Melodrama, Morbidity, and Unthinking Sympathy: Gaskell's *Mary Barton* and *Ruth'*, in *Tainted Souls and Painted Faces: The Rhetoric of Fallenness in Victorian Culture* (1993); Ruth Y. Jenkins, 'To "Stand with Christ against the World": Gaskell's Sentimental Social Agenda', in *Reclaiming Myths of Power: Women Writers and the Victorian Spiritual Crisis* (1995); Terence Wright, 'Women, Death and Integrity: *Ruth'*, in *Elizabeth Gaskell: 'We Are Not Angels': Realism, Gender, Values* (1995).

This edition is based on the first edition of *Ruth*, published on 10 January 1853 by Chapman & Hall, in three volumes. The volume division marks three main divisions in Ruth's life: to her arrival in Eccleston; to the return of Bellingham; and to her death. Chapman & Hall paid Gaskell £500 for the copyright, a considerable advance on their £100 for Gaskell's first novel, *Mary Barton*. The first edition has been collated with the 1855 one-volume Cheap Edition, also published by Chapman & Hall, for which Gaskell made corrections. *Ruth* was subsequently republished in two volumes (1857) by Smith, Elder, to whom Gaskell moved for the publication of *The Life of Charlotte Brontë* earlier that year, and in one volume (1861), again by Smith, Elder. For the 1855 Cheap Edition Gaskell seems to have made a number of minor corrections, mostly to punctuation. She also, though, at Dickens's suggestion in a letter to her of 3 May 1853, omitted Ruth's use of 'sir' in addressing Bellingham while in Wales. More substantially, she omitted two paragraphs from near the end of the novel, presumably because they anticipate or detract from the effect of the conclusion (p. 372, from 'Almost as soon as they' to 'how it fared with *her* child').

Substantive corrections in the present edition are very few. Three are accepted from the 1855 Cheap Edition: p. 15, 'a' in 'with a strange'; p. 98, 'lithe' for 'little' (an easy misreading in 1853 of Gaskell's handwriting); p. 336, 'dour' for 'dear' (unlikely to be a misreading of the copy of 1853 from which the 1855 volume was set, and appropriate to Bradshaw). Three substantive corrections are editorial: p. 70, 'bedroom' for 'sick room' (Ruth has been excluded from the sick room; A. W. Ward made this change in his Knutsford edition of 1906); 'Thank you so much' for 'Thank you much' (p. 109); and p. 136, 'Then there was' for 'Then was' (Ward, 1906, gives 'There was'). Corrections in the 1855 Cheap Edition of obvious misprints in the 1853 First Edition have been accepted and a few other misprints silently corrected. 'Mimie' as the familiar form of Jemima (rather than 'Minnie') has been imposed consistently and the pronouns of God capitalized throughout. The use of certain forms of punctuation, especially to introduce dialogue set off on a separate line, has been made consistent. Punctuation that normally falls outside quotation marks (for example, a question mark stemming from the narrator rather than the character's speech or thought) has been regularly placed outside. Some punctuation (for instance, question and exclamation marks) has been accepted from 1855 (about 50 examples) and some editorially imposed (about 100). This edition follows Penguin house-style in the use of single inverted commas, and in the omission of full stops after abbreviations. The novel's original three-volume division is indicated in the text; chapters, though, are through-numbered rather than starting again at one in each volume.

My thanks to the production staff, not least my copy-editors Imelda Messenger and Christine Collins, whose speed and efficiency saved me from error and inconsistency.

Facsimile title-page of the first edition

RUTH.

A Novel.

BY THE AUTHOR OF "MARY BARTON."

Drop, drop slow tears!
  And bathe those beauteous feet,
Which brought from heaven
  The news and Prince of peace.
Cease not, wet eyes,
  For mercy to entreat:
To cry for vengeance
  Sin doth never cease.
In your deep floods
  Drown all my faults and fears;
Nor let His eye
  See sin, but through my tears.
                    Phineas Fletcher.

IN THREE VOLUMES.

VOL. I.

LONDON:

CHAPMAN AND HALL, 193, PICCADILLY.

1853.

NOTICE.—*The Author of this work reserves the right of publishing a Translation in France.*

Drop, drop, slow tears!
   And bathe those beauteous feet,
Which brought from heaven
   The news and Prince of peace.
Cease not, wet eyes,
   For mercy to entreat:
To cry for vengeance
   Sin doth never cease.
In your deep floods
   Drown all my faults and fears;
Nor let His eye
   See sin, but through my tears.

Phineas Fletcher[1]

VOLUME I

CHAPTER I

There is an assize-town[1] in one of the eastern counties which was much distinguished by the Tudor sovereigns, and, in consequence of their favour and protection, attained a degree of importance that surprises the modern traveller.

A hundred years ago, its appearance was that of picturesque grandeur. The old houses, which were the temporary residences of such of the county-families as contented themselves with the gaieties of a provincial town, crowded the streets and gave them the irregular but noble appearance yet to be seen in the cities of Belgium. The sides of the streets had a quaint richness, from the effect of the gables, and the stacks of chimneys which cut against the blue sky above; while, if the eye fell lower down, the attention was arrested by all kinds of projections in the shape of balcony and oriel; and it was amusing to see the infinite variety of windows that had been crammed into the walls long before Mr Pitt's days of taxation.[2] The streets below suffered from all these projections and advanced stories above; they were dark, and ill-paved with large, round, jolting pebbles, and with no side-path protected by kerbstones; there were no lamp-posts for long winter nights; and no regard was paid to the wants of the middle class, who neither drove about in coaches of their own, nor were carried by their own men in their own sedans into the very halls of their friends. The professional men and their wives, the shopkeepers and their spouses, and all such people, walked about at considerable peril both night and day. The broad unwieldy carriages hemmed them up against the houses in the narrow streets. The inhospitable houses projected their flights of steps almost into the carriage-way, forcing pedestrians again into the danger they had avoided for twenty or thirty paces. Then, at night, the only light was derived from the glaring, flaring oil-lamps hung above the doors of the more aristocratic mansions; just allowing space for the passers-by to become visible, before they again disappeared into the darkness, where it was no uncommon thing for robbers to be in waiting for their prey.

The traditions of those bygone times, even to the smallest social particular, enable one to understand more clearly the circumstances which contributed to the formation of character. The daily life into which people are born, and into which they are absorbed before they are well aware, forms chains which only one in a hundred has moral strength enough to despise, and to break when the right time comes – when an inward necessity for independent individual action arises, which is superior to all outward conventionalities. Therefore it is well to know what were the chains of daily domestic habit which were the natural leading-strings of our forefathers before they learnt to go alone.

The picturesqueness of those ancient streets has departed now. The Astleys, the Dunstans, the Waverhams – names of power in that district – go up duly to London in the season, and have sold their residences in the county-town fifty years ago, or more. And when the county-town lost its attraction for the Astleys, the Dunstans, the Waverhams, how could it be supposed that the Domvilles, the Bextons, and the Wildes would continue to go and winter there in their second-rate houses, and with their increased expenditure? So the grand old houses stood empty awhile; and then speculators ventured to purchase, and to turn the deserted mansions into many smaller dwellings, fitted for professional men, or even (bend your ear lower, lest the shade of Marmaduke, first Baron Waverham, hear) into shops!

Even that was not so very bad, compared with the next innovation on the old glories. The shopkeepers found out that the once fashionable street was dark, and that the dingy light did not show off their goods to advantage; the surgeon could not see to draw his patients' teeth; the lawyer had to ring for candles an hour earlier than he was accustomed to do when living in a more plebeian street. In short, by mutual consent, the whole front of one side of the street was pulled down, and rebuilt in the flat, mean, unrelieved style of George the Third. The body of the houses was too solidly grand to submit to alteration; so people were occasionally surprised, after passing through a common-place-looking shop, to find themselves at the foot of a grand carved oaken staircase, lighted by a window of stained glass, storied all over with armorial bearings.

Up such a stair – past such a window (through which the moonlight fell on her with a glory of many colours) – Ruth Hilton passed wearily one January night, now many years ago. I call it night; but, strictly speaking, it was morning. Two o'clock in the morning chimed forth the old bells of St Saviour's. And yet more than a dozen girls still sat in the room into which Ruth entered, stitching away as if for very life, not daring to gape, or show any outward manifestation of sleepiness. They only sighed a little when Ruth told Mrs Mason the hour of the night, as the result of her errand, for they knew that, stay up as late as they might, the work-hours of the next day must begin at eight, and their young limbs were very weary.

Mrs Mason worked away as hard as any of them; but she was older and tougher; and, besides, the gains were hers. But even she perceived that some rest was needed. 'Young ladies! there will be an interval allowed of half an hour. Ring the bell, Miss Sutton. Martha shall bring you up some bread and cheese, and beer. You will be so good as to eat it standing – away from the dresses – and to have your hands washed ready for work when I return. In half an hour,' said she once more, very distinctly; and then she left the room.

It was curious to watch the young girls as they instantaneously availed themselves of Mrs Mason's absence. One fat, particularly heavy-looking damsel, laid her head on her folded arms and was asleep in a moment; refusing to be wakened for her share in the frugal supper, but springing up with a frightened look at the sound of Mrs Mason's returning footstep, even while it was still far off on the echoing stairs. Two or three others huddled over the scanty fireplace, which, with every possible economy of space, and no attempt whatever at anything of grace or ornament, was inserted in the slight, flat-looking wall, that had been run up by the present owner of the property to portion off this division of the grand old drawing-room of the mansion. Some employed the time in eating their bread and cheese, with as measured and incessant a motion of the jaws (and almost as stupidly placid an expression of countenance), as you may see in cows ruminating in the first meadow you happen to pass.

Some held up admiringly the beautiful ball-dress in progress, while others examined the effect, backing from the object to be criticised in the true artistic manner. Others stretched themselves into all sorts of postures to relieve the weary muscles; one or two gave vent to all the yawns, coughs, and sneezes that had been pent up so long in the presence of Mrs Mason. But Ruth Hilton sprang to the large old window, and pressed against it as a bird presses against the bars of its cage. She put back the blind, and gazed into the quiet moonlight night. It was doubly light – almost as much so as day – for everything was covered with the deep snow which had been falling silently ever since the evening before. The window was in a square recess; the old strange little panes of glass had been replaced by those which gave more light. A little distance off, the feathery branches of a larch waved softly to and fro in the scarcely perceptible night-breeze. Poor old larch! the time had been when it had stood in a pleasant lawn, with the tender grass creeping caressingly up to its very trunk; but now the lawn was divided into yards and squalid back premises, and the larch was pent up and girded about with flag-stones. The snow lay thick on its boughs, and now and then fell noiselessly down. The old stables had been added to, and altered into a dismal street of mean-looking houses, back to back with the ancient mansions. And over all these changes from grandeur to squalor, bent down the purple heavens with their unchanging splendour!

Ruth pressed her hot forehead against the cold glass, and strained her aching eyes in gazing out on the lovely sky of a winter's night. The impulse was strong upon her to snatch up a shawl, and wrapping it round her head, to sally forth and enjoy the glory; and time was when that impulse would have been instantly followed; but now, Ruth's eyes filled with tears, and she stood quite still, dreaming of the days that were gone. Some one touched her shoulder while her thoughts were far away, remembering past January nights, which had resembled this, and were yet so different.

'Ruth, love,' whispered a girl, who had unwillingly distinguished herself by a long hard fit of coughing, 'come and have some supper. You don't know yet how it helps one through the night.'

'One run – one blow of the fresh air would do me more good,' said Ruth.

'Not such a night as this,' replied the other, shivering at the very thought.

'And why not such a night as this, Jenny?' answered Ruth. 'Oh! at home I have many a time run up the lane all the way to the mill, just to see the icicles hang on the great wheel, and when I was once out, I could hardly find in my heart to come in, even to mother, sitting by the fire; – even to mother,' she added, in a low, melancholy tone, which had something of inexpressible sadness in it. 'Why, Jenny!' said she, rousing herself, but not before her eyes were swimming in tears, 'own, now, that you never saw those dismal, hateful, tumble-down old houses there look half so – what shall I call them? almost beautiful – as they do now, with that soft, pure, exquisite covering; and if they are so improved, think of what trees, and grass, and ivy, must be on such a night as this.'

Jenny could not be persuaded into admiring the winter's night, which to her came only as a cold and dismal time, when her cough was more troublesome, and the pain in her side worse than usual. But she put her arm round Ruth's neck, and stood by her; glad that the orphan apprentice, who was not yet inured to the hardship of a dressmaker's workroom, should find so much to give her pleasure in such a common occurrence as a frosty night.

They remained deep in separate trains of thought till Mrs Mason's step was heard, when each returned, supperless but refreshed, to her seat.

Ruth's place was the coldest and the darkest in the room, although she liked it the best; she had instinctively chosen it for the sake of the wall opposite to her, on which was a remnant of the beauty of the old drawing-room, which must once have been magnificent, to judge from the faded specimen left. It was divided into panels of pale sea-green, picked out with white and gold; and on these panels were painted – were thrown with the careless, triumphant hand of a master – the most lovely wreaths of flowers, profuse and luxuriant beyond description, and so real-looking, that you could almost fancy you smelt their fragrance, and heard the south wind go softly rustling in and out among the crimson roses – the branches of purple and white lilac – the floating golden-tressed laburnum boughs. Besides these, there were stately white lilies, sacred to the Virgin – hollyhocks, fraxinella, monk's-hood, pansies, primroses; every flower which blooms profusely in charming old-fashioned country gardens was there, depicted among its graceful foliage, but not in the wild disorder in which I have enumerated them. At the bottom of the panel lay a holly-branch, whose stiff straightness was ornamented by a twining drapery of English ivy and mistletoe and winter aconite; while down either side hung pendant garlands of spring and autumn flowers; and, crowning all, came gorgeous summer with the sweet musk-roses, and the rich-coloured flowers of June and July.

Surely Monnoyer,[3] or whoever the dead and gone artist might be, would have been gratified to know the pleasure his handiwork, even in its wane, had power to give to the heavy heart of a young girl; for they conjured up visions of other sister-flowers that grew, and blossomed, and withered away in her early home.

Mrs Mason was particularly desirous that her workwomen should exert themselves to-night, for, on the next, the annual hunt-ball was to take place. It was the one gaiety of the town since the assize-balls had been discontinued. Many were the dresses she had promised should be sent home 'without fail' the next morning; she had not let one slip through her fingers, for fear, if it did, it might fall into the hands of the rival dressmaker, who had just established herself in the very same street.

She determined to administer a gentle stimulant to the flagging spirits, and with a little preliminary cough to attract attention, she began:

'I may as well inform you, young ladies, that I have been requested this year, as on previous occasions, to allow some of my young people to attend in the ante-chamber of the assembly-room with sandal ribbon,[4] pins, and such little matters, and to be ready to repair any accidental injury to the ladies' dresses. I shall send four – of the most diligent.' She laid a marked emphasis on the last words, but without much effect; they were too sleepy to care for any of the pomps and vanities,[5] or, indeed, for any of the comforts of this world, excepting one sole thing – their beds.

Mrs Mason was a very worthy woman, but, like many other worthy women, she had her foibles; and one (very natural to her calling) was to pay an extreme regard to appearances. Accordingly, she had already selected in her own mind the four girls who were most likely to do credit to the 'establishment'; and these were secretly determined upon, although it was very well to promise the reward to the most diligent. She was really not aware of the falseness of this conduct; being an adept in that species of sophistry with which people persuade themselves that what they wish to do is right.

At last there was no resisting the evidence of weariness. They were told to go to bed; but even that welcome command was languidly obeyed. Slowly they folded up their work, heavily they moved about, until at length all was put away, and they trooped up the wide, dark staircase.

'Oh! how shall I get through five years of these terrible nights! in that close room! and in that oppressive stillness! which lets every sound of the thread be heard as it goes eternally backwards and forwards,' sobbed out Ruth, as she threw herself on her bed, without even undressing herself.

'Nay, Ruth, you know it won't be always as it has been to-night. We often get to bed by ten o'clock and by-and-by you won't mind the closeness of the room. You're worn out to-night, or you would not have minded the sound of the needle; I never hear it. Come, let me unfasten you,' said Jenny.

'What is the use of undressing? We must be up again and at work in three hours.'

'And in those three hours you may get a great deal of rest, if you will but undress yourself and fairly go to bed. Come, love.'

Jenny's advice was not resisted; but before Ruth went to sleep she said:

'Oh! I wish I was not so cross and impatient. I don't think I used to be.'

'No, I am sure not. Most new girls get impatient at first; but it goes off, and they don't care much for anything after a while. Poor child! she's asleep already,' said Jenny to herself.

She could not sleep or rest. The tightness at her side was worse than usual. She almost thought she ought to mention it in her letters home; but then she remembered the premium[6] her father had struggled hard to pay, and the large family, younger than herself, that had to be cared for, and she determined to bear on, and trust that when the warm weather came both the pain and the cough would go away. She would be prudent about herself.

What was the matter with Ruth? She was crying in her sleep as if her heart would break. Such agitated slumber could be no rest; so Jenny wakened her.

'Ruth! Ruth!'

'Oh, Jenny!' said Ruth, sitting up in bed, and pushing back the masses of hair that were heating her forehead, 'I thought I saw mamma by the side of the bed, coming, as she used to do, to see if I were asleep and comfortable; and when I tried to take hold of her, she went away and left me alone – I don't know where; so strange!'

'It was only a dream; you know you'd been talking about her to me, and you're feverish with sitting up late. Go to sleep again, and I'll watch, and waken you if you seem uneasy.'

'But you'll be so tired. Oh, dear! dear!' Ruth was asleep again, even while she sighed.

Morning came, and though their rest had been short, the girls arose refreshed.

'Miss Sutton, Miss Jennings, Miss Booth, and Miss Hilton, you will see that you are ready to accompany me to the shire-hall by eight o'clock.'

One or two of the girls looked astonished, but the majority, having anticipated the selection, and knowing from experience the unexpressed rule by which it was made, received it with the sullen indifference which had become their feeling with regard to most events – a deadened sense of life, consequent upon their unnatural mode of existence, their sedentary days, and their frequent nights of late watching.

But to Ruth it was inexplicable. She had yawned, and loitered, and looked off at the beautiful panel, and lost herself in thoughts of home, until she fully expected the reprimand which at any other time she would have been sure to receive, and now, to her surprise, she was singled out as one of the most diligent!

Much as she longed for the delight of seeing the noble shire-hall – the boast of the county – and of catching glimpses of the dancers, and hearing the band; much as she longed for some variety to the dull monotonous life she was leading, she could not feel happy to accept a privilege, granted, as she believed, in ignorance of the real state of the case; so she startled her companions by rising abruptly and going up to Mrs Mason, who was finishing a dress which ought to have been sent home two hours before:

'If you please, Mrs Mason, I was not one of the most diligent; I am afraid – I believe – I was not diligent at all. I was very tired; and I could not help thinking, and when I think, I can't attend to my work.' She stopped, believing she had sufficiently explained her meaning; but Mrs Mason would not understand, and did not wish for any further elucidation.

'Well, my dear, you must learn to think and work, too; or, if you can't do both, you must leave off thinking. Your guardian, you know, expects you to make great progress in your business, and I am sure you won't disappoint him.'

But that was not to the point. Ruth stood still an instant, although Mrs Mason resumed her employment in a manner which any one but a 'new girl' would have known to be intelligible enough, that she did not wish for any more conversation just then.

'But as I was not diligent I ought not to go, ma'am. Miss Wood was far more industrious than I, and many of the others.'

'Tiresome girl!' muttered Mrs Mason; 'I've half a mind to keep her at home for plaguing me so.' But, looking up, she was struck afresh with the remarkable beauty which Ruth possessed; such a credit to the house, with her waving outline of figure, her striking face, with dark eyebrows and dark lashes, combined with auburn hair and a fair complexion. No! diligent or idle, Ruth Hilton must appear to-night.

'Miss Hilton,' said Mrs Mason, with stiff dignity, 'I am not accustomed (as these young ladies can tell you) to have my decisions questioned. What I say, I mean; and I have my reasons. So sit down, if you please, and take care and be ready by eight. Not a word more,' as she fancied she saw Ruth again about to speak.

'Jenny, you ought to have gone, not me,' said Ruth, in no low voice to Miss Wood, as she sat down by her.

'Hush! Ruth. I could not go if I might, because of my cough. I would rather give it up to you than any one, if it were mine to give. And suppose it is, and take the pleasure as my present, and tell me every bit about it when you come home to-night.'

'Well! I shall take it in that way, and not as if I'd earned it, which I haven't. So thank you. You can't think how I shall enjoy it now. I did work diligently for five minutes last night, after I heard of it, I wanted to go so much. But I could not keep it up. Oh, dear! and I shall really hear a band! and see the inside of that beautiful shire-hall!'

CHAPTER II

In due time that evening, Mrs Mason collected her 'young ladies' for an inspection of their appearance before proceeding to the shire-hall. Her eager, important, hurried manner of summoning them was not unlike that of a hen clucking her chickens together; and to judge from the close investigation they had to undergo, it might have been thought that their part in the evening's performance was to be far more important than that of temporary ladies'-maids.

'Is that your best frock, Miss Hilton?' asked Mrs Mason, in a half-dissatisfied tone, turning Ruth about; for it was only her Sunday black silk, and was somewhat worn and shabby.

'Yes, ma'am,' answered Ruth, quietly.

'Oh! indeed. Then it will do' (still the half-satisfied tone). 'Dress, young ladies, you know is a very secondary consideration. Conduct is everything. Still, Miss Hilton, I think you should write and ask your guardian to send you money for another gown. I am sorry I did not think of it before.'

'I do not think he would send any if I wrote,' answered Ruth, in a low voice. 'He was angry when I wanted a shawl, when the cold weather set in.'

Mrs Mason gave her a little push of dismissal, and Ruth fell into the ranks by her friend, Miss Wood.

'Never mind, Ruthie; you're prettier than any of them,' said a merry, good-natured girl, whose plainness excluded her from any of the envy of rivalry.

'Yes; I know I am pretty,' said Ruth, sadly, 'but I am sorry I have no better gown, for this is very shabby. I am ashamed of it myself, and I can see Mrs Mason is twice as much ashamed. I wish I need not go. I did not know we should have to think about our own dress at all, or I should not have wished to go.'

'Never mind, Ruth,' said Jenny, 'you've been looked at now, and Mrs Mason will soon be too busy to think about you and your gown.'

'Did you hear Ruth Hilton say she knew she was pretty?' whispered one girl to another, so loudly that Ruth caught the words.

'I could not help knowing,' answered she, simply, 'for many people have told me so.'

At length these preliminaries were over, and they were walking briskly through the frosty air; the free motion was so inspiriting that Ruth almost danced along, and quite forgot all about shabby gowns and grumbling guardians. The shire-hall was even more striking than she had expected. The sides of the staircase were painted with figures that showed ghostly in the dim light, for only their faces looked out of the dark dingy canvas, with a strange fixed stare of expression.

The young milliners had to arrange their wares on tables in the ante-room, and make all ready before they could venture to peep into the ball-room, where the musicians were already tuning their instruments, and where one or two char-women (strange contrast! with their dirty, loose attire, and their incessant chatter, to the grand echoes of the vaulted room) were completing the dusting of benches and chairs.

They quitted the place as Ruth and her companions entered. They had talked lightly and merrily in the ante-room, but now their voices were hushed, awed by the old magnificence of the vast apartment. It was so large, that objects showed dim at the further end, as through a mist. Full-length figures of county worthies hung around, in all varieties of costume, from the days of Holbein to the present time. The lofty roof was indistinct, for the lamps were not fully lighted yet; while through the richly-painted Gothic window at one end the moonbeams fell, many-tinted, on the floor, and mocked with their vividness the struggles of the artificial light to illuminate its little sphere.

High above sounded the musicians, fitfully trying some strain of which they were not certain. Then they stopped playing and talked, and their voices sounded goblin-like in their dark recess, where candles were carried about in an uncertain wavering manner, reminding Ruth of the flickering zig-zag motion of the will-o'-the-wisp.

Suddenly the room sprang into the full blaze of light, and Ruth felt less impressed with its appearance, and more willing to obey Mrs Mason's sharp summons to her wandering flock, than she had been when it was dim and mysterious. They had presently enough to do in rendering offices of assistance to the ladies who thronged in, and whose voices drowned all the muffled sound of the band Ruth had longed so much to hear. Still, if one pleasure was less, another was greater than she had anticipated.

'On condition' of such a number of little observances that Ruth thought Mrs Mason would never have ended enumerating them, they were allowed during the dances to stand at a side-door and watch. And what a beautiful sight it was! Floating away to that bounding music – now far away, like garlands of fairies, now near, and showing as lovely women, with every ornament of graceful dress – the *élite* of the county danced on, little caring whose eyes gazed and were dazzled. Outside all was cold, and colourless, and uniform, one coating of snow over all. But inside it was warm, and glowing, and vivid; flowers scented the air, and wreathed the head, and rested on the bosom, as if it were midsummer. Bright colours flashed on the eye and were gone, and succeeded by others as lovely in the rapid movement of the dance. Smiles dimpled every face, and low tones of happiness murmured indistinctly through the room in every pause of the music.

Ruth did not care to separate the figures that formed a joyous and brilliant whole; it was enough to gaze, and dream of the happy smoothness of the lives in which such music, and such profusion of flowers, of jewels, elegance of every description, and beauty of all shapes and hues, were every-day things. She did not want to know who the people were; although to hear a catalogue of names seemed to be the great delight of most of her companions.

In fact, the enumeration rather disturbed her; and to avoid the shock of too rapid a descent into the common-place world of Miss Smiths and Mr Thomsons, she returned to her post in the ante-room. There she stood thinking, or dreaming. She was startled back to actual life by a voice close to her. One of the dancing young ladies had met with a misfortune. Her dress, of some gossamer material, had been looped up by nosegays of flowers, and one of these had fallen off in the dance, leaving her gown to trail. To repair this, she had begged her partner to bring her to the room where the assistants should have been. None were there but Ruth.

'Shall I leave you?' asked the gentleman. 'Is my absence necessary?'

'Oh, no!' replied the lady. 'A few stitches will set all to rights. Besides, I dare not enter that room by myself.' So far she spoke sweetly and prettily. But now she addressed Ruth. 'Make haste. Don't keep me an hour.' And her voice became cold and authoritative.

She was very pretty, with long dark ringlets and sparkling black eyes. These had struck Ruth in the hasty glance she had taken, before she knelt down to her task. She also saw that the gentleman was young and elegant.

'Oh, that lovely galoppe! How I long to dance to it! Will it never be done? What a frightful time you are taking; and I'm dying to return in time for this galoppe!'

By way of showing a pretty child-like impatience, she began to beat time with her feet to the spirited air the band was playing. Ruth could not darn the rent in her dress with this continual motion, and she looked up to remonstrate. As she threw her head back for this purpose, she caught the eye of the gentleman who was standing by; it was so expressive of amusement at the airs and graces of his pretty partner, that Ruth was infected by the feeling, and had to bend her face down to conceal the smile that mantled there. But not before he had seen it; and not before his attention had been thereby drawn to consider the kneeling figure, that, habited in black up to the throat, with the noble head bent down to the occupation in which she was engaged, formed such a contrast to the flippant, bright, artificial girl who sat to be served with an air as haughty as a queen on her throne.

'Oh, Mr Bellingham! I'm ashamed to detain you so long. I had no idea any one could have spent so much time over a little tear. No wonder Mrs Mason charges so much for dress-making, if her work-women are so slow.'

It was meant to be witty, but Mr Bellingham looked grave. He saw the scarlet colour of annoyance flush to that beautiful cheek which was partially presented to him. He took a candle from the table, and held it so that Ruth had more light. She did not look up to thank him, for she felt ashamed that he should have seen the smile which she had caught from him.

'I am sorry I have been so long, ma'am,' said she, gently, as she finished her work. 'I was afraid it might tear out again if I did not do it carefully.' She rose.

'I would rather have had it torn than have missed that charming galoppe,' said the young lady, shaking out her dress as a bird shakes its plumage. 'Shall we go, Mr Bellingham?' looking up at him.

He was surprised that she gave no word or sign of thanks to the assistant. He took up a camelia that some one had left on the table.

'Allow me, Miss Duncombe, to give this in your name to this young lady, as thanks for her dexterous help.'

'Oh – of course,' said she.

Ruth received the flower silently, but with a grave, modest motion of her head. They had gone, and she was once more alone. Presently, her companions returned.

'What was the matter with Miss Duncombe? Did she come here?' asked they.

'Only her lace dress was torn, and I mended it,' answered Ruth, quietly.

'Did Mr Bellingham come with her? They say he's going to be married to her. Did he come, Ruth?'

'Yes,' said Ruth, and relapsed into silence.

Mr Bellingham danced on gaily and merrily through the night, and flirted with Miss Duncombe, as he thought good. But he looked often to the side-door where the milliner's apprentices stood; and once he recognised the tall, slight figure, and the rich auburn hair of the girl in black; and then his eye sought for the camelia. It was there, snowy white in her bosom. And he danced on more gaily than ever.

The cold grey dawn was drearily lighting up the streets when Mrs Mason and her company returned home. The lamps were extinguished, yet the shutters of the shops and dwelling-houses were not opened. All sounds had an echo unheard by day. One or two houseless beggars sat on door-steps, and, shivering, slept with heads bowed on their knees, or resting against the cold hard support afforded by the wall.

Ruth felt as if a dream had melted away, and she were once more in the actual world. How long it would be, even in the most favourable chance, before she should again enter the shire-hall! or hear a band of music! or even see again those bright happy people – as much without any semblance of care or woe as if they belonged to another race of beings! Had they ever to deny themselves a wish, much less a want? Literally and figuratively, their lives seemed to wander through flowery pleasure-paths. Here was cold, biting, mid-winter for her, and such as her – for those poor beggars almost a season of death; but to Miss Duncombe and her companions, a happy, merry time, when flowers still bloomed, and fires crackled, and comforts and luxuries were piled around them like fairy gifts. What did they know of the meaning of the word, so terrific to the poor? What was winter to them? But Ruth fancied that Mr Bellingham looked as if he could understand the feelings of those removed from him by circumstance and station. He had drawn up the windows of his carriage, it is true, with a shudder.

Ruth, then, had been watching him.

Yet she had no idea that any association made her camelia precious to her. She believed it was solely on account of its exquisite beauty that she tended it so carefully. She told Jenny every particular of its presentation, with open, straight-looking eye, and without the deepening of a shade of colour.

'Was it not kind of him? You can't think how nicely he did it, just when I was a little bit mortified by her ungracious ways.'

'It was very nice, indeed,' replied Jenny. 'Such a beautiful flower! I wish it had some scent.'

'I wish it to be exactly as it is; it is perfect. So pure!' said Ruth, almost clasping her treasure as she placed it in water. 'Who is Mr Bellingham?'

'He is son to that Mrs Bellingham of the Priory, for whom we made the grey satin pelisse,'[1] answered Jenny, sleepily.

'That was before my time,' said Ruth. But there was no answer. Jenny was asleep.

It was long before Ruth followed her example. Even on a winter day, it was clear morning light that fell upon her face as she smiled in her slumber. Jenny would not waken her, but watched her face with admiration; it was so lovely in its happiness.

'She is dreaming of last night,' thought Jenny.

It was true she was; but one figure flitted more than all the rest through her visions. He presented flower after flower to her in that baseless morning dream, which was all too quickly ended. The night before, she had seen her dead mother in her sleep, and she wakened, weeping. And now she dreamed of Mr Bellingham, and smiled.

And yet, was this a more evil dream than the other?

The realities of life seemed to cut more sharply against her heart than usual that morning. The late hours of the preceding nights, and perhaps the excitement of the evening before, had indisposed her to bear calmly the rubs and crosses which beset all Mrs Mason's young ladies at times.

For Mrs Mason, though the first dressmaker in the county, was human after all; and suffered, like her apprentices, from the same causes that affected them. This morning she was disposed to find fault with everything, and everybody. She seemed to have risen with the determination of putting the world and all that it contained (her world, at least) to rights before night; and abuses and negligences, which had long passed unreproved, or winked at, were to-day to be dragged to light, and sharply reprimanded. Nothing less than perfection would satisfy Mrs Mason at such times.

She had her ideas of justice, too; but they were not divinely beautiful and true ideas; they were something more resembling a grocer's, or tea-dealer's ideas of equal right. A little over-indulgence last night was to be balanced by a good deal of over-severity to-day; and this manner of rectifying previous errors fully satisfied her conscience.

Ruth was not inclined for, or capable of, much extra exertion; and it would have tasked all her powers to have pleased her superior. The workroom seemed filled with sharp calls. 'Miss Hilton! where have you put the blue Persian?[2] Whenever things are mislaid, I know it has been Miss Hilton's evening for siding away!'[3]

'Miss Hilton was going out last night, so I offered to clear the workroom for her. I will find it directly, ma'am,' answered one of the girls.

'Oh, I am well aware of Miss Hilton's custom of shuffling off her duties upon any one who can be induced to relieve her,' replied Mrs Mason.

Ruth reddened, and tears sprang to her eyes; but she was so conscious of the falsity of the accusation, that she rebuked herself for being moved by it, and, raising her head, gave a proud look round, as if in appeal to her companions.

'Where is the skirt of Lady Farnham's dress? The flounces not put on! I am surprised! May I ask to whom this work was entrusted yesterday?' inquired Mrs Mason, fixing her eyes on Ruth.

'I was to have done it, but I made a mistake, and had to undo it. I am very sorry.'

'I might have guessed, certainly. There is little difficulty, to be sure, in discovering, when work has been neglected or spoilt, into whose hands it has fallen.'

Such were the speeches which fell to Ruth's share on this day of all days, when she was least fitted to bear them with equanimity.

In the afternoon it was necessary for Mrs Mason to go a few miles into the country. She left injunctions, and orders, and directions, and prohibitions without end; but at last she was gone, and in the relief of her absence, Ruth laid her arms on the table, and, burying her head, began to cry aloud, with weak, unchecked sobs.

'Don't cry, Miss Hilton,' – 'Ruthie, never mind the old dragon,' – 'How will you bear on for five years, if you don't spirit yourself up not to care a straw for what she says?' – were some of the modes of comfort and sympathy administered by the young work-women.

Jenny, with a wiser insight into the grievance and its remedy, said:

'Suppose Ruth goes out instead of you, Fanny Barton, to do the errands. The fresh air will do her good; and you know you dislike the cold east winds, while Ruth says she enjoys frost and snow, and all kinds of shivery weather.'

Fanny Barton was a great sleepy-looking girl, huddling over the fire. No one so willing as she to relinquish the walk on this bleak afternoon, when the east wind blew keenly down the street, drying up the very snow itself. There was no temptation to come abroad, for those who were not absolutely obliged to leave their warm rooms; indeed, the dusk hour showed that it was the usual tea-time for the humble inhabitants of that part of the town through which Ruth had to pass on her shopping expedition. As she came to the high ground just above the river, where the street sloped rapidly down to the bridge, she saw the flat country beyond all covered with snow, making the black dome of the cloud-laden sky appear yet blacker; as if the winter's night had never fairly gone away, but had hovered on the edge of the world all through the short bleak day. Down by the bridge (where there was a little shelving bank, used as a landing-place for any pleasure-boats that could float on that shallow stream) some children were playing, and defying the cold; one of them had got a large washing-tub, and with the use of a broken oar kept steering and pushing himself hither and thither in the little creek, much to the admiration of his companions, who stood gravely looking on, immovable in their attentive observation of the hero, although their faces were blue with cold, and their hands crammed deep into their pockets with some faint hope of finding warmth there. Perhaps they feared that, if they unpacked themselves from their lumpy attitudes and began to move about, the cruel wind would find its way into every cranny of their tattered dress. They were all huddled up, and still; with eyes intent on the embryo sailor. At last, one little man, envious of the reputation that his playfellow was acquiring by his daring, called out:

'I'll set thee a craddy,[4] Tom! Thou dar'n't go over yon black line in the water, out into the real river.'

Of course the challenge was not to be refused, and Tom paddled away towards the dark line, beyond which the river swept with smooth, steady current. Ruth (a child in years herself) stood at the top of the declivity watching the adventurer, but as unconscious of any danger as the group of children below. At their playfellow's success, they broke through the calm gravity of observation into boisterous marks of applause, clapping their hands, and stamping their impatient little feet, and shouting, 'Well done, Tom; thou hast done it rarely!'

Tom stood in childish dignity for a moment, facing his admirers; then, in an instant, his washing-tub boat was whirled round, and he lost his balance, and fell out; and both he and his boat were carried away slowly, but surely, by the strong full river which eternally moved onwards to the sea.

The children shrieked aloud with terror; and Ruth flew down to the little bay, and far into its shallow waters, before she felt how useless such an action was, and that the sensible plan would have been to seek for efficient help. Hardly had this thought struck her, when, louder and sharper than the sullen roar of the stream that was ceaselessly and unrelentingly flowing on, came the splash of a horse galloping through the water in which she was standing. Passed her like lightning – down in the stream, swimming along with the current – a stooping rider – an outstretched grasping arm – a little life redeemed, and a child saved to those who loved it! Ruth stood dizzy and sick with emotion while all this took place; and when the rider turned his swimming horse, and slowly breasted up the river to the landing-place, she recognised him as the Mr Bellingham of the night before. He carried the unconscious child across his horse; the body hung in so lifeless a manner that Ruth believed it was dead, and her eyes were suddenly blinded with tears. She waded back to the beach, to the point towards which Mr Bellingham was directing his horse.

'Is he dead?' asked she, stretching out her arms to receive the little fellow; for she instinctively felt that the position in which he hung was not the most conducive to returning consciousness, if, indeed, it would ever return.

'I think not,' answered Mr Bellingham, as he gave the child to her, before springing off his horse. 'Is he your brother? Do you know who he is?'

'Look!' said Ruth, who had sat down upon the ground, the better to prop the poor lad, 'his hand twitches! he lives! oh, sir, he lives! Whose boy is he?' (to the people, who came hurrying and gathering to the spot at the rumour of an accident).

'He's old Nelly Brownson's,' said they. 'Her grandson.'

'We must take him into a house directly,' said she. 'Is his home far off?'

'No, no; it's just close by.'

'One of you go for a doctor at once,' said Mr Bellingham, authoritatively, 'and bring him to the old woman's without delay. You must not hold him any longer,' he continued, speaking to Ruth, and remembering her face now for the first time; 'your dress is dripping wet already. Here! you fellow, take him up, d'ye see!'

But the child's hand had nervously clenched Ruth's dress, and she would not have him disturbed. She carried her heavy burden very tenderly towards a mean little cottage indicated by the neighbours; an old crippled woman was coming out of the door, shaking all over with agitation.

'Dear heart!' said she, 'he's the last of 'em all, and he's gone afore me.'

'Nonsense,' said Mr Bellingham, 'the boy is alive, and likely to live.'

But the old woman was helpless and hopeless, and insisted on believing that her grandson was dead; and dead he would have been if it had not been for Ruth, and one or two of the more sensible neighbours, who, under Mr Bellingham's directions, bustled about, and did all that was necessary until animation was restored.

'What a confounded time these people are in fetching the doctor,' said Mr Bellingham to Ruth, between whom and himself a sort of silent understanding had sprung up from the circumstance of their having been the only two (besides mere children) who had witnessed the accident, and also the only two to whom a certain degree of cultivation had given the power of understanding each other's thoughts and even each other's words.

'It takes so much to knock an idea into such stupid people's heads. They stood gaping and asking which doctor they were to go for, as if it signified whether it was Brown or Smith, so long as he had his wits about him. I have no more time to waste here either; I was on the gallop when I caught sight of the lad; and now he has fairly sobbed and opened his eyes, I see no use in my staying in this stifling atmosphere. May I trouble you with one thing? Will you be so good as to see that the little fellow has all that he wants? If you'll allow me, I'll leave you my purse,' continued he, giving it to Ruth, who was only too glad to have this power entrusted to her of procuring one or two requisites which she had perceived to be wanted. But she saw some gold between the net-work; she did not like the charge of such riches.

'I shall not want so much, really, sir. One sovereign will be plenty – more than enough. May I take that out, and I will give you back what is left of it when I see you again? or, perhaps I had better send it to you, sir?'

'I think you had better keep it all at present. Oh! what a horrid dirty place this is; insufferable two minutes longer. You must not stay here; you'll be poisoned with this abominable air. Come towards the door, I beg. Well, if you think one sovereign will be enough, I will take my purse; only, remember you apply to me if you think they want more.'

They were standing at the door, where some one was holding Mr Bellingham's horse. Ruth was looking at him with her earnest eyes (Mrs Mason and her errands quite forgotten in the interest of the afternoon's event), her whole thoughts bent upon rightly understanding and following out his wishes for the little boy's welfare; and until now this had been the first object in his own mind. But at this moment the strong perception of Ruth's exceeding beauty came again upon him. He almost lost the sense of what he was saying, he was so startled into admiration. The night before, he had not seen her eyes; and now they looked straight and innocently full at him, grave, earnest, and deep. But when she instinctively read the change in the expression of his countenance, she dropped her large white veiling lids; and he thought her face was lovelier still.

The irresistible impulse seized him to arrange matters so that he might see her again before long.

'No!' said he. 'I see it would be better that you should keep the purse. Many things may be wanted for the lad which we cannot calculate upon now. If I remember rightly, there are three sovereigns and some loose change; I shall, perhaps, see you again in a few days, when, if there be any money left in the purse, you can restore it to me.'

'Oh, yes, sir,' said Ruth, alive to the magnitude of the wants to which she might have to administer, and yet rather afraid of the responsibility implied in the possession of so much money.

'Is there any chance of my meeting you again in this house?' asked he.

'I hope to come whenever I can, sir; but I must run in errand-times, and I don't know when my turn may be.'

'Oh' – he did not fully understand this answer – 'I should like to know how you think the boy is going on, if it is not giving you too much trouble; do you ever take walks?'

'Not for walking's sake, sir.'

'Well!' said he, 'you go to church, I suppose? Mrs Mason does not keep you at work on Sundays, I trust?'

'Oh, no, sir. I go to church regularly.'

'Then, perhaps, you will be so good as to tell me what church you go to, and I will meet you there next Sunday afternoon?'

'I go to St Nicholas', sir. I will take care and bring you word how the boy is, and what doctor they get; and I will keep an account of the money I spend.'

'Very well; thank you. Remember, I trust to you.'

He meant that he relied on her promise to meet him; but Ruth thought that he was referring to the responsibility of doing the best she could for the child. He was going away, when a fresh thought struck him, and he turned back into the cottage once more, and addressed Ruth, with a half-smile on his countenance:

'It seems rather strange, but we have no one to introduce us; my name is Bellingham – yours is – ?'

'Ruth Hilton, sir,' she answered, in a low voice, for now that the conversation no longer related to the boy, she felt shy and restrained.

He held out his hand to shake hers, and just as she gave it to him, the old grandmother came tottering up to ask some question. The interruption jarred upon him, and made him once more keenly alive to the closeness of the air, and the squalor and dirt by which he was surrounded.

'My good woman,' said he to Nelly Brownson, 'could you not keep your place a little neater and cleaner? It is more fit for pigs than human beings. The air in this room is quite offensive, and the dirt and filth is really disgraceful.'

By this time he was mounted, and, bowing to Ruth, he rode away.

Then the old woman's wrath broke out.

'Who may you be, that knows no better manners than to come into a poor woman's house to abuse it? – fit for pigs, indeed! What d'ye call yon fellow?'

'He is Mr Bellingham,' said Ruth, shocked at the old woman's apparent ingratitude. 'It was he that rode into the water to save your grandson. He would have been drowned but for Mr Bellingham. I thought once they would both have been swept away by the current, it was so strong.'

'The river is none so deep, either,' the old woman said, anxious to diminish as much as possible the obligation she was under to one who had offended her. 'Some one else would have saved him, if this fine young spark had never been here. He's an orphan, and God watches over orphans,[5] they say. I'd rather it had been any one else as had picked him out, than one who comes into a poor body's house only to abuse it.'

'He did not come in only to abuse it,' said Ruth, gently. 'He came with little Tom; he only said it was not quite so clean as it might be.'

'What! you're taking up the cry, are you? Wait till you are an old woman like me, crippled with rheumatiz, and a lad to see after like Tom, who is always in mud when he isn't in water; and his food and mine to scrape together (God knows we're often short, and do the best I can), and water to fetch up that steep brow.'

She stopped to cough; and Ruth judiciously changed the subject, and began to consult the old woman as to the wants of her grandson, in which consultation they were soon assisted by the medical man.

When Ruth had made one or two arrangements with a neighbour, whom she asked to procure the most necessary things, and had heard from the doctor that all would be right in a day or two, she began to quake at the recollection of the length of time she had spent at Nelly Brownson's, and to remember, with some affright, the strict watch kept by Mrs Mason over her apprentices' out-goings and in-comings on working-days.[6] She hurried off to the shops, and tried to recall her wandering thoughts to the respective merits of pink and blue as a match to lilac, found she had lost her patterns, and went home with ill-chosen things, and in a fit of despair at her own stupidity.

The truth was, that the afternoon's adventure filled her mind; only, the figure of Tom (who was now safe, and likely to do well) was receding into the background, and that of Mr Bellingham becoming more prominent than it had been. His spirited and natural action of galloping into the water to save the child, was magnified by Ruth into the most heroic deed of daring; his interest about the boy was tender, thoughtful benevolence in her eyes, and his careless liberality of money was fine generosity; for she forgot that generosity implies some degree of self-denial. She was gratified, too, by the power of dispensing comfort he had entrusted to her, and was busy with Alnaschar visions[7] of wise expenditure, when the necessity of opening Mrs Mason's house-door summoned her back into actual present life, and the dread of an immediate scolding.

For this time, however, she was spared; but spared for such a reason that she would have been thankful for some blame in preference to her impunity. During her absence, Jenny's difficulty of breathing had suddenly become worse, and the girls had, on their own responsibility, put her to bed, and were standing round her in dismay, when Mrs Mason's return home (only a few minutes before Ruth arrived) fluttered them back into the workroom.

And now all was confusion and hurry; a doctor to be sent for; a mind to be unburdened of directions for a dress to a fore-woman, who was too ill to understand; scoldings to be scattered with no illiberal hand amongst a group of frightened girls, hardly sparing the poor invalid herself for her inopportune illness. In the middle of all this turmoil, Ruth crept quietly to her place, with a heavy saddened heart at the indisposition of the gentle fore-woman. She would gladly have nursed Jenny herself, and often longed to do it, but she could not be spared. Hands, unskilful in fine and delicate work, would be well enough qualified to tend the sick, until the mother arrived from home. Meanwhile, extra diligence was required in the workroom; and Ruth found no opportunity of going to see little Tom, or to fulfil the plans for making him and his grandmother more comfortable, which she had proposed to herself. She regretted her rash promise to Mr Bellingham, of attending to the little boy's welfare; all that she could do, was done by means of Mrs Mason's servant, through whom she made inquiries, and sent the necessary help.

The subject of Jenny's illness was the prominent one in the house. Ruth told of her own adventure, to be sure, but when she was at the very crisis of the boy's fall into the river, the more fresh and vivid interest of some tidings of Jenny was brought into the room, and Ruth ceased, almost blaming herself for caring for anything besides the question of life or death to be decided in that very house.

Then a pale, gentle-looking woman was seen moving softly about; and it was whispered that this was the mother come to nurse her child. Everybody liked her, she was so sweet-looking, and gave so little trouble, and seemed so patient, and so thankful for any inquiries about her daughter, whose illness, it was understood, although its severity was mitigated, was likely to be long and tedious. While all the feelings and thoughts relating to Jenny were predominant, Sunday arrived. Mrs Mason went the accustomed visit to her father's, making some little show of apology to Mrs Wood for leaving her and her daughter; the apprentices dispersed to the various friends with whom they were in the habit of spending the day; and Ruth went to St Nicholas', with a sorrowful heart, depressed on account of Jenny, and self-reproachful at having rashly undertaken what she had been unable to perform.

As she came out of church, she was joined by Mr Bellingham. She had half hoped that he might have forgotten the arrangement, and yet she wished to relieve herself of her responsibility. She knew his step behind her, and the contending feelings made her heart beat hard, and she longed to run away.

'Miss Hilton, I believe,' said he, overtaking her, and bowing forward, so as to catch a sight of her rose-red face. 'How is our little sailor going on? Well, I trust, from the symptoms the other day.'

'I believe, sir, he is quite well now. I am very sorry, but I have not been able to go and see him. I am so sorry – I could not help it. But I have got one or two things through another person. I have put them down on this slip of paper; and here is your purse, sir, for I am afraid I can do nothing more for him. We have illness in the house, and it makes us very busy.'

Ruth had been so much accustomed to blame of late, that she almost anticipated some remonstrance or reproach now, for not having fulfilled her promise better. She little guessed that Mr Bellingham was far more busy trying to devise some excuse for meeting her again, during the silence that succeeded her speech, than displeased with her for not bringing a more particular account of the little boy, in whom he had ceased to feel any interest.

She repeated, after a minute's pause:

'I am very sorry I have done so little, sir.'

'Oh, yes, I am sure you have done all you could. It was thoughtless in me to add to your engagements.'

'He is displeased with me,' thought Ruth, 'for what he believes to have been neglect of the boy, whose life he risked his own to save. If I told all, he would see that I could not do more; but I cannot tell him all the sorrows and worries that have taken up my time.'

'And yet I am tempted to give you another little commission, if it is not taking up too much of your time, and presuming too much on your good nature,' said he, a bright idea having just struck him. 'Mrs Mason lives in Heneage Place, does not she? My mother's ancestors lived there; and once, when the house was being repaired, she took me in to show me the old place. There was an old hunting-piece painted on a panel over one of the chimney-pieces; the figures were portraits of my ancestors. I have often thought I should like to purchase it, if it still remained there. Can you ascertain this for me, and bring me word next Sunday?'

'Oh, yes, sir,' said Ruth, glad that this commission was completely within her power to execute, and anxious to make up for her previous seeming neglect. 'I'll look directly I get home, and ask Mrs Mason to write and let you know.'

'Thank you,' said he, only half satisfied; 'I think perhaps, however, it might be as well not to trouble Mrs Mason about it: you see, it would compromise me, and I am not quite determined to purchase the picture; if you would ascertain whether the painting is there, and tell me, I would take a little time to reflect, and afterwards I could apply to Mrs Mason myself.'

'Very well, sir, I will see about it.' So they parted.

Before the next Sunday, Mrs Wood had taken her daughter to her distant home, to recruit in that quiet place. Ruth watched her down the street from an upper window, and, sighing deep and long, returned to the workroom, whence the warning voice and gentle wisdom had departed.

CHAPTER III

Mr Bellingham attended afternoon service at St Nicholas' church the next Sunday. His thoughts had been far more occupied by Ruth than hers by him, although his appearance upon the scene of her life was more an event to her than it was to him. He was puzzled by the impression she had produced on him, though he did not in general analyse the nature of his feelings, but simply enjoyed them with the delight which youth takes in experiencing new and strong emotion.

He was old compared to Ruth, but young as a man; hardly three-and-twenty. The fact of his being an only child had given him, as it does to many, a sort of inequality in those parts of the character which are usually formed by the number of years that a person has lived.

The unevenness of discipline to which only children are subjected; the thwarting, resulting from over-anxiety; the indiscreet indulgence, arising from a love centred all in one object – had been exaggerated in his education, probably from the circumstance that his mother (his only surviving parent) had been similarly situated to himself.

He was already in possession of the comparatively small property he inherited from his father. The estate on which his mother lived was her own; and her income gave her the means of indulging or controlling him, after he had grown to man's estate, as her wayward disposition and her love of power prompted her.

Had he been double-dealing in his conduct towards her, had he condescended to humour her in the least, her passionate love for him would have induced her to strip herself of all her possessions to add to his dignity or happiness. But although he felt the warmest affection for her, the regardlessness which she had taught him (by example, perhaps, more than by precept) of the feelings of others, was continually prompting him to do things that she, for the time being, resented as mortal affronts. He would mimic the clergyman she specially esteemed, even to his very face; he would refuse to visit her schools for months and months, and, when wearied into going at last, revenge himself by puzzling the children with the most ridiculous questions (gravely put) that he could imagine.

All these boyish tricks annoyed and irritated her far more than the accounts which reached her of more serious misdoings at college and in town. Of these grave offences she never spoke; of the smaller misdeeds she hardly ever ceased speaking.

Still, at times, she had great influence over him, and nothing delighted her more than to exercise it. The submission of his will to hers was sure to be liberally rewarded; for it gave her great happiness to extort, from his indifference or his affection, the concessions which she never sought by force of reason, or by appeals to principle – concessions which he frequently withheld, solely for the sake of asserting his independence of her control.

She was anxious for him to marry Miss Duncombe. He cared little or nothing about it – it was time enough to be married ten years hence;

and so he was dawdling through some months of his life – sometimes flirting with the nothing-loth Miss Duncombe, sometimes plaguing, and sometimes delighting his mother, at all times taking care to please himself – when he first saw Ruth Hilton, and a new, passionate, hearty feeling shot through his whole being. He did not know why he was so fascinated by her. She was very beautiful, but he had seen others equally beautiful, and with many more *agaceries*[1] calculated to set off the effect of their charms.

There was, perhaps, something bewitching in the union of the grace and loveliness of womanhood with the *naïveté*, simplicity, and innocence of an intelligent child. There was a spell in the shyness, which made her avoid and shun all admiring approaches to acquaintance. It would be an exquisite delight to attract and tame her wildness, just as he had often allured and tamed the timid fawns in his mother's park.

By no over-bold admiration, or rash, passionate word, would he startle her; and, surely, in time she might be induced to look upon him as a friend, if not something nearer and dearer still.

In accordance with this determination, he resisted the strong temptation of walking by her side the whole distance home after church. He only received the intelligence she brought respecting the panel with thanks, spoke a few words about the weather, bowed, and was gone. Ruth believed she should never see him again; and, in spite of sundry self-upbraidings for her folly, she could not help feeling as if a shadow were drawn over her existence for several days to come.

Mrs Mason was a widow, and had to struggle for the sake of the six or seven children left dependent on her exertions; thus there was some reason, and great excuse, for the pinching economy which regulated her household affairs.

On Sundays she chose to conclude that all her apprentices had friends who would be glad to see them to dinner, and give them a welcome reception for the remainder of the day; while she, and those of her children who were not at school, went to spend the day at her father's house, several miles out of the town. Accordingly, no dinner was cooked on Sundays for the young work-women; no fires were lighted in any rooms to which they had access. On this morning they breakfasted in Mrs Mason's own parlour, after which the room was closed against them through the day by some understood, though unspoken pro-hibition.

What became of such as Ruth, who had no home and no friends in that large, populous, desolate town? She had hitherto commissioned the servant, who went to market on Saturdays for the family, to buy her a bun or biscuit, whereon she made her fasting dinner in the deserted workroom; sitting in her walking-dress to keep off the cold, which clung to her in spite of shawl and bonnet. Then she would sit at the window, looking out on the dreary prospect till her eyes were often blinded by tears; and, partly to shake off thoughts and recollections, the indulgence in which she felt to be productive of no good, and partly to have some ideas to dwell upon during the coming week beyond those suggested by the constant view of the same room, she would carry her Bible, and place herself in the window-seat on the wide landing, which commanded the street in front of the house. From thence she could see the irregular grandeur of the place; she caught a view of the grey church-tower, rising hoary and massive into mid-air; she saw one or two figures loiter along on the sunny side of the street, in all the enjoyment of their fine clothes and Sunday leisure; and she imagined histories for them, and tried to picture to herself their homes and their daily doings.

And before long, the bells swung heavily in the church-tower, and struck out with musical clang the first summons to afternoon church.

After church was over, she used to return home to the same window-seat, and watch till the winter twilight was over and gone, and the stars came out over the black masses of houses. And then she would steal down to ask for a candle, as a companion to her in the deserted workroom. Occasionally the servant would bring her up some tea; but of late Ruth had declined taking any, as she had discovered she was robbing the kind-hearted creature of part of the small provision left out for her by Mrs Mason. She sat on, hungry and cold, trying to read her Bible, and to think the old holy thoughts which had been her childish meditations at her mother's knee, until one after another the apprentices returned, weary with their day's enjoyment, and their week's late watching; too weary to make her in any way a partaker of their pleasure by entering into details of the manner in which they had spent their day.

And last of all, Mrs Mason returned; and, summoning her 'young people' once more into the parlour, she read a prayer before dismissing them to bed. She always expected to find them all in the house when she came home, but asked no questions as to their proceedings through the day; perhaps, because she dreaded to hear that one or two had occasionally nowhere to go, and that it would be sometimes necessary to order a Sunday's dinner, and leave a lighted fire on that day.

For five months Ruth had been an inmate at Mrs Mason's, and such had been the regular order of the Sundays. While the fore-woman stayed there, it is true, she was ever ready to give Ruth the little variety of hearing of recreations in which she was no partaker; and however tired Jenny might be at night, she had ever some sympathy to bestow on Ruth for the dull length of day she had passed. After her departure, the monotonous idleness of the Sunday seemed worse to bear than the incessant labour of the work-days; until the time came when it seemed to be a recognised hope in her mind, that on Sunday afternoons she should see Mr Bellingham, and hear a few words from him as from a friend who took an interest in her thoughts and proceedings during the past week.

Ruth's mother had been the daughter of a poor curate in Norfolk, and, early left without parents or home, she was thankful to marry a respectable farmer, a good deal older than herself. After their marriage, however, everything seemed to go wrong. Mrs Hilton fell into a delicate state of health, and was unable to bestow the ever-watchful attention to domestic affairs, so requisite in a farmer's wife. Her husband had a series of misfortunes – of a more important kind than the death of a whole brood of turkeys from getting among the nettles,[2] or the year of bad cheeses spoilt by a careless dairy-maid – which were the consequences (so the neighbours said) of Mr Hilton's mistake in marrying a delicate fine lady. His crops failed; his horses died; his barn took fire; in short, if he had been in any way a remarkable character, one might have supposed him to be the object of an avenging fate, so successive were the evils which pursued him; but as he was only a somewhat common-place farmer, I believe we must attribute his calamities to some want in his character of the one quality required to act as key-stone to many excellencies. While his wife lived, all worldly misfortunes seemed as nothing to him; her strong sense and lively faculty of hope upheld him from despair; her sympathy was always ready, and the invalid's room had an atmosphere of peace and encouragement, which affected all who entered it. But when Ruth was about twelve, one morning in the busy hay-time, Mrs Hilton was left alone for some hours. This had often happened before, nor had she seemed weaker than usual when they had gone forth to the field; but on their return, with merry voices, to fetch the dinner prepared for the haymakers, they found an unusual silence brooding over the house; no low voice called out gently to welcome them, and ask after the day's progress; and, on entering the little parlour, which was called Mrs Hilton's and was sacred to her, they found her lying dead on her accustomed sofa. Quite calm and peaceful she lay; there had been no struggle at last; the struggle was for the survivors, and one sank under it. Her husband did not make much ado at first, at least, not in outward show; her memory seemed to keep in check all external violence of grief; but, day by day, dating from his wife's death, his mental powers decreased. He was still a hale-looking elderly man, and his bodily health appeared as good as ever; but he sat for hours in his easy-chair, looking into the fire, not moving, nor speaking unless when it was absolutely necessary to answer repeated questions. If Ruth, with coaxings and draggings, induced him to come out with her, he went with measured steps around his fields, his head bent to the ground with the same abstracted, unseeing look; never smiling – never changing the expression of his face, not even to one of deeper sadness, when anything occurred which might be supposed to remind him of his dead wife. But in this abstraction from all outward things, his worldly affairs went ever lower down. He paid money away, or received it, as if it had been so much water; the gold mines of Potosi[3] could not have touched the deep grief of his soul; but God in His mercy knew the sure balm, and sent the Beautiful Messenger to take the weary one home.[4]

After his death, the creditors were the chief people who appeared to take any interest in the affairs; and it seemed strange to Ruth to see people, whom she scarcely knew, examining and touching all that she had been accustomed to consider as precious and sacred. Her father had made his will at her birth. With the pride of newly and late-acquired paternity, he had considered the office of guardian to his little darling as one which would have been an additional honour to the lord-lieutenant of the county; but as he had not the pleasure of his lordship's acquaintance, he selected the person of most consequence amongst those whom he did know; not any very ambitious appointment, in those days of comparative prosperity; but certainly the flourishing maltster of Skelton was a little surprised, when, fifteen years later, he learnt that he was executor to a will bequeathing many vanished hundreds of pounds, and guardian to a young girl whom he could not remember ever to have seen.

He was a sensible, hard-headed man of the world; having a very fair proportion of conscience as consciences go; indeed, perhaps more than many people; for he had some ideas of duty extending to the circle beyond his own family; and did not, as some would have done, decline acting altogether, but speedily summoned the creditors, examined into the accounts, sold up the farming-stock, and discharged all the debts; paid about 80*l.* into the Skelton bank for a week, while he inquired for a situation or apprenticeship of some kind for poor heart-broken Ruth; heard of Mrs Mason's; arranged all with her in two short conversations; drove over for Ruth in his gig; waited while she and the old servant packed up her clothes; and grew very impatient while she ran, with her eyes streaming with tears, round the garden, tearing off in a passion of love whole boughs of favourite China and damask roses, late flowering against the casement-window of what had been her mother's room. When she took her seat in the gig, she was little able, even if she had been inclined, to profit by her guardian's lectures on economy and self-reliance; but she was quiet and silent, looking forward with longing to the night-time, when, in her bedroom, she might give way to all her passionate sorrow at being wrenched from the home where she had lived with her parents, in that utter absence of any anticipation of change, which is either the blessing or the curse of childhood. But at night there were four other girls in her room, and she could not cry before them. She watched and waited till one by one dropped off to sleep, and then she buried her face in the pillow, and shook with sobbing grief; and then she paused to conjure up, with fond luxuriance, every recollection of the happy days, so little valued in their uneventful peace while they lasted, so passionately regretted when once gone for ever; to remember every look and word of the dear mother, and to moan afresh over the change caused by her death; – the first clouding in of Ruth's day of life. It was Jenny's sympathy on this first night, when awakened by Ruth's irrepressible agony, that had made the bond between them. But Ruth's loving disposition, continually sending forth fibres in search of nutriment, found no other object for regard among those of her daily life to compensate for the want of natural ties.

But, almost insensibly, Jenny's place in Ruth's heart was filled up; there was some one who listened with tender interest to all her little revelations; who questioned her about her early days of happiness, and, in return, spoke of his own childhood – not so golden in reality as

Ruth's, but more dazzling, when recounted with stories of the beautiful cream-coloured Arabian pony, and the old picture-gallery in the house, and avenues, and terraces, and fountains in the garden, for Ruth to paint, with all the vividness of imagination, as scenery and background for the figure which was growing by slow degrees most prominent in her thoughts.

It must not be supposed that this was effected all at once, though the intermediate stages have been passed over. On Sunday, Mr Bellingham only spoke to her to receive the information about the panel; nor did he come to St Nicholas' the next, nor yet the following Sunday. But the third he walked by her side a little way, and, seeing her annoyance, he left her; and then she wished for him back again, and found the day very dreary, and wondered why a strange undefined feeling had made her imagine she was doing wrong in walking alongside of one so kind and good as Mr Bellingham; it had been very foolish of her to be self-conscious all the time, and if ever he spoke to her again she would not think of what people might say, but enjoy the pleasure which his kind words and evident interest in her might give. Then she thought it was very likely he never would notice her again, for she knew that she had been very rude with her short answers; it was very provoking that she had behaved so rudely. She would be sixteen in another month, and she was still childish and awkward. Thus she lectured herself, after parting with Mr Bellingham; and the consequence was, that on the following Sunday she was ten times as blushing and conscious, and (Mr Bellingham thought) ten times more beautiful than ever. He suggested, that instead of going straight home through High-Street, she should take the round by the Leasowes; at first she declined, but then, suddenly wondering and questioning herself why she refused a thing which was, as far as reason and knowledge (*her* knowledge) went, so innocent, and which was certainly so tempting and pleasant, she agreed to go the round; and when she was once in the meadows that skirted the town, she forgot all doubt and awkwardness – nay, almost forgot the presence of Mr Bellingham – in her delight at the new tender beauty of an early spring day in February. Among the last year's brown ruins, heaped together by the wind in the hedgerows, she found the fresh, green, crinkled leaves and pale star-like flowers of the primroses. Here and there a golden celandine made brilliant the sides of the little brook that (full of water in 'February fill-dyke') bubbled along by the side of the path; the sun was low in the horizon, and once, when they came to a higher part of the Leasowes, Ruth burst into an exclamation of delight at the evening glory of mellow light which was in the sky behind the purple distance, while the brown leafless woods in the foreground derived an almost metallic lustre from the golden mist and haze of sunset. It was but three-quarters of a mile round by the meadows, but somehow it took them an hour to walk it. Ruth turned to thank Mr Bellingham for his kindness in taking her home by this beautiful way, but his look of admiration at her glowing, animated face, made her suddenly silent; and, hardly wishing him good-by, she quickly entered the house with a beating, happy, agitated heart.

'How strange it is,' she thought that evening, 'that I should feel as if this charming afternoon's walk were, somehow, not exactly wrong, but yet as if it were not right. Why can it be? I am not defrauding Mrs Mason of any of her time; that I know would be wrong; I am left to go where I like on Sundays; I have been to church, so it can't be because I have missed doing my duty. If I had gone this walk with Jenny, I wonder whether I should have felt as I do now. There must be something wrong in me, myself, to feel so guilty when I have done nothing which is not right; and yet I can thank God for the happiness I have had in this charming spring walk, which dear mamma used to say was a sign when pleasures were innocent and good for us.'

She was not conscious, as yet, that Mr Bellingham's presence had added any charm to the ramble; and when she might have become aware of this, as, week after week, Sunday after Sunday, loitering ramble after loitering ramble succeeded each other, she was too much absorbed with one set of thoughts to have much inclination for self-questioning.

'Tell me everything, Ruth, as you would to a brother; let me help you, if I can, in your difficulties,' he said to her one afternoon. And he really did try to understand, and to realise, how an insignificant and paltry person like Mason the dressmaker could be an object of dread, and regarded as a person having authority, by Ruth. He flamed up with indignation when, by way of impressing him with Mrs Mason's power and consequence, Ruth spoke of some instance of the effects of her employer's displeasure. He declared his mother should never have a gown made again by such a tyrant – such a Mrs Brownrigg;[5] that he would prevent all his acquaintances from going to such a cruel dressmaker; till Ruth was alarmed at the threatened consequences of her one-sided account, and pleaded for Mrs Mason as earnestly as if a young man's menace of this description were likely to be literally fulfilled.

'Indeed, sir, I have been very wrong; if you please, sir, don't be so angry. She is often very good to us; it is only sometimes she goes into a passion; and we are very provoking, I dare say. I know I am for one. I have often to undo my work, and you can't think how it spoils anything (particularly silk) to be unpicked; and Mrs Mason has to bear all the blame. Oh! I am sorry I said anything about it. Don't speak to your mother about it, pray, sir. Mrs Mason thinks so much of Mrs Bellingham's custom.'

'Well, I won't this time' – recollecting that there might be some awkwardness in accounting to his mother for the means by which he had obtained his very correct information as to what passed in Mrs Mason's workroom – 'but if ever she does so again, I'll not answer for myself.'

'I will take care and not tell again, sir,' said Ruth, in a low voice.

'Nay, Ruth, you are not going to have secrets from me, are you? Don't you remember your promise to consider me as a brother? Go on telling me everything that happens to you, pray; you cannot think how much interest I take in all your interests. I can quite fancy that charming home at Milham you told me about last Sunday. I can almost fancy Mrs Mason's workroom; and that, surely, is a proof either of the strength of my imagination, or of your powers of description.'

Ruth smiled. 'It is, indeed, sir. Our workroom must be so different to anything you ever saw. I think you must have passed through Milham often on your way to Lowford.'

'Then you don't think it is any stretch of fancy to have so clear an idea as I have of Milham Grange? On the left hand of the road, is it, Ruth?'

'Yes, sir, just over the bridge, and up the hill where the elm-trees meet overhead and make a green shade; and then comes the dear old Grange, that I shall never see again.'

'Never! Nonsense, Ruthie; it is only six miles off; you may see it any day. It is not an hour's ride.'

'Perhaps I may see it again when I am grown old; I did not think exactly what "never" meant; it is so very long since I was there, and I don't see any chance of my going for years and years, at any rate.'

'Why, Ruth, you – we may go next Sunday afternoon, if you like.'

She looked up at him with a lovely light of pleasure in her face at the idea. 'How, sir? Can I walk it between afternoon-service and the time Mrs Mason comes home? I would go for only one glimpse; but if I could get into the house – oh, sir! if I could just see mamma's room again!'

He was revolving plans in his head for giving her this pleasure, and he had also his own in view. If they went in any of his carriages, the loitering charm of the walk would be lost; and they must, to a certain degree, be encumbered by, and exposed to, the notice of servants.

'Are you a good walker, Ruth? Do you think you can manage six miles? If we set off at two o'clock, we shall be there by four, without hurrying; or say half-past four. Then we might stay two hours, and you could show me all the old walks and old places you love, and we could still come leisurely home. Oh, it's all arranged directly!'

'But do you think it would be right, sir? It seems as if it would be such a great pleasure, that it must be in some way wrong.'

'Why, you little goose, what can be wrong in it?'

'In the first place, I miss going to church by setting out at two,' said Ruth, a little gravely.

'Only for once. Surely you don't see any harm in missing church for once? You will go in the morning, you know.'

'I wonder if Mrs Mason would think it right – if she would allow it?'

'No, I dare say not. But you don't mean to be governed by Mrs Mason's notions of right and wrong. She thought it right to treat that poor girl Palmer in the way you told me about. You would think that wrong, you know, and so would every one of sense and feeling. Come, Ruth, don't pin your faith on any one, but judge for yourself. The pleasure is perfectly innocent; it is not a selfish pleasure either, for I shall enjoy it to the full as much as you will. I shall like to see the places where you spent your childhood; I shall almost love them as much as you do.' He had dropped his voice; and spoke in low, persuasive tones. Ruth hung down her head, and blushed with exceeding happiness; but she could not speak, even to urge her doubts afresh. Thus it was in a manner settled.

How delightfully happy the plan made her through the coming week! She was too young when her mother died to have received any cautions or words of advice respecting *the* subject of a woman's life – if, indeed, wise parents ever directly speak of what, in its depth and power, cannot be put into words – which is a brooding spirit with no definite form or shape that men should know it, but which is there, and present before we have recognised and realised its existence. Ruth was innocent and snow-pure. She had heard of falling in love, but did not know the signs and symptoms thereof; nor, indeed, had she troubled her head much about them. Sorrow had filled up her days, to the exclusion of all lighter thoughts than the consideration of present duties, and the remembrance of the happy time which had been. But the interval of blank, after the loss of her mother and during her father's life-in-death, had made her all the more ready to value and cling to sympathy – first from Jenny, and now from Mr Bellingham. To see her home again, and to see it with him; to show him (secure of his interest) the haunts of former times, each with its little tale of the past – of dead and gone events! – No coming shadow threw its gloom over this week's dream of happiness – a dream which was too bright to be spoken about, to common and indifferent ears.

CHAPTER IV

Sunday came, as brilliant as if there were no sorrow, or death, or guilt in the world; a day or two of rain had made the earth fresh and brave as the blue heavens above. Ruth thought it was too strong a realisation of her hopes, and looked for an over-clouding at noon; but the glory endured, and at two o'clock she was in the Leasowes, with a beating heart full of joy, longing to stop the hours, which would pass too quickly through the afternoon.

They sauntered through the fragrant lanes, as if their loitering would prolong the time, and check the fiery-footed steeds galloping apace[1] towards the close of the happy day. It was past five o'clock before they came to the great mill-wheel, which stood in Sabbath idleness, motionless in a brown mass of shade, and still wet with yesterday's immersion in the deep transparent water beneath. They clambered the little hill, not yet fully shaded by the overarching elms; and then Ruth checked Mr Bellingham, by a slight motion of the hand which lay within his arm, and glanced up into his face to see what that face should express as it looked on Milham Grange, now lying still and peaceful in its afternoon shadows. It was a house of after-thoughts; building materials were plentiful in the neighbourhood, and every successive owner had found a necessity for some addition or projection, till it was a picturesque mass of irregularity – of broken light and shadow – which, as a whole, gave a full and complete idea of a 'Home'. All its gables and nooks were blended and held together by the tender green of the climbing roses and young creepers. An old couple were living in the house until it should be let, but they dwelt in the back part, and never used the front door; so the little birds had grown tame and familiar, and perched upon the window-sills and porch, and on the old stone cistern which caught the water from the roof.

They went silently through the untrimmed garden, full of the pale-coloured flowers of spring. A spider had spread her web over the front door. The sight of this conveyed a sense of desolation to Ruth's heart; she thought it was possible the state-entrance had never been used since her father's dead body had been borne forth, and, without speaking a word, she turned abruptly away, and went round the house to another door. Mr Bellingham followed without questioning, little understanding her feelings, but full of admiration for the varying expression called out upon her face.

The old woman had not yet returned from church, or from the weekly gossip or neighbourly tea which succeeded. The husband sat in the kitchen, spelling the psalms for the day in his Prayer-book, and reading the words out aloud – a habit he had acquired from the double solitude of his life, for he was deaf. He did not hear the quiet entrance of the pair, and they were struck with the sort of ghostly echo which seems to haunt half-furnished and uninhabited houses. The verses he was reading were the following:

'Why art thou so vexed, O my soul: and why art thou so disquieted within me?

'O put thy trust in God: for I will yet thank him, which is the help of my countenance, and my God.'[2]

And when he had finished he shut the book, and sighed with the satisfaction of having done his duty. The words of holy trust, though perhaps they were not fully understood, carried a faithful peace down into the depths of his soul. As he looked up, he saw the young couple standing on the middle of the floor. He pushed his iron-rimmed spectacles on to his forehead, and rose to greet the daughter of his old master and ever-honoured mistress.

'God bless thee, lass; God bless thee! My old eyes are glad to see thee again.'

Ruth sprang forward to shake the horny hand stretched forward in the action of blessing. She pressed it between both of hers, as she rapidly poured out questions. Mr Bellingham was not altogether comfortable at seeing one whom he had already begun to appropriate as his own, so tenderly familiar with a hard-featured, meanly-dressed day-labourer. He sauntered to the window, and looked out into the grass-grown farm-yard; but he could not help overhearing some of the conversation, which seemed to him carried on too much in the tone of equality. 'And who's yon?' asked the old labourer at last. 'Is he your sweetheart? Your missis's son, I reckon. He's a spruce young chap, any how.'

Mr Bellingham's 'blood of all the Howards'[3] rose and tingled about his ears, so that he could not hear Ruth's answer. It began by 'Hush, Thomas; pray hush!' but how it went on he did not catch. The idea of his being Mrs Mason's son! It was really too ridiculous; but, like most things which are 'too ridiculous,' it made him very angry. He was hardly himself again when Ruth shyly came to the window-recess and asked him if he would like to see the house-place, into which the front door entered; many people thought it very pretty, she said, half timidly, for his face had unconsciously assumed a hard and haughty expression, which he could not instantly soften down. He followed her, however; but before he left the kitchen he saw the old man standing, looking at Ruth's companion with a strange, grave air of dissatisfaction.

They went along one or two zig-zag damp-smelling stone passages, and then entered the house-place, or common sitting-room for a farmer's family in that part of the country. The front door opened into it, and several other apartments issued out of it, such as the dairy, the state bedroom (which was half-parlour as well), and a small room which had been appropriated to the late Mrs Hilton, where she sat, or more frequently lay, commanding through the open door the comings and goings of her household. In those days the house-place had been a cheerful room, full of life, with the passing to and fro of husband, child, and servants; with a great merry wood-fire crackling and blazing away every evening, and hardly let out in the very heat of summer; for with the thick stone walls, and the deep window-seats, and the drapery of vine-leaves and ivy, that room, with its flag-floor, seemed always to want the sparkle and cheery warmth of a fire. But now the green shadows from without seemed to have become black in the uninhabited desolation. The oaken shovel-board,[4] the heavy dresser, and the carved cupboards, were now dull and damp, which were formerly polished up to the brightness of a looking-glass, where the fire-blaze was for ever glinting; they only added to the oppressive gloom; the flag-floor was wet with heavy moisture. Ruth stood gazing into the room, seeing nothing of what was present. She saw a vision of former days – an evening in the days of her childhood; her father sitting in the 'master's corner' near the fire, sedately smoking his pipe, while he dreamily watched his wife and child; her mother reading to her, as she sat on a little stool at her feet. It was gone – all gone into the land of shadows; but for the moment it seemed so present in the old room, that Ruth believed her actual life to be the dream. Then, still silent, she went on into her mother's parlour. But there, the bleak look of what had once been full of peace and mother's love, struck cold on her heart. She uttered a cry, and threw herself down by the sofa, hiding her face in her hands, while her frame quivered with her repressed sobs.

'Dearest Ruth, don't give way so. It can do no good; it cannot bring back the dead,' said Mr Bellingham, distressed at witnessing her distress.

'I know it cannot,' murmured Ruth; 'and that is why I cry.[5] I cry because nothing will ever bring them back again.' She sobbed afresh, but more gently, for his kind words soothed her, and softened, if they could not take away, her sense of desolation.

'Come away; I cannot have you stay here, full of painful associations as these rooms must be. Come –' raising her with gentle violence – 'show me your little garden you have often told me about. Near the window of this very room, is it not? See how well I remember everything you tell me.'

He led her round through the back part of the house into the pretty old-fashioned garden. There was a sunny border just under the windows, and clipped box and yew-trees by the grass-plat, further away from the house; and she prattled again of her childish adventures and solitary plays. When they turned round they saw the old man, who had hobbled out with the help of his stick, and was looking at them with the same grave, sad look of anxiety.

Mr Bellingham spoke rather sharply.

'Why does that old man follow us about in that way? It is excessively impertinent of him, I think.'

'Oh, don't call old Thomas impertinent. He is so good and kind, he is like a father to me. I remember sitting on his knee many and many a time when I was a child, whilst he told me stories out of the "Pilgrim's Progress". He taught me to suck up milk through a straw. Mamma was very fond of him, too. He used to sit with us always in the evenings when papa was away at market, for mamma was rather afraid of having no man in the house, and used to beg old Thomas to stay; and he would take me on his knee, and listen just as attentively as I did while mamma read aloud.'

'You don't mean to say you have sat upon that old fellow's knee?'

'Oh, yes! many and many a time.'

Mr Bellingham looked graver than he had done while witnessing Ruth's passionate emotion in her mother's room. But he lost his sense of indignity in admiration of his companion as she wandered among the flowers, seeking for favourite bushes or plants, to which some history or remembrance was attached. She wound in and out in natural, graceful, wavy lines between the luxuriant and overgrown shrubs, which were fragrant with a leafy smell of spring growth; she went on, careless of watching eyes, indeed unconscious, for the time, of their existence. Once she stopped to take hold of a spray of jessamine, and softly kiss it; it had been her mother's favourite flower.

Old Thomas was standing by the horse-mount, and was also an observer of all her goings on. But, while Mr Bellingham's feeling was that of passionate admiration mingled with a selfish kind of love, the old man gazed with tender anxiety, and his lips moved in words of blessing:

'She's a pretty creature, with a glint of her mother about her; and she's the same kind lass as ever. Not a bit set up with yon fine manty-maker's shop[6] she's in. I misdoubt that young fellow though, for all she called him a real gentleman, and checked me when I asked if he was her sweetheart. If his are not sweetheart's looks, I've forgotten all my young days. Here! they're going, I suppose. Look! he wants her to go without a word to the old man; but she is none so changed as that, I reckon.'

Not Ruth, indeed! She never perceived the dissatisfied expression of

Mr Bellingham's countenance, visible to the old man's keen eye; but came running up to Thomas to send her love to his wife, and to shake him many times by the hand.

'Tell Mary I'll make her such a fine gown, as soon as ever I set up for myself; it shall be all in the fashion, big gigot sleeves,[7] that she shall not know herself in them! Mind you tell her that, Thomas, will you?'

'Ay, that I will, lass; and I reckon she'll be pleased to hear thou hast not forgotten thy old merry ways. The Lord bless thee – the Lord lift up the light of His countenance upon thee.'

Ruth was half-way towards the impatient Mr Bellingham when her old friend called her back. He longed to give her a warning of the danger that he thought she was in, and yet he did not know how. When she came up, all he could think of to say was a text; indeed, the language of the Bible was the language in which he thought, whenever his ideas went beyond practical every-day life into expressions of emotion or feeling. 'My dear, remember the devil goeth about as a roaring lion, seeking whom he may devour;[8] remember that, Ruth.'

The words fell on her ear, but gave no definite idea. The utmost they suggested was the remembrance of the dread she felt as a child when this verse came into her mind, and how she used to imagine a lion's head with glaring eyes peering out of the bushes in a dark shady part of the wood, which, for this reason, she had always avoided, and even now could hardly think of without a shudder. She never imagined that the grim warning related to the handsome young man who awaited her with a countenance beaming with love, and tenderly drew her hand within his arm.

The old man sighed as he watched them away. 'The Lord may help her to guide her steps aright. He may. But I'm afeard she's treading in perilous places. I'll put my missis up to going to the town and getting speech of her, and telling her a bit of her danger. An old motherly woman like our Mary will set about it better nor a stupid fellow like me.'

The poor old labourer prayed long and earnestly that night for Ruth. He called it 'wrestling for her soul'; and I think that his prayers were heard, for 'God judgeth not as man judgeth.'[9]

Ruth went on her way, all unconscious of the dark phantoms of the future that were gathering around her; her melancholy turned, with the pliancy of childish years, at sixteen not yet lost, into a softened manner which was infinitely charming. By-and-by she cleared up into sunny happiness. The evening was still and full of mellow light, and the new-born summer was so delicious that, in common with all young creatures, she shared its influence and was glad.

They stood together at the top of a steep ascent, 'the hill' of the hundred.[10] At the summit there was a level space, sixty or seventy yards square, of unenclosed and broken ground, over which the golden bloom of the gorse cast a rich hue, while its delicious scent perfumed the fresh and nimble air. On one side of this common, the ground sloped down to a clear bright pond, in which were mirrored the rough sand-cliffs that rose abrupt on the opposite bank; hundreds of martens found a home there, and were now wheeling over the transparent water, and dipping in their wings in their evening sport. Indeed, all sorts of birds seemed to haunt the lonely pool; the water wagtails were scattered around its margin, the linnets perched on the topmost sprays of the gorse-bushes, and other hidden warblers sang their vespers on the uneven ground beyond. On the far side of the green waste, close by the road, and well placed for the requirements of horses or their riders who might be weary with the ascent of the hill, there was a public-house, which was more of a farm than an inn. It was a long, low building, rich in dormer-windows[11] on the weather side, which were necessary in such an exposed situation, and with odd projections and unlooked-for gables on every side; there was a deep porch in front, on whose hospitable benches a dozen persons might sit and enjoy the balmy air. A noble sycamore grew right before the house, with seats all round it ('such tents the patriarchs loved');[12] and a nondescript sign hung from a branch on the side next to the road, which, being wisely furnished with an interpretation, was found to mean King Charles in the oak.[13]

Near this comfortable, quiet, unfrequented inn, there was another pond, for household and farm-yard purposes, from which the cattle were drinking, before returning to the fields after they had been milked. Their very motions were so lazy and slow, that they served to fill up the mind with the sensation of dreamy rest. Ruth and Mr Bellingham plunged through the broken ground to regain the road near the wayside inn. Hand-in-hand, now pricked by the far-spreading gorse, now ankle-deep in sand; now pressing the soft, thick heath, which should make so brave an autumn show; and now over wild thyme and other fragrant herbs, they made their way, with many a merry laugh. Once on the road, at the summit, Ruth stood silent, in breathless delight at the view before her. The hill fell suddenly down into the plain, extending for a dozen miles or more. There was a clump of dark Scotch firs close to them, which cut clear against the western sky, and threw back the nearest levels into distance. The plain below them was richly wooded, and was tinted by the young tender hues of the earliest summer, for all the trees of the wood had donned their leaves except the cautious ash, which here and there gave a soft, pleasant greyness to the landscape. Far away in the champaign were spires, and towers, and stacks of chimneys belonging to some distant hidden farm-house, which were traced downwards through the golden air by the thin columns of blue smoke sent up from the evening fires. The view was bounded by some rising ground in deep purple shadow against the sunset sky.

When first they stopped, silent with sighing pleasure, the air seemed full of pleasant noises; distant church-bells made harmonious music with the little singing-birds near at hand; nor were the lowings of the cattle, nor the calls of the farm-servants discordant, for the voices seemed to be hushed by the brooding consciousness of the Sabbath. They stood loitering before the house, quietly enjoying the view. The clock in the little inn struck eight, and it sounded clear and sharp in the stillness.

'Can it be so late?' asked Ruth.

'I should not have thought it possible,' answered Mr Bellingham. 'But, never mind, you will be at home long before nine. Stay, there is a shorter road, I know, through the fields; just wait a moment, while I go in and ask the exact way.' He dropped Ruth's arm, and went into the public-house.

A gig had been slowly toiling up the sandy hill behind, unperceived by the young couple, and now it reached the table-land, and was close upon them as they separated. Ruth turned round, when the sound of the horse's footsteps came distinctly as he reached the level. She faced Mrs Mason!

They were not ten – no, not five yards apart. At the same moment they recognised each other, and, what was worse, Mrs Mason had clearly seen, with her sharp, needle-like eyes, the attitude in which Ruth had stood with the young man who had just quitted her. Ruth's hand had been lying in his arm, and fondly held there by his other hand.

Mrs Mason was careless about the circumstances of temptation into which the girls entrusted to her as apprentices were thrown, but severely intolerant if their conduct was in any degree influenced by the force of these temptations. She called this intolerance 'keeping up the character of her establishment'. It would have been a better and more Christian thing, if she had kept up the character of her girls by tender vigilance and maternal care.

This evening, too, she was in an irritated state of temper. Her brother had undertaken to drive her round by Henbury, in order to give her the unpleasant information of the misbehaviour of her eldest son, who was an assistant in a draper's shop in a neighbouring town. She was full of indignation against want of steadiness, though not willing to direct her indignation against the right object – her ne'er-do-well darling. While she was thus charged with anger (for her brother justly defended her son's master and companions from her attacks), she saw Ruth standing with a lover, far away from home, at such a time in the evening, and she boiled over with intemperate displeasure.

'Come here directly, Miss Hilton,' she exclaimed, sharply. Then, dropping her voice to low, bitter tones of concentrated wrath, she said to the trembling, guilty Ruth:

'Don't attempt to show your face at my house again after this conduct. I saw you, and your spark too. I'll have no slurs on the character of my apprentices. Don't say a word. I saw enough. I shall write and tell your guardian to-morrow.'

The horse started away, for he was impatient to be off, and Ruth was left standing there, stony, sick, and pale, as if the lightning had torn up the ground beneath her feet. She could not go on standing, she was so sick and faint; she staggered back to the broken sand-bank, and sank down, and covered her face with her hands.

'My dearest Ruth! are you ill? Speak, darling! My love, my love, do speak to me!'

What tender words after such harsh ones! They loosened the fountain of Ruth's tears, and she cried bitterly.

'Oh! did you see her – did you hear what she said?'

'She! Who, my darling? Don't sob so, Ruth; tell me what it is. Who has been near you? – who has been speaking to you to make you cry so?'

'Oh, Mrs Mason.' And there was a fresh burst of sorrow.

'You don't say so; are you sure? I was not away five minutes.'

'Oh, yes, sir, I'm quite sure. She was so angry; she said I must never show my face there again. Oh, dear! what shall I do?'

It seemed to the poor child as if Mrs Mason's words were irrevocable, and that, being so, she was shut out from every house. She saw how much she had done that was deserving of blame, now when it was too late to undo it. She knew with what severity and taunts Mrs Mason had often treated her for involuntary failings, of which she had been quite unconscious; and now she had really done wrong, and shrank with terror from the consequences. Her eyes were so blinded by the fast-falling tears, she did not see (nor had she seen, would she have been able to interpret) the change in Mr Bellingham's countenance, as he stood silently watching her. He was silent so long, that even in her sorrow she began to wonder that he did not speak, and to wish to hear his soothing words once more.

'It is very unfortunate,' he began, at last; and then he stopped; then he began again: 'It is very unfortunate; for, you see, I did not like to name it to you before, but, I believe – I have business, in fact, which obliges me to go to town to-morrow – to London, I mean; and I don't know when I shall be able to return.'

'To London!' cried Ruth; 'are you going away? Oh, Mr Bellingham!' She wept afresh, giving herself up to the desolate feeling of sorrow, which absorbed all the terror she had been experiencing at the idea of Mrs Mason's anger. It seemed to her at this moment as though she could have borne everything but his departure; but she did not speak again; and after two or three minutes had elapsed, he spoke – not in his natural careless voice, but in a sort of constrained agitated tone.

'I can hardly bear the idea of leaving you, my own Ruth. In such distress, too; for where you can go I do not know at all. From all you have told me of Mrs Mason, I don't think she is likely to mitigate her severity in your case.'

No answer, but tears quietly, incessantly flowing. Mrs Mason's displeasure seemed a distant thing; his going away was the present distress. He went on:

'Ruth, would you go with me to London? My darling, I cannot leave you here without a home; the thought of leaving you at all is pain enough, but in these circumstances – so friendless, so homeless – it is impossible. You must come with me, love, and trust to me.'

Still, she did not speak. Remember how young, and innocent, and motherless she was! It seemed to her as if it would be happiness enough to be with him; and as for the future, he would arrange and decide for that. The future lay wrapped in a golden mist, which she did not care to penetrate; but if he, her sun, was out of sight, and gone, the golden mist became dark heavy gloom, through which no hope could come. He took her hand.

'Will you not come with me? Do you not love me enough to trust me? Oh, Ruth' (reproachfully), 'can you not trust me?'

She had stopped crying, but was sobbing sadly.

'I cannot bear this, love. Your sorrow is absolute pain to me; but it is worse to feel how indifferent you are – how little you care about our separation.'

He dropped her hand. She burst into a fresh fit of crying.

'I may have to join my mother in Paris; I don't know when I shall see you again. Oh, Ruth!' said he, vehemently, 'do you love me at all?'

She said something in a very low voice; he could not hear it, though he bent down his head – but he took her hand again.

'What was it you said, love? Was it not that you did love me? My darling, you do! I can tell it by the trembling of this little hand; then, you will not suffer me to go away alone and unhappy, most anxious about you? There is no other course open to you; my poor girl has no friends to receive her. I will go home directly, and return in an hour with a carriage. You make me too happy by your silence, Ruth.'

'Oh, what can I do?' exclaimed Ruth. 'Mr Bellingham, you should help me, and instead of that you only bewilder me.'

'How, my dearest Ruth? Bewilder you! It seems so clear to me. Look at the case fairly! Here you are, an orphan, with only one person to love you, poor child! – thrown off, for no fault of yours, by the only creature on whom you have a claim, that creature a tyrannical, in-flexible woman; what is more natural (and, being natural, more right) than that you should throw yourself upon the care of the one who loves you dearly – who would go through fire and water for you – who would shelter you from all harm? Unless, indeed, as I suspect, you do not care for him. If so, Ruth, if you do not care for me, we had better part – I will leave you at once; it will be better for me to go, if you do not care for me.'

He said this very sadly (it seemed so to Ruth, at least), and made as though he would have drawn his hand from hers, but now she held it with soft force.

'Don't leave me, please, sir. It is very true I have no friend but you. Don't leave me, please. But, oh! do tell me what I must do!'

'Will you do it if I tell you? If you will trust me, I will do my very best for you. I will give you my best advice. You see your position: Mrs Mason writes and gives her own exaggerated account to your guardian; he is bound by no great love to you, from what I have heard you say, and throws you off; I, who might be able to befriend you – through my mother, perhaps – I, who could at least comfort you a little (could not I, Ruth?), am away, far away, for an indefinite time; that is your position at present. Now, what I advise is this. Come with me into this little inn; I will order tea for you – (I am sure you require it sadly) – and I will leave you there, and go home for the carriage. I will return in an hour at the latest. Then we are together, come what may; that is enough for me, is it not for you, Ruth? Say, yes – say it ever so low, but give me the delight of hearing it. Ruth, say yes.'

Low and soft, with much hesitation, came the 'Yes;' the fatal word of which she so little imagined the infinite consequences. The thought of being with him was all and everything.

'How you tremble, my darling! You are cold, love! Come into the house, and I'll order tea directly, and be off.'

She rose, and, leaning on his arm, went into the house. She was shaking and dizzy with the agitation of the last hour. He spoke to the civil farmer-landlord, who conducted them into a neat parlour, with windows opening into the garden at the back of the house. They had admitted much of the evening's fragrance through their open casements, before they were hastily closed by the attentive host.

'Tea, directly, for this lady!' The landlord vanished.

'Dearest Ruth, I must go; there is not an instant to be lost. Promise me to take some tea, for you are shivering all over, and deadly pale with the fright that abominable woman has given you. I must go; I shall be back in half an hour – and then no more partings, darling.'

He kissed her pale cold face, and went away. The room whirled round before Ruth; it was a dream – a strange, varying, shifting dream – with the old home of her childhood for one scene, with the terror of Mrs Mason's unexpected appearance for another; and then, strangest, dizziest, happiest of all, there was the consciousness of his love, who was all the world to her; and the remembrance of the tender words, which still kept up their low soft echo in her heart.

Her head ached so much that she could hardly see; even the dusky twilight was a dazzling glare to her poor eyes; and when the daughter of the house brought in the sharp light of the candles, preparatory for tea, Ruth hid her face in the sofa pillows with a low exclamation of pain.

'Does your head ache, miss?' asked the girl, in a gentle, sympathising voice. 'Let me make you some tea, miss, it will do you good. Many's the time poor mother's headaches were cured by good strong tea.'

Ruth murmured acquiescence; the young girl (about Ruth's own age, but who was the mistress of the little establishment, owing to her mother's death) made tea, and brought Ruth a cup to the sofa where she lay. Ruth was feverish and thirsty, and eagerly drank it off, although she could not touch the bread-and-butter which the girl offered her. She felt better and fresher, though she was still faint and weak.

'Thank you,' said Ruth. 'Don't let me keep you; perhaps you are busy. You have been very kind, and the tea has done me a great deal of good.'

The girl left the room. Ruth became as hot as she had previously been cold, and went and opened the window, and leant out into the still, sweet, evening air. The bush of sweet-briar, underneath the window, scented the place, and the delicious fragrance reminded her of her old home. I think scents affect and quicken the memory more than either sights or sound; for Ruth had instantly before her eyes the little garden beneath the window of her mother's room, with the old man leaning on his stick, watching her, just as he had done, not three hours before, on that very afternoon.

'Dear old Thomas! He and Mary would take me in, I think; they would love me all the more if I were cast off. And Mr Bellingham would, perhaps, not be so very long away; and he would know where to find me if I stayed at Milham Grange. Oh, would it not be better to go to them? I wonder if he would be very sorry! I could not bear to make him sorry, so kind as he has been to me; but I do believe it would be better to go to them, and ask their advice, at any rate. He would follow me there; and I could talk over what I had better do, with the three best friends I have in the world – the only friends I have.'

She put on her bonnet, and opened the parlour door; but then she saw the square figure of the landlord standing at the open house-door, smoking his evening pipe, and looming large and distinct against the dark air and landscape beyond. Ruth remembered the cup of tea she had drank; it must be paid for, and she had no money with her. She feared that he would not let her quit the house without paying. She thought that she would leave a note for Mr Bellingham, saying where she was gone, and how she had left the house in debt, for (like a child) all dilemmas appeared of equal magnitude to her; and the difficulty of passing the landlord while he stood there, and of giving him an explanation of the circumstances (as far as such explanation was due to him), appeared insuperable, and as awkward, and fraught with inconvenience, as far more serious situations. She kept peeping out of her room, after she had written her little pencil note, to see if the outer door was still obstructed. There he stood, motionless, enjoying his pipe, and looking out into the darkness which gathered thick with the coming night. The fumes of the tobacco were carried by the air into the house, and brought back Ruth's sick headache. Her energy left her; she became stupid and languid, and incapable of spirited exertion; she modified her plan of action, to the determination of asking Mr Bellingham to take her to Milham Grange, to the care of her humble friends, instead of to London. And she thought, in her simplicity, that he would instantly consent when he had heard her reasons.

She started up. A carriage dashed up to the door. She hushed her beating heart, and tried to stop her throbbing head to listen. She heard him speaking to the landlord, though she could not distinguish what he said; heard the jingling of money, and, in another moment, he was in the room, and had taken her arm to lead her to the carriage.

'Oh, sir! I want you to take me to Milham Grange,' said she, holding back. 'Old Thomas would give me a home.'

'Well, dearest, we'll talk of all that in the carriage; I am sure you will listen to reason. Nay, if you will go to Milham, you must go in the carriage,' said he, hurriedly. She was little accustomed to oppose the wishes of any one – obedient and docile by nature, and unsuspicious and innocent of any harmful consequences. She entered the carriage, and drove towards London.

CHAPTER V

The June of 18— had been glorious and sunny, and full of flowers; but July came in with pouring rain, and it was a gloomy time for travellers and for weather-bound tourists, who lounged away the days in touching up sketches, dressing flies, and reading over again for the twentieth time the few volumes they had brought with them. A number of the *Times*, five days old, had been in constant demand, in all the sitting-rooms of a certain inn in a little mountain village of North Wales,[1] through a long July morning. The valleys around were filled with thick cold mist, which had crept up the hillsides till the hamlet itself was folded in its white dense curtain, and from the inn windows nothing was seen of the beautiful scenery around. The tourists who thronged the rooms might as well have been 'wi' their dear little bairnies at hame'; and so some of them seemed to think, as they stood, with their faces flattened against the window-panes, looking abroad in search of an event to fill up the dreary time. How many dinners were hastened that day, by way of getting through the morning, let the poor Welsh kitchen-maid say! The very village children kept in-doors; or if one or two more adventurous stole out into the land of temptation and puddles, they were soon clutched back by angry and busy mothers.

It was only four o'clock, but most of the inmates of the inn thought it must be between six and seven, the morning had seemed so long – so many hours had passed since dinner – when a Welsh car,[2] drawn by two horses, rattled briskly up to the door. Every window of the ark was crowded with faces at the sound; the leathern curtains were undrawn to their curious eyes, and out sprang a gentleman, who carefully assisted a well-cloaked-up lady into the little inn, despite the landlady's assurances of not having a room to spare.

The gentleman (it was Mr Bellingham) paid no attention to the speeches of the hostess, but quietly superintended the unpacking of the carriage, and paid the postilion; then, turning round with his face to the light, he spoke to the landlady, whose voice had been rising during the last five minutes:

'Nay, Jenny, you're strangely altered, if you can turn out an old friend on such an evening as this. If I remember right, Pen trê Voelas is twenty miles across the bleakest mountain road I ever saw.'

'Indeed, sir, and I did not know you; Mr Bellingham, I believe. Indeed, sir, Pen trê Voelas is not above eighteen miles – we only charge for eighteen; it may not be much above seventeen; and we're quite full, indeed, more's the pity.'

'Well, but Jenny, to oblige me, an old friend, you can find lodgings out for some of your people – that house across, for instance.'

'Indeed, sir, and it's at liberty; perhaps you would not mind lodging there yourself. I could get you the best rooms, and send over a trifle or so of furniture, if they wern't as you'd wish them to be.'

'No, Jenny! here I stay. You'll not induce me to venture over into those rooms, whose dirt I know of old. Can't you persuade some one who is not an old friend to move across? Say, if you like, that I had written beforehand to bespeak the rooms. Oh, I know you can manage it – I know your good-natured ways.'

'Indeed, sir – well, I'll see, if you and the lady will just step into the back-parlour, sir – there's no one there just now – the lady is keeping her bed to-day for a cold, and the gentleman is having a rubber at whist in number three. I'll see what I can do.'

'Thank you, thank you! Is there a fire? if not, one must be lighted. Come, Ruthie, come.'

He led the way into a large bow-windowed room, which looked gloomy enough that afternoon, but which I have seen bright and buoyant with youth and hope within, and sunny lights creeping down the purple mountain slope, and stealing over the green, soft meadows, till they reached the little garden, full of roses and lavender bushes, lying close under the window. I have seen – but I shall see no more.

'I did not know you had been here before,' said Ruth, as Mr Bellingham helped her off with her cloak.

'Oh, yes; three years ago I was here on a reading party. We were here above two months, attracted by Jenny's kind heart and oddities; but driven away finally by the insufferable dirt. However, for a week or two it won't much signify.'

'But can she take us in, sir? I thought I heard her saying her house was full.'

'Oh, yes – I dare say it is; but I shall pay her well; she can easily make excuses to some poor devil, and send him over to the other side; and, for a day or two, so that we have shelter, it does not much signify.'

'Could not we go to the house on the other side, sir?'

'And have our meals carried across to us in a half-warm state, to say nothing of having no one to scold for bad cooking! You don't know these out-of-the-way Welsh inns yet, Ruthie.'

'No! I only thought it seemed rather unfair,' said Ruth, gently; but she did not end her sentence, for Mr Bellingham formed his lips into a whistle, and walked to the window to survey the rain.

The remembrance of his former good payment prompted many little lies of which Mrs Morgan was guilty that afternoon, before she succeeded in turning out a gentleman and lady, who were only planning to remain till the ensuing Saturday at the outside, so, if they did fulfil their threat, and leave on the next day, she would be no very great loser.

These household arrangements complete, she solaced herself with tea in her own little parlour, and shrewdly reviewed the circumstances of Mr Bellingham's arrival.

'Indeed! and she's not his wife,' thought Jenny, 'that's clear as day. His wife would have brought her maid, and given herself twice as many airs about the sitting-rooms; while this poor miss never spoke, but kept as still as a mouse. Indeed, and young men will be young men; and, as long as their fathers and mothers shut their eyes, it's none of my business to go about asking questions.'

In this manner they settled down to a week's enjoyment of that Alpine country. It was most true enjoyment to Ruth. It was opening a new sense; vast ideas of beauty and grandeur filled her mind at the sight of the mountains now first beheld in full majesty. She was almost overpowered by the vague and solemn delight; but by-and-by her love for them equalled her awe, and in the night-time she would softly rise, and steal to the window to see the white moonlight, which gave a new aspect to the everlasting hills that girdle the mountain village.

Their breakfast-hour was late, in accordance with Mr Bellingham's tastes and habits; but Ruth was up betimes, and out and away, brushing the dewdrops from the short crisp grass; the lark sung high above her head, and she knew not if she moved or stood still, for the grandeur of this beautiful earth absorbed all idea of separate and individual existence. Even rain was a pleasure to her. She sat in the window-seat of their parlour (she would have gone out gladly, but that such a proceeding annoyed Mr Bellingham, who usually at such times lounged away the listless hours on a sofa, and relieved himself by abusing the weather); she saw the swift fleeting showers come athwart the sunlight like a rush of silver arrows; she watched the purple darkness on the heathery mountain side, and then the pale golden gleam which succeeded. There was no change or alteration of nature that had not its own peculiar beauty in the eyes of Ruth; but if she had complained of the changeable climate, she would have pleased Mr Bellingham more; her admiration and her content made him angry, until her pretty motions and loving eyes soothed down his impatience.

'Really, Ruth,' he exclaimed one day, when they had been imprisoned by rain a whole morning, 'one would think you had never seen a shower of rain before; it quite wearies me to see you sitting there watching this detestable weather with such a placid countenance; and for the last two hours you have said nothing more amusing or interesting than – "Oh, how beautiful!" or, "There's another cloud coming across Moel Wynn."'

Ruth left her seat very gently, and took up her work. She wished she had the gift of being amusing; it must be dull for a man accustomed to all kinds of active employments to be shut up in the house. She was recalled from her absolute self-forgetfulness. What could she say to interest Mr Bellingham? While she thought, he spoke again:

'I remember when we were reading here three years ago, we had a week of just such weather as this; but Howard and Johnson were capital whist-players, and Wilbraham not bad, so we got through the days famously. Can you play *écarté*, Ruth, or picquet?'

'No, sir; I have sometimes played at beggar-my-neighbour,'[3] answered Ruth, humbly, regretting her own deficiencies.

He murmured impatiently, and there was silence for another half hour. Then he sprang up, and rang the bell violently. 'Ask Mrs Morgan for a pack of cards. Ruthie, I'll teach you *écarté*,' said he.

But Ruth was stupid, not so good as a dummy, he said; and it was no fun betting against himself. So the cards were flung across the table – on the floor – anywhere. Ruth picked them up. As she rose, she sighed a little with the depression of spirits consequent upon her own want of power to amuse and occupy him she loved.

'You're pale, love!' said he, half repenting of his anger at her blunders

over the cards. 'Go out before dinner; you know you don't mind this
cursed weather; and see that you come home full of adventures to relate.
Come, little blockhead! give me a kiss, and begone.'

She left the room with a feeling of relief; for if he were dull without
her, she should not feel responsible, and unhappy at her own stupidity.
The open air, that kind soothing balm which gentle mother Nature
offers to us all in our seasons of depression, relieved her. The rain had
ceased, though every leaf and blade was loaded with trembling glittering
drops. Ruth went down to the circular dale, into which the brown-
foaming mountain river fell and made a deep pool, and, after resting
there for a while, ran on between broken rocks down to the valley below.
The waterfall was magnificent, as she had anticipated; she longed to
extend her walk to the other side of the stream, so she sought the
stepping-stones, the usual crossing-place, which were overshadowed by
trees, a few yards from the pool. The waters ran high and rapidly, as
busy as life, between the pieces of grey rock; but Ruth had no fear, and
went lightly and steadily on. About the middle, however, there was a
great gap; either one of the stones was so covered with water as to be
invisible, or it had been washed lower down; at any rate, the spring
from stone to stone was long, and Ruth hesitated for a moment before
taking it. The sound of rushing waters was in her ears to the exclusion
of every other noise; her eyes were on the current running swiftly below
her feet; and thus she was startled to see a figure close before her on
one of the stones, and to hear a voice offering help.

She looked up and saw a man, who was apparently long past middle
life, and of the stature of a dwarf; a second glance accounted for the
low height of the speaker, for then she saw he was deformed. As the
consciousness of this infirmity came into her mind, it must have told
itself in her softened eyes, for a faint flush of colour came into the pale
face of the deformed gentleman, as he repeated his words:

'The water is very rapid; will you take my hand? Perhaps I can help
you.'

Ruth accepted the offer, and with this assistance she was across in a
moment. He made way for her to precede him in the narrow wood
path, and then silently followed her up the glen.

When they had passed out of the wood into the pasture-land beyond,
Ruth once more turned to mark him. She was struck afresh with the
mild beauty of the face, though there was something in the countenance

which told of the body's deformity, something more and beyond the
pallor of habitual ill-health, something of a quick spiritual light in the
deep-set eyes, a sensibility about the mouth; but altogether, though a
peculiar, it was a most attractive face.

'Will you allow me to accompany you if you are going the round by
Cwm Dhu, as I imagine you are? The hand-rail is blown away from
the little wooden bridge by the storm last night, and the rush of waters
below may make you dizzy; and it is really dangerous to fall there, the
stream is so deep.'

They walked on without much speech. She wondered who her
companion might be. She should have known him, if she had seen him
among the strangers at the inn; and yet he spoke English too well to be
a Welshman; he knew the country and the paths so perfectly, he must
be a resident; and so she tossed him from England to Wales and back
again in her imagination.

'I only came here yesterday,' said he, as a widening in the path
permitted them to walk abreast. 'Last night I went to the higher waterfalls;
they are most splendid.'

'Did you go out in all that rain?' asked Ruth, timidly.

'Oh, yes. Rain never hinders me from walking. Indeed, it gives a
new beauty to such a country as this. Besides, my time for my excursion
is so short, I cannot afford to waste a day.'

'Then, you do not live here?' asked Ruth.

'No! my home is in a very different place. I live in a busy town,
where at times it is difficult to feel the truth that

> There are in this loud stunning tide
>   Of human care and crime,
> With whom the melodies abide
>   Of th' everlasting chime;
> Who carry music in their heart
> Through dusky lane and crowded mart,
> Plying their task with busier feet,
> Because their secret souls a holy strain repeat.[4]

I have an annual holiday, which I generally spend in Wales; and often
in this immediate neighbourhood.'

'I do not wonder at your choice,' replied Ruth. 'It is a beautiful
country.'

'It is, indeed; and I have been inoculated by an old innkeeper at Conway with a love for its people, and history, and traditions. I have picked up enough of the language to understand many of their legends; and some are very fine and awe-inspiring, others very poetic and fanciful.'

Ruth was too shy to keep up the conversation by any remark of her own, although his gentle, pensive manner was very winning.

'For instance,' said he, touching a long bud-laden stem of fox-glove in the hedge-side, at the bottom of which one or two crimson speckled flowers were bursting from their green sheaths, 'I dare say, you don't know what makes this fox-glove bend and sway so gracefully. You think it is blown by the wind, don't you?' He looked at her with a grave smile, which did not enliven his thoughtful eyes, but gave an inexpressible sweetness to his face.

'I always thought it was the wind. What is it?' asked Ruth, innocently.

'Oh, the Welsh tell you that this flower is sacred to the fairies, and that it has the power of recognising them, and all spiritual beings who pass by, and that it bows in deference to them as they waft along. Its Welsh name is Maneg Ellyllyn – the good people's glove; and hence, I imagine, our folk's-glove or fox-glove.'

'It's a very pretty fancy,' said Ruth, much interested, and wishing that he would go on, without expecting her to reply.

But they were already at the wooden bridge; he led her across, and then, bowing his adieu, he had taken a different path even before Ruth had thanked him for his attention.

It was an adventure to tell Mr Bellingham, however; and it roused and amused him till dinner-time came, after which he sauntered forth with a cigar.

'Ruth,' said he, when he returned, 'I've seen your little hunchback. He looks like Riquet-with-the-Tuft.[5] He's not a gentleman, though. If it had not been for his deformity, I should not have made him out from your description; you called him a gentleman.'

'And don't you, sir?' asked Ruth, surprised.

'Oh, no! he's regularly shabby and seedy in his appearance; lodging, too, the ostler told me, over that horrible candle and cheese shop, the smell of which is insufferable twenty yards off – no gentleman could endure it; he must be a traveller or artist, or something of that kind.'

'Did you see his face, sir?' asked Ruth.

'No; but a man's back – his *tout ensemble* has character enough in it to decide his rank.'

'His face was very singular; quite beautiful!' said she, softly; but the subject did not interest Mr Bellingham, and he let it drop.

CHAPTER VI

The next day the weather was brave and glorious; a perfect 'bridal of the earth and sky';[1] and every one turned out of the inn to enjoy the fresh beauty of nature. Ruth was quite unconscious of being the object of remark; and, in her light rapid passings to and fro, had never looked at the doors and windows, where many watchers stood observing her, and commenting upon her situation or her appearance.

'She's a very lovely creature,' said one gentleman, rising from the breakfast-table to catch a glimpse of her, as she entered from her morning's ramble. 'Not above sixteen, I should think. Very modest and innocent-looking in her white gown!'

His wife, busy administering to the wants of a fine little boy, could only say (without seeing the young girl's modest ways, and gentle, down-cast countenance):

'Well! I do think it's a shame such people should be allowed to come here. To think of such wickedness under the same roof! Do come away, my dear, and don't flatter her by such notice.'

The husband returned to the breakfast-table; he smelt the broiled ham and eggs, and he heard his wife's commands. Whether smelling or hearing had most to do in causing his obedience, I cannot tell; perhaps you can.

'Now, Harry, go and see if nurse and baby are ready to go out with you. You must lose no time this beautiful morning.'

Ruth found Mr Bellingham was not yet come down; so she sallied out for an additional half hour's ramble. Flitting about through the village, trying to catch all the beautiful sunny peeps at the scenery between the cold stone houses, which threw the radiant distance into aërial perspective far away, she passed by the little shop; and, just issuing from it, came the nurse and baby, and little boy. The baby sat in placid dignity in her nurse's arms, with a face of queenly calm. Her fresh, soft, peachy complexion was really tempting; and Ruth, who was always fond of children, went up to coo and to smile at the little thing, and, after some 'peep-booing', she was about to snatch a kiss, when Harry, whose face had been reddening ever since the play began, lifted up his sturdy little right arm and hit Ruth a great blow on the face.

'Oh, for shame, sir!' said the nurse, snatching back his hand; 'how dare you do that to the lady who is so kind as to speak to Sissy!'

'She's not a lady!' said he, indignantly. 'She's a bad, naughty girl – mamma said so, she did; and she sha'n't kiss our baby.'

The nurse reddened in her turn. She knew what he must have heard; but it was awkward to bring it out, standing face to face with the elegant young lady.

'Children pick up such notions, ma'am,' said she at last, apologetically to Ruth, who stood, white and still, with a new idea running through her mind.

'It's no notion; it's true, nurse; and I heard you say it yourself. Go away, naughty woman!' said the boy, in infantile vehemence of passion to Ruth.

To the nurse's infinite relief, Ruth turned away, humbly and meekly, with bent head, and slow, uncertain steps. But as she turned, she saw the mild sad face of the deformed gentleman, who was sitting at the open window above the shop; he looked sadder and graver than ever; and his eyes met her glance with an expression of deep sorrow. And so, condemned alike by youth and age, she stole with timid step into the house. Mr Bellingham was awaiting her coming in the sitting-room. The glorious day restored all his buoyancy of spirits. He talked gaily away, without pausing for a reply; while Ruth made tea, and tried to calm her heart, which was yet beating with the agitation of the new ideas she had received from the occurrence of the morning. Luckily for her, the only answers required for some time were monosyllables; but those few words were uttered in so depressed and mournful a tone, that at last they struck Mr Bellingham with surprise and displeasure, as the condition of mind they unconsciously implied did not harmonise with his own.

'Ruth, what is the matter this morning? You really are very provoking. Yesterday, when everything was gloomy, and you might have been aware that I was out of spirits, I heard nothing but expressions of delight; to-day, when every creature under heaven is rejoicing, you look most deplorable and woe-begone. You really should learn to have a little sympathy.'

The tears fell quickly down Ruth's cheeks, but she did not speak. She could not put into words the sense she was just beginning to entertain of the estimation in which she was henceforward to be held. She thought he would be as much grieved as she was at what had taken place that morning; she fancied she should sink in his opinion if she told him how others regarded her; besides, it seemed ungenerous to dilate upon the suffering of which he was the cause.

'I will not,' thought she, 'embitter his life; I will try and be cheerful. I must not think of myself so much. If I can but make him happy, what need I care for chance speeches?'

Accordingly, she made every effort possible to be as light-hearted as he was; but, somehow, the moment she relaxed, thoughts would intrude, and wonders would force themselves upon her mind; so that altogether she was not the gay and bewitching companion Mr Bellingham had previously found her.

They sauntered out for a walk. The path they chose led to a wood on the side of a hill, and they entered, glad of the shade of the trees. At first it appeared like any common grove, but they soon came to a deep descent, on the summit of which they stood, looking down on the tree-tops, which were softly waving far beneath their feet. There was a path leading sharp down, and they followed it; the ledge of rock made it almost like going down steps, and their walk grew into a bounding, and their bounding into a run, before they reached the lowest plane. A green gloom reigned there; it was the still hour of noon; the little birds were quiet in some leafy shade. They went on a few yards, and then they came to a circular pool over-shadowed by the trees, whose highest boughs had been beneath their feet a few minutes before. The pond was hardly below the surface of the ground, and there was nothing like a bank on any side. A heron was standing there motionless, but when he saw them he flapped his wings and slowly rose, and soared above the green heights of the wood up into the very sky itself, for at that depth the trees appeared to touch the round white clouds which brooded over the earth. The speed-well grew in the shallowest water of the pool, and all around its margin, but the flowers were hardly seen at first, so deep was the green shadow cast by the trees. In the very middle of the pond the sky was mirrored clear and dark, a blue which looked as if a black void lay behind.

'Oh, there are water-lilies,' said Ruth, her eye catching on the farther side. 'I must go and get some.'

'No; I will get them for you. The ground is spongy all round there. Sit still, Ruth; this heap of grass will make a capital seat.'

He went round, and she waited quietly for his return. When he came back he took off her bonnet, without speaking, and began to place his flowers in her hair. She was quite still while he arranged her coronet, looking up in his face with loving eyes, with a peaceful composure. She knew that he was pleased from his manner, which had the joyousness of a child playing with a new toy, and she did not think twice of his occupation. It was pleasant to forget everything except his pleasure. When he had decked her out, he said:

'There, Ruth! now you'll do. Come and look at yourself in the pond. Here, where there are no weeds. Come.'

She obeyed, and could not help seeing her own loveliness; it gave her a sense of satisfaction for an instant, as the sight of any other beautiful object would have done, but she never thought of associating it with herself. She knew that she was beautiful; but that seemed abstract, and removed from herself. Her existence was in feeling, and thinking, and loving.

Down in that green hollow they were quite in harmony. Her beauty was all that Mr Bellingham cared for, and it was supreme. It was all he recognised of her, and he was proud of it. She stood in her white dress against the trees which grew around; her face was flushed into a brilliancy of colour which resembled that of a rose in June; the great, heavy, white flowers drooped on either side of her beautiful head, and if her brown hair was a little disordered, the very disorder only seemed to add a grace. She pleased him more by looking so lovely than by all her tender endeavours to fall in with his varying humour.

But when they left the wood, and Ruth had taken out her flowers, and resumed her bonnet, as they came near the inn, the simple thought of giving him pleasure was not enough to secure Ruth's peace. She became pensive and sad, and could not rally into gaiety.

'Really, Ruth,' said he, that evening, 'you must not encourage your-self in this habit of falling into melancholy reveries without any cause.

You have been sighing twenty times during the last half hour. Do be a little cheerful. Remember, I have no companion but you in this out-of-the-way place.'

'I am very sorry, sir,' said Ruth, her eyes filling with tears; and then she remembered that it was very dull for him to be alone with her, heavy-hearted as she had been all day. She said in a sweet, penitent tone:

'Would you be so kind as to teach me one of those games at cards you were speaking about yesterday, sir? I would do my best to learn.'

Her soft, murmuring voice won its way. They rang for the cards, and he soon forgot that there was such a thing as depression or gloom in the world, in the pleasure of teaching such a beautiful ignoramus the mysteries of card-playing.

'There!' said he, at last, 'that's enough for one lesson. Do you know, little goose, your blunders have made me laugh myself into one of the worst headaches I have had for years.'

He threw himself on the sofa, and in an instant she was by his side.

'Let me put my cool hands on your forehead,' she begged; 'that used to do mamma good.'

He lay still, his face away from the light, and not speaking. Presently he fell asleep. Ruth put out the candles, and sat patiently by him for a long time, fancying he would awaken refreshed. The room grew cold in the night air; but Ruth dared not rouse him from what appeared to be sound, restoring slumber. She covered him with her shawl, which she had thrown over a chair on coming in from their twilight ramble. She had ample time to think; but she tried to banish thought. At last, his breathing became quick and oppressed, and, after listening to it for some minutes with increasing affright, Ruth ventured to awaken him. He seemed stupefied and shivery. Ruth became more and more terrified; all the household were asleep except one servant-girl, who was wearied out of what little English she had knowledge of in more waking hours, and could only answer, 'Iss, indeed, ma'am,' to any question put to her by Ruth.

She sat by the bedside all night long. He moaned and tossed, but never spoke sensibly. It was a new form of illness to the miserable Ruth. Her yesterday's suffering went into the black distance of long-past years. The present was all-in-all. When she heard people stirring, she went in search of Mrs Morgan, whose shrewd sharp manners, unsoftened by inward respect for the poor girl, had awed Ruth even when Mr Bellingham was by to protect her.

'Mrs Morgan,' she said, sitting down in the little parlour appropriated to the landlady, for she felt her strength suddenly desert her – 'Mrs Morgan, I'm afraid Mr Bellingham is very ill;' – here she burst into tears, but instantly checking herself, 'Oh, what must I do?' continued she; 'I don't think he has known anything all through the night, and he looks so strange and wild this morning.'

She gazed up into Mrs Morgan's face, as if reading an oracle.

'Indeed, miss, ma'am, and it's a very awkward thing. But don't cry, that can do no good, 'deed it can't. I'll go and see the poor young man myself, and then I can judge if a doctor is wanting.'

Ruth followed Mrs Morgan up-stairs. When they entered the sick-room Mr Bellingham was sitting up in bed, looking wildly about him, and as he saw them, he exclaimed:

'Ruth! Ruth! come here; I won't be left alone!' and then he fell down exhausted on the pillow. Mrs Morgan went up and spoke to him, but he did not answer or take any notice.

'I'll send for Mr Jones, my dear, 'deed and I will; we'll have him here in a couple of hours, please God.'

'Oh, can't he come sooner?' asked Ruth, wild with terror.

' 'Deed no! he lives at Llanglâs when he's at home, and that's seven mile away, and he may be gone a round eight or nine mile on the other side Llanglâs; but I'll send a boy on the pony directly.'

Saying this, Mrs Morgan left Ruth alone. There was nothing to be done, for Mr Bellingham had again fallen into heavy sleep. Sounds of daily life began, bells rang, breakfast-services clattered up and down the passages, and Ruth sat on shivering by the bedside in that darkened room. Mrs Morgan sent her breakfast up-stairs by a chambermaid, but Ruth motioned it away in her sick agony, and the girl had no right to urge her to partake of it. That alone broke the monotony of the long morning. She heard the sound of merry parties setting out on excursions, on horseback or in carriages; and once, stiff and wearied, she stole to the window, and looked out on one side of the blind; but the day looked bright and discordant to her aching, anxious heart. The gloom of the darkened room was better and more befitting.

It was some hours after he was summoned before the doctor made his appearance. He questioned his patient, and, receiving no coherent

answer, he asked Ruth concerning the symptoms, but when she questioned him in turn he only shook his head and looked grave. He made
a sign to Mrs Morgan to follow him out of the room, and they went
down to her parlour, leaving Ruth in a depth of despair, lower than she
could have thought it possible there remained for her to experience, an
hour before.

'I am afraid this is a bad case,' said Mr Jones to Mrs Morgan in
Welsh. 'A brain-fever has evidently set in.'

'Poor young gentleman! poor young man! He looked the very picture
of health!'

'That very appearance of robustness will, in all probability, make his
disorder more violent. However, we must hope for the best, Mrs Morgan.
Who is to attend upon him? He will require careful nursing. Is that
young lady his sister? She looks too young to be his wife?'

'No, indeed! Gentlemen like you must know, Mr Jones, that we can't
always look too closely into the ways of young men who come to our
houses. Not but what I'm sorry for her, for she's an innocent, inoffensive
young creature. I always think it right, for my own morals, to put a little
scorn into my manners when such as her come to stay here; but, indeed,
she's so gentle, I've found it hard work to show the proper contempt.'

She would have gone on to her inattentive listener if she had not
heard a low tap at the door, which recalled her from her morality, and
Mr Jones from his consideration of the necessary prescriptions.

'Come in!' said Mrs Morgan, sharply. And Ruth came in. She was
white and trembling; but she stood in that dignity which strong feeling,
kept down by self-command, always imparts.

'I wish you, sir, to be so kind as to tell me, clearly and distinctly,
what I must do for Mr Bellingham. Every direction you give me shall
be most carefully attended to. You spoke about leeches – I can put them
on, and see about them. Tell me everything, sir, that you wish to have
done!'

Her manner was calm and serious, and her countenance and deport-
ment showed that the occasion was calling out strength sufficient to
meet it. Mr Jones spoke with a deference which he had not thought of
using up-stairs, even while he supposed her to be the sister of the invalid.
Ruth listened gravely; she repeated some of the injunctions, in order
that she might be sure that she fully comprehended them, and then,
bowing, left the room.

'She is no common person,' said Mr Jones. 'Still she is too young to have the responsibility of such a serious case. Have you any idea where his friends live, Mrs Morgan?'

'Indeed and I have. His mother, as haughty a lady as you would wish to see, came travelling through Wales last year; she stopped here, and, I warrant you, nothing was good enough for her; she was real quality. She left some clothes and books behind her (for the maid was almost as fine as the mistress, and little thought of seeing after her lady's clothes, having a taste for going to see scenery along with the man-servant), and we had several letters from her. I have them locked in the drawers in the bar, where I keep such things.'

'Well! I should recommend your writing to the lady, and telling her her son's state.'

'It would be a favour, Mr Jones, if you would just write it yourself. English writing comes so strange to my pen.'

The letter was written, and, in order to save time, Mr Jones took it to the Llanglâs post-office.

CHAPTER VII

Ruth put away every thought of the past or future; everything that could unfit her for the duties of the present. Exceeding love supplied the place of experience. She never left the room after the first day; she forced herself to eat, because his service needed her strength. She did not indulge in any tears, because the weeping she longed for would make her less able to attend upon him. She watched, and waited, and prayed: prayed with an utter forgetfulness of self, only with a consciousness that God was all powerful, and that he, whom she loved so much, needed the aid of the Mighty One.

Day and night, the summer night, seemed merged into one. She lost count of time in the hushed and darkened room. One morning Mrs Morgan beckoned her out; and she stole on tiptoe into the dazzling gallery, on one side of which the bedrooms opened.

'She's come,' whispered Mrs Morgan, looking very much excited, and forgetting that Ruth had never heard that Mrs Bellingham had been summoned.

'Who is come?' asked Ruth. The idea of Mrs Mason flashed through her mind – but with a more terrible, because a more vague dread, she heard that it was his mother; the mother of whom he had always spoken as a person whose opinion was to be regarded more than that of any other individual.

'What must I do? Will she be angry with me?' said she, relapsing into her child-like dependence on others; and feeling that even Mrs Morgan was some one to stand between her and Mrs Bellingham.

Mrs Morgan herself was a little perplexed. Her morality was rather shocked at the idea of a proper real lady like Mrs Bellingham discovering that she had winked at the connexion between her son and Ruth. She was quite inclined to encourage Ruth in her inclination to shrink out of Mrs Bellingham's observation, an inclination which arose from no definite consciousness of having done wrong, but principally from the representations she had always heard of the lady's awfulness. Mrs Bellingham swept into her son's room as if she were unconscious what poor young creature had lately haunted it; while Ruth hurried into some unoccupied bedroom, and, alone there, she felt her self-restraint suddenly give way, and burst into the saddest, most utterly wretched weeping she had ever known. She was worn out with watching, and exhausted by passionate crying, and she lay down on the bed and fell asleep. The day passed on; she slumbered unnoticed and unregarded; she awoke late in the evening with a sense of having done wrong in sleeping so long; the strain upon her responsibility had not yet left her. Twilight was closing fast around; she waited until it had become night, and then she stole down to Mrs Morgan's parlour.

'If you please, may I come in?' asked she.

Jenny Morgan was doing up the hieroglyphics which she called her accounts; she answered sharp enough, but it was a permission to enter, and Ruth was thankful for it.

'Will you tell me how he is? Do you think I may go back to him?'

'No, indeed, that you may not. Nest, who has made his room tidy these many days, is not fit to go in now. Mrs Bellingham has brought her own maid, and the family nurse, and Mr Bellingham's man; such a tribe of servants, and no end to packages; water-beds coming by the carrier, and a doctor from London coming down to-morrow, as if featherbeds and Mr Jones was not good enough. Why, she won't let a soul of us into the room; there's no chance for you!'

Ruth sighed. 'How is he?' she inquired, after a pause.

'How can I tell, indeed, when I'm not allowed to go near him? Mr Jones said to-night was a turning point; but I doubt it, for it is four days since he was taken ill, and who ever heard of a sick person taking a turn on an even number of days? It's alway on the third, or the fifth, or seventh, or so on. He'll not turn till to-morrow night, take my word for it, and their fine London doctor will get all the credit, and honest Mr Jones will be thrown aside. I don't think he will get better myself, though – Gelert does not howl for nothing. My patience! what's the matter with the girl? – Lord, child, you're never going to faint, and be ill on my hands?' Her sharp voice recalled Ruth from the sick unconsciousness that had been creeping over her as she listened to the latter part of this speech. She sat down and could not speak – the room whirled round and round – her white feebleness touched Mrs Morgan's heart.

'You've had no tea, I guess. Indeed, and the girls are very careless.' She rang the bell with energy, and seconded her pull by going to the door and shouting out sharp directions, in Welsh, to Nest and Gwen, and three or four other rough, kind, slatternly servants.

They brought her tea, which was comfortable, according to the idea of comfort prevalent in that rude hospitable place; there was plenty to eat, too much, indeed, for it revolted the appetite it was intended to provoke. But the heartiness with which the kind rosy waiter pressed her to eat, and the scolding Mrs Morgan gave her, when she found the buttered toast untouched (toast on which she had herself desired that the butter might not be spared), did Ruth more good than the tea. She began to hope, and to long for the morning when hope might have become certainty. It was all in vain that she was told that the room she had been in all day was at her service; she did not say a word, but she was not going to bed that night, of all nights in the year, when life or death hung trembling in the balance. She went into the bedroom till the bustling house was still, and heard busy feet passing to and fro into the room she might not enter; and voices, imperious, though hushed down to a whisper, ask for innumerable things. Then there was silence; and when she thought that all were dead asleep, except the watchers, she stole out into the gallery. On the other side were two windows, cut into the thick stone wall, and flower-pots were placed on the shelves thus formed, where great, untrimmed, straggling geraniums grew, and strove to reach the light. The window near Mr Bellingham's door was open; the soft, warm-scented night-air came sighing in in faint gusts, and then was still. It was summer; there was no black darkness in the twenty-four hours; only the light grew dusky, and colour disappeared from objects, of which the shape and form remained distinct. A soft grey oblong of barred light fell on the flat wall opposite to the windows, and deeper grey shadows marked out the tracery of the plants, more graceful thus than in reality. Ruth crouched where no light fell. She sat on the ground close by the door; her whole existence was absorbed in listening: all was still; it was only her heart beating with the strong, heavy, regular sound of a hammer. She wished she could stop its rushing, incessant clang. She heard a rustle of a silken gown, and knew it ought not to have been worn in a sick room;[1] for her senses seemed to have passed into the keeping of the invalid, and to feel only as he felt. The noise was probably occasioned by some change of posture in the watcher inside, for it was once more dead-still. The soft wind outside sank with a low, long, distant moan among the windings of the hills, and lost itself there, and came no more again. But Ruth's heart beat loud. She rose with as little noise as if she were a vision, and crept to the open window to try and lose the nervous listening for the ever-recurring sound. Out beyond, under the calm sky, veiled with a mist rather than with a cloud, rose the high, dark outlines of the mountains, shutting in that village as if it lay in a nest. They stood, like giants, solemnly watching for the end of Earth and Time. Here and there a black round shadow reminded Ruth of some 'Cwm', or hollow, where she and her lover had rambled in sun and in gladness. She then thought the land enchanted into everlasting brightness and happiness; she fancied, then, that into a region so lovely no bale or woe could enter, but would be charmed away and disappear before the sight of the glorious guardian mountains. Now she knew the truth, that earth has no barrier which avails against agony. It comes lightning-like down from heaven, into the mountain house and the town garret; into the palace and into the cottage. The garden lay close under the house; a bright spot enough by day; for in that soil, whatever was planted grew and blossomed in spite of neglect. The white roses glimmered out in the dusk all the night through; the red were lost in shadow. Between the low boundary of the garden and the hills swept one or two green meadows; Ruth looked into the grey darkness till she traced each separate wave of outline. Then she heard a little restless bird chirp out of its wakefulness from a nest in the ivy round the walls of the house. But the mother-bird spread her soft feathers, and hushed it into silence. Presently, however, many little birds began to scent the coming dawn, and rustled among the leaves, and chirruped loud and clear. Just above the horizon, too, the mist became a silvery grey cloud hanging on the edge of the world; presently it turned shimmering white; and then, in an instant, it flushed into rose, and the mountain tops sprang into heaven, and bathed in the presence of the shadow of God.[2] With a bound, the sun of a molten fiery red came above the horizon, and immediately thousands of little birds sang out for joy, and a soft chorus of mysterious, glad murmurs came forth from the earth; the low whispering wind left its hiding-place among the clefts and hollows of the hills, and wandered among the rustling herbs and trees, waking the flower-buds to the life of another day. Ruth gave a sigh of relief that the night was over and gone; for she knew that soon suspense would be ended, and the verdict known, whether for life or for death. She grew faint and sick with anxiety; it almost seemed as if she must go into the room and learn the truth. Then she heard movements, but they were not sharp or rapid, as if prompted by any emergency; then, again, it was still. She sat curled up upon the floor, with her head thrown back against the wall, and her hands clasped round her knees. She had yet to wait. Meanwhile, the invalid was slowly rousing himself from a long, deep, sound, health-giving sleep. His mother had sat by him the night through, and was now daring to change her position for the first time; she was even venturing to give directions in a low voice to the old nurse, who had dozed away in an arm-chair, ready to obey any summons of her mistress. Mrs Bellingham went on tiptoe towards the door, and chiding herself because her stiff, weary limbs made some slight noise. She had an irrepressible longing for a few minutes' change of scene after her night of watching. She felt that the crisis was over; and the relief to her mind made her conscious of every bodily feeling and irritation, which had passed unheeded as long as she had been in suspense.

She slowly opened the door. Ruth sprang upright at the first sound of the creaking handle. Her very lips were stiff and unpliable with the force of the blood which rushed to her head. It seemed as if she could not form words. She stood right before Mrs Bellingham. 'How is he, madam?'

Mrs Bellingham was for a moment surprised at the white apparition which seemed to rise out of the ground. But her quick proud mind understood it all in an instant. This was the girl, then, whose profligacy had led her son astray; had raised up barriers in the way of her favourite scheme of his marriage with Miss Duncombe; nay, this was the real cause of his illness, his mortal danger at this present time, and of her bitter, keen anxiety. If, under any circumstances, Mrs Bellingham could have been guilty of the ill-breeding of not answering a question, it was now; and for a moment she was tempted to pass on in silence. Ruth could not wait; she spoke again:

'For the love of God, madam, speak! How is he? Will he live?'

If she did not answer her, she thought the creature was desperate enough to force her way into his room. So she spoke:

'He has slept well: he is better.'

'Oh! my God, I thank thee,' murmured Ruth, sinking back against the wall.

It was too much to hear this wretched girl thanking God for her son's life; as if, in fact, she had any lot or part in him, and to dare to speak to the Almighty on her son's behalf! Mrs Bellingham looked at her with cold, contemptuous eyes, whose glances were like ice-bolts, and made Ruth shiver up away from them.

'Young woman, if you have any propriety or decency left, I trust that you will not dare to force yourself into his room.'

She stood for a moment as if awaiting an answer, and half expecting it to be a defiance. But she did not understand Ruth. She did not imagine the faithful trustfulness of her heart. Ruth believed that if Mr Bellingham was alive and likely to live, all was well. When he wanted her, he would send for her, ask for her, yearn for her, till every one would yield before his steadfast will. At present she imagined that he was probably too weak to care or know who was about him; and though it would have been an infinite delight to her to hover and brood around him, yet it was of him she thought and not of herself. She gently drew herself on one side to make way for Mrs Bellingham to pass.

By-and-by Mrs Morgan came up. Ruth was still near the door, from which it seemed as if she could not tear herself away.

'Indeed, miss, and you must not hang about the door in this way; it is not pretty manners. Mrs Bellingham has been speaking very sharp and cross about it, and I shall lose the character of my inn if people take to talking as she does. Did not I give you a room last night to keep in, and never be seen or heard of; and did I not tell you what a particular lady Mrs Bellingham was, but you must come out here right in her way? Indeed, it was not pretty, nor grateful to me, Jenny Morgan, and that I must say.'

Ruth turned away like a chidden child. Mrs Morgan followed her to her room, scolding as she went; and then, having cleared her heart after her wont by uttering hasty words, her real kindness made her add, in a softened tone:

'You stop up here like a good girl. I'll send you your breakfast by-and-by, and let you know from time to time how he is; and you can go out for a walk, you know: but if you do, I'll take it as a favour if you'll go out by the side door. It will, maybe, save scandal.'

All that day long, Ruth kept herself close prisoner in the room to which Mrs Morgan accorded her; all that day, and many succeeding days. But at nights, when the house was still, and even the little brown mice had gathered up the crumbs, and darted again to their holes, Ruth stole out, and crept to his door to catch, if she could, the sound of his beloved voice. She could tell by its tones how he felt, and how he was getting on, as well as any of the watchers in the room. She yearned and pined to see him once more; but she had reasoned herself down into something like patience. When he was well enough to leave his room, when he had not always one of the nurses with him, then he would send for her, and she would tell him how very patient she had been for his dear sake. But it was long to wait even with this thought of the manner in which the waiting would end. Poor Ruth! her faith was only building up vain castles in the air; they towered up into heaven, it is true, but, after all, they were but visions.

CHAPTER VIII

If Mr Bellingham did not get rapidly well, it was more owing to the morbid querulous fancy attendant on great weakness than from any unfavourable medical symptom. But he turned away with peevish loathing from the very sight of food, prepared in the slovenly manner which had almost disgusted him when he was well. It was of no use telling him that Simpson, his mother's maid, had superintended the preparation at every point. He offended her by detecting something offensive and to be avoided in her daintiest messes, and made Mrs Morgan mutter many a hasty speech, which, however, Mrs Bellingham thought it better not to hear until her son should be strong enough to travel.

'I think you are better to-day,' said she, as his man wheeled his sofa to the bedroom window. 'We shall get you down-stairs to-morrow.'

'If it were to get away from this abominable place, I could go down to-day; but I believe I'm to be kept prisoner here for ever. I shall never get well here, I'm sure.'

He sank back on his sofa in impatient despair. The surgeon was announced, and eagerly questioned by Mrs Bellingham as to the possibility of her son's removal; and he, having heard the same anxiety for the same end expressed by Mrs Morgan in the regions below, threw no great obstacles in the way. After the doctor had taken his departure, Mrs Bellingham cleared her throat several times. Mr Bellingham knew the prelude of old, and winced with nervous annoyance.

'Henry, there is something I must speak to you about; an unpleasant subject, certainly, but one which has been forced upon me by the very girl herself; you must be aware to what I refer without giving me the pain of explaining myself.'

Mr Bellingham turned himself sharply round to the wall, and prepared himself for a lecture by concealing his face from her notice; but she herself was in too nervous a state to be capable of observation.

'Of course,' she continued, 'it was my wish to be as blind to the whole affair as possible, though you can't imagine how Mrs Mason has blazoned it abroad; all Fordham rings with it: but of course it could not be pleasant, or, indeed, I may say correct, for me to be aware that a person of such improper character was under the same – I beg your pardon, dear Henry, what do you say?'

'Ruth is no improper character, mother; you do her injustice!'

'My dear boy, you don't mean to uphold her as a paragon of virtue!'

'No, mother, but I led her wrong; I—'

'We will let all discussions into the cause or duration of her present character drop, if you please,' said Mrs Bellingham, with the sort of dignified authority which retained a certain power over her son – a power which originated in childhood, and which he only defied when he was roused into passion. He was too weak in body to oppose himself to her, and fight the ground inch by inch. 'As I have implied, I do not wish to ascertain your share of blame; from what I saw of her one morning, I am convinced of her forward, intrusive manners, utterly without shame, or even common modesty.'

'What are you referring to?' asked Mr Bellingham, sharply.

'Why, when you were at the worst, and I had been watching you all night, and had just gone out in the morning for a breath of fresh air, this girl pushed herself before me, and insisted upon speaking to me. I really had to send Mrs Morgan to her before I could return to your room. A more impudent, hardened manner, I never saw.'

'Ruth was neither impudent nor hardened; she was ignorant enough, and might offend from knowing no better.'

He was getting weary of the discussion, and wished it had never been begun. From the time he had become conscious of his mother's presence, he had felt the dilemma he was in, in regard to Ruth, and various plans had directly crossed his brain; but it had been so troublesome to weigh and consider them all properly, that they had been put aside to be settled when he grew stronger. But this difficulty in which he was placed by his connexion with Ruth, associated the idea of her in his mind with annoyance and angry regret at the whole affair. He wished, in the languid way in which he wished and felt everything not immediately relating to his daily comfort, that he had never seen her. It was a most awkward, a most unfortunate affair. Notwithstanding this annoyance connected with and arising out of Ruth, he would not submit to hear her abused; and something in his manner impressed this on his mother, for she immediately changed her mode of attack.

'We may as well drop all dispute as to the young woman's manners;

but I suppose you do not mean to defend your connexion with her; I suppose you are not so lost to all sense of propriety as to imagine it fit or desirable that your mother and this degraded girl should remain under the same roof, liable to meet at any hour of the day?' She waited for an answer, but no answer came.

'I ask you a simple question; is it, or is it not desirable?'

'I suppose it is not,' he replied, gloomily.

'And *I* suppose, from your manner, that you think the difficulty would be best solved by my taking my departure, and leaving you with your vicious companion?'

Again no answer, but inward and increasing annoyance, of which Mr Bellingham considered Ruth the cause. At length he spoke:

'Mother, you are not helping me in my difficulty. I have no desire to banish you, nor to hurt you, after all your care for me. Ruth has not been so much to blame as you imagine, that I must say; but I do not wish to see her again, if you can tell me how to arrange it otherwise, without behaving unhandsomely. Only spare me all this worry while I am so weak. I put myself in your hands. Dismiss her, as you wish it; but let it be done handsomely, and let me hear no more about it; I cannot bear it; let me have a quiet life, without being lectured while I am pent up here, and unable to shake off unpleasant thoughts.'

'My dear Henry, rely upon me.'

'No more, mother; it's a bad business, and I can hardly avoid blaming myself in the matter; I don't want to dwell upon it.'

'Don't be too severe in your self-reproaches while you are so feeble, dear Henry; it is right to repent, but I have no doubt in my own mind she led you wrong with her artifices. But, as you say, everything should be done handsomely. I confess I was deeply grieved when I first heard of the affair, but since I have seen the girl – Well! I'll say no more about her, since I see it displeases you; but I am thankful to God that you see the error of your ways.'

She sat silent, thinking for a little while, and then sent for her writing-case, and began to write. Her son became restless, and nervously irritated.

'Mother,' he said, 'this affair worries me to death. I can not shake off the thoughts of it.'

'Leave it to me, I'll arrange it satisfactorily.'

'Could we not leave to-night? I should not be so haunted by this annoyance in another place. I dread seeing her again, because I fear a scene; and yet I believe I ought to see her, in order to explain.'

'You must not think of such a thing, Henry,' said she, alarmed at the very idea. 'Sooner than that, we will leave in half-an-hour, and try to get to Pen trê Voelas to-night. It is not yet three, and the evenings are very long. Simpson should stay and finish the packing; she could go straight to London and meet us there. Macdonald and nurse could go with us. Could you bear twenty miles, do you think?'

Anything to get rid of his uneasiness. He felt that he was not behaving as he should do, to Ruth, though the really right never entered his head. But it would extricate him from his present dilemma, and save him many lectures; he knew that his mother, always liberal where money was concerned, would 'do the thing handsomely', and it would always be easy to write and give Ruth what explanation he felt inclined, in a day or two; so he consented, and soon lost some of his uneasiness in watching the bustle of the preparation for their departure.

All this time Ruth was quietly spending in her room, beguiling the waiting, weary hours, with pictures of the meeting at the end. Her room looked to the back, and was in a side-wing away from the principal state apartments, consequently she was not roused to suspicion by any of the commotion; but, indeed, if she had heard the banging of doors, the sharp directions, the carriage wheels, she would still not have suspected the truth; her own love was too faithful.

It was four o'clock and past, when some one knocked at her door, and, on entering, gave her a note, which Mrs Bellingham had left. That lady had found some difficulty in wording it, so as to satisfy herself, but it was as follows:

'My son, on recovering from his illness, is, I thank God, happily conscious of the sinful way in which he has been living with you. By his earnest desire, and in order to avoid seeing you again, we are on the point of leaving this place; but, before I go, I wish to exhort you to repentance, and to remind you that you will not have your own guilt alone upon your head, but that of any young man whom you may succeed in entrapping into vice. I shall pray that you may turn to an honest life, and I strongly recommend you, if indeed you are not "dead in trespasses and sins",[1] to enter some penitentiary. In accordance with my son's wishes, I forward you in this envelope a bank-note of fifty pounds.

'MARGARET BELLINGHAM.'

Was this the end of all? Had he, indeed, gone? She started up, and asked this last question of the servant, who, half guessing at the purport of the note, had lingered about the room, curious to see the effect produced.

'Iss, indeed, miss; the carriage drove from the door as I came up-stairs. You'll see it now on the Yspytty road, if you'll please to come to the window of No. 24.'

Ruth started up and followed the chambermaid. Ay, there it was, slowly winding up the steep white road, on which it seemed to move at a snail's pace.

She might overtake him – she might – she might speak one farewell word to him, print his face on her heart with a last look – nay, when he saw her he might retract, and not utterly, for ever, leave her. Thus she thought; and she flew back to her room, and snatching up her bonnet, ran, tying the strings with her trembling hands as she went down the stairs, out at the nearest door, little heeding the angry words of Mrs Morgan; for the hostess, more irritated at Mrs Bellingham's severe upbraiding at parting, than mollified by her ample payment, was offended by the circumstance of Ruth, in her wild haste, passing through the prohibited front door.

But Ruth was away before Mrs Morgan had finished her speech, out and away, scudding along the road, thought-lost in the breathless rapidity of her motion. Though her heart and head beat almost to bursting, what did it signify if she could but overtake the carriage? It was a nightmare, constantly evading the most passionate wishes and endeavours, and constantly gaining ground. Every time it was visible it was in fact more distant, but Ruth would not believe it. If she could but gain the summit of that weary everlasting hill, she believed that she could run again, and would soon be nigh upon the carriage. As she ran, she prayed with wild eagerness; she prayed that she might see his face once more, even if she died on the spot before him. It was one of those prayers which God is too merciful to grant; but despairing and wild as it was, Ruth put her soul into it, and prayed it again, and yet again.

Wave above wave of the ever-rising hills were gained, were crossed, and at last Ruth struggled up to the very top and stood on the bare table of moor, brown and purple, stretching far away till it was lost in the haze of the summer afternoon; the white road was all flat before her, but the carriage she sought and the figure she sought had disappeared. There was no human being there; a few wild, black-faced mountain sheep quietly grazing near the road, as if it were long since they had been disturbed by the passing of any vehicle, was all the life she saw on the bleak moorland.

She threw herself down on the ling by the side of the road, in despair. Her only hope was to die, and she believed she was dying. She could not think; she could believe anything. Surely life was a horrible dream, and God would mercifully awaken her from it? She had no penitence, no consciousness of error or offence; no knowledge of any one circumstance but that he was gone. Yet afterwards, long afterwards, she remembered the exact motion of a bright green beetle busily meandering among the wild thyme near her, and she recalled the musical, balanced, wavering drop of a skylark into her nest near the heather-bed where she lay. The sun was sinking low, the hot air had ceased to quiver near the hotter earth, when she bethought her once more of the note which she had impatiently thrown down before half mastering its contents. 'Oh, perhaps,' she thought, 'I have been too hasty. There may be some words of explanation from him on the other side of the page, to which, in my blind anguish, I never turned. I will go and find it.'

She lifted herself heavily and stiffly from the crushed heather. She stood dizzy and confused with her change of posture; and was so unable to move at first, that her walk was but slow and tottering; but, by-and-by, she was tasked and goaded by thoughts which forced her into rapid motion, as if, by it, she could escape from her agony. She came down on the level ground, just as many gay or peaceful groups were sauntering leisurely home with hearts at ease; with low laughs and quiet smiles, and many an exclamation at the beauty of the summer evening.

Ever since her adventure with the little boy and his sister, Ruth had habitually avoided encountering these happy – innocents, may I call them? – these happy fellow-mortals! And even now, the habit grounded on sorrowful humiliation had power over her; she paused, and then, on looking back, she saw more people who had come into the main road from a side path. She opened a gate into a pasture-field, and crept up to the hedge-bank until all should have passed by, and she could steal into the inn unseen. She sat down on the sloping turf by the roots of an old hawthorn-tree which grew in the hedge; she was still tearless with hot burning eyes; she heard the merry walkers pass by; she heard the footsteps of the village children, as they ran along to their evening play;

she saw the small black cows come into the fields after being milked; and life seemed yet abroad. When would the world be still and dark, and fit for such a deserted, desolate creature as she was? Even in her hiding-place she was not long at peace. The little children, with their curious eyes peering here and there, had peeped through the hedge, and through the gate, and now they gathered from all the four corners of the hamlet, and crowded round the gate; and one more adventurous than the rest, had run into the field to cry, 'Gi' me a halfpenny,' which set the example to every little one, emulous of his boldness; and there, where she sat, low on the ground, and longing for the sure hiding-place earth gives to the weary, the children kept running in, and pushing one another forwards, and laughing. Poor things; their time had not come for understanding what sorrow is. Ruth would have begged them to leave her alone, and not madden her utterly; but they knew no English save the one eternal 'Gi' me a halfpenny.' She felt in her heart that there was no pity anywhere. Suddenly, while she thus doubted God, a shadow fell across her garments, on which her miserable eyes were bent. She looked up. The deformed gentleman she had twice before seen, stood there. He had been attracted by the noisy little crowd, and had questioned them in Welsh, but not understanding enough of the language to comprehend their answers, he had obeyed their signs, and entered the gate to which they pointed. There he saw the young girl whom he had noticed at first for her innocent beauty, and the second time for the idea he had gained respecting her situation; there he saw her, crouched up like some hunted creature, with a wild, scared look of despair, which almost made her lovely face seem fierce; he saw her dress soiled and dim, her bonnet crushed and battered with her tossings to and fro on the moorland bed; he saw the poor, lost wanderer, and when he saw her, he had compassion on her.

There was some look of heavenly pity in his eyes, as gravely and sadly they met her upturned gaze, which touched her stony heart. Still looking at him, as if drawing some good influence from him, she said low and mournfully, 'He has left me, sir! – sir, he has indeed – he has gone and left me!'

Before he could speak a word to comfort her, she had burst into the wildest, dreariest crying ever mortal cried. The settled form of the event, when put into words, went sharp to her heart; her moans and sobs wrung his soul; but as no speech of his could be heard, if he had been able to decide what best to say, he stood by her in apparent calmness, while she, wretched, wailed and uttered her woe. But when she lay worn out, and stupefied into silence, she heard him say, to himself, in a low voice:

'Oh, my God! for Christ's sake, pity her!'

Ruth lifted up her eyes, and looked at him with a dim perception of the meaning of his words. She regarded him fixedly in a dreamy way, as if they struck some chord in her heart, and she were listening to its echo; and so it was. His pitiful look, or his words, reminded her of the childish days when she knelt at her mother's knee and she was only conscious of a straining, longing desire to recall it all.

He let her take her time, partly because he was powerfully affected himself by all the circumstances, and by the sad pale face upturned to his; and partly by an instinctive consciousness that the softest patience was required. But suddenly she startled him, as she herself was startled into a keen sense of the suffering agony of the present; she sprang up and pushed him aside, and went rapidly towards the gate of the field. He could not move as quickly as most men, but he put forth his utmost speed. He followed across the road, on to the rocky common; but as he went along, with his uncertain gait, in the dusk gloaming, he stumbled, and fell over some sharp projecting stone. The acute pain which shot up his back forced a short cry from him; and, when bird and beast are hushed into rest and the stillness of night is over all, a high-pitched sound, like the voice of pain, is carried far in the quiet air. Ruth, speeding on in her despair, heard the sharp utterance, and stopped suddenly short. It did what no remonstrance could have done; it called her out of herself. The tender nature was in her still, in that hour when all good angels seemed to have abandoned her. In the old days she could never bear to hear or see bodily suffering in any of God's meanest creatures, without trying to succour them; and now, in her rush to the awful death of the suicide, she stayed her wild steps, and turned to find from whom that sharp sound of anguish had issued.

He lay among the white stones, too faint with pain to move, but with an agony in his mind far keener than any bodily pain, as he thought that by his unfortunate fall he had lost all chance of saving her. He was almost overpowered by his intense thankfulness when he saw her white figure pause, and stand listening, and turn again with slow footsteps, as if searching for some lost thing. He could hardly speak, but he made a sound which, though his heart was inexpressibly glad, was like a groan. She came quickly towards him.

'I am hurt,' said he; 'do not leave me;' his disabled and tender frame was overcome by the accident and the previous emotions, and he fainted away. Ruth flew to the little mountain stream, the dashing sound of whose waters had been tempting her, but a moment before, to seek forgetfulness in the deep pool into which they fell. She made a basin of her joined hands, and carried enough of the cold fresh water back to dash into his face and restore him to consciousness. While he still kept silence, uncertain what to say best fitted to induce her to listen to him, she said softly:

'Are you better, sir? – are you very much hurt?'

'Not very much; I am better. Any quick movement is apt to cause me a sudden loss of power in my back, and I believe I stumbled over some of these projecting stones. It will soon go off, and you will help me to go home, I am sure.'

'Oh, yes! Can you go now? I am afraid of your lying too long on this heather; there is a heavy dew.'

He was so anxious to comply with her wish, and not weary out her thought for him, and so turn her back upon herself, that he tried to rise. The pain was acute, and this she saw.

'Don't hurry yourself, sir; I can wait.'

Then came across her mind the recollection of the business that was thus deferred, but the few homely words which had been exchanged between them seemed to have awakened her from her madness. She sat down by him, and, covering her face with her hands, cried mournfully and unceasingly. She forgot his presence, and yet she had a consciousness that some one looked for her kind offices, that she was wanted in the world, and must not rush hastily out of it. The consciousness did not take this definite form, it did not become a thought, but it kept her still, and it was gradually soothing her.

'Can you help me to rise now?' said he, after a while. She did not speak, but she helped him up, and then he took her arm, and she led him tenderly through all the little velvet paths, where the turf grew short and soft between the rugged stones. Once more on the highway, they slowly passed along in the moonlight. He guided her by a slight motion of the arm, through the more unfrequented lanes, to his lodgings at the shop; for he thought for her, and conceived the pain she would have in seeing the lighted windows of the inn. He leant more heavily on her arm, as they awaited the opening of the door.

'Come in,' said he, not relaxing his hold, and yet dreading to tighten it, lest she should defy restraint, and once more rush away.

They went slowly into the little parlour behind the shop. The bonny-looking hostess, Mrs Hughes by name, made haste to light the candle, and then they saw each other, face to face. The deformed gentleman looked very pale, but Ruth looked as if the shadow of death[2] was upon her.

CHAPTER IX

Mrs Hughes bustled about with many a sympathetic exclamation, now in pretty broken English, now in more fluent Welsh, which sounded as soft as Russian or Italian, in her musical voice. Mr Benson, for that was the name of the hunchback, lay on the sofa, thinking; while the tender Mrs Hughes made every arrangement for his relief from pain. He had lodged with her for three successive years, and she knew and loved him.

Ruth stood in the little bow-window, looking out. Across the moon, and over the deep blue heavens, large, torn, irregular-shaped clouds went hurrying, as if summoned by some storm-spirit. The work they were commanded to do was not here; the mighty gathering-place lay eastward, immeasurable leagues, and on they went, chasing each other over the silent earth, now black, now silver-white at one transparent edge, now with the moon shining like Hope through their darkest centre, now again with a silver lining; and now, utterly black, they sailed lower in the lift, and disappeared behind the immovable mountains; they were rushing in the very direction in which Ruth had striven and struggled to go that afternoon; they, in their wild career, would soon pass over the very spot where he (her world's he) was lying sleeping, or perhaps not sleeping, perhaps thinking of her. The storm was in her mind, and rent and tore her purposes into forms as wild and irregular as the heavenly shapes she was looking at. If, like them, she could pass the barrier horizon in the night, she might overtake him.

Mr Benson saw her look, and read it partially. He saw her longing gaze outwards upon the free, broad world, and thought that the syren waters,[1] whose deadly music yet rang in his ears, were again tempting her. He called her to him, praying that his feeble voice might have power.

'My dear young lady, I have much to say to you; and God has taken my strength from me now when I most need it. – Oh, I sin to speak so – but, for His sake, I implore you to be patient here, if only till to-morrow morning.' He looked at her, but her face was immovable, and she did not speak. She could not give up her hope, her chance, her liberty till to-morrow.

'God help me,' said he, mournfully, 'my words do not touch her;' and, still holding her hand, he sank back on the pillows. Indeed, it was true that his words did not vibrate in her atmosphere. The storm-spirit raged there, and filled her heart with the thought that she was an outcast; and the holy words, 'for His sake', were answered by the demon, who held possession, with a blasphemous defiance of the merciful God:

'What have I to do with Thee?'[2]

He thought of every softening influence of religion which over his own disciplined heart had power, but put them aside as useless. Then the still small voice[3] whispered, and he spake:

'In your mother's name, whether she be dead or alive, I command you to stay here until I am able to speak to you.'

She knelt down at the foot of the sofa, and shook it with her sobs. Her heart was touched, and he hardly dared to speak again. At length he said:

'I know you will not go – you could not – for her sake. You will not, will you?'

'No,' whispered Ruth; and then there was a great blank in her heart. She had given up her chance. She was calm, in the utter absence of all hope.

'And now you will do what I tell you?' said he, gently, but, unconsciously to himself, in the tone of one who has found the hidden spell by which to rule spirits.

She slowly said, 'Yes.' But she was subdued.

He called Mrs Hughes. She came from her adjoining shop.

'You have a bedroom within yours, where your daughter used to sleep, I think? I am sure you will oblige me, and I shall consider it as a great favour, if you will allow this young lady to sleep there to-night. Will you take her there now? Go, my dear. I have full trust in your promise not to leave until I can speak to you.' His voice died away to silence; but as Ruth rose from her knees at his bidding, she looked at his face through her tears. His lips were moving in earnest, unspoken prayer, and she knew it was for her.

That night, although his pain was relieved by rest, he could not sleep; and, as in fever, the coming events kept unrolling themselves before him in every changing and fantastic form. He met Ruth in all possible places and ways, and addressed her in every manner he could imagine most calculated to move and affect her to penitence and virtue. Towards morning he fell asleep, but the same thoughts haunted his dreams; he spoke, but his voice refused to utter aloud; and she fled, relentless, to the deep, black pool.

But God works in His own way.

The visions melted into deep, unconscious sleep. He was awakened by a knock at the door, which seemed a repetition of what he had heard in his last sleeping moments.

It was Mrs Hughes. She stood at the first word of permission within the room.

'Please, sir, I think the young lady is very ill indeed, sir; perhaps you would please to come to her.'

'How is she ill?' said he, much alarmed.

'Quite quiet-like, sir; but I think she is dying, that's all, indeed, sir!'

'Go away, I will be with you directly,' he replied, his heart sinking within him.

In a very short time he was standing with Mrs Hughes by Ruth's bedside. She lay as still as if she were dead, her eyes shut, her wan face numbed into a fixed anguish of expression. She did not speak when they spoke, though after a while they thought she strove to do so. But all power of motion and utterance had left her. She was dressed in everything, except her bonnet, as she had been the day before; although sweet, thoughtful Mrs Hughes had provided her with nightgear, which lay on the little chest of drawers that served as a dressing-table. Mr Benson lifted up her arm to feel her feeble, fluttering pulse; and when he let go her hand, it fell upon the bed in a dull heavy way, as if she were already dead.

'You gave her some food?' said he, anxiously, to Mrs Hughes.

'Indeed, and I offered her the best in the house, but she shook her poor pretty head, and only asked if I would please to get her a cup of water. I brought her some milk though, and 'deed, I think she'd rather have had the water; but not to seem sour and cross, she took some milk.' By this time Mrs Hughes was fairly crying.

'When does the doctor come up here?'

'Indeed, sir, and he's up nearly every day now, the inn is so full.'

'I'll go for him. And can you manage to undress her and lay her in bed? Open the window too, and let in the air; if her feet are cold, put bottles of hot water to them.'

It was a proof of the true love, which was the nature of both, that it never crossed their minds to regret that this poor young creature had been thus thrown upon their hands. On the contrary, Mrs Hughes called it 'a blessing'.

'It blesseth him that gives, and him that takes.'[4]

CHAPTER X

At the inn everything was life and bustle. Mr Benson had to wait long in Mrs Morgan's little parlour before she could come to him, and he kept growing more and more impatient. At last she made her appearance and heard his story.

People may talk as they will about the little respect that is paid to virtue, unaccompanied by the outward accidents of wealth or station; but I rather think it will be found that in the long run, true and simple virtue always has its proportionate reward in the respect and reverence of every one whose esteem is worth having. To be sure, it is not rewarded after the way of the world as mere worldly possessions are, with low obeisance and lip-service; but all the better and more noble qualities in the hearts of others make ready and go forth to meet it on its approach, provided only it be pure, simple, and unconscious of its own existence.

Mr Benson had little thought for outward tokens of respect just then, nor had Mrs Morgan much time to spare; but she smoothed her ruffled brow, and calmed her bustling manner, as soon as ever she saw who it was that awaited her; for Mr Benson was well known in the village where he had taken up his summer holiday among the mountains year after year, always a resident at the shop, and seldom spending a shilling at the inn.

Mrs Morgan listened patiently – for her.

'Mr Jones will come this afternoon. But it is a shame you should be troubled with such as her. I had but little time yesterday, but I guessed there was something wrong, and Gwen has just been telling me her bed has not been slept in. They were in a pretty hurry to be gone yesterday, for all that the gentleman was not fit to travel, to my way of thinking; indeed, William Wynn, the post-boy, said he was weary enough before he got to the end of that Yspytty road; and he thought they would have to rest there a day or two before they could go further than Pen trê Voelas. Indeed, and anyhow, the servant is to follow them with the baggage this very morning; and now I remember, William Wynn said they would wait for her. You'd better write a note, Mr Benson, and tell them her state.'

It was good, though unpalatable advice. It came from one accustomed to bring excellent, if unrefined sense, to bear quickly upon any emergency, and to decide rapidly. She was, in truth, so little accustomed to have her authority questioned, that before Mr Benson had made up his mind, she had produced paper, pens, and ink from the drawer in her bureau, placed them before him, and was going to leave the room.

'Leave the note on this shelf, and trust me that it goes by the maid. The boy that drives her there in the car shall bring you an answer back.'

She was gone before he could rally his scattered senses enough to remember that he had not the least idea of the name of the party to whom he was to write. The quiet leisure and peace of his little study at home favoured his habit of reverie and long deliberation, just as her position as mistress of an inn obliged her to quick, decisive ways.

Her advice, though good in some points, was unpalatable in others. It was true that Ruth's condition ought to be known by those who were her friends; but were these people to whom he was now going to write, friends? He knew there was a rich mother, and a handsome, elegant son; and he had also some idea of the circumstances which might a little extenuate their mode of quitting Ruth. He had wide enough sympathy to understand that it must have been a most painful position in which the mother had been placed, on finding herself under the same roof with a girl, who was living with her son as Ruth was. And yet he did not like to apply to her; to write to the son was still more out of the question, as it seemed like asking him to return. But through one or the other lay the only clue to her friends, who certainly ought to be made acquainted with her position. At length he wrote:

'MADAM,

'I write to tell you of the condition of the poor young woman' – (here came a long pause of deliberation) – 'who accompanied your son on his arrival here, and who was left behind on your departure yesterday. She is lying (as it appears to me) in a very dangerous state at my lodgings; and, if I may suggest, it would be kind to allow your maid to return and attend upon her until she is sufficiently recovered to be restored to her friends, if, indeed, they could not come to take charge of her themselves.

'I remain, madam,

'Your obedient servant,

'THURSTAN BENSON.'

The note was very unsatisfactory after all his consideration, but it was the best he could do. He made inquiry of a passing servant as to the lady's name, directed the note, and placed it on the indicated shelf. He then returned to his lodgings, to await the doctor's coming, and the postboy's return. There was no alteration in Ruth; she was as one stunned into unconsciousness; she did not move her posture, she hardly breathed. From time to time Mrs Hughes wetted her mouth with some liquid, and there was a little mechanical motion of the lips; that was the only sign of life she gave. The doctor came and shook his head, – 'a thorough prostration of strength, occasioned by some great shock on the nerves,' – and prescribed care and quiet, and mysterious medicines, but acknowledged that the result was doubtful, very doubtful. After his departure, Mr Benson took his Welsh grammar and tried again to master the ever-puzzling rules for the mutations of letters; but it was of no use, for his thoughts were absorbed by the life-in-death condition of the young creature, who was lately bounding and joyous.

The maid and the luggage, the car and the driver, had arrived before noon at their journey's end, and the note had been delivered. It annoyed Mrs Bellingham exceedingly. It was the worst of these kind of connexions, there was no calculating the consequences; they were never ending. All sorts of claims seemed to be established, and all sorts of people to step in to their settlement. The idea of sending her maid! Why, Simpson would not go if she asked her. She soliloquized thus while reading the letter; and then, suddenly turning round to the favourite attendant, who had been listening to her mistress's remarks with no inattentive ear, she asked:

'Simpson, would you go and nurse this creature, as this—' she looked at the signature, 'Mr Benson, whoever he is, proposes?'

'Me! no, indeed, ma'am,' said the maid, drawing herself up, stiff in her virtue. 'I'm sure, ma'am, you would not expect it of me; I could never have the face to dress a lady of character again.'

'Well, well! don't be alarmed; I cannot spare you; by the way, just attend to the strings on my dress, the chambermaid here pulled them into knots, and broke them terribly, last night. It is awkward though, very,' said she, relapsing into a musing fit over the condition of Ruth.

'If you'll allow me, ma'am, I think I might say something that would alter the case. I believe, ma'am, you put a bank-note into the letter to the young woman yesterday?'

Mrs Bellingham bowed acquiescence, and the maid went on:

'Because, ma'am, when the little deformed man wrote that note (he's Mr Benson, ma'am), I have reason to believe neither he nor Mrs Morgan knew of any provision being made for the young woman. Me and the chambermaid found your letter and the bank-note lying quite promiscuous, like waste paper, on the floor of her room; for I believe she rushed out like mad after you left.'

'That, as you say, alters the case. This letter, then, is principally a sort of delicate hint that some provision ought to have been made, which is true enough, only it has been attended to already. What became of the money?'

'Law, ma'am! do you ask? Of course, as soon as I saw it, I picked it up and took it to Mrs Morgan, in trust for the young person.'

'Oh, that's right. What friends has she? Did you ever hear from Mason? – perhaps they ought to know where she is.'

'Mrs Mason did tell me, ma'am, she was an orphan; with a guardian who was noways akin, and who washed his hands of her when she ran off; but Mrs Mason was sadly put out, and went into hysterics, for fear you would think she had not seen after her enough, and that she might lose your custom; she said it was no fault of hers, for the girl was always a forward creature, boasting of her beauty, and saying how pretty she was, and striving to get where her good looks could be seen and admired, – one night in particular, ma'am, at a county ball; and how Mrs Mason had found out she used to meet Mr Bellingham at an old woman's house, who was a regular old witch, ma'am, and lives in the lowest part of the town, where all the bad characters haunt.'

'There! that's enough,' said Mrs Bellingham, sharply, for the maid's chattering had outrun her tact; and in her anxiety to vindicate the character of her friend Mrs Mason by blackening that of Ruth, she had forgotten that she a little implicated her mistress's son, whom his proud mother did not like to imagine as ever passing through a low and degraded part of the town.

'If she has no friends, and is the creature you describe (which is confirmed by my own observation), the best place for her is, as I said before, the Penitentiary. Her fifty pounds will keep her a week or so, if she is really unable to travel, and pay for her journey; and if on her return to Fordham she will let me know, I will undertake to obtain her admission immediately.'

'I'm sure it's well for her she has to do with a lady who will take any interest in her, after what has happened.'

Mrs Bellingham called for her writing-desk, and wrote a few hasty lines to be sent back by the post-boy, who was on the point of starting:

'Mrs Bellingham presents her compliments to her unknown correspondent, Mr Benson, and begs to inform him of a circumstance of which she believes he was ignorant when he wrote the letter with which she has been favoured; namely, that provision to the amount of 50l. was left for the unfortunate young person who is the subject of Mr Benson's letter. This sum is in the hands of Mrs Morgan, as well as a note from Mrs Bellingham to the miserable girl, in which she proposes to procure her admission into the Fordham Penitentiary, the best place for such a character, as by this profligate action she has forfeited the only friend remaining to her in the world. This proposition, Mrs Bellingham repeats; and they are the young woman's best friends who most urge her to comply with the course now pointed out.'

'Take care Mr Bellingham hears nothing of this Mr Benson's note,' said Mrs Bellingham, as she delivered the answer to her maid; 'he is so sensitive just now that it would annoy him sadly, I am sure.'

CHAPTER XI

You have now seen the note which was delivered into Mr Benson's hands, as the cool shades of evening stole over the glowing summer sky. When he had read it, he again prepared to write a few hasty lines before the post went out. The postboy was even now sounding his horn through the village as a signal for letters to be ready; and it was well that Mr Benson, in his long morning's meditation, had decided upon the course to be pursued, in case of such an answer as that which he had received from Mrs Bellingham. His present note was as follows:

'DEAR FAITH,

'You must come to this place directly, where I earnestly desire you and your advice. I am well myself, so do not be alarmed. I have no time for explanation, but I am sure you will not refuse me; let me trust that I shall see you on Saturday at the latest. You know the mode by which I came; it is the best both for expedition and cheapness. Dear Faith, do not fail me.

'Your affectionate brother,

THURSTAN BENSON.

'P.S. – I am afraid the money I left may be running short. Do not let this stop you. Take my Facciolati[1] to Johnson's, he will advance upon it; it is the third row, bottom shelf. Only come.'

When this letter was despatched he had done all he could; and the next two days passed like a long monotonous dream of watching, thought, and care, undisturbed by any event, hardly by the change from day to night, which, now the harvest moon was at her full, was scarcely perceptible. On Saturday morning the answer came:

'DEAREST THURSTAN,

'Your incomprehensible summons has just reached me, and I obey, thereby proving my right to my name of Faith. I shall be with you almost as soon as this letter. I cannot help feeling anxious, as well as curious. I have money enough, and it is well I have; for Sally, who guards your room like a dragon, would rather see me walk the whole way, than have any of your things disturbed.

'Your affectionate sister,

'FAITH BENSON.'

It was a great relief to Mr Benson to think that his sister would so soon be with him. He had been accustomed from childhood to rely on her prompt judgment and excellent sense; and to her care he felt that Ruth ought to be consigned, as it was too much to go on taxing good Mrs Hughes with night watching and sick nursing, with all her other claims on her time. He asked her once more to sit by Ruth, while he went to meet his sister.

The coach passed by the foot of the steep ascent which led up to Llan-dhu. He took a boy to carry his sister's luggage when she arrived; they were too soon at the bottom of the hill, and the boy began to make ducks and drakes in the shallowest part of the stream, which there flowed glassy and smooth, while Mr Benson sat down on a great stone, under the shadow of an alder-bush which grew where the green flat meadow skirted the water. It was delightful to be once more in the open air, and away from the scenes and thoughts which had been pressing on him for the last three days. There was a new beauty in everything: from the blue mountains which glimmered in the distant sunlight, down to the flat, rich, peaceful vale, with its calm round shadows, where he sat. The very margin of white pebbles which lay on the banks of the stream had a sort of cleanly beauty about it. He felt calmer and more at ease than he had done for some days; and yet, when he began to think, it was rather a strange story which he had to tell his sister, in order to account for his urgent summons. Here was he, sole friend and guardian of a poor sick girl, whose very name he did not know; about whom all that he did know was, that she had been the mistress of a man who had deserted her, and that he feared – he believed – she had contemplated suicide. The offence, too, was one for which his sister, good and kind as she was, had little compassion. Well, he must appeal to her love for him, which was a very unsatisfactory mode of proceeding, as he would far rather have had her interest in the girl founded on reason, or some less personal basis than showing it merely because her brother wished it.

The coach came slowly rumbling over the stony road. His sister was outside, but got down in a brisk active way, and greeted her brother heartily and affectionately. She was considerably taller than he was, and must have been very handsome; her black hair was parted plainly over her forehead, and her dark expressive eyes and straight nose still retained the beauty of her youth. I do not know whether she was older than her brother, but, probably owing to his infirmity requiring her care, she had something of a mother's manner towards him.

'Thurstan, you are looking pale! I do not believe you are well, whatever you may say. Have you had the old pain in your back?'

'No – a little – never mind that, dearest Faith. Sit down here, while I send the boy up with your box.' And then, with some little desire to show his sister how well he was acquainted with the language, he blundered out his directions in very grammatical Welsh; so grammatical, in fact, and so badly pronounced, that the boy, scratching his head, made answer:

'Dim Saesoneg.'[2]

So he had to repeat it in English.

'Well, now, Thurstan, here I sit as you bid me. But don't try me too long; tell me why you sent for me.'

Now came the difficulty, and oh! for a seraph's tongue, and a seraph's powers of representation![3] But there was no seraph at hand, only the soft running waters singing a quiet tune, and predisposing Miss Benson to listen with a soothed spirit to any tale, not immediately involving her brother's welfare, which had been the cause of her seeing that lovely vale.

'It is an awkward story to tell, Faith, but there is a young woman lying ill at my lodgings whom I wanted you to nurse.'

He thought he saw a shadow on his sister's face, and detected a slight change in her voice as she spoke.

'Nothing very romantic, I hope, Thurstan. Remember, I cannot stand much romance; I always distrust it.'

'I don't know what you mean by romance. The story is real enough, and not out of the common way, I'm afraid.'

He paused; he did not get over the difficulty.

'Well, tell it me at once, Thurstan. I am afraid you have let some one, or perhaps only your own imagination, impose upon you; but don't try my patience too much; you know I've no great stock.'

'Then I'll tell you. The young girl was brought to the inn here by a gentleman, who has left her; she is very ill, and has no one to see after her.'

Miss Benson had some masculine tricks, and one was whistling a long low whistle when surprised or displeased. She had often found it a useful vent for feelings, and she whistled now. Her brother would rather she had spoken.

'Have you sent for her friends?' she asked, at last.

'She has none.'

Another pause and another whistle, but rather softer and more wavering than the last.

'How is she ill?'

'Pretty nearly as quiet as if she were dead. She does not speak, or move, or even sigh.'

'It would be better for her to die at once, I think.'

'Faith!'

That one word put them right. It was spoken in the tone which had authority over her; it was so full of grieved surprise and mournful upbraiding. She was accustomed to exercise a sway over him, owing to her greater decision of character; and, probably, if everything were traced to its cause, to her superior vigour of constitution; but at times she was humbled before his pure, childlike nature, and felt where she was inferior. She was too good and true to conceal this feeling, or to resent its being forced upon her. After a time she said:

'Thurstan, dear, let us go to her.'

She helped him with tender care, and gave him her arm up the long and tedious hill; but when they approached the village, without speaking a word on the subject, they changed their position, and she leant (apparently) on him. He stretched himself up into as vigorous a gait as he could, when they drew near to the abodes of men.

On the way they had spoken but little. He had asked after various members of his congregation, for he was a Dissenting minister in a country-town, and she had answered; but they neither of them spoke of Ruth, though their minds were full of her.

Mrs Hughes had tea ready for the traveller on her arrival. Mr Benson chafed a little internally, at the leisurely way in which his sister sipped and sipped, and paused to tell him some trifling particular respecting home affairs, which she had forgotten before.

'Mr Bradshaw has refused to let the children associate with the Dixons any longer, because one evening they played at acting charades.'

'Indeed; – a little more bread and butter, Faith?'

'Thank you. This Welsh air does make one hungry. Mrs Bradshaw is paying poor old Maggie's rent, to save her from being sent into the workhouse.'

'That's right. Won't you have another cup of tea?'

'I have had two. However, I think I'll take another.'

Mr Benson could not refrain from a little sigh as he poured it out. He thought he had never seen his sister so deliberately hungry and thirsty before. He did not guess that she was feeling the meal rather a respite from a distasteful interview, which she was aware was awaiting her at its conclusion. But all things come to an end, and so did Miss Benson's tea.

'Now, will you go and see her?'

'Yes.'

And so they went. Mrs Hughes had pinned up a piece of green calico, by way of a Venetian blind, to shut out the afternoon sun; and in the light thus shaded lay Ruth, still, and wan, and white. Even with her brother's account of Ruth's state, such death-like quietness startled Miss Benson – startled her into pity for the poor lovely creature who lay thus stricken and felled. When she saw her, she could no longer imagine her to be an impostor, or a hardened sinner; such prostration of woe belonged to neither. Mr Benson looked more at his sister's face than at Ruth's; he read her countenance as a book.

Mrs Hughes stood by, crying.

Mr Benson touched his sister, and they left the room together.

'Do you think she will live?' asked he.

'I cannot tell,' said Miss Benson, in a softened voice. 'But how young she looks! quite a child, poor creature! When will the doctor come, Thurstan? Tell me all about her; you have never told me the particulars.'

Mr Benson might have said, she had never cared to hear them before, and had rather avoided the subject; but he was too happy to see this awakening of interest in his sister's warm heart to say anything in the least reproachful. He told her the story as well as he could; and, as he felt it deeply, he told it with heart's eloquence; and as he ended and looked at her, there were tears in the eyes of both.

'And what does the doctor say?' asked she, after a pause.

'He insists upon quiet; he orders medicines and strong broth. I cannot tell you all; Mrs Hughes can. She has been so truly good. "Doing good, hoping for nothing again." '[4]

'She looks very sweet and gentle. I shall sit up to-night, and watch her myself; and I shall send you and Mrs Hughes early to bed, for you have both a worn look about you I don't like. Are you sure the effect of that fall has gone off? Do you feel anything of it in your back still?

After all, I owe her something for turning back to your help. Are you sure she was going to drown herself?'

'I cannot be sure, for I have not questioned her. She has not been in a state to be questioned; but I have no doubt whatever about it. But you must not think of sitting up after your journey, Faith.'

'Answer me, Thurstan. Do you feel any bad effect from that fall?'

'No, hardly any. Don't sit up, Faith, to-night!'

'Thurstan, it's no use talking, for I shall; and, if you go on opposing me, I dare say I shall attack your back, and put a blister on it.[5] Do tell me what that "hardly any" means. Besides, to set you quite at ease, you know I have never seen mountains before, and they fill me and oppress me so much that I could not sleep; I must keep awake this first night, and see that they don't fall on the earth and overwhelm it. And now answer my questions about yourself.'

Miss Benson had the power, which some people have, of carrying her wishes through to their fulfilment; her will was strong, her sense was excellent, and people yielded to her – they did not know why. Before ten o'clock she reigned sole power and potentate[6] in Ruth's little chamber. Nothing could have been better devised for giving her an interest in the invalid. The very dependence of one so helpless upon her care inclined her heart towards her. She thought she perceived a slight improvement in the symptoms during the night, and she was a little pleased that this progress should have been made while she reigned monarch of the sickroom. Yes, certainly there was an improvement. There was more consciousness in the look of the eyes, although the whole countenance still retained its painful traces of acute suffering, manifested in an anxious, startled, uneasy aspect. It was broad morning light, though barely five o'clock, when Miss Benson caught the sight of Ruth's lips moving, as if in speech. Miss Benson stooped down to listen.

'Who are you?' asked Ruth, in the faintest of whispers.

'Miss Benson – Mr Benson's sister,' she replied.

The words conveyed no knowledge to Ruth; on the contrary, weak as a babe in mind and body as she was, her lips began to quiver, and her eyes to show a terror similar to that of any little child who wakens in the presence of a stranger, and sees no dear, familiar face of mother or nurse to reassure its trembling heart.

Miss Benson took her hand in hers, and began to stroke it caressingly.

'Don't be afraid, dear; I'm a friend come to take care of you. Would you like some tea now, my love?'

The very utterance of these gentle words was unlocking Miss Benson's heart. Her brother was surprised to see her so full of interest, when he came to inquire later on in the morning. It required Mrs Hughes's persuasions, as well as his own, to induce her to go to bed for an hour or two after breakfast; and, before she went, she made them promise that she should be called when the doctor came. He did not come until late in the afternoon. The invalid was rallying fast, though rallying to a consciousness of sorrow, as was evinced by the tears which came slowly rolling down her pale sad cheeks – tears which she had not the power to wipe away.

Mr Benson had remained in the house all day to hear the doctor's opinion; and now that he was relieved from the charge of Ruth by his sister's presence, he had the more time to dwell upon the circumstances of her case – so far as they were known to him. He remembered his first sight of her; her lithe figure swaying to and fro as she balanced herself on the slippery stones, half smiling at her own dilemma, with a bright happy light in the eyes that seemed like a reflection from the glancing waters sparkling below. Then he recalled the changed, affrighted look of those eyes as they met his, after the child's rebuff of her advances; – how that little incident filled up the tale at which Mrs Hughes had hinted, in a kind of sorrowful way, as if loth (as a Christian should be) to believe evil. Then that fearful evening, when he had only just saved her from committing suicide, and that night-mare sleep! And now, lost, forsaken, and but just delivered from the jaws of death, she lay dependent for everything on his sister and him, – utter strangers a few weeks ago. Where was her lover? Could he be easy and happy? Could he grow into perfect health, with these great sins pressing on his conscience with a strong and hard pain? Or had he a conscience?

Into whole labyrinths of social ethics Mr Benson's thoughts wandered, when his sister entered suddenly and abruptly.

'What does the doctor say? Is she better?'

'Oh, yes! she's better,' answered Miss Benson, sharp and short. Her brother looked at her in dismay. She bumped down into a chair in a cross, disconcerted manner. They were both silent for a few minutes; only Miss Benson whistled and clucked alternately.

'What is the matter, Faith? You say she is better.'

'Why, Thurstan, there is something so shocking the matter, that I cannot tell you.'

Mr Benson changed colour with affright. All things possible and impossible crossed his mind, but the right one. I said 'all things possible'; I made a mistake. He never believed Ruth to be more guilty than she seemed.

'Faith, I wish you would tell me, and not bewilder me with those noises of yours,' said he, nervously.

'I beg your pardon; but something so shocking has just been discovered – I don't know how to word it – she will have a child. The doctor says so.'

She was allowed to make noises unnoticed for a few minutes. Her brother did not speak. At last she wanted his sympathy.

'Isn't it shocking, Thurstan? You might have knocked me down with a straw when he told me.'

'Does she know?'

'Yes; and I am not sure that that isn't the worst part of all.'

'How? – what do you mean?'

'Oh! I was just beginning to have a good opinion of her, but I'm afraid she is very depraved. After the doctor was gone, she pulled the bed-curtain aside, and looked as if she wanted to speak to me. (I can't think how she heard, for we were close to the window, and spoke very low.) Well, I went to her, though I really had taken quite a turn against her. And she whispered, quite eagerly, "Did he say I should have a baby?" Of course, I could not keep it from her; but I thought it my duty to look as cold and severe as I could. She did not seem to understand how it ought to be viewed, but took it just as if she had a right to have a baby. She said, "Oh, my God, I thank Thee! Oh, I will be so good!" I had no patience with her then, so I left the room.'

'Who is with her?'

'Mrs Hughes. She is not seeing the thing in a moral light, as I should have expected.'

Mr Benson was silent again. After some time he began:

'Faith, I don't see this affair quite as you do. I believe I am right.'

'You surprise me, brother! I don't understand you.'

'Wait awhile! I want to make my feelings very clear to you, but I don't know where to begin, or how to express myself.'

'It is, indeed, an extraordinary subject for us to have to talk about;

but if once I get clear of this girl, I'll wash my hands of all such cases again.'

Her brother was not attending to her; he was reducing his own ideas to form.

'Faith, do you know I rejoice in this child's advent?'

'May God forgive you, Thurstan! – if you know what you are saying. But, surely, it is a temptation, dear Thurstan.'

'I do not think it is a delusion. The sin appears to me to be quite distinct from its consequences.'

'Sophistry – and a temptation,' said Miss Benson, decidedly.

'No, it is not,' said her brother, with equal decision. 'In the eye of God, she is exactly the same as if the life she has led had left no trace behind. We knew her errors before, Faith.'

'Yes, but not this disgrace – this badge of her shame!'

'Faith, Faith! let me beg of you not to speak so of the little innocent babe, who may be God's messenger to lead her back to Him. Think again of her first words – the burst of nature from her heart! Did she not turn to God, and enter into a covenant with Him – "I will be so good"? Why, it draws her out of herself! If her life has hitherto been self-seeking and wickedly thoughtless, here is the very instrument to make her forget herself, and be thoughtful for another. Teach her (and God will teach her, if man does not come between) to reverence her child; and this reverence will shut out sin, – will be purification.'

He was very much excited; he was even surprised at his own excitement; but his thoughts and meditations through the long afternoon had prepared his mind for this manner of viewing the subject.

'These are quite new ideas to me,' said Miss Benson, coldly. 'I think you, Thurstan, are the first person I ever heard rejoicing over the birth of an illegitimate child. It appears to me, I must own, rather questionable morality.'

'I do not rejoice. I have been all this afternoon mourning over the sin which has blighted this young creature; I have been dreading lest, as she recovered consciousness, there should be a return of her despair. I have been thinking of every holy word, every promise to the penitent – of the tenderness which led the Magdalen aright.[7] I have been feeling, severely and reproachfully, the timidity which has hitherto made me blink all encounter[8] with evils of this particular kind. Oh, Faith! once for all, do not accuse me of questionable morality, when I am trying more than ever I did in my life to act as my blessed Lord would have done.'

He was very much agitated. His sister hesitated, and then she spoke more softly than before.

'But, Thurstan, everything might have been done to "lead her right" (as you call it), without this child, this miserable offspring of sin.'

'The world has, indeed, made such children miserable, innocent as they are; but I doubt if this be according to the will of God, unless it be His punishment for the parents' guilt; and even then the world's way of treatment is too apt to harden the mother's natural love into something like hatred. Shame, and the terror of friends' displeasure, turn her mad – defile her holiest instincts; and, as for the fathers – God forgive them! I cannot – at least, not just now.'

Miss Benson thought on what her brother said. At length she asked, 'Thurstan (remember I'm not convinced), how would you have this girl treated according to your theory?'

'It will require some time, and much Christian love, to find out the best way. I know I'm not very wise; but the way I think it would be right to act in, would be this –' He thought for some time before he spoke, and then said:

'She has incurred a responsibility – that we both acknowledge. She is about to become a mother, and have the direction and guidance of a little tender life. I fancy such a responsibility must be serious and solemn enough, without making it into a heavy and oppressive burden, so that human nature recoils from bearing it. While we do all we can to strengthen her sense of responsibility, I would likewise do all we can to make her feel that it is responsibility for what may become a blessing.'

'Whether the children are legitimate or illegitimate?' asked Miss Benson, dryly.

'Yes!' said her brother, firmly. 'The more I think, the more I believe I am right. No one,' said he, blushing faintly as he spoke, 'can have a greater recoil from profligacy than I have. You yourself have not greater sorrow over this young creature's sin than I have: the difference is this, you confuse the consequences with the sin.'

'I don't understand metaphysics.'

'I am not aware that I am talking metaphysics. I can imagine that if the present occasion be taken rightly, and used well, all that is good in her may be raised to a height unmeasured but by God; while all that is evil and dark may, by His blessing, fade and disappear in the pure light of her child's presence. Oh, Father! listen to my prayer, that her redemption may date from this time. Help us to speak to her in the loving spirit of thy Holy Son!'

The tears were full in his eyes; he almost trembled in his earnestness. He was faint with the strong power of his own conviction, and with his inability to move his sister. But she was shaken. She sat very still for a quarter of an hour or more, while he leaned back, exhausted by his own feelings.

'The poor child!' said she, at length – 'the poor, poor child! what it will have to struggle through and endure! Do you remember Thomas Wilkins, and the way he threw the registry of his birth and baptism back in your face? Why, he would not have the situation; he went to sea and was drowned, rather than present the record of his shame.'

'I do remember it all. It has often haunted me. She must strengthen her child to look to God, rather than to man's opinion. It will be the discipline, the penance, she has incurred. She must teach it to be (humanly speaking) self-dependent.'

'But after all,' said Miss Benson (for she had known and esteemed poor Thomas Wilkins, and had mourned over his untimely death, and the recollection thereof softened her) – 'after all, it might be concealed. The very child need never know its illegitimacy.'

'How?' asked her brother.

'Why – we know so little about her yet; but in that letter, it said she had no friends; – now, could she not go into quite a fresh place, and be passed off as a widow?'

Ah, tempter! unconscious tempter! Here was a way of evading the trials for the poor little unborn child, of which Mr Benson had never thought. It was the decision – the pivot, on which the fate of years moved; and he turned it the wrong way. But it was not for his own sake. For himself, he was brave enough to tell the truth; for the little helpless baby, about to enter a cruel, biting world, he was tempted to evade the difficulty. He forgot what he had just said, of the discipline and the penance to the mother consisting in strengthening her child to meet, trustfully and bravely, the consequences of her own weakness. He remembered more clearly the wild fierceness, the Cain-like look,[9] of

Thomas Wilkins, as the obnoxious word in the baptismal registry told him that he must go forth branded into the world, with his hand against every man's, and every man's against him.

'How could it be managed, Faith?'

'Nay, I must know much more, which she alone can tell us, before I can see how it is to be managed. It is certainly the best plan.'

'Perhaps it is,' said her brother, thoughtfully, but no longer clearly or decidedly; and so the conversation dropped.

Ruth moved the bed-curtain aside, in her soft manner, when Miss Benson re-entered the room; she did not speak, but she looked at her as if she wished her to come near. Miss Benson went and stood by her. Ruth took her hand in hers and kissed it; then, as if fatigued even by this slight movement, she fell asleep.

Miss Benson took up her work, and thought over her brother's speeches. She was not convinced, but she was softened and bewildered.

CHAPTER XII

Miss Benson continued in an undecided state of mind for the two next days; but on the third, as they sat at breakfast, she began to speak to her brother.

'That young creature's name is Ruth Hilton.'

'Indeed! how did you find it out?'

'From herself, of course. She is much stronger. I slept with her last night, and I was aware she was awake long before I liked to speak, but at last I began. I don't know what I said, or how it went on, but I think it was a little relief to her to tell me something about herself. She sobbed and cried herself to sleep; I think she is asleep now.'

'Tell me what she said about herself.'

'Oh, it was really very little; it was evidently a most painful subject. She is an orphan, without brother or sister, and with a guardian, whom, I think she said, she never saw but once. He apprenticed her (after her father's death) to a dressmaker. This Mr Bellingham got acquainted with her, and they used to meet on Sunday afternoons. One day they were late, lingering on the road, when the dressmaker came up by accident. She seems to have been very angry, and not unnaturally so. The girl took fright at her threats, and the lover persuaded her to go off with him to London, there and then. Last May, I think it was. That's all.'

'Did she express any sorrow for her error?'

'No, not in words, but her voice was broken with sobs, though she tried to make it steady. After a while she began to talk about her baby, but shyly, and with much hesitation. She asked me, how much I thought she could earn as a dressmaker, by working very, very hard; and that brought us round to her child. I thought of what you had said, Thurstan, and I tried to speak to her as you wished me. I am not sure if it was right; I am doubtful in my own mind still.'

'Don't be doubtful, Faith! Dear Faith, I thank you for your kindness.'

'There is really nothing to thank me for. It is almost impossible to help being kind to her; there is something so meek and gentle about her, so patient, and so grateful!'

'What does she think of doing?'

'Poor child! she thinks of taking lodgings – very cheap ones, she says; there she means to work night and day to earn enough for her child. For, she said to me, with such pretty earnestness, "It must never know want, whatever I do. I have deserved suffering, but it will be such a little innocent darling!" Her utmost earnings would not be more than seven or eight shillings a week, I'm afraid; and then she is so young and so pretty!'

'There is that fifty pounds Mrs Morgan brought me, and those two letters. Does she know about them yet?'

'No; I did not like to tell her till she is a little stronger. Oh, Thurstan! I wish there was not this prospect of a child. I cannot help it. I do – I could see a way in which we might help her, if it were not for that.'

'How do you mean?'

'Oh, it's no use thinking of it, as it is! Or else we might have taken her home with us, and kept her till she had got a little dress-making in the congregation, but for this meddlesome child; that spoils everything. You must let me grumble to you, Thurstan. I was very good to her, and spoke as tenderly and respectfully of the little thing as if it were the Queen's,[1] and born in lawful matrimony.'

'That's right, my dear Faith! Grumble away to me, if you like. I'll forgive you, for the kind thought of taking her home with us. But do you think her situation is an insuperable objection?'

'Why, Thurstan! – it's so insuperable, it puts it quite out of the question.'

'How? – that's only repeating your objection. Why is it out of the question?'

'If there had been no child coming, we might have called her by her right name – Miss Hilton; that's one thing. Then, another is, the baby in our house. Why, Sally would go distraught!'

'Never mind Sally. If she were an orphan relation of our own, left widowed,' said he, pausing, as if in doubt. 'You yourself suggested she should be considered as a widow, for the child's sake. I'm only taking up your ideas, dear Faith. I respect you for thinking of taking her home; it is just what we ought to do. Thank you for reminding me of my duty.'

'Nay, it was only a passing thought. Think of Mr Bradshaw. Oh! I tremble at the thought of his grim displeasure.'

'We must think of a higher than Mr Bradshaw. I own I should be a very coward, if he knew. He is so severe, so inflexible. But after all he sees so little of us; he never comes to tea, you know, but is always engaged when Mrs Bradshaw comes. I don't think he knows of what our household consists.'

'Not know Sally? Oh yes, but he does. He asked Mrs Bradshaw one day, if she knew what wages we gave her, and said we might get a far more efficient and younger servant for the money. And, speaking about money, think what our expenses would be if we took her home for the next six months.'

That consideration was a puzzling one; and both sat silent and perplexed for a time. Miss Benson was as sorrowful as her brother, for she was becoming as anxious as he was to find it possible that her plan could be carried out.

'There's the fifty pounds,' said he, with a sigh of reluctance at the idea.

'Yes, there's the fifty pounds,' echoed his sister, with the same sadness in her tone. 'I suppose it is hers.'

'I suppose it is; and, being so, we must not think who gave it to her. It will defray her expenses. I am very sorry, but I think we must take it.'

'It would never do to apply to him under the present circumstances,' said Miss Benson, in a hesitating manner.

'No, that we won't,' said her brother, decisively. 'If she consents to let us take care of her, we will never let her stoop to request anything from him, even for his child. She can live on bread and water. We can all live on bread and water rather than that.'

'Then I will speak to her and propose the plan. Oh, Thurstan! from a child you could persuade me to anything! I hope I am doing right. However much I oppose you at first, I am sure to yield soon, almost in proportion to my violence at first. I think I am very weak.'

'No, not in this instance. We are both right; I, in the way in which the child ought to be viewed; you, dear good Faith, for thinking of taking her home with us. God bless you, dear, for it!'

When Ruth began to sit up (and the strange, new, delicious prospect of becoming a mother seemed to give her some mysterious source of strength, so that her recovery was rapid and swift from that time), Miss Benson brought her the letters and the bank-note.

'Do you recollect receiving this letter, Ruth?' asked she, with grave gentleness. Ruth changed colour, and took it and read it again without making any reply to Miss Benson. Then she sighed, and thought a while; and then took up and read the second note – the note which Mrs Bellingham had sent to Mr Benson in answer to his. After that she took up the bank-note and turned it round and round, but not as if she saw it. Miss Benson noticed that her fingers trembled sadly, and that her lips were quivering for some time before she spoke.

'If you please, Miss Benson, I should like to return this money.'

'Why, my dear?'

'I have a strong feeling against taking it. While he,' said she, deeply blushing, and letting her large white lids drop down and veil her eyes, 'loved me, he gave me many things – my watch – oh, many things; and I took them from him gladly and thankfully because he loved me – for I would have given him anything – and I thought of them as signs of love. But this money pains my heart. He has left off loving me, and has gone away. This money seems – oh, Miss Benson – it seems as if he could comfort me, for being forsaken, by money.' And at that word, the tears so long kept back and repressed, forced their way like rain.

She checked herself, however, in the violence of her emotion, for she thought of her child.

'So, will you take the trouble of sending it back to Mrs Bellingham?'

'That I will, my dear. I am glad of it, that I am! They don't deserve to have the power of giving: they don't deserve that you should take it.'

Miss Benson went and enclosed it up, there and then; simply writing these words in the envelope, 'From Ruth Hilton.'

'And now we wash our hands of these Bellinghams,' said she, triumphantly. But Ruth looked tearful and sad; not about returning the note, but from the conviction that the reason she had given for the ground of her determination was true – he no longer loved her.

To cheer her, Miss Benson began to speak of the future. Miss Benson was one of those people who, the more she spoke of a plan in its details, and the more she realised it in her own mind, the more firmly she became a partisan of the project. Thus she grew warm and happy in the idea of taking Ruth home; but Ruth remained depressed and languid under the conviction that he no longer loved her. No home, no future, but the thought of her child, could wean her from this sorrow. Miss Benson was a little piqued; and this pique showed itself afterwards in talking to her brother of the morning's proceedings in the sick-chamber.

'I admired her at the time for sending away her fifty pounds so proudly; but I think she has a cold heart: she hardly thanked me at all for my proposal of taking her home with us.'

'Her thoughts are full of other things just now; and people have such different ways of showing feeling: some by silence, some by words. At any rate, it is unwise to expect gratitude.'

'What do you expect – not indifference or ingratitude?'

'It is better not to expect or calculate consequences. The longer I live, the more fully I see that. Let us try simply to do right actions, without thinking of the feelings they are to call out in others. We know that no holy or self-denying effort can fall to the ground vain and useless;[2] but the sweep of eternity is large, and God alone knows when the effect is to be produced. We are trying to do right now, and to feel right; don't let us perplex ourselves with endeavouring to map out how she should feel, or how she should show her feelings.'

'That's all very fine, and I dare say very true,' said Miss Benson, a little chagrined. 'But "a bird in the hand is worth two in the bush"; and I would rather have had one good, hearty "Thank you", now, for all I have been planning to do for her, than the grand effects you promise me in the "sweep of eternity". Don't be grave and sorrowful, Thurstan, or I'll go out of the room. I can stand Sally's scoldings, but I can't bear your look of quiet depression whenever I am a little hasty or impatient. I had rather you would give me a good box on the ear.'

'And I would often rather you would speak, if ever so hastily, instead of whistling. So, if I box your ears when I am vexed with you, will you promise to scold me when you are put out of the way, instead of whistling?'

'Very well! that's a bargain. You box, and I scold. But, seriously, I began to calculate our money when she so cavalierly sent off the fifty-pound note (I can't help admiring her for it), and I am very much afraid we shall not have enough to pay the doctor's bill, and take her home with us.'

'She must go inside the coach, whatever we do,' said Mr Benson, decidedly. 'Who's there? Come in! Oh! Mrs Hughes! Sit down.'

'Indeed, sir, and I cannot stay; but the young lady has just made me find up her watch for her, and asked me to get it sold to pay the doctor, and the little things she has had since she came; and please, sir, indeed, I don't know where to sell it nearer than Caernarvon.'

'That is good of her,' said Miss Benson, her sense of justice satisfied; and, remembering the way in which Ruth had spoken of the watch, she felt what a sacrifice it must have been to resolve to part with it.

'And her goodness just helps us out of our dilemma,' said her brother; who was unaware of the feelings with which Ruth regarded her watch, or, perhaps, he might have parted with his Facciolati.

Mrs Hughes patiently awaited their leisure for answering her practical question. Where could the watch be sold? Suddenly her face brightened.

'Mr Jones, the doctor, is just going to be married, perhaps he would like nothing better than to give this pretty watch to his bride; indeed, and I think it's very likely; and he'll pay money for it as well as letting alone his bill. I'll ask him, sir, at any rate.'

Mr Jones was only too glad to obtain possession of so elegant a present at so cheap a rate. He even, as Mrs Hughes had foretold, 'paid money for it;' more than was required to defray the expenses of Ruth's accommodation, as most of the articles of food she had were paid for at the time by Mr or Miss Benson, but they strictly forbade Mrs Hughes to tell Ruth of this.

'Would you object to my buying you a black gown?' said Miss Benson to her, the day after the sale of the watch. She hesitated a little, and then went on:

'My brother and I think it would be better to call you – as if in fact you were – a widow. It will save much awkwardness, and it will spare your child much—' 'mortification', she was going to have added, but that word did not exactly do. But, at the mention of her child, Ruth started and turned ruby-red; as she always did when allusion was made to it.

'Oh, yes! certainly. Thank you so much for thinking of it. Indeed,' said she, very low, as if to herself, 'I don't know how to thank you for all you are doing; but I do love you, and will pray for you, if I may.'

'If you may, Ruth!' repeated Miss Benson, in a tone of surprise.

'Yes, if I may. If you will let me pray for you.'

'Certainly, my dear. My dear Ruth, you don't know how often I sin; I do so wrong, with my few temptations. We are both of us great sinners in the eyes of the Most Holy; let us pray for each other. Don't speak so again, my dear; at least, not to me.'

Miss Benson was actually crying. She had always looked upon herself as so inferior to her brother in real goodness; had seen such heights above her, that she was distressed by Ruth's humility. After a short time she resumed the subject.

'Then I may get you a black gown? – and we may call you Mrs Hilton?'

'No; not Mrs Hilton!' said Ruth, hastily.

Miss Benson, who had hitherto kept her eyes averted from Ruth's face from a motive of kindly delicacy, now looked at her with surprise.

'Why not?' asked she.

'It was my mother's name,' said Ruth, in a low voice. 'I had better not be called by it.'

'Then, let us call you by my mother's name,' said Miss Benson, tenderly. 'She would have— But I'll talk to you about my mother some other time. Let me call you Mrs Denbigh. It will do very well, too. People will think you are a distant relation.'

When she told Mr Benson of this choice of name, he was rather sorry; it was like his sister's impulsive kindness – impulsive in everything – and he could imagine how Ruth's humility had touched her. He was sorry, but he said nothing.

And now the letter was written home, announcing the probable arrival of the brother and sister on a certain day, 'with a distant relation, early left a widow,' as Miss Benson expressed it. She desired the spare-room might be prepared, and made every provision she could think of for Ruth's comfort; for Ruth still remained feeble and weak.

When the black gown, at which she had stitched away incessantly, was finished – when nothing remained but to rest for the next day's journey – Ruth could not sit still. She wandered from window to window, learning off each rock and tree by heart. Each had its tale, which it was agony to remember; but which it would have been worse agony to forget. The sound of running waters she heard that quiet evening was in her ears as she lay on her death-bed; so well had she learnt their tune.

And now all was over. She had driven in to Llan-dhu, sitting by her lover's side, living in the bright present, and strangely forgetful of the past or the future; she had dreamed out her dream, and she had awakened from the vision of love. She walked slowly and sadly down the long hill, her tears fast falling, but as quickly wiped away; while she strove to make steady the low quivering voice which was often called upon to answer some remark of Miss Benson's.

They had to wait for the coach. Ruth buried her face in some flowers which Mrs Hughes had given her on parting; and was startled when the mail drew up with a sudden pull, which almost threw the horses on their haunches. She was placed inside, and the coach had set off again, before she was fully aware that Mr and Miss Benson were travelling on the outside; but it was a relief to feel she might now cry without exciting their notice. The shadow of a heavy thunder-cloud was on the valley, but the little upland village-church (that showed the spot in which so much of her life had passed)[3] stood out clear in the sunshine. She grudged the tears that blinded her as she gazed. There was one passenger, who tried after a while to comfort her.

'Don't cry, miss,' said the kind-hearted woman. 'You're parting from friends, maybe? Well, that's bad enough, but when you come to my age, you'll think none of it. Why, I've three sons, and they're soldiers and sailors, all of them – here, there, and everywhere. One is in America, beyond seas; another is in China, making tea; and another is at Gibraltar, three miles from Spain; and yet, you see, I can laugh and eat and enjoy myself. I sometimes think I'll try and fret a bit, just to make myself a better figure; but, Lord! it's no use, it's against my nature; so I laugh and grow fat again. I'd be quite thankful for a fit of anxiety as would make me feel easy in my clothes, which them manty-makers will make so tight I'm fairly throttled.'

Ruth durst cry no more; it was no relief, now she was watched and noticed, and plied with a sandwich or a gingerbread each time she looked sad. She lay back with her eyes shut, as if asleep, and went on, and on, the sun never seeming to move from his high place in the sky, nor the bright hot day to show the least sign of waning. Every now and then, Miss Benson scrambled down, and made kind inquiries of the pale, weary Ruth; and once they changed coaches, and the fat old lady left her with a hearty shake of the hand.

'It is not much further now,' said Miss Benson, apologetically, to Ruth. 'See! we are losing sight of the Welsh mountains. We have about eighteen miles of plain, and then we come to the moors and the rising ground, amidst which Eccleston lies.⁴ I wish we were there, for my brother is sadly tired.'

The first wonder in Ruth's mind was, why then, if Mr Benson was so tired, did they not stop where they were for the night; for she knew little of the expenses of a night at an inn. The next thought was, to beg that Mr Benson would take her place inside the coach, and allow her to mount up by Miss Benson. She proposed this, and Miss Benson was evidently pleased.

'Well, if you're not tired, it would be a rest and a change for him, to be sure; and if you were by me I could show you the first sight of Eccleston, if we reach there before it is quite dark.'

So Mr Benson got down, and changed places with Ruth.

She hardly yet understood the numerous small economies which he and his sister had to practise – the little daily self-denials, – all endured so cheerfully, and simply, that they had almost ceased to require an effort, and it had become natural to them to think of others before themselves. Ruth had not understood that it was for economy that their places had been taken on the outside of the coach, while hers, as an invalid requiring rest, was to be the inside; and that the biscuits which supplied the place of a dinner were, in fact, chosen because the difference in price between the two would go a little way towards fulfilling their plan for receiving her as an inmate. Her thought about money had been hitherto a child's thought; the subject had never touched her; but afterwards, when she had lived a little while with the Bensons, her eyes were opened, and she remembered their simple kindness on the journey, and treasured the remembrance of it in her heart.

A low grey cloud was the first sign of Eccleston; it was the smoke of the town hanging over the plain. Beyond the place where she was expected to believe it existed, arose round, waving uplands; nothing to the fine outlines of the Welsh mountains, but still going up nearer to heaven than the rest of the flat world into which she had now entered. Rumbling stones, lamp-posts, a sudden stop, and they were in the town of Eccleston; and a strange, uncouth voice, on the dark side of the coach, was heard to say:

'Be ye there, measter?'

'Yes, yes!' said Miss Benson, quickly. 'Did Sally send you, Ben? Get the ostler's lantern, and look out the luggage.'

CHAPTER XIII

Miss Benson had resumed every morsel of the briskness which she had rather lost in the middle of the day; her foot was on her native stones, and a very rough set they were, and she was near her home and among known people. Even Mr Benson spoke very cheerfully to Ben, and made many inquiries of him respecting people whose names were strange to Ruth. She was cold, and utterly weary. She took Miss Benson's offered arm, and could hardly drag herself as far as the little quiet street in which Mr Benson's house was situated. The street was so quiet that their footsteps sounded like a loud disturbance, and announced their approach as effectually as the 'trumpet's lordly blare' did the coming of Abdallah.[1] A door flew open, and a lighted passage stood before them. As soon as they had entered, a stout elderly servant emerged from behind the door, her face radiant with welcome.

'Eh, bless ye! are ye back again? I thought I should ha' been lost without ye.'

She gave Mr Benson a hearty shake of the hand, and kissed Miss Benson warmly; then, turning to Ruth, she said, in a loud whisper:

'Who's yon?'

Mr Benson was silent, and walked a step onwards. Miss Benson said boldly out:

'The lady I named in my note, Sally – Mrs Denbigh, a distant relation.'

'Ay, but you said hoo was a widow. Is this chit a widow?'

'Yes, this is Mrs Denbigh,' answered Miss Benson.

'If I'd been her mother, I'd ha' given her a lollypop instead on a husband. Hoo looks fitter for it.'

'Hush! Sally, Sally! Look, there's your master trying to move that heavy box.' Miss Benson calculated well when she called Sally's attention to her master; for it was believed by every one, and by Sally herself, that his deformity was owing to a fall he had had, when he was scarcely more than a baby, and entrusted to her care – a little nurse-girl, as she then was, not many years older than himself. For years, the poor girl had cried herself to sleep on her pallet-bed, moaning over the blight her carelessness had brought upon her darling; nor was this self-reproach diminished by the forgiveness of the gentle mother, from whom Thurstan Benson derived so much of his character. The way in which comfort stole into Sally's heart, was in the gradually-formed resolution that she would never leave him nor forsake him, but serve him faithfully all her life long; and she had kept to her word. She loved Miss Benson, but she almost worshipped the brother. The reverence for him was in her heart, however, and did not always show itself in her manners. But if she scolded him herself, she allowed no one else that privilege. If Miss Benson differed from her brother, and ventured to think his sayings or doings might have been improved, Sally came down upon her like a thunder-clap.

'My goodness gracious, Master Thurstan, when will you learn to leave off meddling with other folks' business? Here, Ben! help me up with these trunks.'

The little narrow passage was cleared, and Miss Benson took Ruth into the sitting-room. There were only two sitting-rooms on the ground-floor, one behind the other. Out of the back room the kitchen opened, and for this reason the back parlour was used as the family sitting-room; or else, being, with its garden aspect, so much the pleasanter of the two, both Sally and Miss Benson would have appropriated it for Mr Benson's study. As it was, the front room, which looked to the street, was his room; and many a person coming for help – help of which giving money was the lowest kind – was admitted, and let forth by Mr Benson, unknown to any one else in the house. To make amends for his having the least cheerful room on the ground-floor, he had the garden bedroom, while his sister slept over his study. There were two more rooms again over these, with sloping ceilings, though otherwise large and airy. The attic looking into the garden was the spare bedroom; while the front belonged to Sally. There was no room over the kitchen, which was, in fact, a supplement to the house. The sitting-room was called by the pretty, old-fashioned name of the parlour, while Mr Benson's room was styled the study.

The curtains were drawn in the parlour; there was a bright fire and a clean hearth; indeed, exquisite cleanliness seemed the very spirit of the household, for the door which was open to the kitchen showed a delicately-white and spotless floor, and bright glittering tins, on which the ruddy firelight danced.

From the place in which Ruth sat she could see all Sally's movements; and though she was not conscious of close or minute observation at the time (her body being weary, and her mind full of other thoughts), yet it was curious how faithfully that scene remained depicted on her memory in after years. The warm light filled every corner of the kitchen, in strong distinction to the faint illumination of the one candle in the parlour, whose radiance was confined, and was lost in the dead folds of window-curtains, carpet, and furniture. The square, stout, bustling figure, neat and clean in every respect, but dressed in the peculiar, old-fashioned costume of the county, namely, a dark-striped linsey-woolsey petticoat, made very short, displaying sturdy legs in woollen stockings beneath; a loose kind of jacket called there a 'bedgown', made of pink print; a snow-white apron and cap, both of linen, and the latter made in the shape of a 'mutch';[2] – these articles completed Sally's costume, and were painted on Ruth's memory. Whilst Sally was busied in preparing tea, Miss Benson took off Ruth's things; and the latter instinctively felt that Sally, in the midst of her movements, was watching their proceedings. Occasionally she also put in a word in the conversation, and these little sentences were uttered quite in the tone of an equal, if not of a superior. She had dropped the more formal 'you', with which at first she had addressed Miss Benson, and thou'd her quietly and habitually.

All these particulars sank unconsciously into Ruth's mind; but they did not rise to the surface, and become perceptible, for a length of time. She was weary, and much depressed. Even the very kindness that ministered to her was overpowering. But over the dark, misty moor a little light shone, – a beacon; and on that she fixed her eyes, and struggled out of her present deep dejection – the little child that was coming to her!

Mr Benson was as languid and weary as Ruth, and was silent during all this bustle and preparation. His silence was more grateful to Ruth than Miss Benson's many words, although she felt their kindness. After tea, Miss Benson took her up-stairs to her room. The white dimity bed, and the walls, stained green, had something of the colouring and purity of effect of a snowdrop; while the floor, rubbed with a mixture that turned it into a rich dark-brown, suggested the idea of the garden-mould out of which the snowdrop grows. As Miss Benson helped the pale Ruth to undress, her voice became less full-toned and hurried; the hush of approaching night subdued her into a softened, solemn kind of tenderness, and the murmured blessing sounded like granted prayer.

When Miss Benson came down-stairs, she found her brother reading some letters which had been received during his absence. She went and softly shut the door of communication between the parlour and the kitchen; and then, fetching a grey worsted stocking which she was knitting, sat down near him, her eyes not looking at her work but fixed on the fire; while the eternal rapid click of the knitting-needles broke the silence of the room, with a sound as monotonous and incessant as the noise of a hand-loom. She expected him to speak, but he did not. She enjoyed an examination into, and discussion of, her feelings; it was an interest and amusement to her, while he dreaded and avoided all such conversation. There were times when his feelings, which were always earnest, and sometimes morbid, burst forth, and defied control, and overwhelmed him; when a force was upon him compelling him to speak. But he, in general, strove to preserve his composure, from a fear of the compelling pain of such times, and the consequent exhaustion. His heart had been very full of Ruth all day long, and he was afraid of his sister beginning the subject; so he read on, or seemed to do so, though he hardly saw the letter he held before him. It was a great relief to him when Sally threw open the middle door with a bang, which did not indicate either calmness of mind or sweetness of temper.

'Is yon young woman going to stay any length o' time with us?' asked she of Miss Benson.

Mr Benson put his hand gently on his sister's arm, to check her from making any reply, while he said:

'We cannot exactly tell, Sally. She will remain until after her confinement.'

'Lord bless us and save us! – a baby in the house! Nay, then my time's come, and I'll pack up and begone. I never could abide them things. I'd sooner have rats in the house.'

Sally really did look alarmed.

'Why, Sally!' said Mr Benson, smiling, 'I was not much more than a baby when you came to take care of me.'

'Yes, you were, Master Thurstan; you were a fine bouncing lad of three year old and better.'

Then she remembered the change she had wrought in the 'fine bouncing lad', and her eyes filled with tears, which she was too proud to wipe away with her apron; for, as she sometimes said to herself, 'she could not abide crying before folk.'

'Well, it's no use talking, Sally,' said Miss Benson, too anxious to speak to be any longer repressed. 'We've promised to keep her, and we must do it; you'll have none of the trouble, Sally, so don't be afraid.'

'Well, I never! as if I minded trouble! You might ha' known me better nor that. I've scoured master's room twice over, just to make the boards look white, though the carpet is to cover them, and now you go and cast up about me minding my trouble. If them's the fashions you've learnt in Wales, I'm thankful I've never been there.'

Sally looked red, indignant, and really hurt. Mr Benson came in with his musical voice and soft words of healing.

'Faith knows you don't care for trouble, Sally; she is only anxious about this poor young woman, who has no friends but ourselves. We know there will be more trouble in consequence of her coming to stay with us; and I think, though we never spoke about it, that in making our plans we reckoned on your kind help, Sally, which has never failed us yet when we needed it.'

'You've twice the sense of your sister, Master Thurstan, that you have. Boys always has. It's truth there will be more trouble, and I shall have my share on't, I reckon. I can face it if I'm told out and out, but I cannot abide the way some folk has of denying there's trouble or pain to be met; just as if their saying there was none, would do away with it.

Some folk treats one like a babby, and I don't like it. I'm not meaning *you*, Master Thurstan.'

'No, Sally, you need not say that. I know well enough who you mean when you say "some folk". However, I admit I was wrong in speaking as if you minded trouble, for there never was a creature minded it less. But I want you to like Mrs Denbigh,' said Miss Benson.

'I dare say I should, if you'd let me alone. I did na like her sitting down in master's chair. Set her up, indeed, in an arm-chair wi' cushions! Wenches in my day were glad enough of stools.'

'She was tired to-night,' said Mr Benson. 'We are all tired; so if you have done your work, Sally, come in to reading.'

The three quiet people knelt down side by side, and two of them prayed earnestly for 'them that had gone astray'.[3] Before ten o'clock, the household were in bed.

Ruth, sleepless, weary, restless with the oppression of a sorrow which she dared not face and contemplate bravely, kept awake all the early part of the night. Many a time did she rise, and go to the long casement window, and look abroad over the still and quiet town – over the grey-stone walls, and chimneys, and old high-pointed roofs – on to the far-away hilly line of the horizon, lying calm under the bright moonshine. It was late in the morning when she woke from her long-deferred slumbers; and when she went down-stairs, she found Mr and Miss Benson awaiting her in the parlour. That homely, pretty, old-fashioned little room! How bright and still and clean it looked! The window (all the windows at the back of the house were casements) was open, to let in the sweet morning air, and streaming eastern sunshine. The long jessamine sprays, with their white-scented stars, forced themselves almost into the room. The little square garden beyond, with grey-stone walls all round, was rich and mellow in its autumnal colouring, running from deep crimson hollyhocks up to amber and gold nasturtiums, and all toned down by the clear and delicate air. It was so still, that the gossamer-webs, laden with dew, did not tremble or quiver in the least; but the sun was drawing to himself the sweet incense of many flowers, and the parlour was scented with the odours of mignionette and stocks. Miss Benson was arranging a bunch of China and damask roses in an old-fashioned jar; they lay, all dewy and fresh, on the white breakfast-cloth when Ruth entered. Mr Benson was reading in some large folio. With gentle morning speech they greeted her; but the quiet repose of the scene was instantly broken by Sally popping in from the kitchen, and glancing at Ruth with sharp reproach. She said:

'I reckon I may bring in breakfast, now?' with a strong emphasis on the last word.

'I am afraid I am very late,' said Ruth.

'Oh, never mind,' said Mr Benson, gently. 'It was our fault for not telling you our breakfast hour. We always have prayers at half-past seven; and, for Sally's sake, we never vary from that time; for she can so arrange her work, if she knows the hour of prayers, as to have her mind calm and untroubled.'

'Ahem!' said Miss Benson, rather inclined to 'testify' against the invariable calmness of Sally's mind at any hour of the day; but her brother went on as if he did not hear her.

'But the breakfast does not signify being delayed a little; and I am sure you were sadly tired with your long day yesterday.'

Sally came slapping in, and put down some withered, tough, dry toast, with –

'It's not my doing if it is like leather;' but as no one appeared to hear her, she withdrew to her kitchen, leaving Ruth's cheeks like crimson at the annoyance she had caused.

All day long, she had that feeling common to those who go to stay at a fresh house among comparative strangers: a feeling of the necessity that she should become accustomed to the new atmosphere in which she was placed, before she could move and act freely; it was, indeed, a purer ether, a diviner air,[4] which she was breathing in now, than what she had been accustomed to for long months. The gentle, blessed mother, who had made her childhood's home holy ground, was in her very nature so far removed from any of earth's stains and temptations, that she seemed truly one of those

> Who ask not if Thine eye
> Be on them; who, in love and truth,
> Where no misgiving is, rely
> Upon the genial sense of youth.[5]

In the Bensons' house there was the same unconsciousness of individual merit, the same absence of introspection and analysis of motive, as there had been in her mother; but it seemed that their lives were pure and good, not merely from a lovely and beautiful nature, but from some law, the obedience to which was, of itself, harmonious peace, and which governed them almost implicitly, and with as little questioning on their part, as the glorious stars which haste not, rest not, in their eternal obedience. This household had many failings: they were but human, and, with all their loving desire to bring their lives into harmony with the will of God, they often erred and fell short; but, somehow, the very errors and faults of one individual served to call out higher excellencies in another, and so they re-acted upon each other, and the result of short discords was exceeding harmony and peace. But they had themselves no idea of the real state of things; they did not trouble themselves with marking their progress by self-examination; if Mr Benson did sometimes, in hours of sick incapacity for exertion, turn inwards, it was to cry aloud with almost morbid despair, 'God be merciful to me a sinner!'[6] But he strove to leave his life in the hands of God, and to forget himself.

Ruth sat still and quiet through the long first day. She was languid and weary from her journey; she was uncertain what help she might offer to give in the household duties, and what she might not. And, in her languor and in her uncertainty, it was pleasant to watch the new ways of the people among whom she was placed. After breakfast, Mr Benson withdrew to his study, Miss Benson took away the cups and saucers, and leaving the kitchen door open, talked sometimes to Ruth, sometimes to Sally, while she washed them up. Sally had up-stairs duties to perform, for which Ruth was thankful, as she kept receiving rather angry glances for her unpunctuality as long as Sally remained down-stairs. Miss Benson assisted in the preparation for the early dinner, and brought some kidney-beans to shred into a basin of bright, pure spring-water, which caught and danced in the sunbeams as she sat near the open casement of the parlour, talking to Ruth of things and people which as yet the latter did not understand, and could not arrange and comprehend. She was like a child who gets a few pieces of a dissected map, and is confused until a glimpse of the whole unity is shown him. Mr and Mrs Bradshaw were the centre pieces in Ruth's map; their children, their servants, were the accessories; and one or two other names were occasionally mentioned. Ruth wondered and almost wearied at Miss Benson's perseverance in talking to her about people whom she did not know; but, in truth, Miss Benson heard the long-drawn, quivering sighs which came from the poor heavy heart, when it was left to silence, and had leisure to review the past; and her quick accustomed ear caught also the low mutterings of the thunder in the distance, in the shape of Sally's soliloquies, which, like the asides at a theatre, were intended to be heard. Suddenly, Miss Benson called Ruth out of the room, up-stairs into her own bed-chamber, and then began rummaging in little old-fashioned boxes, drawn out of an equally old-fashioned bureau, half desk, half table, and wholly drawers.

'My dear, I've been very stupid and thoughtless. Oh! I'm so glad I thought of it before Mrs Bradshaw came to call. Here it is!' and she pulled out an old wedding-ring, and hurried it on Ruth's finger. Ruth hung down her head, and reddened deep with shame; her eyes smarted with the hot tears that filled them. Miss Benson talked on, in a nervous hurried way:

'It was my grandmother's; it's very broad; they made them so then, to hold a posy inside: there's one in that:

> Thine own sweetheart
> Till death doth part,

I think it is. There, there! Run away, and look as if you'd always worn it.'

Ruth went up to her room, and threw herself down on her knees by the bedside, and cried as if her heart would break; and then, as if a light had come down into her soul, she calmed herself and prayed – no words can tell how humbly, and with what earnest feeling. When she came down, she was tear-stained and wretchedly pale; but even Sally looked at her with new eyes, because of the dignity with which she was invested by an earnestness of purpose which had her child for its object. She sat and thought, but she no longer heaved those bitter sighs which had wrung Miss Benson's heart in the morning. In this way the day wore on; early dinner, early tea seemed to make it preternaturally long to Ruth; the only event was some unexplained absence of Sally's, who had disappeared out of the house in the evening, much to Miss Benson's surprise, and somewhat to her indignation.

At night, after Ruth had gone up to her room, this absence was explained to her at least. She had let down her long waving glossy hair, and was standing absorbed in thought in the middle of the room, when she heard a round clumping knock at her door, different from that given by the small knuckles of delicate fingers, and in walked Sally, with a judge-like severity of demeanour, holding in her hand two widow's caps[7] of commonest make and coarsest texture. Queen Eleanor herself, when she presented the bowl to Fair Rosamond,[8] had not a more relentless purpose stamped on her demeanour than had Sally at this moment. She walked up to the beautiful, astonished Ruth, where she stood in her long, soft, white dressing-gown, with all her luxuriant brown hair hanging dishevelled down her figure, and thus Sally spoke:

'Missus – or miss, as the case may be – I've my doubts as to you. I'm not going to have my master and Miss Faith put upon, or shame come near them. Widows wears these sort o' caps, and has their hair cut off; and whether widows wears wedding-rings or not, they shall have their hair cut off – they shall. I'll have no half work in this house. I've lived with the family forty-nine year come Michaelmas, and I'll not see it disgraced by any one's fine long curls. Sit down and let me snip off your hair, and let me see you sham decently in a widow's cap to-morrow, or I'll leave the house. Whatten's come over Miss Faith, as used to be as mim[9] a lady as ever was, to be taken by such as you, I dunnot know. Here! sit down with ye, and let me crop you.'

She laid no light hand on Ruth's shoulder; and the latter, partly intimidated by the old servant, who had hitherto only turned her vixen lining to observation, and partly because she was broken-spirited enough to be indifferent to the measure proposed, quietly sat down. Sally produced the formidable pair of scissors that always hung at her side, and began to cut in a merciless manner. She expected some remonstrance or some opposition, and had a torrent of words ready to flow forth at the least sign of rebellion; but Ruth was still and silent, with meekly-bowed head, under the strange hands that were shearing her beautiful hair into the clipped shortness of a boy's. Long before she had finished, Sally had some slight misgivings as to the fancied necessity of her task; but it was too late, for half the curls were gone, and the rest must now come off. When she had done, she lifted up Ruth's face by placing her hand under the round white chin. She gazed into the countenance, expecting to read some anger there, though it had not come out in words; but she only met the large, quiet eyes, that looked at her with sad gentleness out of their finely-hollowed orbits. Ruth's soft, yet dignified submission, touched Sally with compunction, though she did not choose to show the change in her feelings. She tried to hide it, indeed, by stooping to pick up the long bright tresses; and, holding them up admiringly, and letting them drop down and float on the air (like the pendent branches of the weeping birch), she said: 'I thought we should ha' had some crying – I did. They're pretty curls enough; you've not been so bad to let them be cut off neither. You see, Master Thurstan is no wiser than a babby in some things; and Miss Faith just lets him have his own way; so it's all left to me to keep him out of scrapes. I'll wish you a very good night. I've heard many a one say as long hair was not wholesome. Good night.'

But in a minute she popped her head into Ruth's room once more:

'You'll put on them caps to-morrow morning. I'll make you a present on them.'

Sally had carried away the beautiful curls, and she could not find it in her heart to throw such lovely chestnut tresses away, so she folded them up carefully in paper, and placed them in a safe corner of her drawer.

END OF VOL. I

VOLUME II

CHAPTER XIV

Ruth felt very shy when she came down (at half-past seven) the next morning, in her widow's cap. Her smooth, pale face, with its oval untouched by time, looked more young and child-like than ever, when contrasted with the head-gear usually associated with ideas of age. She blushed very deeply as Mr and Miss Benson showed the astonishment, which they could not conceal, in their looks. She said in a low voice to Miss Benson:

'Sally thought I had better wear it.'

Miss Benson made no reply; but was startled at the intelligence, which she thought was conveyed in this speech, of Sally's acquaintance with Ruth's real situation. She noticed Sally's looks particularly this morning. The manner in which the old servant treated Ruth, had in it far more of respect than there had been the day before; but there was a kind of satisfied way of braving out Miss Benson's glances which made the latter uncertain and uncomfortable.

She followed her brother into his study.

'Do you know, Thurstan, I am almost certain Sally suspects.'

Mr Benson sighed. That deception grieved him, and yet he thought he saw its necessity.

'What makes you think so?' asked he.

'Oh! many little things. It was her odd way of ducking her head about, as if to catch a good view of Ruth's left hand, that made me think of the wedding-ring; and once, yesterday, when I thought I had made up quite a natural speech, and was saying how sad it was for so young a creature to be left a widow, she broke in with "widow be farred!"[1] in a very strange, contemptuous kind of manner.'

'If she suspects, we had far better tell her the truth, at once. She will never rest till she finds it out, so we must make a virtue of necessity.'

'Well, brother, you shall tell her then, for I am sure I daren't. I don't mind doing the thing, since you talked to me that day, and since I have got to know Ruth; but I do mind all the clatter people will make about it.'

'But Sally is not "people".'

'Oh, I see it must be done; she'll talk as much as all the other persons put together, so that's the reason I call her "people". Shall I call her?' (For the house was too homely and primitive to have bells.)

Sally came, fully aware of what was now going to be told her, and determined not to help them out in telling their awkward secret, by understanding the nature of it before it was put into the plainest language. In every pause, when they hoped she had caught the meaning they were hinting at, she persisted in looking stupid and perplexed, and in saying 'Well,' as if quite unenlightened as to the end of the story.

When it was all complete and before her, she said, honestly enough:

'It's just as I thought it was; and I think you may thank me for having had the sense to put her into widow's caps, and clip off that bonny brown hair that was fitter for a bride in lawful matrimony than for such as her. She took it very well, though. She was as quiet as a lamb, and I clipped her pretty roughly at first. I must say, though, if I'd ha' known who your visitor was, I'd ha' packed up my things and cleared myself out of the house before such as her came into it. As it's done, I suppose I must stand by you, and help you through with it; I only hope I sha'n't lose my character, – and me a parish clerk's daughter!'

'Oh, Sally! people know you too well to think any ill of you,' said Miss Benson, who was pleased to find the difficulty so easily got over; for, in truth, Sally had been much softened by the unresisting gentleness with which Ruth had submitted to the 'clipping' of the night before.

'If I'd been with you, Master Thurstan, I'd ha' seen sharp after you, for you're always picking up some one or another as nobody else would touch with a pair of tongs. Why, there was that Nelly Brandon's child as was left at our door, if I hadn't gone to th' overseer[2] we should have had that Irish tramp's babby saddled on us for life; but I went off and told th' overseer, and th' mother was caught.'

'Yes,' said Mr Benson, sadly, 'and I often lie awake and wonder what is the fate of that poor little thing, forced back on the mother who tried to get quit of it. I often doubt whether I did right; but it's no use thinking about it now.'

'I'm thankful it isn't,' said Sally; 'and now, if we've talked doctrine long enough, I'll go make th' beds. Yon girl's secret is safe enough for me.'

Saying this she left the room, and Miss Benson followed. She found Ruth busy washing the breakfast-things; and they were done in so quiet and orderly a manner, that neither Miss Benson nor Sally, both particular enough, had any of their little fancies or prejudices annoyed. She seemed to have an instinctive knowledge of the exact period when her help was likely to become a hindrance, and withdrew from the busy kitchen just at the right time.

That afternoon, as Miss Benson and Ruth sat at their work, Mrs and Miss Bradshaw called. Miss Benson was so nervous as to surprise Ruth, who did not understand the probable and possible questions which might be asked respecting any visitor at the minister's house. Ruth went on sewing, absorbed in her own thoughts, and glad that the conversation between the two elder ladies and the silence of the younger one, who sat at some distance from her, gave her an opportunity of retreating into the haunts of memory; and soon the work fell from her hands, and her eyes were fixed on the little garden beyond, but she did not see its flowers or its walls; she saw the mountains which girdled Llan-dhu, and saw the sun rise from behind their iron outline, just as it had done – how long ago? was it months or was it years? – since she had watched the night through, crouched up at *his* door. Which was the dream and which the reality? that distant life, or this? His moans rang more clearly in her ears than the buzzing of the conversation between Mrs Bradshaw and Miss Benson.

At length the subdued, scared-looking little lady and her bright-eyed silent daughter rose to take leave; Ruth started into the present, and stood up and curtseyed, and turned sick at heart with sudden recollection.

Miss Benson accompanied Mrs Bradshaw to the door; and in the passage gave her a long explanation of Ruth's (fictitious) history. Mrs Bradshaw looked so much interested and pleased, that Miss Benson enlarged a little more than was necessary, and rounded off her invention with one or two imaginary details, which, she was quite unconscious, were overheard by her brother through the half-open study door.

She was rather dismayed when he called her into his room after Mrs Bradshaw's departure, and asked her what she had been saying about Ruth?

'Oh! I thought it was better to explain it thoroughly – I mean, to tell the story we wished to have believed once for all – you know we agreed about that, Thurstan?' deprecatingly.

'Yes; but I heard you saying you believed her husband had been a young surgeon, did I not?'

'Well, Thurstan, you know he must have been something; and young surgeons are so in the way of dying, it seemed very natural. Besides,' said she, with sudden boldness, 'I do think I've a talent for fiction, it is so pleasant to invent, and make the incidents dovetail together; and after all, if we are to tell a lie, we may as well do it thoroughly, or else it's of no use. A bungling lie would be worse than useless. And, Thurstan – it may be very wrong – but I believe – I am afraid I enjoy not being fettered by truth. Don't look so grave. You know it is necessary, if ever it was, to tell falsehoods now; and don't be angry with me because I do it well.'

He was shading his eyes with his hand, and did not speak for some time. At last he said:

'If it were not for the child, I would tell all; but the world is so cruel. You don't know how this apparent necessity for falsehood pains me, Faith, or you would not invent all these details, which are so many additional lies.'

'Well, well! I will restrain myself if I have to talk about Ruth again. But Mrs Bradshaw will tell every one who need to know. You don't wish me to contradict it, Thurstan, surely – it was such a pretty, probable story.'

'Faith! I hope God will forgive us if we are doing wrong; and pray, dear, don't add one unnecessary word that is not true.'

Another day elapsed, and then it was Sunday: and the house seemed filled with a deep peace. Even Sally's movements were less hasty and abrupt. Mr Benson seemed invested with a new dignity, which made his bodily deformity be forgotten in his calm, grave composure of spirit. Every trace of week-day occupation was put away; the night before, a bright new handsome tablecloth had been smoothed down over the table, and the jars had been freshly filled with flowers. Sunday was a festival and a holyday in the house. After the very early breakfast, little feet pattered into Mr Benson's study, for he had a class for boys – a sort of domestic Sunday-school, only that there was more talking between teacher and pupils, than dry, absolute lessons going on. Miss Benson, too, had her little, neat-tippeted[3] maidens sitting with her in the parlour; and she was far more particular in keeping them to their reading and spelling, than her brother was with his boys. Sally, too, put in her word of instruction from the kitchen, helping, as she fancied, though her assistance was often rather *mal-àpropos*; for instance, she called out, to a little fat, stupid, roly-poly girl, to whom Miss Benson was busy explaining the meaning of the word quadruped:

'Quadruped, a thing wi' four legs, Jenny; a chair is a quadruped, child!'

But Miss Benson had a deaf manner sometimes when her patience was not too severely tried, and she put it on now. Ruth sat on a low hassock, and coaxed the least of the little creatures to her, and showed it pictures till it fell asleep in her arms, and sent a thrill through her, at the thought of the tiny darling who would lie on her breast before long, and whom she would have to cherish and to shelter from the storms of the world.

And then she remembered, that she was once white and sinless as the wee lassie who lay in her arms; and she knew that she had gone astray. By-and-by the children trooped away, and Miss Benson summoned her to put on her things for chapel.

The chapel[4] was up a narrow street, or rather *cul-de-sac*, close by. It stood on the outskirts of the town, almost in fields. It was built about the time of Matthew and Philip Henry,[5] when the Dissenters were afraid of attracting attention or observation, and hid their places of worship in obscure and out-of-the-way parts of the towns in which they were built. Accordingly, it often happened, as in the present case, that the buildings immediately surrounding, as well as the chapels themselves, looked as if they carried you back to a period a hundred and fifty years ago. The chapel had a picturesque and old-world look, for luckily the congregation had been too poor to rebuild it, or new-face it in George the Third's time. The staircases which led to the galleries were outside, at each end of the building, and the irregular roof and worn stone-steps looked grey and stained by time and weather. The grassy hillocks, each with a little upright head-stone, were shaded by a grand old wych-elm. A lilac-bush or two, a white rose-tree, and a few laburnums, all old and gnarled enough, were planted round the chapel yard; and the casement windows of the chapel were made of heavy-leaded, diamond-shaped panes, almost covered with ivy, producing a green gloom, not without its solemnity, within. This ivy was the home of an infinite number of little birds, which twittered and warbled, till it might have been thought that they were emulous of the power of praise possessed by the human creatures within, with such earnest, long-drawn strains did this crowd of winged songsters rejoice and be glad in their beautiful gift of life. The interior of the building was plain and simple as plain and simple could be. When it was fitted up, oak-timber was much cheaper than it is now, so the wood-work was all of that description; but roughly hewed, for the early builders had not much wealth to spare. The walls were whitewashed, and were recipients of the shadows of the beauty without; on their 'white plains'[6] the tracery of the ivy might be seen, now still, now stirred by the sudden flight of some little bird. The congregation consisted of here and there a farmer with his labourers, who came down from the uplands beyond the town to worship where their fathers worshipped, and who loved the place because they knew how much those fathers had suffered for it, although they never troubled themselves with the reason why they left the parish church; of a few shopkeepers, far more thoughtful and reasoning, who were Dissenters from conviction, unmixed with old ancestral association; and of one or two families of still higher worldly station. With many poor, who were drawn there by love for Mr Benson's character, and by a feeling that the faith which made him what he was could not be far wrong, for the base of the pyramid, and with Mr Bradshaw for its apex, the congregation stood complete.

The country people came in sleeking down their hair, and treading with earnest attempts at noiseless lightness of step over the floor of the aisle; and by-and-by, when all were assembled, Mr Benson followed, unmarshalled and unattended. When he had closed the pulpit-door, and knelt in prayer for an instant or two, he gave out a psalm from the dear old Scottish paraphrase,[7] with its primitive inversion of the simple perfect Bible words; and a kind of precentor stood up, and, having sounded the note on a pitch-pipe, sang a couple of lines by way of indicating the tune; then all the congregation stood up, and sang aloud, Mr Bradshaw's great bass voice being half a note in advance of the others, in accordance with his place of precedence as principal member of the congregation. His powerful voice was like an organ very badly played, and very much out of tune; but as he had no ear, and no diffidence, it pleased him very much to hear the fine loud sound. He was a tall, large-boned, iron man; stern, powerful, and authoritative in appearance; dressed in clothes of the finest broadcloth, and scrupulously ill-made, as if to show that he was indifferent to all outward things. His wife was sweet and gentle-looking, but as if she was thoroughly broken into submission.

Ruth did not see this, or hear aught but the words which were reverently – oh, how reverently! – spoken by Mr Benson. He had had Ruth present in his thoughts all the time he had been preparing for his Sunday duty; and he had tried carefully to eschew everything which she might feel as an allusion to her own case. He remembered how the Good Shepherd, in Poussin's beautiful picture,[8] tenderly carried the lambs which had wearied themselves by going astray, and felt how like tenderness was required towards poor Ruth. But where is the chapter which does not contain something which a broken and contrite spirit may not apply to itself? And so it fell out that, as he read, Ruth's heart was smitten, and she sank down, and down, till she was kneeling on the floor of the pew, and speaking to God in the spirit, if not in the words of the Prodigal Son: 'Father! I have sinned against Heaven and before Thee, and am no more worthy to be called Thy child!'[9] Miss Benson was thankful (although she loved Ruth the better for this self-abandonment) that the minister's seat was far in the shade of the gallery. She tried to look most attentive to her brother, in order that Mr Bradshaw might not suspect anything unusual, while she stealthily took hold of Ruth's passive hand, as it lay helpless on the cushion, and pressed it softly and tenderly. But Ruth sat on the ground, bowed down and crushed in her sorrow, till all was ended.

Miss Benson loitered in her seat, divided between the consciousness that she, as *locum tenens* for the minister's wife, was expected to be at the door to receive the kind greetings of many after her absence from home, and her unwillingness to disturb Ruth, who was evidently praying, and, by her quiet breathing, receiving grave and solemn influences into her soul. At length she rose up, calm and composed even to dignity. The chapel was still and empty; but Miss Benson heard the buzz of voices in the chapel-yard without. They were probably those of people waiting for her; and she summoned courage, and taking Ruth's arm in hers, and holding her hand affectionately, they went out into the broad daylight. As they issued forth, Miss Benson heard Mr Bradshaw's strong bass voice speaking to her brother, and winced, as she knew he would be wincing, under the broad praise, which is impertinence, however little it may be intended or esteemed as such.

'Oh, yes! – my wife told me yesterday about her – her husband was a surgeon; my father was a surgeon too, as I think you have heard. Very much to your credit, I must say, Mr Benson, with your limited means, to burden yourself with a poor relation. Very creditable indeed.'

Miss Benson glanced at Ruth; she either did not hear or did not understand, but passed on into the awful sphere of Mr Bradshaw's observation unmoved. He was in a bland and condescending humour of universal approval, and when he saw Ruth, he nodded his head in token of satisfaction. That ordeal was over, Miss Benson thought, and in the thought rejoiced.

'After dinner, you must go and lie down, my dear,' said she, untying Ruth's bonnet-strings, and kissing her. 'Sally goes to church again, but you won't mind staying alone in the house. I am sorry we have so many people to dinner, but my brother will always have enough on Sundays for any old or weak people, who may have come from a distance, to stay and dine with us; and to-day they all seem to have come, because it is his first Sabbath at home.'

In this way Ruth's first Sunday passed over.

CHAPTER XV

'Here is a parcel for you, Ruth!' said Miss Benson on the Tuesday morning.

'For me!' said Ruth, all sorts of rushing thoughts and hopes filling her mind, and turning her dizzy with expectation. If it had been from 'him', the new-born resolutions would have had a hard struggle for existence.

'It is directed "Mrs Denbigh",' said Miss Benson, before giving it up. 'It is in Mrs Bradshaw's handwriting;' and, far more curious than Ruth, she awaited the untying of the close-knotted string. When the paper was opened, it displayed a whole piece of delicate cambric-muslin; and there was a short note from Mrs Bradshaw to Ruth, saying her husband had wished her to send this muslin in aid of any preparations Mrs Denbigh might have to make. Ruth said nothing, but coloured up, and sat down again to her employment.

'Very fine muslin, indeed,' said Miss Benson, feeling it, and holding it up against the light, with the air of a connoisseur; yet all the time she was glancing at Ruth's grave face. The latter kept silence, and showed no wish to inspect her present further. At last she said, in a low voice:

'I suppose I may send it back again?'

'My dear child! send it back to Mr Bradshaw! You'd offend him for life. You may depend upon it, he means it as a mark of high favour!'

'What right had he to send it me?' asked Ruth, still in her quiet voice.

'What right? Mr Bradshaw thinks— I don't know exactly what you mean by "right".'

Ruth was silent for a moment, and then said:

'There are people to whom I love to feel that I owe gratitude – gratitude which I cannot express, and had better not talk about – but I cannot see why a person whom I do not know should lay me under an obligation. Oh! don't say I must take this muslin, please, Miss Benson!'

What Miss Benson might have said if her brother had not just then entered the room, neither he nor any other person could tell; but she felt his presence was most opportune, and called him in as umpire. He had come hastily, for he had much to do; but he no sooner heard the case than he sat down, and tried to draw some more explicit declaration of her feeling from Ruth, who had remained silent during Miss Benson's explanation.

'You would rather send this present back?' said he.

'Yes,' she answered, softly. 'Is it wrong?'

'Why do you want to return it?'

'Because I feel as if Mr Bradshaw had no right to offer it me.'

Mr Benson was silent.

'It's beautifully fine,' said Miss Benson, still examining the piece.

'You think that it is a right which must be earned?'

'Yes,' said she, after a minute's pause. 'Don't you?'

'I understand what you mean. It is a delight to have gifts made to you by those whom you esteem and love, because then such gifts are merely to be considered as fringes to the garment[1] – as inconsiderable additions to the mighty treasure of their affection, adding a grace, but no additional value, to what before was precious, and proceeding as naturally out of that as leaves burgeon out upon the trees; but you feel it to be different when there is no regard for the giver to idealise the gift – when it simply takes its stand among your property as so much money's value. Is this it, Ruth?'

'I think it is. I never reasoned why I felt as I did; I only knew that Mr Bradshaw's giving me a present hurt me, instead of making me glad.'

'Well, but there is another side of the case we have not looked at yet – we must think of that, too. You know who said, "Do unto others as ye would that they should do unto you"?[2] Mr Bradshaw may not have had that in his mind when he desired his wife to send you this; he may have been self-seeking, and only anxious to gratify his love of patronising – that is the worst motive we can give him; and that would be no excuse for your thinking only of yourself, and returning his present.'

'But you would not have me pretend to be obliged?' asked Ruth.

'No, I would not. I have often been similarly situated to you, Ruth; Mr Bradshaw has frequently opposed me on the points on which I feel the warmest – am the most earnestly convinced. He, no doubt, thinks me Quixotic, and often speaks of me, and to me, with great contempt when he is angry. I suppose he has a little fit of penitence afterwards, or perhaps he thinks he can pay for ungracious speeches by a present; so, formerly, he invariably sent me something after these occasions. It was a time, of all others, to feel as you are doing now; but I became convinced it would be right to accept them, giving only the very cool thanks which I felt. This omission of all show of much gratitude had the best effect – the presents have much diminished; but if the gifts have lessened, the unjustifiable speeches have decreased in still greater proportion, and I am sure we respect each other more. Take this muslin, Ruth, for the reason I named; and thank him as your feelings prompt you. Overstrained expressions of gratitude always seem like an endeavour to place the receiver of these expressions in the position of debtor for future favours. But you won't fall into this error.'

Ruth listened to Mr Benson; but she had not yet fallen sufficiently into the tone of his mind to understand him fully. She only felt that he comprehended her better than Miss Benson, who once more tried to reconcile her to her present, by calling her attention to the length and breadth thereof.

'I will do what you wish me,' she said, after a little pause of thoughtfulness. 'May we talk of something else?'

Mr Benson saw that his sister's frame of mind was not particularly congenial with Ruth's, any more than Ruth's was with Miss Benson's; and, putting aside all thought of returning to the business which had appeared to him so important when he came into the room (but which principally related to himself), he remained above an hour in the parlour, interesting them on subjects far removed from the present, and left them at the end of that time soothed and calm.

But the present gave a new current to Ruth's ideas. Her heart was as yet too sore to speak, but her mind was crowded with plans. She asked Sally to buy her (with the money produced by the sale of a ring or two) the coarsest linen, the homeliest dark blue print, and similar materials; on which she set busily to work to make clothes for herself; and as they were made, she put them on; and as she put them on, she gave a grace to each, which such homely material and simple shaping had never had before. Then the fine linen and delicate soft white muslin, which she had chosen in preference to more expensive articles of dress when Mr Bellingham had given her *carte blanche* in London, were cut into small garments, most daintily stitched and made ready for the little creature, for whom in its white purity of soul nothing could be too precious.

The love which dictated this extreme simplicity and coarseness of attire, was taken for stiff, hard economy by Mr Bradshaw, when he deigned to observe it. And economy by itself, without any soul or spirit in it to make it living and holy, was a great merit in his eyes. Indeed, Ruth altogether found favour with him.[3] Her quiet manner, subdued by an internal consciousness of a deeper cause for sorrow than he was aware of, he interpreted into a very proper and becoming awe of him. He looked off from his own prayers to observe how well she attended to hers at chapel; when he came to any verse in the hymn relating to immortality or a future life, he sung it unusually loud, thinking he should thus comfort her in her sorrow for her deceased husband. He desired Mrs Bradshaw to pay her every attention she could; and even once remarked, that he thought her so respectable a young person that he should not object to her being asked to tea the next time Mr and Miss Benson came. He added, that he thought, indeed, Benson had looked last Sunday as if he rather hoped to get an invitation; and it was right to encourage the ministers, and to show them respect, even though their salaries were small. The only thing against this Mrs Denbigh was the circumstance of her having married too early, and without any provision for a family. Though Ruth pleaded delicacy of health, and declined accompanying Mr and Miss Benson on their visit to Mr Bradshaw, she still preserved her place in his esteem; and Miss Benson had to call a little upon her 'talent for fiction' to spare Ruth from the infliction of further presents, in making which his love of patronising delighted.

The yellow and crimson leaves came floating down on the still October air; November followed, bleak and dreary; it was more cheerful when the earth put on her beautiful robe of white, which covered up all the grey naked stems, and loaded the leaves of the hollies and evergreens each with its burden of feathery snow. When Ruth sank down to languor and sadness, Miss Benson trotted up-stairs, and rummaged up every article of spare or worn-out clothing, and bringing down a variety of strange materials, she tried to interest Ruth in making them up into garments for the poor. But though Ruth's fingers flew through the work, she still sighed with thought and remembrance. Miss Benson was at first disappointed, and then she was angry. When she heard the low, long sigh, and saw the dreamy eyes filling with glittering tears, she would say, 'What is the matter, Ruth?' in a half-reproachful tone, for the sight of suffering was painful to her; she had done all in her power to remedy it; and, though she acknowledged a cause beyond her reach for Ruth's deep sorrow, and, in fact, loved and respected her all the more for these manifestations of grief, yet at the time they irritated her. Then Ruth would snatch up the dropped work, and stitch away with drooping eyes, from which the hot tears fell fast; and Miss Benson was then angry with herself, yet not at all inclined to agree with Sally when she asked her mistress 'why she kept "mithering"[4] the poor lass with asking her for ever what was the matter, as if she did not know well enough.' Some element of harmony was wanting – some little angel of peace, in loving whom all hearts and natures should be drawn together, and their discords hushed.

The earth was still 'hiding her guilty front with innocent snow',[5] when a little baby was laid by the side of the pale white mother. It was a boy; beforehand she had wished for a girl, as being less likely to feel the want of a father – as being what a mother, worse than widowed, could most effectually shelter. But now she did not think or remember this. What it was, she would not have exchanged for a wilderness of girls.[6] It was her own, her darling, her individual baby, already, though not an hour old, separate and sole in her heart, strangely filling up its measure with love and peace, and even hope. For here was a new, pure, beautiful, innocent life, which she fondly imagined, in that early passion of maternal love, she could guard from every touch of corrupting sin by ever watchful and most tender care. And *her* mother had thought the same, most probably; and thousands of others think the same, and pray to God to purify and cleanse their souls, that they may be fit guardians for their little children. Oh, how Ruth prayed, even while she was yet too weak to speak; and how she felt the beauty and significance of the words, 'Our Father!'

She was roused from this holy abstraction by the sound of Miss Benson's voice. It was very much as if she had been crying.

'Look, Ruth!' it said, softly, 'my brother sends you these. They are the first snowdrops in the garden.' And she put them on the pillow by Ruth; the baby lay on the opposite side.

'Won't you look at him?' said Ruth; 'he is so pretty!'

Miss Benson had a strange reluctance to see him. To Ruth, in spite of all that had come and gone, she was reconciled – nay, more, she was deeply attached; but over the baby there hung a cloud of shame and disgrace. Poor little creature, her heart was closed against it – firmly, as she thought. But she could not resist Ruth's low faint voice, nor her pleading eyes, and she went round to peep at him as he lay on his mother's arm, as yet his shield and guard.

'Sally says he will have black hair, she thinks,' said Ruth. 'His little hand is quite a man's, already. Just feel how firmly he closes it;' and with her own weak fingers she opened his little red fist, and taking Miss Benson's reluctant hand, placed one of her fingers in his grasp. That baby-touch called out her love; the doors of her heart were thrown open wide for the little infant to go in and take possession.

'Ah, my darling!' said Ruth, falling back weak and weary. 'If God will but spare you to me, never mother did more than I will. I have done you a grievous wrong – but, if I may but live, I will spend my life in serving you!'

'And in serving God!' said Miss Benson, with tears in her eyes. 'You must not make him into an idol, or God will, perhaps, punish you through him.'

A pang of affright shot through Ruth's heart at these words; had she already sinned and made her child into an idol, and was there punishment already in store for her through him? But then the internal voice whispered that God was 'Our Father', and that He knew our frame, and knew how natural was the first outburst of a mother's love; so, although she treasured up the warning, she ceased to affright herself for what had already gushed forth.

'Now go to sleep, Ruth,' said Miss Benson, kissing her, and darkening the room. But Ruth could not sleep; if her heavy eyes closed, she opened them again with a start, for sleep seemed to be an enemy stealing from her the consciousness of being a mother. That one thought excluded all remembrance and all anticipation, in those first hours of delight.

But soon remembrance and anticipation came. Then there was the natural want of the person, who alone could take an interest similar in kind, though not in amount, to the mother's. And sadness grew like a giant in the still watches of the night, when she remembered that there would be no father to guide and strengthen the child, and place him in a favourable position for fighting the hard 'Battle of Life'. She hoped and believed that no one would know the sin of his parents; and that that struggle might be spared to him. But a father's powerful care and mighty guidance would never be his; and then, in those hours of spiritual purification, came the wonder and the doubt of how far the real father would be the one to whom, with her desire of heaven for her child, whatever might become of herself, she would wish to entrust him. Slight speeches, telling of a selfish, worldly nature, unnoticed at the time, came back upon her ear, having a new significance. They told of a low standard, of impatient self-indulgence, of no acknowledgment of things spiritual and heavenly. Even while this examination was forced upon her, by the new spirit of maternity that had entered into her, and made her child's welfare supreme, she hated and reproached herself for the necessity there seemed upon her of examining and judging the absent father of her child. And so the compelling presence that had taken possession of her, wearied her into a kind of feverish slumber; in which she dreamt that the innocent babe that lay by her side in soft ruddy slumber, had started up into man's growth, and, instead of the pure and noble being whom she had prayed to present as her child to 'Our Father in heaven', he was a repetition of his father; and, like him, lured some maiden (who in her dream seemed strangely like herself, only

more utterly sad and desolate even than she) into sin, and left her there
to even a worse fate than that of suicide. For Ruth believed there was
a worse. She dreamt she saw the girl, wandering, lost; and that she saw
her son in high places, prosperous – but with more than blood on his
soul. She saw her son dragged down by the clinging girl into some pit
of horrors into which she dared not look, but from whence his father's
voice was heard, crying aloud, that in his day and generation he had
not remembered the words of God, and that now he was 'tormented
in this flame'.[7] Then she started in sick terror, and saw, by the dim
rushlight,[8] Sally, nodding in an arm-chair by the fire; and felt her little
soft warm babe, nestled up against her breast, rocked by her heart,
which yet beat hard from the effects of the evil dream. She dared not
go to sleep again, but prayed. And every time she prayed, she asked
with a more complete wisdom, and a more utter and self-forgetting
faith. Little child! thy angel was with God, and drew her nearer and
nearer to Him, whose face is continually beheld by the angels of little
children.[9]

CHAPTER XVI

Sally and Miss Benson took it in turns to sit up, or rather, they took it
in turns to nod by the fire; for if Ruth was awake she lay very still in
the moonlight calm of her sick bed. That time resembled a beautiful
August evening, such as I have seen. The white, snowy, rolling mist
covers up under its great sheet all trees and meadows, and tokens of
earth; but it cannot rise high enough to shut out the heavens, which on
such nights seem bending very near, and to be the only real and present
objects; and so near, so real and present, did heaven, and eternity, and
God seem to Ruth, as she lay encircling her mysterious holy child.

One night Sally found out she was not asleep.

'I'm a rare hand at talking folks to sleep,' said she. 'I'll try on thee,
for thou must get strength by sleeping and eating. What must I talk to
thee about, I wonder. Shall I tell thee a love story or a fairy story, such
as I've telled Master Thurstan many a time and many a time, for all

his father set his face again fairies, and called it vain talking; or shall I tell you the dinner I once cooked, when Mr Harding, as was Miss Faith's sweetheart, came unlooked for, and we'd nought in the house but a neck of mutton, out of which I made seven dishes, all with a different name?'

'Who was Mr Harding?' asked Ruth.

'Oh, he was a grand gentleman from Lunnon, as had seen Miss Faith, and been struck by her pretty looks when she was out on a visit, and came here to ask her to marry him. She said, "No, she would never leave Master Thurstan, as could never marry;" but she pined a deal at after he went away. She kept up afore Master Thurstan, but I seed her fretting, though I never let on that I did, for I thought she'd soonest get over it and be thankful at after she'd the strength to do right. However, I've no business to be talking of Miss Benson's concerns. I'll tell you of my own sweethearts and welcome, or I'll tell you of the dinner, which was the grandest thing I ever did in my life, but I thought a Lunnoner should never think country folks knew nothing; and, my word! I puzzled him with his dinner. I'm doubting whether to this day he knows whether what he was eating was fish, flesh, or fowl. Shall I tell you how I managed?'

But Ruth said she would rather hear about Sally's sweethearts, much to the disappointment of the latter, who considered the dinner by far the greatest achievement.

'Well, you see, I don't know as I should calt them sweethearts; for excepting John Rawson, who was shut up in a mad-house the next week, I never had what you may call a downright offer of marriage but once. But I had once; and so I may say I had a sweetheart. I was beginning to be afeard though, for one likes to be axed; that's but civility; and I remember, after I had turned forty, and afore Jeremiah Dixon had spoken, I began to think John Rawson had perhaps not been so very mad, and that I'd done ill to lightly his offer,[1] as a madman's, if it was to be the only one I was ever to have; I don't mean as I'd have had him, but I thought, if it was to come o'er again, I'd speak respectful of him to folk, and say it were only his way to go about on-all-fours, but that he was a sensible man in most things. However, I'd had my laugh, and so had others, at my crazy lover, and it was late now to set him up as a Solomon. However, I thought it would be no bad thing to be tried again; but I little thought the trial would come when it did. You see,

Saturday night is a leisure night in counting-houses[2] and such-like places, while it's the busiest of all for servants. Well! it was a Saturday night, and I'd my baize apron on, and the tails of my bed-gown pinned together behind, down on my knees, pipeclaying the kitchen,[3] when a knock comes to the back door. "Come in!" says I; but it knocked again, as if it were too stately to open the door for itself; so I got up, rather cross, and opened the door; and there stood Jerry Dixon, Mr Holt's head-clerk; only he was not head-clerk then. So I stood, stopping up the door, fancying he wanted to speak to master; but he kind of pushed past me, and telling me summut about the weather (as if I could not see it for myself), he took a chair, and sat down by the oven. "Cool and easy!" thought I; meaning hisself, not his place, which I knew must be pretty hot. Well! it seemed no use standing waiting for my gentleman to go; not that he had much to say either; but he kept twirling his hat round and round, and smoothing the nap on't with the back of his hand. So at last I squatted down to my work, and thinks I, I shall be on my knees all ready if he puts up a prayer, for I knew he was a Methodee[4] by bringing-up, and had only lately turned to master's way of thinking; and them Methodees are terrible hands at unexpected prayers when one least looks for 'em. I can't say I like their way of taking one by surprise, as it were; but then I'm a parish clerk's daughter, and could never demean myself to dissenting fashions, always save and except Master Thurstan's, bless him. However, I'd been caught once or twice unawares, so this time I thought I'd be up to it, and I moved a dry duster wherever I went, to kneel upon in case he began when I were in a wet place. By-and-by I thought, if the man would pray it would be a blessing, for it would prevent his sending his eyes after me wherever I went; for when they takes to praying they shuts their eyes, and quivers th' lids in a queer kind o' way – them Dissenters does. I can speak pretty plain to you, for you're bred in the Church like mysel', and must find it as out o' the way as I do to be among dissenting folk. God forbid I should speak disrespectful of Master Thurstan and Miss Faith, though; I never think on them as Church or Dissenters, but just as Christians. But to come back to Jerry. First, I tried always to be cleaning at his back; but when he wheeled round, so as always to face me, I thought I'd try a different game. So, says I, "Master Dixon, I ax your pardon, but I must pipeclay under your chair. Will you please to move?" Well, he moved; and by-and-by I was at him again with the same words; and at after that, again and again, till he were always moving about wi' his chair behind him, like a snail as carries its house on its back. And the great gaupus[5] never seed that I were pipeclaying the same places twice over. At last I got desperate cross, he were so in my way; so I made two big crosses on the tails of his brown coat; for you see, wherever he went, up or down, he drew out the tails of his coat from under him, and stuck them through the bars of the chair; and flesh and blood could not resist pipeclaying them for him; and a pretty brushing he'd have, I reckon, to get it off again. Well! at length he clears his throat uncommon loud; so I spreads my duster, and shuts my eyes all ready; but when nought comed of it, I opened my eyes a little bit to see what he were about. My word! if there he wasn't down on his knees right facing me, staring as hard as he could. Well! I thought it would be hard work to stand that, if he made a long ado; so I shut my eyes again, and tried to think serious, as became what I fancied were coming; but, forgive me! but I thought why couldn't the fellow go in and pray wi' Master Thurstan, as had always a calm spirit ready for prayer, instead o' me, who had my dresser to scour, let alone an apron to iron. At last he says, says he, "Sally! will you oblige me with your hand?" So I thought it were, maybe, Methodee fashion to pray hand in hand; and I'll not deny but I wished I'd washed it better after blackleading the kitchen fire.[6] I thought I'd better tell him it were not so clean as I could wish, so says I, "Master Dixon, you shall have it, and welcome, if I may just go and wash 'em first." But, says he, "My dear Sally, dirty or clean it's all the same to me, seeing I'm only speaking in a figuring way. What I'm asking on my bended knees is, that you'd please to be so kind as to be my wedded wife; week after next will suit me, if it's agreeable to you!" My word! I were up on my feet in an instant! It were odd now, weren't it? I never thought of taking the fellow, and getting married; for all, I'll not deny, I had been thinking it would be agreeable to be axed. But all at once, I couldn't abide the chap. "Sir," says I, trying to look shame-faced as became the occasion, but for all that, feeling a twittering round my mouth that I were afeard might end in a laugh – "Master Dixon, I'm obleeged to you for the compliment, and thank ye all the same, but I think I'd prefer a single life." He looked mighty taken aback; but in a minute he cleared up, and was as sweet as ever. He still kept on his knees, and I wished he'd take himself up; but, I reckon, he thought it would give force to his words; says he, "Think again, my dear Sally.

I've a four-roomed house, and furniture comfortable; and eighty pound a year. You may never have such a chance again." There were truth enough in that, but it was not pretty in the man to say it; and it put me up a bit. "As for that, neither you nor I can tell, Master Dixon. You're not the first chap as I've had down on his knees afore me, axing me to marry him (you see I were thinking of John Rawson, only I thought there were no need to say he were on-all-fours – it were truth he were on his knees, you know), and maybe you'll not be the last. Anyhow, I've no wish to change my condition just now." "I'll wait till Christmas," says he. "I've a pig as will be ready for killing then, so I must get married before that." Well now! would you believe it? the pig were a temptation. I'd a receipt for curing hams, as Miss Faith would never let me try, saying the old way were good enough. However, I resisted. Says I, very stern, because I felt I'd been wavering, "Master Dixon, once for all, pig or no pig, I'll not marry you. And if you'll take my advice, you'll get up off your knees. The flags is but damp yet, and it would be an awkward thing to have rheumatiz just before winter." With that he got up, stiff enough. He looked as sulky a chap as ever I clapped eyes on. And as he were so black and cross, I thought I'd done well (whatever came of the pig) to say "No" to him. "You may live to repent this," says he, very red. "But I'll not be too hard upon ye, I'll give you another chance. I'll let you have the night to think about it, and I'll just call in to hear your second thoughts, after chapel to-morrow." Well now! did ever you hear the like! But that is the way with all of them men, thinking so much of theirselves, and that it's but ask and have. They've never had me, though; and I shall be sixty-one next Martinmas, so there's not much time left for them to try me, I reckon. Well! when Jeremiah said that, he put me up more than ever, and I says, "My first thoughts, second thoughts, and third thoughts is all one and the same; you've but tempted me once, and that was when you spoke of your pig. But of yoursel' you're nothing to boast on, and so I'll bid you good night, and I'll keep my manners, or else, if I told the truth, I should say it had been a great loss of time listening to you. But I'll be civil – so good-night." He never said a word, but went off as black as thunder, slamming the door after him. The master called me in to prayers, but I can't say I could put my mind to them, for my heart was beating so. However, it was a comfort to have had an offer of holy matrimony; and though it flustered me, it made me think more of myself. In the night, I began to wonder if I'd not been cruel and hard to him. You see, I were feverish-like; and the old song of Barbary Allen[7] would keep running in my head, and I thought I were Barbary, and he were young Jemmy Gray, and that maybe he'd die for love of me; and I pictured him to mysel', lying on his death-bed, with his face turned to the wall, "wi' deadly sorrow sighing", and I could ha' pinched mysel' for having been so like cruel Barbary Allen. And when I got up next day, I found it hard to think on the real Jerry Dixon I had seen the night before, apart from the sad and sorrowful Jerry I thought on a-dying, when I were between sleeping and waking. And for many a day I turned sick, when I heard the passing bell, for I thought it were the bell loud-knelling which were to break my heart wi' a sense of what I'd missed in saying "No" to Jerry, and so killing him with cruelty. But in less than a three week, I heard parish bells a-ringing merrily for a wedding; and in the course of the morning, some one says to me, "Hark! how the bells is ringing for Jerry Dixon's wedding!" And, all on a sudden, he changed back again from a heart-broken young fellow, like Jemmy Gray, into a stout, middle-aged man, ruddy-complexioned, with a wart on his left cheek like life!'

Sally waited for some exclamation at the conclusion of her tale; but receiving none, she stepped softly to the bedside, and there lay Ruth, peaceful as death, with her baby on her breast.

'I thought I'd lost some of my gifts if I could not talk a body to sleep,' said Sally, in a satisfied and self-complacent tone.

Youth is strong and powerful, and makes a hard battle against sorrow. So Ruth strove and strengthened, and her baby flourished accordingly; and before the little celandines were out on the hedge-banks, or the white violets had sent forth their fragrance from the border under the south wall of Miss Benson's small garden, Ruth was able to carry her baby into that sheltered place on sunny days.

She often wished to thank Mr Benson and his sister, but she did not know how to tell the deep gratitude she felt, and therefore she was silent. But they understood her silence well. One day, as she watched her sleeping child, she spoke to Miss Benson, with whom she happened to be alone.

'Do you know of any cottage where the people are clean, and where they would not mind taking me in?' asked she.

'Taking you in! What do you mean?' said Miss Benson, dropping her knitting, in order to observe Ruth more closely.

'I mean,' said Ruth, 'where I might lodge with my baby – any very poor place would do, only it must be clean, or he might be ill.'

'And what in the world do you want to go and lodge in a cottage for?' said Miss Benson, indignantly.

Ruth did not lift up her eyes, but she spoke with a firmness which showed that she had considered the subject.

'I think I could make dresses. I know I did not learn as much as I might, but perhaps I might do for servants, and people who are not particular.'

'Servants are as particular as any one,' said Miss Benson, glad to lay hold of the first objection that she could.

'Well! somebody who would be patient with me,' said Ruth.

'Nobody is patient over an ill-fitting gown,' put in Miss Benson. 'There's the stuff spoilt, and what not!'

'Perhaps I could find plain work to do,' said Ruth, very meekly. 'That I can do very well; mamma taught me, and I liked to learn from her. If you would be so good, Miss Benson, you might tell people I could do plain work very neatly, and punctually, and cheaply.'

'You'd get sixpence a day, perhaps,' said Miss Benson, 'and who would take care of baby, I should like to know? Prettily he'd be neglected, would not he? Why, he'd have the croup and the typhus fever in no time, and be burnt to ashes after.'[8]

'I have thought of all. Look how he sleeps! Hush, darling;' for just at this point he began to cry, and to show his determination to be awake, as if in contradiction to his mother's words. Ruth took him up, and carried him about the room while she went on speaking.

'Yes, just now I know he will not sleep; but very often he will, and in the night he always does.'

'And so you'd work in the night and kill yourself, and leave your poor baby an orphan. Ruth! I'm ashamed of you. Now, brother' (Mr Benson had just come in), 'is not this too bad of Ruth; here she is planning to go away and leave us, just as we – as I, at least – have grown so fond of baby, and he's beginning to know me.'

'Where were you thinking of going to, Ruth?' interrupted Mr Benson, with mild surprise.

'Anywhere to be near you and Miss Benson; in any poor cottage where I might lodge very cheaply, and earn my livelihood by taking in plain sewing, and perhaps a little dress-making; and where I could come and see you and dear Miss Benson sometimes and bring baby.'

'If he was not dead before then of some fever, or burn, or scald, poor neglected child; or you had not worked yourself to death with never sleeping,' said Miss Benson.

Mr Benson thought a minute or two, and then he spoke to Ruth.

'Whatever you may do when this little fellow is a year old, and able to dispense with some of a mother's care, let me beg you, Ruth, as a favour to me – as a still greater favour to my sister, is it not, Faith?'

'Yes; you may put it so if you like.'

'To stay with us,' continued he, 'till then. When baby is twelve months old, we'll talk about it again, and very likely before then some opening may be shown us. Never fear leading an idle life, Ruth. We'll treat you as a daughter, and set you all the household tasks; and it is not for your sake that we ask you to stay, but for this little dumb helpless child's; and it is not for our sake that you must stay, but for his.'

Ruth was sobbing.

'I do not deserve your kindness,' said she, in a broken voice; 'I do not deserve it.'

Her tears fell fast and soft like summer rain, but no further word was spoken. Mr Benson quietly passed on to make the inquiry for which he had entered the room.

But when there was nothing to decide upon, and no necessity for entering upon any new course of action, Ruth's mind relaxed from its strung-up state. She fell into trains of reverie, and mournful regretful recollections which rendered her languid and tearful. This was noticed both by Miss Benson and Sally, and as each had kind sympathies, and felt depressed when they saw any one near them depressed, and as each, without much reasoning on the cause or reason for such depression, felt irritated at the uncomfortable state into which they themselves were thrown, they both resolved to speak to Ruth on the next fitting occasion.

Accordingly, one afternoon – the morning of that day had been spent by Ruth in house-work, for she had insisted on Mr Benson's words, and had taken Miss Benson's share of the more active and fatiguing household duties, but she went through them heavily, and as if her heart was far away – in the afternoon when she was nursing her child, Sally, on coming into the back parlour, found her there alone, and easily detected the fact that she was crying.

'Where's Miss Benson?' asked Sally, gruffly.

'Gone out with Mr Benson,' answered Ruth, with an absent sadness in her voice and manner. Her tears, scarce checked while she spoke, began to fall afresh; and as Sally stood and gazed she saw the babe look back in his mother's face, and his little lip begin to quiver, and his open blue eye to grow over-clouded, as with some mysterious sympathy with the sorrowful face bent over him. Sally took him briskly from his mother's arms; Ruth looked up in grave surprise, for in truth she had forgotten Sally's presence, and the suddenness of the motion startled her.

'My bonny boy! are they letting the salt tears drop on thy sweet face before thou'rt weaned! Little somebody knows how to be a mother – I could make a better myself. "Dance, thumbkin, dance – dance, ye merry men every one."[9] Ay, that's it! smile, my pretty. Any one but a child like thee,' continued she, turning to Ruth, 'would have known better than to bring ill-luck on thy babby by letting tears fall on its face before it was weaned. But thou'rt not fit to have a babby, and so I've said many a time. I've a great mind to buy thee a doll, and take thy babby mysel'.'

Sally did not look at Ruth, for she was too much engaged in amusing the baby with the tassel of the string to the window-blind, or else she would have seen the dignity which the mother's soul put into Ruth at that moment. Sally was quelled into silence by the gentle composure, the self-command over her passionate sorrow, which gave to Ruth an unconscious grandeur of demeanour as she came up to the old servant.

'Give him back to me, please. I did not know it brought ill-luck, or if my heart broke I would not have let a tear drop on his face – I never will again. Thank you, Sally,' as the servant relinquished him to her who came in the name of a mother. Sally watched Ruth's grave, sweet smile, as she followed up Sally's play with the tassel, and imitated, with all the docility inspired by love, every movement and sound which had amused her babe.

'Thou'lt be a mother, after all,' said Sally, with a kind of admiration of the control which Ruth was exercising over herself. 'But why talk of thy heart breaking? I don't question thee about what's past and gone; but now thou'rt wanting for nothing, nor thy child either; the time to come is the Lord's and in His hands; and yet thou goest about a-sighing and a-moaning in a way that I can't stand or thole.'[10]

'What do I do wrong?' said Ruth; 'I try to do all I can.'

'Yes, in a way,' said Sally, puzzled to know how to describe her meaning. 'Thou dost it – but there's a right and a wrong way of setting about everything – and to my thinking, the right way is to take a thing up heartily, if it is only making a bed. Why! dear ah me, making a bed may be done after a Christian fashion, I take it, or else what's to come of such as me in heaven, who've had little enough time on earth for clapping ourselves down on our knees for set prayers? When I was a girl, and wretched enough about Master Thurstan, and the crook on his back which came of the fall I gave him, I took to praying and sighing, and giving up the world; and I thought it were wicked to care for the flesh, so I made heavy puddings,[11] and was careless about dinner and the rooms, and thought I was doing my duty, though I did call myself a miserable sinner. But one night, the old missus (Master Thurstan's mother) came in, and sat down by me, as I was a-scolding myself, without thinking of what I was saying; and, says she, "Sally! what are you blaming yourself about, and groaning over? We hear you in the parlour every night, and it makes my heart ache." "Oh, ma'am," says I, "I'm a miserable sinner, and I'm travailing in the new birth."[12] "Was that the reason," says she, "why the pudding was so heavy to-day?" "Oh, ma'am, ma'am," said I, "if you would not think of the things of the flesh, but trouble yourself about your immortal soul." And I sat a-shaking my head to think about her soul. "But," says she, in her sweet-dropping voice, "I do try to think of my soul every hour of the day, if by that you mean trying to do the will of God, but we'll talk now about the pudding; Master Thurstan could not eat it, and I know you'll be sorry for that." Well! I was sorry, but I didn't choose to say so, as she seemed to expect me; so says I, "It's a pity to see children brought up to care for things of the flesh;" and then I could have bitten my tongue out, for the missus looked so grave, and I thought of my darling little lad pining for want of his food. At last, says she, "Sally, do you think God has put us into the world just to be selfish, and do nothing but see after our own souls? or to help one another with heart and hand, as Christ did to all who wanted help?" I was silent, for, you see, she puzzled me. So she went on, "What is that beautiful answer in your Church catechism, Sally?" I were pleased to hear a Dissenter, as I did not think would have done it, speak so knowledgeably about the catechism, and she went on: " 'to do my duty in that station of life unto which it shall please God to call me;'[13] well, your station is a servant, and it is as honourable as a king's, if you look at it right; you are to help and serve others in one way, just as a king is to help others in another. Now what way are you to help and serve, or to do your duty, in that station of life unto which it has pleased God to call you? Did it answer God's purpose, and serve Him, when the food was unfit for a child to eat, and unwholesome for any one?" Well! I would not give it up, I was so pig-headed about my soul; so says I, "I wish folks would be content with locusts and wild honey,[14] and leave other folks in peace to work out their salvation;" and I groaned out pretty loud to think of missus's soul. I often think since she smiled a bit at me; but she said, "Well, Sally, to-morrow, you shall have time to work out your salvation; but as we have no locusts in England, and I don't think they'd agree with Master Thurstan if we had, I will come and make the pudding; but I shall try and do it well, not only for him to like it, but because everything may be done in a right way or a wrong; the right way is to do it as well as we can, as in God's sight; the wrong is to do it in a self-seeking spirit, which either leads us to neglect it to follow out some device of our own for our own ends, or to give up too much time and thought to it both before and after the doing." Well! I thought of all old missus's words this morning, when I saw you making the beds. You sighed so, you could not half shake the pillows; your heart was not in your work; and yet it was the duty God had set you, I reckon; I know it's not the work parsons preach about; though I don't think they go so far off the mark when they read, "whatsoever thy hand findeth to do, that do with all thy might."[15] Just try for a day to think of all the odd jobs as to be done well and truly as in God's sight, not just slurred over anyhow, and you'll go through them twice as cheerfully, and have no thought to spare for sighing or crying.'

Sally bustled off to set on the kettle for tea, and felt half ashamed, in the quiet of the kitchen, to think of the oration she had made in the parlour. But she saw with much satisfaction, that henceforward Ruth nursed her boy with a vigour and cheerfulness that were reflected back from him; and the household work was no longer performed with a languid indifference, as if life and duty were distasteful. Miss Benson had her share in this improvement, though Sally placidly took all the credit to herself. One day as she and Ruth sat together, Miss Benson spoke of the child, and thence went on to talk about her own childhood. By degrees they spoke of education, and the book-learning that forms one part of it; and the result was that Ruth determined to get up early all through the bright summer mornings, to acquire the knowledge hereafter to be given to her child. Her mind was uncultivated, her reading scant; beyond the mere mechanical arts of education she knew nothing; but she had a refined taste, and excellent sense and judgment to separate the true from the false. With these qualities, she set to work under Mr Benson's directions. She read in the early morning the books that he marked out; she trained herself with strict perseverance to do all thoroughly; she did not attempt to acquire any foreign language, although her ambition was to learn Latin, in order to teach it to her boy. Those summer mornings were happy, for she was learning neither to look backwards nor forwards, but to live faithfully and earnestly in the present. She rose while the hedge-sparrow was yet singing his *réveille* to his mate; she dressed and opened her window, shading the soft-blowing air and the sunny eastern light from her baby. If she grew tired, she went and looked at him, and all her thoughts were holy prayers for him. Then she would gaze awhile out of the high upper window on to the moorlands, that swelled in waves one behind the other, in the grey, cool morning light. These were her occasional relaxations, and after them she returned with strength to her work.

CHAPTER XVII

In that body of Dissenters to which Mr Benson belonged, it is not considered necessary to baptise infants[1] as early as the ceremony can be performed; and many circumstances concurred to cause the solemn thanksgiving and dedication of the child (for so these Dissenters looked upon christenings) to be deferred until it was probably somewhere about six months old. There had been many conversations in the little sitting-room between the brother and sister and their *protégée*, which had consisted more of questions betraying a thoughtful wondering kind of ignorance on the part of Ruth, and answers more suggestive than explanatory from Mr Benson; while Miss Benson kept up a kind of running commentary, always simple and often quaint, but with that intuition into the very heart of all things truly religious which is often the gift of those who seem, at first sight, to be only affectionate and sensible. When Mr Benson had explained his own views of what a christening ought to be considered, and, by calling out Ruth's latent feelings into pious earnestness, brought her into a right frame of mind, he felt that he had done what he could to make the ceremony more than a mere form, and to invest it, quiet, humble, and obscure as it must necessarily be in outward shape – mournful and anxious as many of its antecedents had rendered it – with the severe grandeur of an act done in faith and truth.

It was not far to carry the little one, for, as I said, the chapel almost adjoined the minister's house. The whole procession was to have consisted of Mr and Miss Benson, Ruth carrying her babe, and Sally, who felt herself, as a Church-of-England woman, to be condescending and kind in requesting leave to attend a baptism among 'them Dissenters'; but unless she had asked permission, she would not have been desired to attend, so careful was the habit of her master and mistress that she should be allowed that freedom which they claimed for themselves. But they were glad she wished to go; they liked the feeling that all were of one household, and that the interests of one were the interests of all. It produced a consequence, however, which they did not anticipate. Sally was full of the event which her presence was to sanction, and, as it were, to redeem from the character of being utterly schismatic;[2] she spoke about it with an air of patronage to three or four, and among them to some of the servants at Mr Bradshaw's.

Miss Benson was rather surprised to receive a call from Jemima Bradshaw, on the very morning of the day on which little Leonard was to be baptised; Miss Bradshaw was rosy and breathless with eagerness. Although the second in the family, she had been at school when her younger sisters had been christened, and she was now come, in the full warmth of a girl's fancy, to ask if she might be present at the afternoon's service. She had been struck with Mrs Denbigh's grace and beauty at the very first sight, when she had accompanied her mother to call upon the Bensons on their return from Wales; and had kept up an enthusiastic interest in the widow only a little older than herself, whose very reserve and retirement but added to her unconscious power of enchantment.

'Oh, Miss Benson! I never saw a christening; papa says I may go, if you think Mr Benson and Mrs Denbigh would not dislike it; and I will be quite quiet, and sit up behind the door, or anywhere; and that sweet little baby! I should so like to see him christened; is he to be called Leonard, did you say? After Mr Denbigh, is it?'

'No – not exactly,' said Miss Benson, rather discomfited.

'Was not Mr Denbigh's name Leonard, then? Mamma thought it would be sure to be called after him, and so did I. But I may come to the christening, may I not, dear Miss Benson?'

Miss Benson gave her consent with a little inward reluctance. Both her brother and Ruth shared in this feeling, although no one expressed it; and it was presently forgotten.

Jemima stood grave and quiet in the old-fashioned vestry adjoining the chapel, as they entered with steps subdued to slowness. She thought Ruth looked so pale and awed because she was left a solitary parent; but Ruth came to the presence of God, as one who had gone astray, and doubted her own worthiness to be called His child; she came as a mother who had incurred a heavy responsibility, and who entreated His almighty aid to enable her to discharge it; full of passionate, yearning love which craved for more faith in God, to still her distrust and fear of the future that might hang over her darling. When she thought of her boy, she sickened and trembled: but when she heard of God's loving kindness, far beyond all tender mother's love, she was hushed into peace and prayer. There she stood, her fair pale cheek resting on her baby's head, as he slumbered on her bosom; her eyes went slanting down under their half-closed white lids; but their gaze was not on the primitive cottage-like room, it was earnestly fixed on a dim mist, through which she fain would have seen the life that lay before her child; but the mist was still and dense, too thick a veil for anxious human love to penetrate. The future was hid with God.

Mr Benson stood right under the casement window that was placed high up in the room; he was almost in shade, except for one or two marked lights which fell on hair already silvery white; his voice was always low and musical when he spoke to few; it was too weak to speak so as to be heard by many without becoming harsh and strange; but now it filled the little room with a loving sound, like the stock-dove's brooding murmur over her young. He and Ruth forgot all in their earnestness of thought; and when he said 'Let us pray,' and the little congregation knelt down, you might have heard the baby's faint breathing, scarcely sighing out upon the stillness, so absorbed were all in the solemnity. But the prayer was long; thought followed thought, and fear crowded upon fear, and all were to be laid bare before God, and His aid and counsel asked. Before the end, Sally had shuffled quietly out of the vestry into the green chapel-yard, upon which the door opened. Miss Benson was alive to this movement, and so full of curiosity as to what it might mean that she could no longer attend to her brother, and felt inclined to rush off and question Sally, the moment all was ended. Miss Bradshaw hung about the babe and Ruth, and begged to be allowed to carry the child home, but Ruth pressed him to her, as if there was no safe harbour for him but in his mother's breast. Mr Benson saw her feeling, and caught Miss Bradshaw's look of disappointment.

'Come home with us,' said he, 'and stay to tea. You have never drunk tea with us since you went to school.'

'I wish I might,' said Miss Bradshaw, colouring with pleasure. 'But I must ask papa. May I run home, and ask?'

'To be sure, my dear!'

Jemima flew off; and fortunately her father was at home; for her mother's permission would have been deemed insufficient. She received many directions about her behaviour.

'Take no sugar in your tea, Jemima. I am sure the Bensons ought not to be able to afford sugar, with their means. And do not eat much; you can have plenty at home on your return; remember Mrs Denbigh's keep must cost them a great deal.'

So Jemima returned considerably sobered, and very much afraid of her hunger leading her to forget Mr Benson's poverty. Meanwhile Miss Benson and Sally, acquainted with Mr Benson's invitation to Jemima, set about making some capital tea-cakes on which they piqued themselves. They both enjoyed the offices of hospitality; and were glad to place some home-made tempting dainty before their guests.

'What made ye leave the chapel-vestry before my brother had ended?' inquired Miss Benson.

'Indeed, ma'am, I thought master had prayed so long he'd be drouthy.[3] So I just slipped out to put on the kettle for tea.'

Miss Benson was on the point of reprimanding her for thinking of anything besides the object of the prayer, when she remembered how she herself had been unable to attend after Sally's departure for wondering what had become of her; so she was silent.

It was a disappointment to Miss Benson's kind and hospitable expectation when Jemima, as hungry as a hound, confined herself to one piece of the cake which her hostess had had such pleasure in making. And Jemima wished she had not a prophetic feeling all tea-time of the manner in which her father would inquire into the particulars of the meal, elevating his eyebrows at every viand named beyond plain bread-and-butter, and winding up with some such sentence as this: 'Well, I marvel how, with Benson's salary, he can afford to keep such a table.' Sally could have told of self-denial when no one was by, when the left hand did not know what the right hand did,[4] on the part of both her master and mistress, practised without thinking even to themselves that it was either a sacrifice or a virtue, in order to enable them to help those who were in need, or even to gratify Miss Benson's kind, old-fashioned feelings on such occasions as the present, when a stranger came to the house. Her homely, affectionate pleasure in making others comfortable, might have shown that such little occasional extravagances were not waste, but a good work; and were not to be gauged by the standard of money spending. This evening her spirits were damped by Jemima's refusal to eat! Poor Jemima! the cakes were so good, and she was so hungry; but still she refused.

While Sally was clearing away the tea-things, Miss Benson and Jemima accompanied Ruth up-stairs, when she went to put little Leonard to bed.

'A christening is a very solemn service,' said Miss Bradshaw; 'I had no idea it was so solemn. Mr Benson seemed to speak as if he had a weight of care on his heart that God alone could relieve or lighten.'

'My brother feels these things very much,' said Miss Benson, rather wishing to cut short the conversation, for she had been aware of several parts in the prayer which she knew were suggested by the peculiarity and sadness of the case before him.

'I could not quite follow him all through,' continued Jemima. 'What did he mean by saying, "This child, rebuked by the world and bidden to stand apart, Thou wilt not rebuke, but wilt suffer it to come to Thee and be blessed with Thine almighty blessing"?[5] Why is this little darling to be rebuked? I do not think I remember the exact words, but he said something like that.'

'My dear! your gown is dripping wet! it must have dipped into the tub; let me wring it out.'

'Oh, thank you! Never mind my gown!' said Jemima, hastily, and wanting to return to her question; but just then she caught the sight of tears falling fast down the cheeks of the silent Ruth as she bent over her child, crowing and splashing away in his tub. With a sudden consciousness that unwittingly she had touched on some painful chord, Jemima rushed into another subject, and was eagerly seconded by Miss Benson. The circumstance seemed to die away, and leave no trace; but in after-years it rose, vivid and significant, before Jemima's memory. At present it was enough for her, if Mrs Denbigh would let her serve her in every possible way. Her admiration for beauty was keen, and little indulged at home; and Ruth was very beautiful in her quiet mournfulness; her mean and homely dress left her herself only the more open to admiration, for she gave it a charm by her unconscious wearing of it that made it seem like the drapery of an old Greek statue – subordinate to the figure it covered, yet imbued by it with an unspeakable grace. Then the pretended circumstances of her life were such as to catch the imagination of a young romantic girl. Altogether, Jemima could have kissed her hand and professed herself Ruth's slave. She moved away all the articles used at this little *coucher*;[6] she folded up Leonard's day-clothes; she felt only too much honoured when Ruth trusted him to her for a few minutes – only too amply rewarded when Ruth thanked her with a grave, sweet smile, and a grateful look of her loving eyes.

When Jemima had gone away with the servant who was sent to fetch her, there was a little chorus of praise.

'She's a warm-hearted girl,' said Miss Benson. 'She remembers all the old days before she went to school. She is worth two of Mr Richard. They're each of them just the same as they were when they were children, when they broke that window in the chapel, and he ran away home, and she came knocking at our door, with a single knock, just like a beggar's,[7] and I went to see who it was, and was quite startled to see her round, brown, honest face looking up at me, half-frightened, and telling me what she had done, and offering me the money in her savings bank to pay for it. We never should have heard of Master Richard's share in the business if it had not been for Sally.'

'But remember,' said Mr Benson, 'how strict Mr Bradshaw has always been with his children. It is no wonder if poor Richard was a coward in those days.'

'He is now, or I'm much mistaken,' answered Miss Benson. 'And Mr Bradshaw was just as strict with Jemima, and she's no coward. But

I've no faith in Richard. He has a look about him that I don't like. And when Mr Bradshaw was away on business in Holland last year, for those months my young gentleman did not come half as regularly to chapel, and I always believe that story of his being seen out with the hounds at Smithiles.'

'Those are neither of them great offences in a young man of twenty,' said Mr Benson, smiling.

'No! I don't mind them in themselves; but when he could change back so easily to being regular and mim when his father came home, I don't like that.'

'Leonard shall never be afraid of me,' said Ruth, following her own train of thought. 'I will be his friend from the very first; and I will try and learn how to be a wise friend, and you will teach me, won't you, sir?'

'What made you wish to call him Leonard, Ruth?' asked Miss Benson.

'It was my mother's father's name; and she used to tell me about him and his goodness, and I thought if Leonard could be like him—'

'Do you remember the discussion there was about Miss Bradshaw's name, Thurstan? Her father wanting her to be called Hepzibah, but insisting that she was to have a Scripture name at any rate; and Mrs Bradshaw wanting her to be Juliana, after some novel she had read not long before; and at last Jemima was fixed upon, because it would do either for a Scripture name or a name for a heroine out of a book.'

'I did not know Jemima was a Scripture name,' said Ruth.

'Oh yes, it is. One of Job's daughters; Jemima, Kezia, and Keren-Happuch.[8] There are a good many Jemimas in the world, and some Kezias, but I never heard of a Keren-Happuch; and yet we know just as much of one as of another. People really like a pretty name, whether in Scripture or out of it.'

'When there is no particular association with the name,' said Mr Benson.

'Now, I was called Faith after the cardinal virtue; and I like my name, though many people would think it too Puritan; that was according to our gentle mother's pious desire. And Thurstan was called by his name because my father wished it; for, although he was what people called a radical and a democrat in his ways of talking and thinking, he was very proud in his heart of being descended from some old Sir Thurstan, who figured away in the French wars.'[9]

'The difference between theory and practice, thinking and being,' put in Mr Benson, who was in a mood for allowing himself a little social enjoyment. He leaned back in his chair, with his eyes looking at, but not seeing, the ceiling. Miss Benson was clicking away with her eternal knitting-needles, looking at her brother, and seeing him, too. Ruth was arranging her child's clothes against the morrow. It was but their usual way of spending an evening; the variety was given by the different tone which the conversation assumed on the different nights. Yet, somehow, the peacefulness of the time, the window open into the little garden, the scents that came stealing in, and the clear summer heaven above, made the time be remembered as a happy festival by Ruth. Even Sally seemed more placid than usual when she came in to prayers; and she and Miss Benson followed Ruth to her bedroom, to look at the beautiful sleeping Leonard.

'God bless him!' said Miss Benson, stooping down to kiss his little dimpled hand, which lay outside the coverlet, tossed abroad in the heat of the evening.

'Now, don't get up too early, Ruth! Injuring your health will be short-sighted wisdom and poor economy. Good night!'

'Good night, dear Miss Benson. Good night, Sally.' When Ruth had shut her door, she went again to the bed, and looked at her boy till her eyes filled with tears.

'God bless thee, darling! I only ask to be one of His instruments, and not thrown aside as useless – or worse than useless.'

So ended the day of Leonard's christening.

Mr Benson had sometimes taught the children of different people as an especial favour, when requested by them. But then his pupils were only children, and by their progress he was little prepared for Ruth's. She had had early teaching, of that kind which need never be unlearnt, from her mother; enough to unfold many of her powers; they had remained inactive now for several years, but had grown strong in the dark and quiet time. Her tutor was surprised at the bounds by which she surmounted obstacles, the quick perception and ready adaptation of truths and first principles, and her immediate sense of the fitness of things. Her delight in what was strong and beautiful called out her master's sympathy; but, most of all, he admired the complete unconsciousness of uncommon power, or unusual progress. It was less of a wonder than he considered it to be, it is true, for she never thought of comparing what she was now with her former self, much less with another. Indeed, she did not think of herself at all, but of her boy, and what she must learn in order to teach him to be and to do as suited her hope and her prayer. If any one's devotion could have flattered her into self-consciousness, it was Jemima's. Mr Bradshaw never dreamed that his daughter could feel herself inferior to the minister's *protégée*, but so it was; and no knight-errant of old could consider himself more honoured by his ladye's commands than did Jemima, if Ruth allowed her to do anything for her or for her boy. Ruth loved her heartily, even while she was rather annoyed at the open expression Jemima used of admiration.

'Please, I really would rather not be told if people do think me pretty.'

'But it was not merely beautiful; it was sweet-looking and good, Mrs Postlethwaite called you,' replied Jemima.

'All the more I would rather not hear it. I may be pretty, but I know I am not good. Besides, I don't think we ought to hear what is said of us behind our backs.'

Ruth spoke so gravely, that Jemima feared lest she was displeased.

'Dear Mrs Denbigh, I never will admire or praise you again. Only let me love you.'

'And let me love you!' said Ruth, with a tender kiss.

Jemima would not have been allowed to come so frequently if Mr Bradshaw had not been possessed with the idea of patronising Ruth. If the latter had chosen, she might have gone dressed from head to foot in the presents which he wished to make her, but she refused them constantly; occasionally to Miss Benson's great annoyance. But if he could not load her with gifts, he could show his approbation by asking her to his house; and after some deliberation, she consented to accompany Mr and Miss Benson there. The house was square and massy-looking, with a great deal of drab-colour about the furniture. Mrs Bradshaw, in her lack-a-daisical, sweet-tempered way, seconded her husband in his desire of being kind to Ruth; and as she cherished privately a great taste for what was beautiful or interesting, as opposed to her husband's love of the purely useful, this taste of hers had rarely had so healthy and true a mode of gratification as when she watched Ruth's movements about the room, which seemed in its unobtrusiveness and poverty of colour to receive the requisite ornament of light and splendour from Ruth's presence. Mrs Bradshaw sighed, and wished she had a daughter as lovely, about whom to weave a romance; for castle-building, after the manner of the Minerva Press,[10] was the outlet by which she escaped from the pressure of her prosaic life, as Mr Bradshaw's wife. Her perception was only of external beauty, and she was not always alive to that, or she might have seen how a warm, affectionate, ardent nature, free from all envy or carking care of self, gave an unspeakable charm to her plain, bright-faced daughter Jemima, whose dark eyes kept challenging admiration for her friend. The first evening spent at Mr Bradshaw's passed like many succeeding visits there. There was tea, the equipage for which was as handsome and as ugly as money could purchase. Then the ladies produced their sewing, while Mr Bradshaw stood before the fire, and gave the assembled party the benefit of his opinions on many subjects. The opinions were as good and excellent as the opinions of any man can be who sees one side of a case very strongly, and almost ignores the other. They coincided in many points with those held by Mr Benson, but he once or twice interposed with a plea for those who might differ; and then he was heard by Mr Bradshaw with a kind of evident and indulgent pity, such as one feels for a child who unwittingly talks nonsense. By-and-by, Mrs Bradshaw and Miss Benson fell into one *tête-à-tête*, and Ruth and Jemima into another. Two well-behaved but unnaturally quiet children were sent to bed early in the evening, in an authoritative voice, by their father, because one of them had spoken too loud while he was enlarging on an alteration in the tariff. Just before the supper-tray[11] was brought in, a gentleman was announced whom Ruth had never previously seen, but who appeared well known to the rest of the party. It was Mr Farquhar, Mr Bradshaw's partner; he had been on the Continent for the last year, and had only recently returned. He seemed perfectly at home, but spoke little. He leaned back in his chair, screwed up his eyes, and watched everybody; yet there was nothing unpleasant or impertinent in his keenness of observation. Ruth wondered to hear him contradict Mr Bradshaw, and almost expected some rebuff, but Mr Bradshaw, if he did not yield the point, admitted, for the first time that evening, that it was possible something might be said on the other side. Mr Farquhar differed also from Mr Benson, but it was in a more respectful manner than Mr Bradshaw had done. For these reasons, although Mr Farquhar had never spoken to Ruth, she came away with the impression that he was a man to be respected, and perhaps liked.

Sally would have thought herself mightily aggrieved if, on their return, she had not heard some account of the evening. As soon as Miss Benson came in, the old servant began:

'Well, and who was there? and what did they give you for supper?'

'Only Mr Farquhar besides ourselves; and sandwiches, sponge-cake, and wine; there was no occasion for anything more,' replied Miss Benson, who was tired and preparing to go up-stairs.

'Mr Farquhar! Why, they do say he's thinking of Miss Jemima!'

'Nonsense, Sally! why, he's old enough to be her father!' said Miss Benson, half-way up the first flight.

'There's no need for it to be called nonsense, though he may be ten year older,' muttered Sally, retreating towards the kitchen. 'Bradshaw's Betsy knows what she's about, and wouldn't have said it for nothing.'

Ruth wondered a little about it. She loved Jemima well enough to be interested in what related to her; but, after thinking for a few minutes, she decided that such a marriage was, and would ever be, very unlikely.

CHAPTER XVIII

One afternoon, not long after this, Mr and Miss Benson set off to call upon a farmer, who attended the chapel, but lived at some distance from the town. They intended to stay to tea if they were invited, and Ruth and Sally were left to spend a long afternoon together. At first, Sally was busy in her kitchen, and Ruth employed herself in carrying her baby out into the garden. It was now nearly a year since she came to the Bensons'; it seemed like yesterday, and yet as if a life time had gone between. The flowers were budding now, that were all in bloom when she came down, on the first autumnal morning, into the sunny parlour. The yellow jessamine that was then a tender plant, had now taken firm root in the soil, and was sending out strong shoots; the wallflowers, which Miss Benson had sown on the wall a day or two after her arrival, were scenting the air with their fragrant flowers. Ruth knew every plant now; it seemed as though she had always lived here, and always known the inhabitants of the house. She heard Sally singing her accustomed song in the kitchen, a song she never varied over her afternoon's work. It began:

> As I was going to Derby, sir,
> Upon a market-day.[1]

And if music is a necessary element in a song, perhaps I had better call it by some other name.

But the strange change was in Ruth herself. She was conscious of it though she could not define it, and did not dwell upon it. Life had become significant and full of duty to her. She delighted in the exercise of her intellectual powers, and liked the idea of the infinite amount of which she was ignorant; for it was a grand pleasure to learn – to crave, and be satisfied. She strove to forget what had gone before this last twelve months. She shuddered up from contemplating it; it was like a bad, unholy dream. And yet, there was a strange yearning kind of love for the father of the child whom she pressed to her heart, which came, and she could not bid it begone as sinful, it was so pure and natural, even when thinking of it, as in the sight of God. Little Leonard cooed to the flowers, and stretched after their bright colours; and Ruth laid him on the dry turf, and pelted him with the gay petals. He chinked and crowed with laughing delight, and clutched at her cap, and pulled it off. Her short rich curls were golden-brown in the slanting sunlight, and by their very shortness made her look more childlike. She hardly seemed as if she could be the mother of the noble babe over whom she knelt, now snatching kisses, now matching his cheek with rose leaves. All at once, the bells of the old church struck the hour, and far away, high up in the air, began slowly to play the old tune of 'Life let us cherish';[2] they had played it for years – for the life of man – and it always sounded fresh and strange and aërial. Ruth was still in a moment, she knew not why; and the tears came into her eyes as she listened. When it was ended, she kissed her baby, and bade God bless him.

Just then Sally came out, dressed for the evening, with a leisurely look about her. She had done her work, and she and Ruth were to drink tea together in the exquisitely clean kitchen; but while the kettle was boiling, she came out to enjoy the flowers. She gathered a piece of southern-wood,[3] and stuffed it up her nose, by way of smelling it.

'Whatten you call this in your country?' asked she.

'Old-man,' replied Ruth.

'We call it here lad's love. It and peppermint-drops always reminds me of going to church in the country. Here! I'll get you a black currant-leaf to put in the teapot. It gives it a flavour. We had bees once against this wall; but when missus died, we forgot to tell 'em,[4] and put 'em in mourning, and, in course, they swarmed away without our knowing, and the next winter came a hard frost, and they died. Now, I dare say, the water will be boiling; and it's time for little master there to come in, for the dew is falling. See, all the daisies is shutting themselves up.'

Sally was most gracious as a hostess. She quite put on her company manners to receive Ruth in the kitchen. They laid Leonard to sleep on the sofa in the parlour, that they might hear him the more easily, and then they sat quietly down to their sewing by the bright kitchen fire. Sally was, as usual, the talker; and, as usual, the subject was the family of whom for so many years she had formed a part.

'Ay! things was different when I was a girl,' quoth she. 'Eggs was thirty for a shilling, and butter only sixpence a pound. My wage when I came here was but three pound, and I did on it, and was always clean and tidy, which is more than many a lass can say now who gets seven and eight pound a year; and tea was kept for an afternoon drink, and pudding was eaten afore meat in them days, and the upshot was, people paid their debts better; ay, ay! we'n gone backwards, and we thinken we'n gone forrards.'

After shaking her head a little over the degeneracy of the times, Sally returned to a part of the subject on which she thought she had given Ruth a wrong idea.

'You'll not go for to think now that I've not more than three pound a year. I've a deal above that now. First of all, old missus gave me four pound, for she said I were worth it, and I thought in my heart that I were; so I took it without more ado; but after her death, Master Thurstan and Miss Faith took a fit of spending, and says they to me, one day as I carried tea in, "Sally, we think your wages ought to be raised." "What matter what you think!" said I, pretty sharp, for I thought they'd ha' shown more respect to missus if they'd let things stand as they were in her time; and they'd gone and moved the sofa away from the wall to where it stands now, already that very day. So I speaks up sharp, and, says I, "As long as I'm content, I think it's no business of yours to be meddling wi' me and my money matters." But, says Miss Faith (she's always the one to speak first if you'll notice, though it's master that comes in and clinches the matter with some reason she'd never ha' thought of – he were always a sensible lad), "Sally, all the servants in the town have six pound and better, and you have as hard a place as any of 'em." "Did you ever hear me grumble about my work that you talk about it in that way? wait till I grumble," said I, "but don't meddle wi' me till then." So I flung off in a huff; but in the course of the evening, Master Thurstan came in and sat down in the kitchen, and he's such winning ways he wiles one over to anything; and besides, a notion had come into my head – now you'll not tell,' said she, glancing round the room, and hitching her chair nearer to Ruth in a confidential manner; Ruth promised, and Sally went on:

'I thought I should like to be an heiress wi' money, and leave it all to Master and Miss Faith; and I thought if I'd six pound a year I could, maybe, get to be an heiress; all I was feared on was that some chap or other might marry me for my money, but I've managed to keep the fellows off; so I looks mim and grateful, and I thanks Master Thurstan for his offer, and I takes the wages; and what do you think I've done?' asked Sally, with an exultant air.

'What have you done?' asked Ruth.

'Why,' replied Sally, slowly and emphatically, 'I've saved thirty pound! but that's not it. I've getten a lawyer to make me a will; that's it, wench!' said she, slapping Ruth on the back.

'How did you manage it?' asked Ruth.

'Ay, that was it,' said Sally; 'I thowt about it many a night before I hit on the right way. I was afeared the money might be thrown into Chancery[5] if I didn't make it all safe, and yet I could na' ask Master Thurstan. At last and at length, John Jackson, the grocer, had a nephew come to stay a week with him, as was 'prentice to a lawyer in Liverpool; so now was my time, and here was my lawyer. Wait a minute! I could tell you my story better if I had my will in my hand; and I'll scomfish[6] you if ever you go for to tell.'

She held up her hand, and threatened Ruth as she left the kitchen to fetch the will.

When she came back, she brought a parcel tied up in a blue pocket-handkerchief; she sat down, squared her knees, untied the handkerchief, and displayed a small piece of parchment.

'Now, do you know what this is?' said she, holding it up. 'It's parchment, and it's the right stuff to make wills on. People gets into Chancery if they don't make them o' this stuff, and I reckon Tom Jackson thowt he'd have a fresh job on it if he could get it into Chancery; for the rascal went and wrote it on a piece of paper at first, and came and read it me out loud off a piece of paper no better than what one writes letters upon. I were up to him; and, thinks I, come, come, my lad, I'm not a fool, though you may think so; I know a paper will won't stand, but I'll let you run your rig.[7] So I sits and I listens. And would you belie me, he read it out as if it were as clear a business as your giving me that thimble – no more ado, though it were thirty pound! I could understand it mysel' – that were no law for me. I wanted summat to consider about, and for th' meaning to be wrapped up as I wrap up my best gown. So says I, "Tom! it's not on parchment. I mun have it on parchment." "This 'ill do as well," says he. "We'll get it witnessed, and it will stand good." Well! I liked the notion of having it witnessed, and for a while that soothed me; but after a bit, I felt I should like it done according to law, and not plain out as anybody might ha' done it; I mysel', if I could have written. So says I, "Tom! I mun have it on parchment." "Parchment costs money," says he, very grave. "Oh, oh, my lad! are ye there?" thinks I. "That's the reason I'm clipped of law."[8] So says I, "Tom! I mun have it on parchment. I'll pay the money and welcome. It's thirty pound, and what I can lay to it. I'll make it safe. It shall be on parchment, and I'll tell thee what, lad! I'll gie ye sixpence for every good law-word you put in it, sounding like, and not to be caught up as a person runs. Your master had need to be ashamed of you as a 'prentice if you can't do a thing more tradesman-like than this!" Well! he laughed above a bit, but I were firm, and stood to it. So he made it out on parchment. Now, woman, try and read it!' said she, giving it to Ruth.

Ruth smiled, and began to read; Sally listening with rapt attention. When Ruth came to the word 'testatrix', Sally stopped her.

'That was the first sixpence,' said she. 'I thowt he was going to fob me off again wi' plain language; but when that word came, I out wi' my sixpence, and gave it to him on the spot. Now go on.'

Presently Ruth read 'accruing'.

'That was the second sixpence. Four sixpences it were in all, besides six-and-eightpence as we bargained at first, and three-and-fourpence parchment. There! that's what I call a will; witnessed according to law, and all. Master Thurstan will be prettily taken in when I die, and he finds all his extra wage left back to him. But it will teach him it's not so easy as he thinks for, to make a woman give up her way.'

The time was now drawing near when little Leonard might be weaned – the time appointed by all three for Ruth to endeavour to support herself in some way more or less independent of Mr and Miss Benson. This prospect dwelt much in all of their minds, and was in each shaded with some degree of perplexity; but they none of them spoke of it for fear of accelerating the event. If they had felt clear and determined as to the best course to be pursued, they were none of them deficient in courage to commence upon that course at once. Miss Benson would, perhaps, have objected the most to any alteration in their present daily mode of life; but that was because she had the habit of speaking out her thoughts as they arose, and she particularly disliked and dreaded change. Besides this, she had felt her heart open out, and warm towards the little helpless child, in a strong and powerful manner. Nature had intended her warm instincts to find vent in a mother's duties; her heart had yearned after children, and made her restless in her childless state, without her well knowing why; but now, the delight she experienced in tending, nursing, and contriving for the little boy – even contriving to the point of sacrificing many of her cherished whims – made her happy and satisfied and peaceful. It was more difficult to sacrifice her whims than her comforts; but all had been given up when and where required by the sweet lordly baby, who reigned paramount in his very helplessness.

From some cause or other, an exchange of ministers for one Sunday was to be effected with a neighbouring congregation, and Mr Benson went on a short absence from home. When he returned on Monday, he was met at the house-door by his sister, who had evidently been looking out for him some time. She stepped out to greet him.

'Don't hurry yourself, Thurstan! all's well; only I wanted to tell you something. Don't fidget yourself – baby is quite well, bless him! It's only good news. Come into your room, and let me talk a little quietly with you.'

She drew him into his study, which was near the outer door, and then she took off his coat, and put his carpet-bag in a corner, and wheeled a chair to the fire, before she would begin.

'Well, now! to think how often things fall out just as we want them, Thurstan! Have not you often wondered what was to be done with

Ruth when the time came at which we promised her she should earn her living? I am sure you have, because I have so often thought about it myself. And yet I never dared to speak out my fear, because that seemed giving it a shape. And now Mr Bradshaw has put all to rights. He invited Mr Jackson to dinner yesterday, just as we were going into chapel; and then he turned to me and asked me if I would come to tea – straight from afternoon chapel, because Mrs Bradshaw wanted to speak to me. He made it very clear I was not to bring Ruth; and, indeed, she was only too happy to stay at home with baby. And so I went; and Mrs Bradshaw took me into her bedroom, and shut the doors, and said Mr Bradshaw had told her, that he did not like Jemima being so much confined with the younger ones while they were at their lessons, and that he wanted some one above a nursemaid to sit with them while their masters were there – some one who would see about their learning their lessons, and who would walk out with them; a sort of nursery governess I think she meant, though she did not say so; and Mr Bradshaw (for, of course, I saw his thoughts and words constantly peeping out, though he had told her to speak to me) believed that our Ruth would be the very person. Now, Thurstan, don't look so surprised, as if she had never come into your head! I am sure I saw what Mrs Bradshaw was driving at, long before she came to the point; and I could scarcely keep from smiling, and saying, "We'd jump at the proposal" – long before I ought to have known anything about it.'

'Oh, I wonder what we ought to do!' said Mr Benson. 'Or rather, I believe I see what we ought to do, if I durst but do it.'

'Why, what ought we to do?' asked his sister, in surprise.

'I ought to go and tell Mr Bradshaw the whole story—'

'And get Ruth turned out of our house,' said Miss Benson, indignantly.

'They can't make us do that,' said her brother. 'I do not think they would try.'

'Yes, Mr Bradshaw would try; and he would blazon out poor Ruth's sin, and there would not be a chance for her left. I know him well, Thurstan; and why should he be told now, more than a year ago?'

'A year ago, he did not want to put her in a situation of trust about his children.'

'And you think she'll abuse that trust, do you? You've lived a twelvemonth in the house with Ruth, and the end of it is, you think she will do his children harm! Besides, who encouraged Jemima to come to the house so much to see Ruth? Did you not say it would do them both good to see something of each other?'

Mr Benson sat thinking.

'If you had not known Ruth as well as you do – if during her stay with us you had marked anything wrong, or forward, or deceitful, or immodest, I would say at once, don't allow Mr Bradshaw to take her into his house; but still I would say, don't tell of her sin and her sorrow to so severe a man – so unpitiful a judge. But here I ask you, Thurstan, can you, or I, or Sally (quick-eyed as she is), say, that in any one thing we have had true, just occasion to find fault with Ruth? I don't mean that she is perfect – she acts without thinking, her temper is sometimes warm and hasty; but have we any right to go and injure her prospects for life, by telling Mr Bradshaw all we know of her errors – only sixteen when she did so wrong, and never to escape from it all her many years to come – to have the despair which would arise from its being known, clutching her back into worse sin? What harm do you think she can do? What is the risk to which you think you are exposing Mr Bradshaw's children?' She paused, out of breath, her eyes glittering with tears of indignation, and impatient for an answer, that she might knock it to pieces.

'I do not see any danger that can arise,' said he at length, and with slow difficulty, as if not fully convinced. 'I have watched Ruth, and I believe she is pure and truthful; and the very sorrow and penitence she has felt – the very suffering she has gone through – has given her a thoughtful conscientiousness beyond her age.'

'That and the care of her baby,' said Miss Benson, secretly delighted at the tone of her brother's thoughts.

'Ah, Faith! that baby you so much dreaded once, is turning out a blessing, you see,' said Thurstan, with a faint, quiet smile.

'Yes! any one might be thankful, and better too, for Leonard; but how could I tell that it would be like him?'

'But to return to Ruth and Mr Bradshaw. What did you say?'

'Oh! with my feelings, of course, I was only too glad to accept the proposal, and so I told Mrs Bradshaw then; and I afterwards repeated it to Mr Bradshaw, when he asked me if his wife had mentioned their plans. They would understand that I must consult you and Ruth, before it could be considered as finally settled.'

'And have you named it to her?'

'Yes,' answered Miss Benson, half afraid lest he should think she had been too precipitate.

'And what did she say?' asked he, after a little pause of grave silence.

'At first she seemed very glad, and fell into my mood of planning how it should all be managed; how Sally and I should take care of the baby the hours that she was away at Mr Bradshaw's; but by-and-by she became silent and thoughtful, and knelt down by me and hid her face in my lap, and shook a little as if she was crying; and then I heard her speak in a very low smothered voice, for her head was still bent down – quite hanging down, indeed, so that I could not see her face, so I stooped to listen, and I heard her say, "Do you think I should be good enough to teach little girls, Miss Benson?" She said it so humbly and fearfully that all I thought of was how to cheer her, and I answered and asked her if she did not hope to be good enough to bring up her own darling to be a brave Christian man? And she lifted up her head, and I saw her eyes looking wild and wet and earnest, and she said, "With God's help, that will I try to make my child." And I said then, "Ruth, as you strive and as you pray for your own child, so you must strive and pray to make Mary and Elizabeth good, if you are trusted with them." And she said out quite clear, though her face was hidden from me once more, "I will strive, and I will pray." You would not have had any fears, Thurstan, if you could have heard and seen her last night.'

'I have no fear,' said he, decidedly. 'Let the plan go on.' After a minute, he added, 'But I am glad it was so far arranged before I heard of it. My indecision about right and wrong – my perplexity as to how far we are to calculate consequences – grows upon me, I fear.'

'You look tired and weary, dear. You should blame your body rather than your conscience at these times.'

'A very dangerous doctrine.'

The scroll of Fate was closed, and they could not foresee the Future; and yet, if they could have seen it, though they might have shrank fearfully at first, they would have smiled and thanked God when all was done and said.

CHAPTER XIX

The quiet days grew into weeks and months, and even years, without any event to startle the little circle into the consciousness of the lapse of time. One who had known them at the date of Ruth's becoming a governess in Mr Bradshaw's family, and had been absent until the time of which I am now going to tell you, would have noted some changes which had imperceptibly come over all; but he, too, would have thought, that the life which had brought so little of turmoil and vicissitude must have been calm and tranquil, and in accordance with the bygone activity of the town in which their existence passed away.

The alterations that he would have perceived were those caused by the natural progress of time. The Benson home was brightened into vividness by the presence of the little Leonard, now a noble boy of six, large and grand in limb and stature, and with a face of marked beauty and intelligence. Indeed, he might have been considered by many as too intelligent for his years; and often the living with old and thoughtful people gave him, beyond most children, the appearance of pondering over the mysteries which meet the young on the threshold of life, but which fade away as advancing years bring us more into contact with the practical and tangible – fade away and vanish, until it seems to require the agitation of some great storm of the soul before we can again realise spiritual things.

But, at times, Leonard seemed oppressed and bewildered, after listening intent, with grave and wondering eyes, to the conversation around him; at others, the bright animal life shone forth radiant, and no three months' kitten – no foal, suddenly tossing up its heels by the side of its sedate dam, and careering around the pasture in pure mad enjoyment – no young creature of any kind, could show more merriment and gladness of heart.

'For ever in mischief,' was Sally's account of him at such times; but it was not intentional mischief; and Sally herself would have been the first to scold any one else who had used the same words in reference to her darling. Indeed, she was once nearly giving warning, because she thought the boy was being ill-used. The occasion was this: Leonard had for some time shown a strange odd disregard of truth; he invented stories, and told them with so grave a face, that unless there was some internal evidence of their incorrectness (such as describing a cow with a bonnet on), he was generally believed, and his statements, which were given with the full appearance of relating a real occurrence, had once or twice led to awkward results. All the three, whose hearts were pained by this apparent unconsciousness of the difference between truth and falsehood, were unaccustomed to children, or they would have recognised this as a stage through which most infants, who have lively imaginations, pass; and, accordingly, there was a consultation in Mr Benson's study one morning. Ruth was there, quiet, very pale, and with compressed lips, sick at heart as she heard Miss Benson's arguments for the necessity of whipping, in order to cure Leonard of his story-telling. Mr Benson looked unhappy and uncomfortable. Education was but a series of experiments to them all, and they all had a secret dread of spoiling the noble boy, who was the darling of their hearts. And, perhaps, this very intensity of love begot an impatient, unnecessary anxiety, and made them resolve on sterner measures than the parent of a large family (where love was more spread abroad) would have dared to use. At any rate, the vote for whipping carried the day; and even Ruth, trembling and cold, agreed that it must be done; only she asked, in a meek sad voice, if she need be present (Mr Benson was to be the executioner – the scene, the study); and being instantly told that she had better not, she went slowly and languidly up to her room, and kneeling down, she closed her ears, and prayed.

Miss Benson, having carried her point, was very sorry for the child, and would have begged him off; but Mr Benson had listened more to her arguments than now to her pleadings, and only answered, 'If it is right, it shall be done!' He went into the garden, and deliberately, almost as if he wished to gain time, chose and cut off a little switch from the laburnum-tree. Then he returned through the kitchen, and gravely taking the awed and wondering little fellow by the hand, he led him silently into the study, and placing him before him, began an admonition on the importance of truthfulness, meaning to conclude with what he believed to be the moral of all punishment: 'As you cannot remember this of yourself, I must give you a little pain to make you remember it. I am sorry it is necessary, and that you cannot recollect without my doing so.'

But before he had reached this very proper and desirable conclusion, and while he was yet working his way, his heart aching with the terrified look of the child at the solemnly sad face and words of upbraiding, Sally burst in:

'And what may ye be going to do with that fine switch I saw ye gathering, Master Thurstan?' asked she, her eyes gleaming with anger at the answer she knew must come, if answer she had at all.

'Go away, Sally,' said Mr Benson, annoyed at the fresh difficulty in his path.

'I'll not stir never a step till you give me that switch, as you've got for some mischief, I'll be bound.'

'Sally! remember where it is said, "He that spareth the rod, spoileth the child," '[1] said Mr Benson, austerely.

'Ay, I remember; and I remember a bit more than you want me to remember, I reckon. It were King Solomon as spoke them words, and it were King Solomon's son that were King Rehoboam, and no great shakes either. I can remember what is said on him, II Chronicles, xii. chapter, 14th v.: "And he," that's King Rehoboam, the lad that tasted the rod, "did evil, because he prepared not his heart to seek the Lord." I've not been reading my chapters every night for fifty year to be caught napping by a Dissenter, neither!' said she, triumphantly. 'Come along, Leonard.' She stretched out her hand to the child, thinking that she had conquered.

But Leonard did not stir. He looked wistfully at Mr Benson. 'Come!' said she, impatiently. The boy's mouth quivered.

'If you want to whip me, uncle, you may do it. I don't much mind.'

Put in this form, it was impossible to carry out his intentions; and so Mr Benson told the lad he might go – that he would speak to him another time. Leonard went away, more subdued in spirit than if he had been whipped. Sally lingered a moment. She stopped to add: 'I think it's for them without sin to throw stones at a poor child,[2] and cut up good laburnum branches to whip him. I only do as my betters do, when I call Leonard's mother Mrs —' The moment she had said this she was sorry; it was an ungenerous advantage after the enemy had acknowledged himself defeated. Mr Benson dropped his head upon his hands, and hid his face, and sighed deeply.

Leonard flew in search of his mother, as in search of a refuge. If he had found her calm, he would have burst into a passion of crying after his agitation; as it was, he came upon her kneeling and sobbing, and he stood quite still. Then he threw his arms round her neck, and said: 'Mamma! mamma! I will be good – I make a promise; I will speak true – I make a promise.' And he kept his word.

Miss Benson piqued herself upon being less carried away by her love for this child than any one else in the house; she talked severely, and had capital theories; but her severity ended in talk, and her theories would not work. However, she read several books on education, knitting socks for Leonard all the while; and, upon the whole, I think, the hands were more usefully employed than the head, and the good honest heart better than either. She looked older than when we first knew her, but it was a ripe, kindly age that was coming over her. Her excellent practical sense, perhaps, made her a more masculine character than her brother. He was often so much perplexed by the problems of life, that he let the time for action go by; but she kept him in check by her clear, pithy talk, which brought back his wandering thoughts to the duty that lay straight before him, waiting for action; and then he remembered that it was the faithful part to 'wait patiently upon God',[3] and leave the ends in His hands, who alone knows why Evil exists in this world, and why it ever hovers on either side of Good. In this respect, Miss Benson had more faith than her brother – or so it seemed; for quick, resolute action in the next step of Life was all she required, while he deliberated and trembled, and often did wrong from his very deliberation, when his first instinct would have led him right.

But, although decided and prompt as ever, Miss Benson was grown older since the summer afternoon when she dismounted from the coach at the foot of the long Welsh hill that led to Llan-dhu, where her brother awaited her to consult her about Ruth. Though her eye was as bright and straight-looking as ever, quick and brave in its glances, her hair had become almost snowy white; and it was on this point she consulted Sally, soon after the date of Leonard's last untruth. The two were arranging Miss Benson's room one morning, when, after dusting the looking-glass, she suddenly stopped in her operation, and after a close inspection of herself, startled Sally by this speech:

'Sally! I'm looking a great deal older than I used to do!'

Sally, who was busy dilating on the increased price of flour, considered this remark of Miss Benson's as strangely irrelevant to the matter in hand, and only noticed it by a

'To be sure! I suppose we all on us do. But two-and-fourpence a dozen is too much to make us pay for it.'

Miss Benson went on with her inspection of herself, and Sally with her economical projects.

'Sally!' said Miss Benson, 'my hair is nearly white. The last time I looked it was only pepper-and-salt. What must I do?'

'Do – why, what would the wench do?' asked Sally, contemptuously. 'Ye're never going to be taken in, at your time of life, by hair-dyes and such gimcracks, as can only take in young girls whose wisdom-teeth are not cut.'

'And who are not very likely to want them,' said Miss Benson, quietly. 'No! but you see, Sally, it's very awkward having such grey hair, and feeling so young. Do you know, Sally, I've as great a mind for dancing, when I hear a lively tune on the street-organs, as ever; and as great a mind to sing when I'm happy – to sing in my old way, Sally, you know.'

'Ay, you had it from a girl,' said Sally; 'and many a time, when the door's been shut, I did not know if it was you in the parlour, or a big bumble-bee in the kitchen, as was making that drumbling noise. I heard you at it yesterday.'

'But an old woman with grey hair ought not to have a fancy for dancing or singing,' continued Miss Benson.

'Whatten nonsense are ye talking?' said Sally, roused to indignation. 'Calling yoursel' an old woman when you're better than ten years younger than me! and many a girl has grey hair at five-and-twenty.'

'But I'm more than five-and-twenty, Sally – I'm fifty-seven next May!'

'More shame for ye, then, not to know better than to talk of dyeing your hair. I cannot abide such vanities!'

'Oh, dear! Sally, when will you understand what I mean? I want to know how I'm to keep remembering how old I am, so as to prevent myself from feeling so young? I was quite startled just now to see my hair in the glass, for I can generally tell if my cap is straight by feeling. I'll tell you what I'll do – I'll cut off a piece of my grey hair, and plait it together for a marker in my Bible!' Miss Benson expected applause for this bright idea, but Sally only made answer:

'You'll be taking to painting your cheeks next, now you've once thought of dyeing your hair.' So Miss Benson plaited her grey hair in silence and quietness, Leonard holding one end of it while she wove it, and admiring the colour and texture all the time, with a sort of implied dissatisfaction at the auburn colour of his own curls, which was only half-comforted away by Miss Benson's information, that, if he lived long enough, his hair would be like hers.

Mr Benson, who had looked old and frail while he was yet but young, was now stationary as to the date of his appearance. But there was something more of nervous restlessness in his voice and ways than formerly; that was the only change six years had brought to him. And as for Sally, she chose to forget age and the passage of years altogether, and had as much work in her, to use her own expression, as she had at sixteen; nor was her appearance very explicit as to the flight of time. Fifty, sixty, or seventy, she might be – not more than the last, not less than the first – though her usual answer to any circuitous inquiry as to her age was now (what it had been for many years past), 'I'm feared I shall never see thirty again.'

Then as to the house. It was not one where the sitting-rooms are refurnished every two or three years; not now, even (since Ruth came to share their living) a place where, as an article grew shabby or worn, a new one was purchased. The furniture looked poor, and the carpets almost threadbare; but there was such a dainty spirit of cleanliness abroad, such exquisite neatness of repair, and altogether so bright and cheerful a look about the rooms – everything so above-board – no shifts to conceal poverty under flimsy ornament – that many a splendid drawing-room would give less pleasure to those who could see evidences of character in inanimate things. But whatever poverty there might be in the house, there was full luxuriance in the little square wall-encircled garden, on two sides of which the parlour and kitchen looked. The laburnum-tree, which when Ruth came was like a twig stuck into the ground, was now a golden glory in spring, and a pleasant shade in summer. The wild hop, that Mr Benson had brought home from one of his country rambles, and planted by the parlour-window, while Leonard was yet a baby in his mother's arms, was now a garland over the casement, hanging down long tendrils, that waved in the breezes, and threw pleasant shadows and traceries, like some old Bacchanalian carving,[4] on the parlour-walls, at 'morn or dusky eve'.[5] The yellow rose had clambered up to the window of Mr Benson's bedroom, and its blossom-laden branches were supported by a jargonelle pear-tree rich in autumnal fruit.

But, perhaps, in Ruth herself there was the greatest external change; for of the change which had gone on in her heart, and mind, and soul, or if there had been any, neither she nor any one around her was conscious; but sometimes Miss Benson did say to Sally, 'How very handsome Ruth is grown!' To which Sally made ungracious answer, 'Yes! she's well enough. Beauty is deceitful, and favour a snare, and I'm thankful the Lord has spared me from such man-traps and spring-guns.' But even Sally could not help secretly admiring Ruth. If her early brilliancy of colouring was gone, a clear ivory skin, as smooth as satin, told of complete and perfect health, and was as lovely, if not so striking in effect, as the banished lilies and roses. Her hair had grown darker and deeper, in the shadow that lingered in its masses; her eyes, even if you could have guessed that they had shed bitter tears in their day, had a thoughtful spiritual look about them, that made you wonder at their depth, and look – and look again. The increase of dignity in her face had been imparted to her form. I do not know if she had grown taller since the birth of her child, but she looked as if she had. And although she had lived in a very humble home, yet there was something about either it or her, or the people amongst whom she had been thrown during the last few years, which had so changed her, that whereas, six or seven years ago, you would have perceived that she was not altogether a lady by birth and education, yet now she might have been placed among the highest in the land, and would have been taken by the most critical judge for their equal, although ignorant of their conventional etiquette – an ignorance which she would have acknowledged in a simple, childlike way, being unconscious of any false shame.

Her whole heart was in her boy. She often feared that she loved him too much – more than God Himself – yet she could not bear to pray to have her love for her child lessened. But she would kneel down by his little bed at night – at the deep, still midnight – with the stars that kept watch over Rizpah[6] shining down upon her, and tell God what I have now told you, that she feared she loved her child too much, yet could not, would not, love him less; and speak to Him of her one treasure as she could speak to no earthly friend. And so, unconsciously, her love for her child led her up to love to God, to the All-knowing, who read her heart.

It might be superstition – I dare say it was – but, somehow, she never lay down to rest without saying, as she looked her last on her boy, 'Thy will, not mine, be done';[7] and even while she trembled and shrank with infinite dread from sounding the depths of what that will might be, she felt as if her treasure were more secure to waken up rosy and bright in the morning, as one over whose slumbers God's holy angels had watched, for the very words which she had turned away in sick terror from realising the night before.

Her daily absence at her duties to the Bradshaw children only ministered to her love for Leonard. Everything does minister to love when its foundation lies deep in a true heart, and it was with an exquisite pang of delight that, after a moment of vague fear

> (Oh, mercy! to myself I said,
> If Lucy should be dead!),[8]

she saw her child's bright face of welcome as he threw open the door every afternoon on her return home. For it was his silently-appointed work to listen for her knock, and rush breathless to let her in. If he were in the garden, or up-stairs among the treasurers of the lumber-room, either Miss Benson, or her brother, or Sally, would fetch him to his happy little task; no one so sacred as he to the allotted duty. And the joyous meeting was not deadened by custom, to either mother or child.

Ruth gave the Bradshaws the highest satisfaction, as Mr Bradshaw often said both to her and to the Bensons; indeed, she rather winced under his pompous approbation. But his favourite recreation was patronising; and when Ruth saw how quietly and meekly Mr Benson submitted to gifts and praise, when an honest word of affection, or a tacit, implied acknowledgment of equality, would have been worth everything said and done, she tried to be more meek in spirit, and to recognise the good that undoubtedly existed in Mr Bradshaw. He was richer and more prosperous than ever; – a keen, far-seeing man of business, with an undisguised contempt for all who failed in the success which he had achieved. But it was not alone those who were less fortunate in obtaining wealth than himself that he visited with severity of judgment; every moral error or delinquency came under his unsparing comment. Stained by no vice himself, either in his own eyes or in that of any human being who cared to judge him, having nicely and wisely proportioned and adapted his means to his ends, he could afford to speak and act with a severity which was almost sanctimonious in its ostentation of thankfulness as to himself. Not a misfortune or a sin was brought to light but Mr Bradshaw could trace it to its cause in some former mode of action, which he had long ago foretold would lead to shame. If another's son turned out wild or bad, Mr Bradshaw had little sympathy; it might have been prevented by a stricter rule, or more religious life at home; young Richard Bradshaw was quiet and steady, and other fathers might have had sons like him if they had taken the same pains to enforce obedience. Richard was an only son, and yet Mr Bradshaw might venture to say, he had never had his own way in his life. Mrs Bradshaw was, he confessed (Mr Bradshaw did not dislike confessing his wife's errors), rather less firm than he should have liked with the girls; and with some people, he believed, Jemima was rather headstrong; but to his wishes, she had always shown herself obedient. All children were obedient, if their parents were decided and authoritative; and every one would turn out well, if properly managed. If they did not prove good, they must take the consequences of their errors.

Mrs Bradshaw murmured faintly at her husband when his back was turned; but if his voice was heard, or his footsteps sounded in the distance, she was mute, and hurried her children into the attitude or action most pleasing to their father. Jemima, it is true, rebelled against this manner of proceeding, which savoured to her a little of deceit; but even she had not, as yet, overcome her awe of her father sufficiently to act independently of him, and according to her own sense of right – or, rather, I should say, according to her own warm passionate impulses. Before him, the wilfulness which made her dark eyes blaze out at times was hushed and still; he had no idea of her self-tormenting, no notion of the almost southern jealousy which seemed to belong to her brunette complexion. Jemima was not pretty, the flatness and shortness of her face made her almost plain; yet most people looked twice at her expressive countenance, at the eyes which flamed or melted at every trifle, at the rich colour which came at every expressed emotion into her usually sallow face, at the faultless teeth which made her smile like a sunbeam. But then, again, when she thought she was not kindly treated, when a suspicion crossed her mind, or when she was angry with herself, her lips were tight-pressed together, her colour was wan and almost livid, and a stormy gloom clouded her eyes as with a film. But before her father her words were few, and he did not notice looks or tones.

Her brother Richard had been equally silent before his father, in boyhood and early youth; but since he had gone to be a clerk in a London house, preparatory to assuming his place as junior partner in Mr Bradshaw's business, he spoke more on his occasional visits at home. And very proper and highly moral was his conversation; set sentences of goodness, which were like the flowers that children stick in the ground, and that have not sprung upwards from roots – deep down in the hidden life and experience of the heart. He was as severe a judge as his father of other people's conduct, but you felt that Mr Bradshaw was sincere in his condemnation of all outward error and vice, and that he would try himself by the same laws as he tried others; somehow, Richard's words were frequently heard with a lurking distrust, and many shook their heads over the pattern son; but then it was those whose sons had gone astray, and been condemned, in no private or tender manner, by Mr Bradshaw, so it might be revenge in them. Still, Jemima felt that all was not right; her heart sympathised in the rebellion against his father's commands, which her brother had confessed to her in an unusual moment of confidence, but her uneasy conscience condemned the deceit which he had practised.

The brother and sister were sitting alone over a blazing Christmas fire, and Jemima held an old newspaper in her hand to shield her face from the hot light. They were talking of family events, when, during a pause, Jemima's eye caught the name of a great actor, who had lately given prominence and life to a character in one of Shakspeare's plays. The criticism in the paper was fine, and warmed Jemima's heart.

'How I should like to see a play!' exclaimed she.

'Should you?' said her brother, listlessly.

'Yes, to be sure! Just hear this!' and she began to read a fine passage of criticism.

'Those newspaper people can make an article out of anything,' said he, yawning. 'I've seen the man myself, and it was all very well, but nothing to make such a fuss about!'

'You! you seen —? Have you seen a play, Richard? Oh, why did you never tell me before? Tell me all about it! Why did you never name seeing — in your letters?'

He half smiled, contemptuously enough. 'Oh! at first it strikes one rather, but after a while one cares no more for the theatre than one does for mince-pies.'

'Oh, I wish I might go to London!' said Jemima, impatiently. 'I've a great mind to ask papa to let me go to the George Smiths', and then I could see —. I would not think him like mince-pies.'

'You must not do any such thing!' said Richard, now neither yawning nor contemptuous. 'My father would never allow you to go to the theatre; and the George Smiths are such old fogeys – they would be sure to tell.'

'How do you go, then? Does my father give you leave?'

'Oh! many things are right for men which are not for girls.'

Jemima sat and pondered. Richard wished he had not been so confidential.

'You need not name it,' said he, rather anxiously.

'Name what?' said she, startled, for her thoughts had gone far a-field.

'Oh, name my going once or twice to the theatre!'

'No, I sha'n't name it!' said she. 'No one here would care to hear it.'

But it was with some little surprise, and almost with a feeling of disgust, that she heard Richard join with her father in condemning some one, and add to Mr Bradshaw's list of offences, by alleging that the young man was a play-goer. He did not think his sister heard his words.

Mary and Elizabeth were the two girls whom Ruth had in charge; they resembled Jemima more than their brother in character. The household rules were occasionally a little relaxed in their favour, for Mary, the elder, was nearly eight years younger than Jemima, and three intermediate children had died. They loved Ruth dearly, made a great pet of Leonard, and had many profound secrets together, most of which related to their wonders if Jemima and Mr Farquhar would ever be married. They watched their sister closely; and every day had some fresh confidence to make to each other, confirming or discouraging to their hopes.

Ruth rose early, and shared the household work with Sally and Miss Benson, till seven; and then she helped Leonard to dress, and had a quiet time alone with him till prayers and breakfast. At nine she was to be at Mr Bradshaw's house. She sat in the room with Mary and Elizabeth during the Latin, the writing, and arithmetic lessons, which they received from masters; then she read, and walked with them, they clinging to her as to an elder sister; she dined with her pupils at the family lunch, and reached home by four. That happy home – those quiet days!

And so the peaceful days passed on into weeks, and months, and years, and Ruth and Leonard grew and strengthened into the riper beauty of their respective ages; while as yet no touch of decay had come on the quaint, primitive elders of the household.

CHAPTER XX

It was no wonder that the lookers-on were perplexed as to the state of affairs between Jemima and Mr Farquhar, for they too were sorely puzzled themselves at the sort of relationship between them. Was it love, or was it not? that was the question in Mr Farquhar's mind. He hoped it was not; he believed it was not; and yet he felt as if it were. There was something preposterous, he thought, in a man, nearly forty years of age, being in love with a girl of twenty. He had gone on reasoning through all the days of his manhood on the idea of a staid, noble-minded wife, grave and sedate, the fit companion in experience of her husband. He had spoken with admiration of reticent characters, full of self-control and dignity; and he hoped – he trusted, that all this time he had not been allowing himself unconsciously to fall in love with a wild-hearted, impetuous girl, who knew nothing of life beyond her father's house, and who chafed under the strict discipline enforced there. For it was rather a suspicious symptom of the state of Mr Farquhar's affections, that he had discovered the silent rebellion which continued in Jemima's heart, unperceived by any of her own family, against the severe laws and opinions of her father. Mr Farquhar shared in these opinions; but in him they were modified, and took a milder form. Still, he approved of much that Mr Bradshaw did and said; and this made it all the more strange that he should wince so for Jemima, whenever anything took place which he instinctively knew that she would dislike. After an evening at Mr Bradshaw's, when Jemima had gone to the very verge of questioning or disputing some of her father's severe judgments, Mr Farquhar went home in a dissatisfied, restless state of mind, which he was almost afraid to analyse. He admired the inflexible integrity – and almost the pomp of principle – evinced by Mr Bradshaw on every occasion; he wondered how it was that Jemima could not see how grand a life might be, whose every action was shaped in obedience to some eternal law; instead of which, he was afraid she rebelled against every law, and was only guided by impulse. Mr Farquhar had been taught to dread impulses as promptings of the devil. Sometimes, if he tried to present her father's opinion before her in another form, so as to bring himself and her rather more into that state of agreement he longed for, she flashed out upon him with the indignation of difference that she dared not show to, or before, her father, as if she had some diviner instinct which taught her more truly than they knew, with all their experience; at least, in her first expressions there seemed something good and fine; but opposition made her angry and irritable, and the arguments which he was constantly provoking (whenever he was with her in her father's absence) frequently ended in some vehemence of expression on her part that offended Mr Farquhar, who did not see how she expiated her anger in tears and self-reproaches when alone in her chamber. Then he would lecture himself severely on the interest he could not help feeling in a wilful girl; he would determine not to interfere with her opinions in future, and yet, the very next time they differed, he strove to argue her into harmony with himself, in spite of all resolutions to the contrary.

Mr Bradshaw saw just enough of this interest which Jemima had excited in his partner's mind, to determine him in considering their future marriage as a settled affair. The fitness of the thing had long ago struck him; her father's partner – so the fortune he meant to give her might continue in the business; a man of such steadiness of character, and such a capital eye for a desirable speculation as Mr Farquhar – just the right age to unite the paternal with the conjugal affection, and consequently the very man for Jemima, who had something unruly in her, which might break out under a *régime* less widely adjusted to the circumstances than was Mr Bradshaw's (in his own opinion) – a house ready-furnished, at a convenient distance from her home – no near relations on Mr Farquhar's side, who might be inclined to consider his residence as their own for an indefinite time, and so add to the household expenses – in short, what could be more suitable in every way? Mr Bradshaw respected the very self-restraint he thought he saw in Mr Farquhar's demeanour, attributing it to a wise desire to wait until trade should be rather more slack, and the man of business more at leisure to become the lover.

As for Jemima, at times she thought she almost hated Mr Farquhar.

'What business has he,' she would think, 'to lecture me? Often I can hardly bear it from papa, and I will not bear it from him. He treats me just like a child, and as if I should lose all my present opinions when I know more of the world. I am sure I should like never to know the world, if it was to make me think as he does, hard man that he is! I wonder what made him take Jem Brown on as gardener again, if he does not believe that above one criminal in a thousand is restored to goodness. I'll ask him, some day, if that was not acting on impulse rather than principle. Poor impulse! how you do get abused! But I will tell Mr Farquhar, I will not let him interfere with me. If I do what papa bids me, no one has a right to notice whether I do it willingly or not.'

So then she tried to defy Mr Farquhar, by doing and saying things that she knew he would disapprove. She went so far that he was seriously grieved, and did not even remonstrate and 'lecture', and then she was disappointed and irritated; for, somehow, with all her indignation at interference, she liked to be lectured by him; not that she was aware of this liking of hers, but still it would have been more pleasant to be scolded than so quietly passed over. Her two little sisters, with their wide-awake eyes, had long ago put things together, and conjectured. Every day they had some fresh mystery together, to be imparted in garden-walks and whispered talks.

'Lizzie, did you see how the tears came into Mimie's eyes when Mr Farquhar looked so displeased when she said good people were always dull? I think she's in love.' Mary said the last words with grave emphasis, and felt like an oracle of twelve years of age.

'I don't,' said Lizzie. 'I know I cry often enough when papa is cross, and I'm not in love with him.'

'Yes! but you don't look as Mimie did.'

'Don't call her Mimie – you know papa does not like it.'

'Yes; but there are so many things papa does not like I can never remember them all. Never mind about that; but listen to something I've got to tell you, if you'll never, never tell.'

'No, indeed I won't, Mary. What is it?'

'Not to Mrs Denbigh?'

'No, not even to Mrs Denbigh.'

'Well, then, the other day – last Friday, Mimie—'

'Jemima!' interrupted the more conscientious Elizabeth.

'Jemima, if it must be so,' jerked out Mary, 'sent me to her desk[1] for an envelope, and what do you think I saw?'

'What?' asked Elizabeth, expecting nothing else than a red-hot Valentine, signed Walter Farquhar, *pro* Bradshaw, Farquhar, & Co.,[2] in full.

'Why, a piece of paper, with dull-looking lines upon it, just like the scientific dialogues; and I remembered all about it. It was once when Mr Farquhar had been telling us that a bullet does not go in a straight line, but in a something curve, and he drew some lines on a piece of paper; and Mimie —'

'Jemima!' put in Elizabeth.

'Well, well! She had treasured it up, and written in a corner, "W. F., April 3rd." Now, that's rather like love, is not it? For Jemima hates useful information just as much as I do, and that's saying a great deal; and yet she had kept this paper, and dated it.'

'If that's all, I know Dick keeps a paper with Miss Benson's name written on it, and yet he's not in love with her; and perhaps Jemima may like Mr Farquhar, and he may not like her. It seems such a little while since her hair was turned up, and he has always been a grave middle-aged man ever since I can recollect; and then, have you never noticed how often he finds fault with her – almost lectures her?'

'To be sure,' said Mary; 'but he may be in love, for all that. Just think how often papa lectures mamma; and yet, of course, they're in love with each other.'

'Well! we shall see,' said Elizabeth.

Poor Jemima little thought of the four sharp eyes that watched her daily course while she sat alone, as she fancied, with her secret in her own room. For, in a passionate fit of grieving, at the impatient hasty temper which had made her so seriously displease Mr Farquhar that he had gone away without remonstrance, without more leave-taking than a distant bow, she had begun to suspect that, rather than not be noticed at all by him, rather than be an object of indifference to him – oh! far rather would she be an object of anger and upbraiding; and the thoughts that followed this confession to herself, stunned and bewildered her; and for once that they made her dizzy with hope, ten times they made her sick with fear. For an instant she planned to become and to be all he could wish her; to change her very nature for him. And then a great gush of pride came over her, and she set her teeth tight together, and determined that he should either love her as she was, or not at all. Unless he could take her with all her faults, she would not care for his regard; 'love' was too noble a word to call such cold calculating feeling as his must be, who went about with a pattern idea in his mind, trying to find a wife to match. Besides, there was something degrading, Jemima thought, in trying to alter herself to gain the love of any human creature. And yet, if he did not care for her, if this late indifference were to last, what a great shroud was drawn over life! Could she bear it?

From the agony she dared not look at, but which she was going to risk encountering, she was aroused by the presence of her mother.

'Jemima! your father wants to speak to you in the dining-room.'

'What for?' asked the girl.

'Oh! he is fidgeted by something Mr Farquhar said to me, and which I repeated. I am sure I thought there was no harm in it, and your father always likes me to tell him what everybody says in his absence.'

Jemima went with a heavy heart into her father's presence.

He was walking up and down the room, and did not see her at first.

'Oh, Jemima! is that you? Has your mother told you what I want to speak to you about?'

'No!' said Jemima. 'Not exactly.'

'She has been telling me, what proves to me how very seriously you must have displeased and offended Mr Farquhar, before he could have expressed himself to her as he did, when he left the house. You know what he said?'

'No!' said Jemima, her heart swelling within her. 'He has no right to say anything about me.' She was desperate, or she durst not have said this before her father.

'No right! – what do you mean, Jemima?' said Mr Bradshaw, turning sharp round. 'Surely you must know that I hope he may one day be your husband; that is to say, if you prove yourself worthy of the excellent training I have given you. I cannot suppose Mr Farquhar would take any undisciplined girl as a wife.'

Jemima held tight by a chair near which she was standing. She did not speak; her father was pleased by her silence – it was the way in which he liked his projects to be received.

'But you cannot suppose,' he continued, 'that Mr Farquhar will consent to marry you—'

'Consent to marry me!' repeated Jemima, in a low tone of brooding indignation; were those the terms upon which her rich, woman's heart was to be given, with a calm consent of acquiescent acceptance, but a little above resignation on the part of the receiver?

' – if you give way to a temper which, although you have never dared to show it to me, I am well aware exists, although I hoped the habits of self-examination I had instilled had done much to cure you of manifesting it. At one time, Richard promised to be the more headstrong of the two; now, I must desire you to take pattern by him. Yes,' he continued, falling into his old train of thought, 'it would be a most fortunate connexion for you in every way. I should have you under my own eye, and could still assist you in the formation of your character, and I should be at hand to strengthen and confirm your principles. Mr Farquhar's connexion with the firm would be convenient and agreeable to me in a pecuniary point of view. He—' Mr Bradshaw was going on in his enumeration of the advantages which he in particular, and Jemima in the second place, would derive from this marriage, when his daughter spoke, at first so low that he could not hear her, as he walked up and down the room with his creaking boots, and he had to stop to listen.

'Has Mr Farquhar ever spoken to you about it?' Jemima's cheek was flushed as she asked the question; she wished that she might have been the person to whom he had first addressed himself.

Mr Bradshaw answered:

'No! not spoken. It has been implied between us for some time. At least, I have been so aware of his intentions that I have made several allusions, in the course of business, to it, as a thing that might take place. He can hardly have misunderstood; he must have seen that I perceived his design, and approved of it,' said Mr Bradshaw, rather doubtfully; as he remembered how very little, in fact, passed between him and his partner which could have reference to the subject, to any but a mind prepared to receive it. Perhaps Mr Farquhar had not really thought of it; but then again, that would imply that his own penetration had been mistaken, a thing not impossible certainly, but quite beyond the range of probability. So he reassured himself, and (as he thought) his daughter, by saying:

'The whole thing is so suitable – the advantages arising from the connexion are so obvious; besides which, I am quite aware, from many little speeches of Mr Farquhar's, that he contemplates marriage at no very distant time; and he seldom leaves Eccleston, and visits few families besides our own – certainly, none that can compare with ours in the advantages you have all received in moral and religious training.' But then Mr Bradshaw was checked in his implied praises of himself (and only himself could be his martingale[3] when he once set out on such a career), by a recollection that Jemima must not feel too secure, as she might become if he dwelt too much on the advantages of her being her father's daughter. Accordingly, he said: 'But you must be aware, Jemima, that you do very little credit to the education I have given you, when you make such an impression as you must have done to-day, before Mr Farquhar could have said what he did of you!'

'What did he say?' asked Jemima, still in the low, husky tone of suppressed anger.

'Your mother says he remarked to her, "What a pity it is, that Jemima cannot maintain her opinions without going into a passion; and what a pity it is, that her opinions are such as to sanction, rather than curb, these fits of rudeness and anger!" '

'Did he say that?' said Jemima, in a still lower tone, not questioning her father, but speaking rather to herself.

'I have no doubt he did,' replied her father, gravely. 'Your mother is in the habit of repeating accurately to me what takes place in my absence; besides which, the whole speech is not one of hers; she has not altered a word in the repetition, I am convinced. I have trained her to habits of accuracy very unusual in a woman.'

At another time, Jemima might have been inclined to rebel against this system of carrying constant intelligence to head-quarters, which she had long ago felt as an insurmountable obstacle to any free communication with her mother; but now, her father's means of acquiring knowledge faded into insignificance before the nature of the information he imparted. She stood quite still, grasping the chair-back, longing to be dismissed.

'I have said enough now, I hope, to make you behave in a becoming manner to Mr Farquhar; if your temper is too unruly to be always under your own control, at least have respect to my injunctions, and take some pains to curb it before him.'

'May I go?' asked Jemima, chafing more and more.

'You may,' said her father. When she left the room he gently rubbed his hands together, satisfied with the effect he had produced, and wondering how it was, that one so well brought up as his daughter,

could ever say or do anything to provoke such a remark from Mr
Farquhar as that which he had heard repeated.

'Nothing can be more gentle and docile than she is when spoken to
in the proper manner. I must give Farquhar a hint,' said Mr Bradshaw
to himself.

Jemima rushed up-stairs, and locked herself into her room. She began
pacing up and down at first, without shedding a tear; but then she
suddenly stopped, and burst out crying with passionate indignation.

'So! I am to behave well, not because it is right – not because it is
right – but to show off before Mr Farquhar. Oh, Mr Farquhar!' said
she, suddenly changing to a sort of upbraiding tone of voice, 'I did not
think so of you an hour ago. I did not think you could choose a wife in
that cold-hearted way, though you did profess to act by rule and line;[4]
but you think to have me, do you? because it is fitting and suitable, and
you want to be married, and can't spare time for wooing' (she was
lashing herself up by an exaggeration of all her father had said). 'And
how often I have thought you were too grand for me! but now I know
better. Now I can believe that all you do is done from calculation; you
are good because it adds to your business credit – you talk in that high
strain about principle because it sounds well, and is respectable – and
even these things are better than your cold way of looking out for a
wife, just as you would do for a carpet, to add to your comforts, and
settle you respectably. But I won't be that wife. You shall see something
of me which shall make you not acquiesce so quietly in the arrangements
of the firm.' She cried too vehemently to go on thinking or speaking.
Then she stopped, and said:

'Only an hour ago I was hoping – I don't know what I was hoping
– but I thought – oh! how I was deceived! – I thought he had a true,
deep, loving, manly heart, which God might let me win; but now I
know he has only a calm, calculating head—'

If Jemima had been vehement and passionate before this conversation with her father, it was better than the sullen reserve she
assumed now whenever Mr Farquhar came to the house. He felt it
deeply; no reasoning with himself took off the pain he experienced. He
tried to speak on the subjects she liked, in the manner she liked, until
he despised himself for the unsuccessful efforts.

He stood between her and her father once or twice, in obvious
inconsistency with his own previously-expressed opinions; and Mr Brad-

shaw piqued himself upon his admirable management, in making Jemima feel that she owed his indulgence or forbearance to Mr Farquhar's interference; but Jemima – perverse, miserable Jemima – thought that she hated Mr Farquhar all the more. She respected her father inflexible, much more than her father pompously giving up to Mr Farquhar's subdued remonstrances on her behalf. Even Mr Bradshaw was perplexed, and shut himself up to consider how Jemima was to be made more fully to understand his wishes and her own interests. But there was nothing to take hold of as a ground for any further conversation with her. Her actions were so submissive that they were spiritless; she did all her father desired; she did it with a nervous quickness and haste, if she thought that otherwise Mr Farquhar would interfere in any way. She wished evidently to owe nothing to him. She had begun by leaving the room when he came in, after the conversation she had had with her father; but at Mr Bradshaw's first expression of his wish that she should remain, she remained – silent, indifferent, inattentive to all that was going on; at least there was this appearance of inattention. She would work away at her sewing as if she were to earn her livelihood by it; the light was gone out of her eyes as she lifted them up heavily before replying to any question, and the eyelids were often swollen with crying.

But in all this there was no positive fault. Mr Bradshaw could not have told her not to do this, or to do that, without her doing it; for she had become much more docile of late.

It was a wonderful proof of the influence Ruth had gained in the family, that Mr Bradshaw, after much deliberation, congratulated himself on the wise determination he had made of requesting her to speak to Jemima, and find out what feeling was at the bottom of all this change in her ways of going on.

He rang the bell.

'Is Mrs Denbigh here?' he inquired of the servant who answered it.

'Yes, sir; she has just come.'

'Beg her to come to me in this room as soon as she can leave the young ladies.'

Ruth came.

'Sit down, Mrs Denbigh, sit down. I want to have a little conversation with you; not about your pupils, they are going on well under your care, I am sure; and I often congratulate myself on the choice I made – I assure you I do. But now I want to speak to you about Jemima. She is very fond of you, and perhaps you could take some opportunity of observing to her – in short, of saying to her, that she is behaving very foolishly – in fact, disgusting Mr Farquhar (who was, I know, inclined to like her) by the sullen, sulky way she behaves in, when he is by.'

He paused for the ready acquiescence he expected. But Ruth did not quite comprehend what was required of her, and disliked the glimpse she had gained of the task very much.

'I hardly understand, sir. You are displeased with Miss Bradshaw's manners to Mr Farquhar.'

'Well, well! not quite that; I am displeased with her manners – they are sulky and abrupt, particularly when he is by – and I want you (of whom she is so fond) to speak to her about it.'

'But I have never had the opportunity of noticing them. Whenever I have seen her, she has been most gentle and affectionate.'

'But I think you do not hesitate to believe me, when I say that I have noticed the reverse,' said Mr Bradshaw, drawing himself up.

'No, sir. I beg your pardon if I have expressed myself so badly as to seem to doubt. But am I to tell Miss Bradshaw that you have spoken of her faults to me?' asked Ruth, a little astonished, and shrinking more than ever from the proposed task.

'If you would allow me to finish what I have got to say, without interruption, I could then tell you what I do wish.'

'I beg your pardon, sir,' said Ruth, gently.

'I wish you to join our circle occasionally in an evening; Mrs Bradshaw shall send you an invitation when Mr Farquhar is likely to be here. Warned by me, and, consequently, with your observation quickened, you can hardly fail to notice instances of what I have pointed out; and then I will trust to your own good sense' (Mr Bradshaw bowed to her at this part of his sentence) 'to find an opportunity to remonstrate with her.'

Ruth was beginning to speak, but he waved his hand for another minute of silence.

'Only a minute, Mrs Denbigh; I am quite aware that, in requesting your presence occasionally in the evening, I shall be trespassing upon the time which is, in fact, your money; you may be assured that I shall not forget this little circumstance, and you can explain what I have said on this head to Benson and his sister.'

'I am afraid I cannot do it,' Ruth began: but while she was choosing words delicate enough to express her reluctance to act as he wished, he had almost bowed her out of the room; and thinking that she was modest in her estimate of her qualifications for remonstrating with his daughter, he added, blandly:

'No one so able, Mrs Denbigh. I have observed many qualities in you – observed when, perhaps, you have little thought it.'

If he had observed Ruth that morning, he would have seen an absence of mind, and depression of spirits, not much to her credit as a teacher; for she could not bring herself to feel, that she had any right to go into the family purposely to watch over and find fault with any one member of it. If she had seen anything wrong in Jemima, Ruth loved her so much that she would have told her of it in private; and with many doubts, how far she was the one to pull out the mote[5] from any one's eye, even in the most tender manner; – she would have had to conquer reluctance before she could have done even this; but there was something indefinably repugnant to her in the manner of acting which Mr Bradshaw had proposed, and she determined not to accept the invitations which were to place her in so false a position.

But as she was leaving the house, after the end of the lessons, while she stood in the hall tying on her bonnet, and listening to the last small confidences of her two pupils, she saw Jemima coming in through the garden-door, and was struck by the change in her looks. The large eyes, so brilliant once, were dim and clouded; the complexion sallow and colourless; a lowering expression was on the dark brow, and the corners of her mouth drooped as with sorrowful thoughts. She looked up, and her eyes met Ruth's.

'Oh! you beautiful creature!' thought Jemima, 'with your still, calm, heavenly face, what are you to know of earth's trials? You have lost your beloved by death – but that is a blessed sorrow; the sorrow I have pulls me down and down, and makes me despise and hate every one – not you, though.' And her face changing to a soft tender look, she went up to Ruth, and kissed her fondly; as if it were a relief to be near some one on whose true pure heart she relied. Ruth returned the caress; and even while she did so, she suddenly rescinded her resolution to keep clear of what Mr Bradshaw had desired her to do. On her way home she resolved, if she could, to find out what were Jemima's secret feelings: and if (as from some previous knowledge she suspected) they were morbid and exaggerated in any way, to try and help her right with all the wisdom which true love gives. It was time that some one should come to still the storm in Jemima's turbulent heart, which was daily and hourly knowing less and less of peace. The irritating difficulty was to separate the two characters, which at two different times she had attributed to Mr Farquhar – the old one, which she had formerly believed to be true, that he was a man acting up to a high standard of lofty principle, and acting up without a struggle (and this last had been the circumstance which had made her rebellious and irritable once); the new one, which her father had excited in her suspicious mind, that Mr Farquhar was cold and calculating in all he did, and that she was to be transferred by the former, and accepted by the latter, as a sort of stock in trade – these were the two Mr Farquhars who clashed together in her mind. And in this state of irritation and prejudice, she could not bear the way in which he gave up his opinions to please her; that was not the way to win her; she liked him far better when he inflexibly and rigidly adhered to his idea of right and wrong, not even allowing any force to temptation, and hardly any grace to repentance, compared with that beauty of holiness[6] which had never yielded to sin. He had been her idol in those days, as she found out now, however much at the time she had opposed him with violence.

As for Mr Farquhar, he was almost weary of himself; no reasoning, even no principle, seemed to have influence over him, for he saw that Jemima was not at all what he approved of in woman. He saw her uncurbed and passionate, affecting to despise the rules of life he held most sacred, and indifferent to, if not positively disliking him; and yet he loved her dearly. But he resolved to make a great effort of will, and break loose from these trammels of sense. And while he resolved, some old recollection would bring her up, hanging on his arm, in all the confidence of early girlhood, looking up in his face with her soft dark eyes, and questioning him upon the mysterious subjects which had so much interest for both of them at that time, although they had become only matter for dissension in these later days.

It was also true, as Mr Bradshaw had said, Mr Farquhar wished to marry, and had not much choice in the small town of Eccleston. He never put this so plainly before himself, as a reason for choosing Jemima, as her father had done to her; but it was an unconscious motive all the same. However, now he had lectured himself into the resolution to make a pretty long absence from Eccleston, and see if, amongst his distant friends, there was no woman more in accordance with his ideal, who could put the naughty, wilful, plaguing Jemima Bradshaw out of his head, if he did not soon perceive some change in her for the better.

A few days after Ruth's conversation with Mr Bradshaw, the invitation she had been expecting, yet dreading, came. It was to her alone. Mr and Miss Benson were pleased at the compliment to her, and urged her acceptance of it. She wished that they had been included; she had not thought it right, or kind to Jemima, to tell them why she was going, and she feared now lest they should feel a little hurt that they were not asked too. But she need not have been afraid. They were glad and proud of the attention to her, and never thought of themselves.

'Ruthie, what gown shall you wear to-night? Your dark-grey one, I suppose?' asked Miss Benson.

'Yes, I suppose so. I never thought of it; but that is my best.'

'Well, then, I shall quill up⁷ a ruff for you. You know I am a famous quiller of net.'

Ruth came down-stairs with a little flush on her cheeks when she was ready to go. She held her bonnet and shawl in her hand, for she knew Miss Benson and Sally would want to see her dressed.

'Is not mamma pretty?' asked Leonard, with a child's pride.

'She looks very nice and tidy,' said Miss Benson, who had an idea that children should not talk or think about beauty.

'I think my ruff looks so nice,' said Ruth, with gentle pleasure. And indeed it did look nice, and set off the pretty round throat most becomingly. Her hair, now grown long and thick, was smoothed as close to her head as its waving nature would allow, and plaited up in a great rich knot low down behind. The grey gown was as plain as plain could be.

'You should have light gloves, Ruth,' said Miss Benson. She went up-stairs, and brought down a delicate pair of Limerick ones,⁸ which had been long treasured up in a walnut-shell.

'They say them gloves is made of chicken's-skins,' said Sally, examining them curiously. 'I wonder how they set about skinning 'em.'

'Here, Ruth,' said Mr Benson, coming in from the garden, 'here's a rose or two for you. I am sorry there are no more; I hoped I should have had my yellow rose out by this time, but the damask and the white are in a warmer corner, and have got the start.'

Miss Benson and Leonard stood at the door, and watched her down the little passage-street till she was out of sight.

She had hardly touched the bell at Mr Bradshaw's door, when Mary and Elizabeth opened it with boisterous glee.

'We saw you coming – we've been watching for you – we want you to come round the garden before tea; papa is not come in yet. Do come!'

She went round the garden with a little girl clinging to each arm. It was full of sunshine and flowers, and this made the contrast between it and the usual large family room (which fronted the north-east, and therefore had no evening sun to light up its cold, drab furniture) more striking than usual. It looked very gloomy. There was the great dining-table, heavy and square; the range of chairs, straight and square; the work-boxes, useful and square; the colouring of walls, and carpet, and curtains, all of the coldest description; everything was handsome, and everything was ugly. Mrs Bradshaw was asleep in her easy-chair when they came in. Jemima had just put down her work, and, lost in thought, she leant her cheek on her hand. When she saw Ruth she brightened a little, and went to her and kissed her. Mrs Bradshaw jumped up at the sound of their entrance, and was wide awake in a moment.

'Oh! I thought your father was here,' said she, evidently relieved to find that he had not come in and caught her sleeping.

'Thank you, Mrs Denbigh, for coming to us to-night,' said she, in the quiet tone in which she generally spoke in her husband's absence. When he was there, a sort of constant terror of displeasing him made her voice sharp and nervous; the children knew that many a thing passed over by their mother when their father was away, was sure to be noticed by her when he was present, and noticed, too, in a cross and querulous manner, for she was so much afraid of the blame which on any occasion of their misbehaviour fell upon her. And yet she looked up to her husband with a reverence, and regard, and a faithfulness of love, which his decision of character was likely to produce on a weak and anxious mind. He was a rest and a support[9] to her, on whom she cast all her responsibilities; she was an obedient, unremonstrating wife to him; no stronger affection had ever brought her duty to him into conflict with any desire of her heart. She loved her children dearly, though they all perplexed her very frequently. Her son was her especial darling, because he very seldom brought her into any scrapes with his father; he was so cautious and prudent, and had the art of 'keeping a calm sough'[10] about any difficulty he might be in. With all her dutiful sense of the obligation, which her husband enforced upon her, to notice and tell him everything that was going wrong in the household, and especially among his children, Mrs Bradshaw, somehow, contrived to be honestly blind to a good deal that was not praiseworthy in Master Richard.

Mr Bradshaw came in before long, bringing with him Mr Farquhar. Jemima had been talking to Ruth with some interest before then; but, on seeing Mr Farquhar, she bent her head down over her work, went a little paler, and turned obstinately silent. Mr Bradshaw longed to command her to speak; but even he had a suspicion that what she might say, when so commanded, might be rather worse in its effect than her gloomy silence; so he held his peace, and a discontented, angry kind of peace it was. Mrs Bradshaw saw that something was wrong, but could not tell what; only she became every moment more trembling, and nervous, and irritable, and sent Mary and Elizabeth off on all sorts of contradictory errands to the servants, and made the tea twice as strong, and sweetened it twice as much as usual, in hopes of pacifying her husband with good things.

Mr Farquhar had gone for the last time, or so he thought. He had resolved (for the fifth time) that he would go and watch Jemima once more, and if her temper got the better of her, and she showed the old sullenness again, and gave the old proofs of indifference to his good opinion, he would give her up altogether, and seek a wife elsewhere. He sat watching her with folded arms, and in silence. Altogether they were a pleasant family party!

Jemima wanted to wind a skein of wool. Mr Farquhar saw it, and came to her, anxious to do her this little service. She turned away pettishly, and asked Ruth to hold it for her.

Ruth was hurt for Mr Farquhar, and looked sorrowfully at Jemima; but Jemima would not see her glance of upbraiding, as Ruth, hoping that she would relent, delayed a little to comply with her request. Mr Farquhar did; and went back to his seat to watch them both. He saw Jemima turbulent and stormy in look; he saw Ruth, to all appearance, heavenly calm as the angels, or with only that little tinge of sorrow which her friend's behaviour had called forth. He saw the unusual beauty of her face and form, which he had never noticed before; and he saw Jemima, with all the brilliancy she once possessed in eyes and complexion, dimmed and faded. He watched Ruth, speaking low and soft to the little girls, who seemed to come to her in every difficulty; and he remarked her gentle firmness when their bedtime came, and they pleaded to stay up longer (their father was absent in his counting-house, or they would not have dared to do so). He liked Ruth's soft, distinct, unwavering 'No! you must go. You must keep to what is right,' far better than the good-natured yielding to entreaty he had formerly admired in Jemima. He was wandering off into this comparison, while Ruth, with delicate and unconscious tact, was trying to lead Jemima into some subject which should take her away from the thoughts, whatever they were, that made her so ungracious and rude.

Jemima was ashamed of herself before Ruth, in a way which she had never been before any one else. She valued Ruth's good opinion so highly, that she dreaded lest her friend should perceive her faults. She put a check upon herself – a check at first; but after a little time she had forgotten something of her trouble, and listened to Ruth, and questioned her about Leonard, and smiled at his little witticisms; and only the sighs, that would come up from the very force of habit, brought back the consciousness of her unhappiness. Before the end of the evening, Jemima had allowed herself to speak to Mr Farquhar in the old way – questioning, differing, disputing. She was recalled to the remembrance of that miserable conversation by the entrance of her father. After that she was silent. But he had seen her face more animated, and bright with a smile, as she spoke to Mr Farquhar; and although he regretted the loss of her complexion (for she was still very pale), he was highly pleased with the success of his project. He never doubted but that Ruth had given her some sort of private exhortation to behave better. He could not have understood the pretty art with which, by simply banishing unpleasant subjects, and throwing a wholesome natural sunlit tone over others, Ruth had insensibly drawn Jemima out of her gloom. He resolved to buy Mrs Denbigh a handsome silk gown the very next day. He did not believe she had a silk gown, poor creature! He had noticed that dark-grey stuff, this long long time, as her Sunday dress. He liked the colour; the silk one should be just the same tinge. Then he thought that it would, perhaps, be better to choose a lighter shade, one which might be noticed as different to the old gown. For he had no doubt she would like to have it remarked, and, perhaps, would not object to tell people that it was a present from Mr Bradshaw – a token of his approbation. He smiled a little to himself as he thought of this additional source of pleasure to Ruth. She, in the mean time, was getting up to go home. While Jemima was lighting the bed-candle[11] at the lamp, Ruth came round to bid good night. Mr Bradshaw could not allow her to remain till the morrow, uncertain whether he was satisfied or not.

'Good night, Mrs Denbigh,' said he. 'Good night. Thank you. I am obliged to you – I am exceedingly obliged to you.'

He laid emphasis on these words, for he was pleased to see Mr Farquhar step forwards to help Jemima in her little office.

Mr Farquhar offered to accompany Ruth home; but the streets that intervened between Mr Bradshaw's and the Chapel-house were so quiet that he desisted, when he learnt from Ruth's manner how much she disliked his proposal. Mr Bradshaw, too, instantly observed:

'Oh! Mrs Denbigh need not trouble you, Farquhar. I have servants at liberty at any moment to attend on her, if she wishes it.'

In fact, he wanted to make hay while the sun shone, and to detain Mr Farquhar a little longer, now that Jemima was so gracious. She went up-stairs with Ruth to help her to put on her things.

'Dear Jemima!' said Ruth, 'I am so glad to see you looking better to-night! You quite frightened me this morning, you looked so ill.'

'Did I?' replied Jemima. 'Oh, Ruth! I have been so unhappy lately. I want you to come and put me to-rights,' she continued, half smiling. 'You know I'm a sort of out-pupil of yours, though we are so nearly of an age. You ought to lecture me, and make me good.'

'Should I, dear?' said Ruth. 'I don't think I'm the one to do it.'

'Oh, yes! you are – you've done me good to-night.'

'Well, if I can do anything for you, tell me what it is?' asked Ruth, tenderly.

'Oh, not now – not now,' replied Jemima. 'I could not tell you here. It's a long story, and I don't know that I can tell you at all. Mamma might come up at any moment, and papa would be sure to ask what we had been talking about so long.'

'Take your own time, love,' said Ruth; 'only remember, as far as I can, how glad I am to help you.'

'You're too good, my darling!' said Jemima, fondly.

'Don't say so,' replied Ruth, earnestly, almost as if she were afraid. 'God knows I am not.'

'Well! we're none of us too good,' answered Jemima; 'I know that. But you *are* very good. Nay, I won't call you so, if it makes you look so miserable. But come away down-stairs.'

With the fragrance of Ruth's sweetness lingering about her, Jemima was her best self during the next half hour. Mr Bradshaw was more and more pleased, and raised the price of the silk, which he was going to give Ruth, sixpence a yard during the time. Mr Farquhar went home through the garden-way, happier than he had been this long time. He even caught himself humming the old refrain:

> On revient, on revient toujours,
> A ses premiers amours.[12]

But as soon as he was aware of what he was doing, he cleared away the remnants of the song into a cough, which was sonorous, if not perfectly real.

CHAPTER XXI

The next morning, as Jemima and her mother sat at their work, it came into the head of the former to remember her father's very marked way of thanking Ruth the evening before.

'What a favourite Mrs Denbigh is with papa!' said she. 'I am sure I don't wonder at it. Did you notice, mamma, how he thanked her for coming here last night?'

'Yes, dear; but I don't think it was all—' Mrs Bradshaw stopped short. She was never certain if it was right or wrong to say anything.

'Not all what?' asked Jemima, when she saw her mother was not going to finish the sentence.

'Not all because Mrs Denbigh came to tea here,' replied Mrs Bradshaw.

'Why, what else could he be thanking her for? What has she done?' asked Jemima, stimulated to curiosity by her mother's hesitating manner.

'I don't know if I ought to tell you,' said Mrs Bradshaw.

'Oh, very well!' said Jemima, rather annoyed.

'Nay, dear! your papa never said I was not to tell; perhaps I may.'

'Never mind! I don't want to hear,' in a piqued tone.

There was silence for a little while. Jemima was trying to think of something else, but her thoughts would revert to the wonder what Mrs Denbigh could have done for her father.

'I think I may tell you, though,' said Mrs Bradshaw, half questioning.

Jemima had the honour not to urge any confidence, but she was too curious to take any active step towards repressing it.

Mrs Bradshaw went on. 'I think you deserve to know. It is partly your doing that papa is so pleased with Mrs Denbigh. He is going to buy her a silk gown this morning, and I think you ought to know why.'

'Why?' asked Jemima.

'Because papa is so pleased to find that you mind what she says.'

'I mind what she says! to be sure I do, and always did. But why should papa give her a gown for that? I think he ought to give it me rather,' said Jemima, half laughing.

'I am sure he would, dear; he will give you one, I am certain, if you want one. He was so pleased to see you like your old self to Mr Farquhar last night. We neither of us could think what had come over you this last month; but now all seems right.'

A dark cloud came over Jemima's face. She did not like this close observation and constant comment upon her manners; and what had Ruth to do with it?

'I am glad you were pleased,' said she, very coldly. Then, after a pause, she added, 'But you have not told me what Mrs Denbigh had to do with my good behaviour.'

'Did not she speak to you about it?' asked Mrs Bradshaw, looking up.

'No; why should she? She has no right to criticise what I do. She would not be so impertinent,' said Jemima, feeling very uncomfortable and suspicious.

'Yes, love! she would have had a right, for papa had desired her to do it.'

'Papa desired her! What do you mean, mamma?'

'Oh, dear! I dare say I should not have told you,' said Mrs Bradshaw, perceiving, from Jemima's tone of voice, that something had gone wrong. 'Only you spoke as if it would be impertinent in Mrs Denbigh, and I am sure she would not do anything that was impertinent. You know, it would be but right for her to do what papa told her; and he said a great deal to her, the other day, about finding out why you were so cross, and bringing you right. And you are right now, dear!' said Mrs Bradshaw, soothingly, thinking that Jemima was annoyed (like a good child) at the recollection of how naughty she had been.

'Then papa is going to give Mrs Denbigh a gown because I was civil to Mr Farquhar last night.'

'Yes, dear!' said Mrs Bradshaw, more and more frightened at Jemima's angry manner of speaking – low-toned, but very indignant.

Jemima remembered, with smouldered anger, Ruth's pleading way of wiling her from her sullenness the night before. Management everywhere! but in this case it was peculiarly revolting; so much so, that she could hardly bear to believe that the seemingly-transparent Ruth had lent herself to it.

'Are you sure, mamma, that papa asked Mrs Denbigh to make me behave differently? It seems so strange.'

'I am quite sure. He spoke to her last Friday morning in the study. I remember it was Friday, because Mrs Dean was working here.'

Jemima remembered now that she had gone into the school-room on the Friday, and found her sisters lounging about, and wondering what papa could possibly want with Mrs Denbigh.

After this conversation, Jemima repulsed all Ruth's timid efforts to ascertain the cause of her disturbance, and to help her if she could. Ruth's tender, sympathising manner, as she saw Jemima daily looking more wretched, was distasteful to the latter in the highest degree. She could not say that Mrs Denbigh's conduct was positively wrong – it might even be quite right; but it was inexpressibly repugnant to her to think of her father consulting with a stranger (a week ago she almost considered Ruth as a sister) how to manage his daughter, so as to obtain the end he wished for; yes, even if that end was for her own good.

She was thankful and glad to see a brown-paper parcel lying on the hall-table, with a note in Ruth's handwriting, addressed to her father. She *knew* what it was, the grey silk dress. That she was sure Ruth would never accept.

No one henceforward could induce Jemima to enter into conversation with Mr Farquhar. She suspected manœuvring in the simplest actions, and was miserable in this constant state of suspicion. She would not allow herself to like Mr Farquhar, even when he said things the most after her own heart. She heard him, one evening, talking with her father about the principles of trade. Her father stood out for the keenest, sharpest work, consistent with honesty; if he had not been her father she would, perhaps, have thought some of his sayings inconsistent with true Christian honesty. He was for driving hard bargains, exacting interest and payment of just bills to a day. That was (he said) the only way in which trade could be conducted. Once allow a margin of uncertainty, or where feelings, instead of maxims, were to be the guide, and all hope of there ever being any good men of business was ended.

'Suppose a delay of a month in requiring payment might save a man's credit – prevent his becoming a bankrupt?' put in Mr Farquhar.

'I would not give it him. I would let him have money to set up again as soon as he had passed the Bankruptcy Court; if he never passed, I might, in some cases, make him an allowance, but I would always keep my justice and my charity separate.'

'And yet charity (in your sense of the word) degrades; justice, tempered with mercy and consideration, elevates.'

'That is not justice – justice is certain and inflexible. No! Mr Farquhar, you must not allow any Quixotic notions to mingle with your conduct as a tradesman.'

And so they went on; Jemima's face glowing with sympathy in all Mr Farquhar said; till once, on looking up suddenly with sparkling eyes, she saw a glance of her father's which told her, as plain as words can say, that he was watching the effect of Mr Farquhar's speeches upon his daughter. She was chilled thenceforward; she thought her father prolonged the argument, in order to call out those sentiments which he knew would most recommend his partner to his daughter. She would so fain have let herself love Mr Farquhar; but this constant manœuvring, in which she did not feel clear that he did not take a passive part, made her sick at heart. She even wished that they might not go through the form of pretending to try to gain her consent to the marriage, if it involved all this premeditated action and speech-making – such moving about of every one into their right places, like pieces at chess. She felt as if she would rather be bought openly, like an Oriental daughter, where no one is degraded in their own eyes by being parties to such a contract. The consequences of all this 'admirable management' of Mr Bradshaw's would have been very unfortunate to Mr Farquhar (who was innocent of all connivance in any of the plots – indeed, would have been as much annoyed at them as Jemima, had he been aware of them), but that the impression made upon him by Ruth on the evening I have so lately described, was deepened by the contrast which her behaviour made to Miss Bradshaw's on one or two more recent occasions.

There was no use, he thought, in continuing attentions so evidently distasteful to Jemima. To her, a young girl hardly out of the school-room, he probably appeared like an old man; and he might even lose the friendship with which she used to regard him, and which was, and ever would be, very dear to him, if he persevered in trying to be considered as a lover. He should always feel affectionately towards her; her very faults gave her an interest in his eyes, for which he had blamed himself most conscientiously and most uselessly when he was looking upon her as his future wife, but which the said conscience would learn to approve of when she sank down to the place of a young friend, over whom he might exercise a good and salutary interest. Mrs Denbigh, if not many months older in years, had known sorrow and cares so early that she was much older in character. Besides, her shy reserve, and her quiet daily walk within the lines of duty, were much in accordance with Mr Farquhar's notion of what a wife should be. Still, it was a wrench to take his affections away from Jemima. If she had not helped him to do so by every means in her power, he could never have accomplished it.

Yes! by every means in her power had Jemima alienated her lover, her beloved – for so he was in fact. And now her quick-sighted eyes saw he was gone for ever – past recall: for did not her jealous, sore heart feel, even before he himself was conscious of the fact, that he was drawn towards sweet, lovely, composed, and dignified Ruth – one who always thought before she spoke (as Mr Farquhar used to bid Jemima do) – who never was tempted by sudden impulse, but walked the world calm and self-governed. What now availed Jemima's reproaches, as she remembered the days when he had watched her with earnest, attentive eyes, as he now watched Ruth; and the times since, when, led astray by her morbid fancy, she had turned away from all his advances!

'It was only in March – last March, he called me "dear Jemima". Ah, don't I remember it well? The pretty nosegay of green-house flowers that he gave me in exchange for the wild daffodils – and how he seemed to care for the flowers I gave him – and how he looked at me, and thanked me – that is all gone and over now.'

Her sisters came in bright and glowing.

'Oh, Jemima, how nice and cool you are, sitting in this shady room!' (she had felt it even chilly). 'We have been such a long walk! We are so tired. It is so hot.'

'Why did you go, then?' said she.

'Oh! we wanted to go. We would not have stayed at home on any account. It has been so pleasant,' said Mary.

'We've been to Scaurside Wood, to gather wild-strawberries,' said Elizabeth. 'Such a quantity! We've left a whole basket-ful, in the dairy. Mr Farquhar says he'll teach us how to dress them in the way he learnt in Germany, if we can get him some hock.[1] Do you think papa will let us have some?'

'Was Mr Farquhar with you?' asked Jemima, a dull light coming into her eyes.

'Yes, we told him this morning that mamma wanted us to take some old linen to the lame man at Scaurside Farm, and that we meant to coax Mrs Denbigh to let us go into the wood and gather strawberries,' said Elizabeth.

'I thought he would make some excuse and come,' said the quick-witted Mary, as eager and thoughtlessness an observer of one love-affair as of another, and quite forgetting that, not many weeks ago, she had fancied an attachment between him and Jemima.

'Did you? I did not,' replied Elizabeth. 'At least I never thought about it. I was quite startled when I heard his horse's feet behind us on the road.'

'He said he was going to the farm, and could take our basket. Was not it kind of him?' Jemima did not answer, so Mary continued:

'You know it's a great pull up to the farm, and we were so hot already. The road was quite white and baked; it hurt my eyes terribly. I was so glad when Mrs Denbigh said we might turn into the wood. The light was quite green there, the branches are so thick overhead.'

'And there are whole beds of wild-strawberries,' said Elizabeth, taking up the tale now Mary was out of breath. Mary fanned herself with her bonnet, while Elizabeth went on:

'You know where the grey rock crops out, don't you, Jemima? Well, there was a complete carpet of strawberry runners. So pretty! And we could hardly step without treading the little bright scarlet berries under foot.'

'We did so wish for Leonard,' put in Mary.

'Yes! but Mrs Denbigh gathered a great many for him. And Mr Farquhar gave her all his.'

'I thought you said he had gone on to Dawson's farm,' said Jemima.

'Oh, yes! he just went up there; and then he left his horse there, like a wise man, and came to us in the pretty, cool, green wood. Oh, Jemima! it was so pretty – little flecks of light coming down here and there through the leaves, and quivering on the ground. You must go with us to-morrow.'

'Yes,' said Mary, 'we're going again to-morrow. We could not gather nearly all the strawberries.'

'And Leonard is to go too, to-morrow.'

'Yes! we thought of such a capital plan. That's to say, Mr Farquhar thought of it – we wanted to carry Leonard up the hill in a king's cushion,[2] but Mrs Denbigh would not hear of it.'

'She said it would tire us so; and yet she wanted him to gather strawberries!'

'And so,' interrupted Mary, for by this time the two girls were almost speaking together, 'Mr Farquhar is to bring him up before him on his horse.'

'You'll go with us, won't you, dear Jemima?' asked Elizabeth; 'it will be at —'

'No! I can't go,' said Jemima, abruptly. 'Don't ask me – I can't.'

The little girls were hushed into silence by her manner; for whatever she might be to those above her in age and position, to those below her Jemima was almost invariably gentle. She felt that they were wondering at her.

'Go up-stairs and take off your things. You know papa does not like you to come into this room in the shoes in which you have been out.'

She was glad to cut her sisters short in the details which they were so mercilessly inflicting – details which she must harden herself to, before she could hear them quietly and unmoved. She saw that she had lost her place as the first object in Mr Farquhar's eyes – a position she had hardly cared for while she was secure in the enjoyment of it; but the charm of it now was redoubled, in her acute sense of how she had forfeited it by her own doing, and her own fault. For if he were the cold, calculating man her father had believed him to be, and had represented him as being to her, would he care for a portionless widow[3] in humble circumstances like Mrs Denbigh; no money, no connexion, encumbered with her boy? The very action which proved Mr Farquhar to be lost to Jemima, reinstated him on his throne in her fancy. And she must go on in hushed quietness, quivering with every fresh token of his preference for another! That other, too, one so infinitely more worthy of him than herself; so that she could not have even the poor comfort of thinking, that he had no discrimination, and was throwing himself away on a common or worthless person. Ruth was beautiful, gentle, good, and conscientious. The hot colour flushed up into Jemima's sallow face as she became aware that, even while she acknowledged these excellencies on Mrs Denbigh's part, she hated her. The recollection of her marble face wearied her even to sickness; the tones of her low voice were irritating from their very softness. Her goodness, undoubted as it was, was more distasteful than many faults which had more savour of human struggle in them.

'What was this terrible demon in her heart?' asked Jemima's better angel. 'Was she, indeed, given up to possession? Was not this the old stinging hatred which had prompted so many crimes? The hatred of all sweet virtues which might win the love denied to us? The old anger that wrought in the elder brother's heart, till it ended in the murder of the gentle Abel, while yet the world was young?'

'Oh, God! help me! I did not know I was so wicked,' cried Jemima aloud in her agony. It had been a terrible glimpse into the dark lurid gulf – the capability for evil, in her heart. She wrestled with the demon, but he would not depart; it was to be a struggle whether or not she was to be given up to him, in this her time of sore temptation.

All the next day long, she sat and pictured the happy strawberry gathering going on, even then, in pleasant Scaurside Wood. Every touch of fancy which could heighten her idea of their enjoyment, and of Mr Farquhar's attention to the blushing, conscious Ruth – every such touch which would add a pang to her self-reproach and keen jealousy, was added by her imagination. She got up and walked about, to try and stop her over-busy fancy by bodily exercise. But she had eaten little all day, and was weak and faint in the intense heat of the sunny garden. Even the long grass walk under the filbert hedge, was parched and dry in the glowing August sun. Yet her sisters found her there when they returned, walking quickly up and down, as if to warm herself on some winter's day. They were very weary; and not half so communicative as on the day before, now that Jemima was craving for every detail to add to her agony.

'Yes! Leonard came up before Mr Farquhar. Oh! how hot it is, Jemima; do sit down, and I'll tell you about it, but I can't if you keep walking so!'

'I can't sit still to-day,' said Jemima, springing up from the turf as soon as she had sat down. 'Tell me! I can hear you while I walk about.'

'Oh! but I can't shout; I can hardly speak I am so tired. Mr Farquhar brought Leonard—'

'You've told me that before,' said Jemima, sharply.

'Well! I don't know what else to tell. Somebody had been since yesterday, and gathered nearly all the strawberries off the grey rock. Jemima! Jemima!' said Elizabeth, faintly, 'I am so dizzy – I think I am ill.'

The next minute the tired girl lay swooning on the grass. It was an outlet for Jemima's fierce energy. With a strength she had never again, and never had known before, she lifted up her fainting sister, and bidding Mary run and clear the way, she carried her in through the open garden-door, up the wide old-fashioned stairs, and laid her on the bed in her own room, where the breeze from the window came softly and pleasantly through the green shade of the vine-leaves and jessamine.

'Give me the water. Run for mamma, Mary,' said Jemima, as she saw that the fainting-fit did not yield to the usual remedy of a horizontal position, and the water-sprinkling.

'Dear! dear Lizzie!' said Jemima, kissing the pale, unconscious face. 'I think you loved me, darling.'

The long walk on the hot day had been too much for the delicate Elizabeth, who was fast outgrowing her strength. It was many days before she regained any portion of her spirit and vigour. After that fainting-fit, she lay listless and weary, without appetite or interest, through the long sunny autumn weather, on the bed or on the couch

in Jemima's room, whither she had been carried at first. It was a comfort
to Mrs Bradshaw to be able at once to discover what it was that had
knocked up Elizabeth; she did not rest easily until she had settled upon
a cause for every ailment or illness in the family. It was a stern consolation
to Mr Bradshaw, during his time of anxiety respecting his daughter, to
be able to blame somebody. He could not, like his wife, have taken
comfort from an inanimate fact; he wanted the satisfaction of feeling
that some one had been in fault, or else this never could have happened.
Poor Ruth did not need his implied reproaches. When she saw her
gentle Elizabeth lying feeble and languid, her heart blamed her for
thoughtlessness, so severely as to make her take all Mr Bradshaw's words
and hints as too light censure for the careless way in which, to please
her own child, she had allowed her two pupils to fatigue themselves
with such long walks. She begged hard to take her share of nursing.
Every spare moment she went to Mr Bradshaw's, and asked, with earnest
humility, to be allowed to pass them with Elizabeth and, as it was often
a relief to have her assistance, Mrs Bradshaw received these entreaties
very kindly, and desired her to go up-stairs, where Elizabeth's pale
countenance brightened when she saw her, but where Jemima sat in
silent annoyance that her own room was now become open ground for
one, whom her heart rose up against, to enter in and be welcomed.
Whether it was that Ruth, who was not an inmate of the house, brought
with her a fresher air, more change of thought to the invalid, I do not
know, but Elizabeth always gave her a peculiarly tender greeting; and
if she had sunk down into languid fatigue, in spite of all Jemima's
endeavours to interest her, she roused up into animation when Ruth
came in with a flower, a book, or a brown and ruddy pear, sending
out the warm fragrance it retained from the sunny garden-wall at
Chapel-house.

The jealous dislike which Jemima was allowing to grow up in her
heart against Ruth was, as she thought, never shown in word or deed.
She was cold in manner, because she could not be hypocritical; but her
words were polite and kind in purport; and she took pains to make her
actions the same as formerly. But rule and line may measure out the
figure of a man; it is the soul that gives it life; and there was no soul, no
inner meaning, breathing out in Jemima's actions. Ruth felt the change
acutely. She suffered from it some time before she ventured to ask what
had occasioned it. But, one day, she took Miss Bradshaw by surprise,

when they were alone together for a few minutes, by asking her if she
had vexed her in any way, she was so changed. It is sad when friendship
has cooled so far as to render such a question necessary. Jemima went
rather paler than usual, and then made answer:

'Changed! How do you mean? How am I changed? What do I say
or do different from what I used to do?'

But the tone was so constrained and cold, that Ruth's heart sank
within her. She knew now, as well as words could have told her, that
not only had the old feeling of love passed away from Jemima, but that
it had gone unregretted, and no attempt had been made to recall it.
Love was very precious to Ruth now, as of old time. It was one of the
faults of her nature to be ready to make any sacrifices for those who
loved her, and to value affection almost above its price. She had yet to
learn the lesson, that it is more blessed to love than to be beloved;[4] and
lonely as the impressible years of her youth had been – without parents,
without brother or sister – it was, perhaps, no wonder that she clung
tenaciously to every symptom of regard, and could not relinquish the
love of any one without a pang.

The doctor who was called in to Elizabeth prescribed sea-air as the
best means of recruiting her strength. Mr Bradshaw, who liked to spend
money ostentatiously, went down straight to Abermouth,[5] and engaged
a house for the remainder of the autumn; for, as he told the medical
man, money was no object to him in comparison with his children's
health; and the doctor cared too little about the mode in which his
remedy was administered, to tell Mr Bradshaw that lodgings would
have done as well, or better, than the complete house he had seen fit
to take. For it was now necessary to engage servants, and take much
trouble, which might have been obviated, and Elizabeth's removal
effected more quietly and speedily, if she had gone into lodgings. As it
was, she was weary of hearing all the planning and talking, and deciding
and undeciding, and re-deciding, before it was possible for her to go.
Her only comfort was in the thought, that dear Mrs Denbigh was to go
with her.

It had not been entirely by way of pompously spending his money
that Mr Bradshaw had engaged this sea-side house. He was glad to get
his little girls and their governess out of the way; for a busy time was
impending, when he should want his head clear for electioneering
purposes,[6] and his house clear for electioneering hospitality. He was the

mover of a project for bringing forward a man, on the Liberal and
Dissenting interest, to contest the election with the old Tory member,
who had on several successive occasions walked over the course,[7] as he
and his family owned half the town, and votes and rent were paid alike
to the landlord.

Kings of Eccleston had Mr Cranworth and his ancestors been this
many a long year; their right was so little disputed that they never
thought of acknowledging the allegiance so readily paid to them. The
old feudal feeling between landowner and tenant did not quake prophetically[8] at the introduction of manufactures; the Cranworth family ignored
the growing power of the manufacturers, more especially as the principal
person engaged in the trade was a Dissenter. But notwithstanding this
lack of patronage from the one great family in the neighbourhood, the
business flourished, increased, and spread wide; and the Dissenting head
thereof looked around, about the time of which I speak, and felt himself
powerful enough to defy the great Cranworth interest even in their
hereditary stronghold, and, by so doing, avenge the slights of many
years – slights which rankled in Mr Bradshaw's mind as much as if he
did not go to chapel twice every Sunday, and pay the largest pew-rent[9]
of any member of Mr Benson's congregation.

Accordingly, Mr Bradshaw had applied to one of the Liberal parliamentary agents[10] in London – a man whose only principle was to do
wrong on the Liberal side; he would not act, right or wrong, for a Tory,
but for a Whig the latitude of his conscience had never yet been
discovered. It was possible Mr Bradshaw was not aware of the character
of this agent; at any rate, he knew he was the man for his purpose,
which was to hear of some one who would come forward as a candidate
for the representation of Eccleston on the Dissenting interest.

'There are in round numbers about six hundred voters,' said he;
'two hundred are decidedly in the Cranworth interest – dare not offend
Mr Cranworth, poor souls! Two hundred more we may calculate upon
as pretty certain – factory hands, or people connected with our trade
in some way or another – who are indignant at the stubborn way in
which Cranworth has contested the right of water;[11] two hundred are
doubtful.'

'Don't much care either way,' said the parliamentary agent. 'Of
course, we must make them care.'

Mr Bradshaw rather shrunk from the knowing look with which this was said. He hoped that Mr Pilson did not mean to allude to bribery; but he did not express this hope, because he thought it would deter the agent from using this means, and it was possible it might prove to be the only way. And if he (Mr Bradshaw) once embarked on such an enterprise, there must be no failure. By some expedient or another, success must be certain, or he could have nothing to do with it.

The parliamentary agent was well accustomed to deal with all kinds and shades of scruples. He was most at home with men who had none; but still he could allow for human weakness; and he perfectly understood Mr Bradshaw.

'I have a notion I know of a man who will just suit your purpose. Plenty of money – does not know what to do with it, in fact – tired of yachting, travelling, wants something new. I heard, through some of the means of intelligence I employ, that not very long ago he was wishing for a seat in Parliament.'

'A Liberal?' said Mr Bradshaw.

'Decidedly. Belongs to a family who were in the Long Parliament[12] in their day.'

Mr Bradshaw rubbed his hands.

'Dissenter?' asked he.

'No, no! Not so far as that. But very lax Church.'

'What is his name?' asked Mr Bradshaw, eagerly.

'Excuse me. Until I am certain that he would like to come forward for Eccleston, I think I had better not mention his name.'

The anonymous gentleman did like to come forward, and his name proved to be Donne. He and Mr Bradshaw had been in correspondence during all the time of Mr Ralph Cranworth's illness, and when he died, everything was arranged ready for a start, even before the Cranworths had determined who should keep the seat warm till the eldest son came of age, for the father was already member for the county.[13] Mr Donne was to come down to canvass in person, and was to take up his abode at Mr Bradshaw's; and therefore it was that the sea-side house, within twenty miles' distance of Eccleston, was found to be so convenient as an infirmary and nursery for those members of his family who were likely to be useless, if not positive encumbrances, during the forthcoming election.

CHAPTER XXII

Jemima did not know whether she wished to go to Abermouth or not. She longed for change. She wearied of the sights and sounds of home. But yet she could not bear to leave the neighbourhood of Mr Farquhar; especially as, if she went to Abermouth, Ruth would in all probability be left to take her holiday at home.

When Mr Bradshaw decided that she was to go, Ruth tried to feel glad that he gave her the means of repairing her fault towards Elizabeth; and she resolved to watch over the two girls most faithfully and carefully, and to do all in her power to restore the invalid to health. But a tremor came over her whenever she thought of leaving Leonard; she had never quitted him for a day, and it seemed to her as if her brooding, constant care, was his natural and necessary shelter from all evils – from very death itself. She would not go to sleep at nights, in order to enjoy the blessed consciousness of having him near her; when she was away from him teaching her pupils, she kept trying to remember his face, and print it deep on her heart, against the time when days and days would elapse without her seeing that little darling countenance. Miss Benson would wonder to her brother that Mr Bradshaw did not propose that Leonard should accompany his mother; he only begged her not to put such an idea into Ruth's head, as he was sure Mr Bradshaw had no thoughts of doing any such thing, yet to Ruth it might be a hope, and then a disappointment. His sister scolded him for being so cold-hearted; but he was full of sympathy, although he did not express it, and made some quiet little sacrifices in order to set himself at liberty to take Leonard a long walking expedition on the day when his mother left Eccleston.

Ruth cried until she could cry no longer, and felt very much ashamed of herself as she saw the grave and wondering looks of her pupils, whose only feeling on leaving home was delight at the idea of Abermouth, and into whose minds the possibility of death to any of their beloved ones never entered. Ruth dried her eyes, and spoke cheerfully as soon as she caught the perplexed expression of their faces; and by the time they arrived at Abermouth, she was as much delighted with all the new scenery as they were, and found it hard work to resist their entreaties to go rambling out on the sea-shore at once; but Elizabeth had undergone more fatigue that day, than she had had before for many weeks, and Ruth was determined to be prudent.

Meanwhile, the Bradshaws' house at Eccleston was being rapidly adapted for electioneering hospitality. The partition-wall between the un-used drawing-room and the school-room was broken down, in order to admit of folding-doors; the 'ingenious' upholsterer of the town (and what town does not boast of the upholsterer full of contrivances and resources, in opposition to the upholsterer of steady capital and no imagination, who looks down with uneasy contempt on ingenuity?) had come in to give his opinion, that 'nothing could be easier than to convert a bath-room into a bedroom, by the assistance of a little drapery to conceal the shower-bath,' the string of which was to be carefully concealed, for fear that the unconscious occupier of the bath-bed might innocently take it for a bell-rope. The professional cook of the town had been already engaged to take up her abode for a month at Mr Bradshaw's, much to the indignation of Betsy, who became a vehement partisan of Mr Cranworth, as soon as ever she heard of the plan of her deposition from sovereign authority in the kitchen, in which she had reigned supreme for fourteen years. Mrs Bradshaw sighed and bemoaned herself in all her leisure moments, which were not many, and wondered why their house was to be turned into an inn for this Mr Donne, when everybody knew that the 'George' was good enough for the Cranworths, who never thought of asking the electors to the Hall; – and they had lived at Cranworth ever since Julius Cæsar's time,[1] and if that was not being an old family, she did not know what was. The excitement soothed Jemima. There was something to do. It was she who planned with the upholsterer; it was she who soothed Betsy into angry silence; it was she who persuaded her mother to lie down and rest, while she herself went out to buy the heterogeneous things required to make the family and house presentable to Mr Donne, and his precursor – the friend of the parliamentary agent. This latter gentleman never appeared himself on the scene of action, but pulled all the strings notwithstanding. The friend was a Mr Hickson, a lawyer – a briefless barrister,[2] some people called him; but he himself professed a great disgust to the law, as a 'great sham', which involved an immensity of underhand action, and truckling and time-serving, and was perfectly encumbered by useless forms and ceremonies, and dead obsolete words. So, instead of putting his shoulder to the wheel to reform the law, he talked eloquently against it, in such a high-priest style,[3] that it was occasionally a matter of surprise how he could ever have made a friend of the parliamentary agent before mentioned. But, as Mr Hickson himself said, it was the very corruptness of the law which he was fighting against, in doing all he could to effect the return of certain members to Parliament; these certain members being pledged to effect a reform in the law, according to Mr Hickson. And, as he once observed confidentially, 'If you had to destroy a hydra-headed monster,[4] would you measure swords with the demon as if he were a gentleman? Would you not rather seize the first weapon that came to hand? And so do I. My great object in life, sir, is to reform the law of England, sir. Once get a majority of Liberal members into the House, and the thing is done. And I consider myself justified, for so high – for, I may say, so holy – an end, in using men's weaknesses to work out my purpose. Of course, if men were angels, or even immaculate – men invulnerable to bribes, we would not bribe.'

'Could you?' asked Jemima, for the conversation took place at Mr Bradshaw's dinner-table, where a few friends were gathered together to meet Mr Hickson; and among them was Mr Benson.

'We neither would nor could,' said the ardent barrister, disregarding in his vehemence the point of the question, and floating on over the bar of argument into the wide ocean of his own eloquence: 'As it is – as the world stands, they who would succeed even in good deeds, must come down to the level of expediency; and therefore, I say once more, if Mr Donne is the man for your purpose, and your purpose is a good one, a lofty one, a holy one' (for Mr Hickson remembered the Dissenting character of his little audience, and privately considered the introduction of the word 'holy' a most happy hit), 'then, I say, we must put all the squeamish scruples which might befit Utopia, or some such place, on one side, and treat men as they are. If they are avaricious, it is not we who have made them so; but as we have to do with them, we must consider their failings in dealing with them; if they have been careless or extravagant, or have had their little peccadilloes, we must administer the screw.[5] The glorious reform of the law will justify, in my idea, all means to obtain the end – that law, from the profession of which I have withdrawn myself from perhaps a too scrupulous conscience!' he concluded softly to himself.

'We are not to do evil that good may come,' said Mr Benson. He was startled at the deep sound of his own voice as he uttered these words; but he had not been speaking for some time, and his voice came forth strong and unmodulated.

'True, sir; most true,' said Mr Hickson, bowing. 'I honour you for the observation.' And he profited by it, insomuch that he confined his further remarks on elections to the end of the table, where he sat near Mr Bradshaw, and one or two equally eager, though not equally influential partisans of Mr Donne's. Meanwhile Mr Farquhar took up Mr Benson's quotation, at the end where he and Jemima sat near to Mrs Bradshaw and him.

'But in the present state of the world, as Mr Hickson says, it is rather difficult to act upon that precept.'

'Oh, Mr Farquhar!' said Jemima, indignantly, the tears springing to her eyes with a feeling of disappointment. For she had been chafing under all that Mr Hickson had been saying, perhaps the more for one or two attempts on his part at a flirtation with the daughter of his wealthy host, which she resented with all the loathing of a pre-occupied heart; and she had longed to be a man, to speak out her wrath at this paltering with right and wrong. She had felt grateful to Mr Benson for his one, clear, short precept, coming down with a divine force against which there was no appeal; and now to have Mr Farquhar taking the side of expediency! It was too bad.

'Nay, Jemima!' said Mr Farquhar, touched, and secretly flattered by the visible pain his speech had given. 'Don't be indignant with me till I have explained myself a little more. I don't understand myself yet; and it is a very intricate question, or so it appears to me, which I was going to put, really, earnestly, and humbly, for Mr Benson's opinion. Now, Mr Benson, may I ask, if you always find it practicable to act strictly in accordance with that principle? For if you do not, I am sure no man living can! Are there not occasions when it is absolutely necessary to wade through evil to good?[6] I am not speaking in the careless, presumptuous way of that man yonder,' said he, lowering his voice, and addressing himself to Jemima more exclusively, 'I am really anxious to hear what Mr Benson will say on the subject, for I know no one to whose candid opinion I should attach more weight.'

But Mr Benson was silent. He did not see Mrs Bradshaw and Jemima leave the room. He was really, as Mr Farquhar supposed him, completely absent, questioning himself as to how far his practice tallied with his principle. By degrees he came to himself; he found the conversation still turned on the election; and Mr Hickson, who felt that he had jarred against the little minister's principles, and yet knew, from the *carte du pays*[7] which the scouts of the parliamentary agent had given him, that Mr Benson was a person to be conciliated, on account of his influence over many of the working people, began to ask him questions with an air of deferring to superior knowledge, that almost surprised Mr Bradshaw, who had been accustomed to treat 'Benson' in a very different fashion, of civil condescending indulgence, just as one listens to a child who can have had no opportunities of knowing better.

At the end of a conversation that Mr Hickson held with Mr Benson, on a subject in which the latter was really interested, and on which he had expressed himself at some length, the young barrister turned to Mr Bradshaw, and said very audibly:

'I wish Donne had been here. This conversation during the last half hour would have interested him almost as much as it has done me.'

Mr Bradshaw little guessed the truth, that Mr Donne was, at that very moment, coaching up[8] the various subjects of public interest at Eccleston, and privately cursing the particular subject on which Mr Benson had been holding forth, as being an unintelligible piece of Quixotism; or the leading Dissenter of the town need not have experienced a pang of jealousy, at the possible future admiration his minister might excite in the possible future member for Eccleston. And if Mr Benson had been clairvoyant, he need not have made an especial subject of gratitude out of the likelihood that he might have an opportunity of so far interesting Mr Donne in the condition of the people of Eccleston as to induce him to set his face against any attempts at bribery.

Mr Benson thought of this, half the night through; and ended by determining to write a sermon on the Christian view of political duties, which might be good for all, both electors and member, to hear on the eve of an election. For Mr Donne was expected at Mr Bradshaw's before the next Sunday; and, of course, as Mr and Miss Benson had settled it, he would appear at the chapel with them on that day. But the stinging conscience refused to be quieted. No present plan of usefulness allayed the aching remembrance of the evil he had done that good might come. Not even the look of Leonard, as the early dawn fell on him, and Mr Benson's sleepless eyes saw the rosy glow on his firm round cheeks; his open mouth, through which the soft long-drawn breath came gently quivering; and his eyes not fully shut, but closed to outward sight – not even the aspect of the quiet innocent child could soothe the troubled spirit.

Leonard and his mother dreamt of each other that night. Her dream of him was one of undefined terror – terror so great that it wakened her up, and she strove not to sleep again, for fear that ominous ghastly dream should return. He, on the contrary, dreamt of her sitting watching and smiling by his bedside, as her gentle self had been many a morning; and when she saw him awake (so it fell out in the dream), she smiled still more sweetly, and bending down she kissed him, and then spread out large, soft, white-feathered wings (which in no way surprised her child – he seemed to have known they were there all along), and sailed away through the open window far into the blue sky of a summer's day. Leonard wakened up then, and remembered how far away she really was – far more distant and inaccessible than the beautiful blue sky to which she had betaken herself in his dream – and cried himself to sleep again.

In spite of her absence from her child, which made one great and abiding sorrow, Ruth enjoyed her sea-side visit exceedingly. In the first place, there was the delight of seeing Elizabeth's daily and almost hourly improvement. Then, at the doctor's express orders, there were so few lessons to be done, that there was time for the long-exploring rambles, which all three delighted in. And when the rain came on and the storms blew, the house with its wild sea-views was equally delightful. It was a large house, built on the summit of a rock, which nearly overhung the shore below; there was, to be sure, a series of zig-zag tacking paths down the face of this rock, but from the house they could not be seen. Old or delicate people would have considered the situation bleak and exposed; indeed, the present proprietor wanted to dispose of it on this very account; but by its present inhabitants, this exposure and bleakness were called by other names, and considered as charms. From every part of the rooms, they saw the grey storms gather on the sea horizon, and put themselves in marching array; and soon the march became a sweep, and the great dome of the heavens was covered with the lurid clouds, between which and the vivid green earth below there seemed to come a purple atmosphere, making the very threatening beautiful; and by-and-by the house was wrapped in sheets of rain, shutting out sky and sea, and inland view; till, of a sudden, the storm was gone by, and the heavy rain-drops glistened in the sun as they hung on leaf and grass, and the 'little birds sang east, and the little birds sang west,'[9] and there was a pleasant sound of running waters all abroad.[10]

'Oh! if papa would but buy this house!' exclaimed Elizabeth, after one such storm, which she had watched silently from the very beginning of the 'little cloud no bigger than a man's hand'.[11]

'Mamma would never like it, I am afraid,' said Mary. 'She would call our delicious gushes of air, draughts, and think we should catch cold.'

'Jemima would be on our side. But how long Mrs Denbigh is! I hope she was near enough to the post-office when the rain came on!'

Ruth had gone to 'the shop' in the little village, about half a mile distant, where all letters were left till fetched. She only expected one, but that one was to tell her of Leonard. She, however, received two; the unexpected one was from Mr Bradshaw, and the news it contained was, if possible, a greater surprise than the letter itself. Mr Bradshaw informed her, that he planned arriving by dinner-time the following Saturday, at Eagle's Crag; and more, that he intended bringing Mr Donne and one or two other gentlemen with him, to spend the Sunday there! The letter went on to give every possible direction regarding the household preparations. The dinner-hour was fixed to be at six,[12] but, of course, Ruth and the girls would have dined long before. The (professional) cook would arrive the day before, laden with all the provisions that could not be obtained on the spot. Ruth was to engage a waiter from the inn, and this it was that detained her so long. While she sat in the little parlour, awaiting the coming of the landlady, she could not help wondering why Mr Bradshaw was bringing this strange gentleman to spend two days at Abermouth, and thus giving himself so much trouble and fuss of preparation.

There were so many small reasons that went to make up the large one which had convinced Mr Bradshaw of the desirableness of this step, that it was not likely that Ruth should guess at one half of them. In the first place, Miss Benson, in the pride and fulness of her heart, had told Mrs Bradshaw what her brother had told her; how he meant to preach upon the Christian view of the duties involved in political rights; and as, of course, Mrs Bradshaw had told Mr Bradshaw, he began to dislike the idea of attending chapel on that Sunday at all; for he had an uncomfortable idea that by the Christian standard – that divine test of the true and pure – bribery would not be altogether approved of; and yet he was tacitly coming round to the understanding that 'packets'[13] would be required, for what purpose both he and Mr Donne were to be supposed to remain ignorant. But it would be very awkward, so near to the time, if he were to be clearly convinced that bribery, however disguised by names and words, was in plain terms a sin. And yet he knew Mr Benson had once or twice convinced him against his will of certain things, which he had thenceforward found it impossible to do, without such great uneasiness of mind, that he had left off doing them, which was sadly against his interest. And if Mr Donne (whom he had intended to take with him to chapel, as fair Dissenting prey) should also become convinced, why the Cranworths would win the day, and he should be the laughing-stock of Eccleston. No! in this one case bribery must be allowed – was allowable; but it was a great pity human nature was so corrupt, and if his member succeeded, he would double his subscription to the schools, in order that the next generation might be taught better. There were various other reasons, which strengthened Mr Bradshaw in the bright idea of going down to Abermouth for the Sunday; some connected with the out-of-door politics, and some with the domestic. For instance, it had been the plan of the house to have a cold dinner on the Sundays[14] – Mr Bradshaw had piqued himself on this strictness – and yet he had an instinctive feeling that Mr Donne was not quite the man to partake of cold meat for conscience' sake with cheerful indifference to his fare.

Mr Donne had, in fact, taken the Bradshaw household a little by surprise. Before he came, Mr Bradshaw had pleased himself with thinking, that more unlikely things had happened than the espousal of his daughter with the member of a small borough. But this pretty airy bubble burst as soon as he saw Mr Donne; and its very existence was forgotten in less than half an hour, when he felt the quiet but incontestible difference of rank and standard that there was, in every respect, between his guest and his own family. It was not through any circumstance so palpable, and possibly accidental, as the bringing down a servant, whom Mr Donne seemed to consider as much a matter of course as a carpet-bag (though the smart gentleman's arrival 'fluttered the Volscians in Corioli'[15] considerably more than his gentle-spoken master's). It was nothing like this; it was something indescribable – a quiet being at ease, and expecting every one else to be so – an attention to women, which was so habitual as to be unconsciously exercised to those subordinate persons in Mr Bradshaw's family – a happy choice of simple and expressive words, some of which it must be confessed were slang, but fashionable slang, and that makes all the difference – a measured, graceful way of utterance, with a style of pronunciation quite different to that of Eccleston. All these put together make but a part of the indescribable whole which unconsciously affected Mr Bradshaw, and established Mr Donne in his estimation as a creature quite different to any he had seen before, and as most unfit to mate with Jemima. Mr Hickson, who had appeared as a model of gentlemanly ease before Mr Donne's arrival, now became vulgar and coarse in Mr Bradshaw's eyes. And yet, such was the charm of that languid, high-bred manner, that Mr Bradshaw 'cottoned'[16] (as he expressed it to Mr Farquhar) to his new candidate at once. He was only afraid lest Mr Donne was too indifferent to all things under the sun,[17] to care whether he gained or lost the election; but he was reassured after the first conversation they had together on the subject. Mr Donne's eye lightened with an eagerness that was almost fierce, though his tones were as musical, and nearly as slow as ever; and when Mr Bradshaw alluded distantly to 'probable expenses' and 'packets,' Mr Donne replied:

'Oh, of course! disagreeable necessity! Better speak as little about such things as possible; other people can be found to arrange all the dirty work. Neither you nor I would like to soil our fingers by it, I am sure. Four thousand pounds are in Mr Pilson's hands, and I shall never inquire what becomes of them; they may, very probably, be absorbed in the law expenses, you know. I shall let it be clearly understood from the hustings, that I most decidedly disapprove of bribery, and leave the rest to Hickson's management. He is accustomed to these sort of things. I am not.'

Mr Bradshaw was rather perplexed by this want of bustling energy on the part of the new candidate; and if it had not been for the four thousand pounds aforesaid, would have doubted whether Mr Donne cared sufficiently for the result of the election. Jemima thought differently. She watched her father's visitor attentively, with something like the curious observation which a naturalist bestows on a new species of animal.

'Do you know what Mr Donne reminds me of, mamma?' said she,

one day, as the two sat at work, while the gentlemen were absent canvassing.

'No! he is not like anybody I ever saw. He quite frightens me, by being so ready to open the door for me if I am going out of the room, and by giving me a chair when I come in. I never saw any one like him. Who is it, Jemima?'

'Not any person – not any human being, mamma,' said Jemima, half smiling. 'Do you remember our stopping at Wakefield once, on our way to Scarborough, and there were horse-races going on some-where, and some of the racers were in the stables at the inn where we dined?'

'Yes! I remember it; but what about that?'

'Why Richard, somehow, knew one of the jockeys, and, as we were coming in from our ramble through the town, this man, or boy, asked us to look at one of the racers he had the charge of.'

'Well, my dear!'

'Well, mamma! Mr Donne is like that horse!'

'Nonsense, Jemima; you must not say so. I don't know what your father would say, if he heard you likening Mr Donne to a brute.'

'Brutes are sometimes very beautiful, mamma. I am sure I should think it a compliment to be likened to a race-horse, such as the one we saw. But the thing in which they are alike, is the sort of repressed eagerness in both.'

'Eager! Why, I should say there never was any one cooler than Mr Donne. Think of the trouble your papa has had this month past, and then remember the slow way in which Mr Donne moves when he is going out to canvass, and the low drawling voice in which he questions the people who bring him intelligence. I can see your papa standing by, ready to shake them to get out their news.'

'But Mr Donne's questions are always to the point, and force out the grain without the chaff. And look at him, if any one tells him ill news about the election! Have you never seen a dull red light come into his eyes? That is like my race-horse. Her flesh quivered all over, at certain sounds and noises which had some meaning to her; but she stood quite still, pretty creature! Now, Mr Donne is just as eager as she was, though he may be too proud to show it. Though he seems so gentle, I almost think he is very headstrong in following out his own will.'

'Well! don't call him like a horse again, for I am sure papa would not like it. Do you know, I thought you were going to say he was like little Leonard, when you asked me who he was like.'

'Leonard! O mamma! he is not in the least like Leonard. He is twenty times more like my race-horse.'

'Now, my dear Jemima, do be quiet. Your father thinks racing so wrong, that I am sure he would be very seriously displeased if he were to hear you.'

To return to Mr Bradshaw, and to give one more of his various reasons for wishing to take Mr Donne to Abermouth. The wealthy Eccleston manufacturer was uncomfortably impressed with an indefinable sense of inferiority to his visitor. It was not in education, for Mr Bradshaw was a well-educated man; it was not in power, for, if he chose, the present object of Mr Donne's life might be utterly defeated; it did not arise from anything overbearing in manner, for Mr Donne was habitually polite and courteous, and was just now anxious to propitiate his host, whom he looked upon as a very useful man. Whatever this sense of inferiority arose from, Mr Bradshaw was anxious to relieve himself of it, and imagined that if he could make more display of his wealth his object would be obtained. Now his house in Eccleston was old-fashioned and ill-calculated to exhibit money's worth. His mode of living, though strained to a high pitch just at this time, he became aware was no more than Mr Donne was accustomed to every day of his life. The first day at dessert, some remark (some opportune remark, as Mr Bradshaw in his innocence had thought) was made regarding the price of pine-apples, which was rather exorbitant that year, and Mr Donne asked Mrs Bradshaw, with quiet surprise, if they had no pinery,[18] as if to be without a pinery were indeed a depth of pitiable destitution. In fact, Mr Donne had been born and cradled in all that wealth could purchase, and so had his ancestors before him for so many generations, that refinement and luxury seemed the natural condition of man, and they that dwelt without were in the position of monsters. The absence was noticed; but not the presence.

Now Mr Bradshaw knew that the house and grounds of Eagle's Crag were exorbitantly dear, and yet he really thought of purchasing them. And as one means of exhibiting his wealth, and so raising himself up to the level of Mr Donne, he thought that if he could take the latter down to Abermouth, and show him the place for which, 'because his little girls had taken a fancy to it,' he was willing to give the fancy-price of fourteen thousand pounds, he should at last make those half-shut dreamy eyes open wide, and their owner confess that, in wealth at least, the Eccleston manufacturer stood on a par with him.

All these mingled motives caused the determination which made Ruth sit in the little inn-parlour of Abermouth during the wild storm's passage.

She wondered if she had fulfilled all Mr Bradshaw's directions. She looked at the letter. Yes! everything was done. And now home with her news, through the wet lane, where the little pools by the roadside reflected the deep blue sky and the round white clouds with even deeper blue and clearer white; and the rain-drops hung so thick on the trees, that even a little bird's flight was enough to shake them down in a bright shower as of rain. When she told the news, Mary exclaimed:

'Oh, how charming! Then we shall see this new member after all!' while Elizabeth added:

'Yes! I shall like to do that. But where must we be? Papa will want the dining-room and this room, and where must we sit?'

'Oh!' said Ruth, 'in the dressing-room next to my room. All that your papa wants always, is that you are quiet and out of the way.'

CHAPTER XXIII

Saturday came. Torn, ragged clouds were driven across the sky. It was not a becoming day for the scenery, and the little girls regretted it much. First they hoped for a change at twelve o'clock, and then at the afternoon tide-turning. But at neither time did the sun show his face.

'Papa will never buy this dear place,' said Elizabeth, sadly, as she watched the weather. 'The sun is everything to it. The sea looks quite leaden to-day, and there is no sparkle on it. And the sands, that were so yellow and sun-speckled on Thursday, are all one dull brown now.'

'Never mind! to-morrow may be better,' said Ruth, cheerily.

'I wonder what time they will come at?' inquired Mary.

'Your papa said they would be at the station[1] at five o'clock. And the landlady at the "Swan" said it would take them half an hour to get here.'

'And they are to dine at six?' asked Elizabeth.

'Yes,' answered Ruth. 'And I think if we had our tea half an hour earlier, at half-past four, and then went out for a walk, we should be nicely out of the way just during the bustle of the arrival and dinner; and we could be in the drawing-room ready against your papa came in after dinner.'

'Oh! that would be nice,' said they; and tea was ordered accordingly.

The south-westerly wind had dropped, and the clouds were stationary, when they went out on the sands. They dug little holes near the in-coming tide, and made canals to them from the water, and blew the light sea-foam against each other; and then stole on tiptoe near to the groups of grey and white sea-gulls, which despised their caution, flying softly and slowly away to a little distance as soon as they drew near. And in all this Ruth was as great a child as any. Only she longed for Leonard with a mother's longing, as indeed she did every day, and all hours of the day. By-and-by the clouds thickened yet more, and one or two drops of rain were felt. It was very little, but Ruth feared a shower for her delicate Elizabeth, and besides, the September evening was fast closing in the dark and sunless day. As they turned homewards in the rapidly increasing dusk, they saw three figures on the sand near the rocks, coming in their direction.

'Papa and Mr Donne!' exclaimed Mary. 'Now we shall see him!'

'Which do you make out is him?' asked Elizabeth.

'Oh! the tall one, to be sure. Don't you see how papa always turns to him, as if he was speaking to him, and not to the other?'

'Who is the other?' asked Elizabeth.

'Mr Bradshaw said that Mr Farquhar and Mr Hickson would come with him. But that is not Mr Farquhar, I am sure,' said Ruth.

The girls looked at each other, as they always did, when Ruth mentioned Mr Farquhar's name; but she was perfectly unconscious both of the look and of the conjectures which gave rise to it.

As soon as the two parties drew near, Mr Bradshaw called out in his strong voice:

'Well, my dears! we found there was an hour before dinner, so we came down upon the sands, and here you are.'

The tone of his voice assured them that he was in a bland and indulgent mood, and the two little girls ran towards him. He kissed them, and shook hands with Ruth; told his companions that these were the little girls who were tempting him to this extravagance of purchasing Eagle's Crag; and then, rather doubtfully, and because he saw that Mr Donne expected it, he introduced 'My daughters' governess, Mrs Denbigh.'

It was growing darker every moment, and it was time they should hasten back to the rocks, which were even now indistinct in the grey haze. Mr Bradshaw held a hand of each of his daughters, and Ruth walked alongside, the two strange gentlemen being on the outskirts of the party.

Mr Bradshaw began to give his little girls some home news. He told them that Mr Farquhar was ill, and could not accompany them; but Jemima and their mamma were quite well.

The gentleman nearest to Ruth spoke to her.

'Are you fond of the sea?' asked he. There was no answer, so he repeated his question in a different form.

'Do you enjoy staying by the sea-side, I should rather ask.'

The reply was 'Yes,' rather breathed out in a deep inspiration than spoken in a sound. The sands heaved and trembled beneath Ruth. The figures near her vanished into strange nothingness; the sounds of their voices were as distant sounds in a dream, while the echo of one voice thrilled through and through. She could have caught at his arm for support, in the awful dizziness which wrapped her up, body and soul. That voice! No! if name, and face, and figure, were all changed, that voice was the same which had touched her girlish heart, which had spoken most tender words of love, which had won, and wrecked her, and which she had last heard in the low mutterings of fever. She dared not look round to see the figure of him who spoke, dark as it was. She knew he was there – she heard him speak in the manner in which he used to address strangers years ago; perhaps she answered him, perhaps she did not – God knew. It seemed as if weights were tied to her feet – as if the steadfast rocks receded – as if time stood still; – it was so long, so terrible, that path across the reeling sand.

At the foot of the rocks they separated. Mr Bradshaw, afraid lest dinner should cool, preferred the shorter way for himself and his friends. On Elizabeth's account, the girls were to take the longer and easier path, which wound upwards through a rocky field, where larks' nests abounded, and where wild thyme and heather were now throwing out their sweets to the soft night-air.

The little girls spoke in eager discussion of the strangers. They appealed to Ruth, but Ruth did not answer, and they were too impatient to convince each other to repeat the question. The first little ascent from the sands to the field surmounted, Ruth sat down suddenly, and covered her face with her hands. This was so unusual – their wishes, their good, was so invariably the rule of motion or of rest in their walks – that the girls, suddenly checked, stood silent and affrighted in surprise. They were still more startled when Ruth wailed aloud some inarticulate words.

'Are you not well, dear Mrs Denbigh?' asked Elizabeth, gently, kneeling down on the grass by Ruth.

She sat facing the west. The low watery twilight was on her face as she took her hands away. So pale, so haggard, so wild and wandering a look, the girls had never seen on human countenance before.

'Well! what are you doing here with me? You should not be with me,' said she, shaking her head slowly.

They looked at each other.

'You are sadly tired,' said Elizabeth, soothingly. 'Come home, and let me help you to bed. I will tell papa you are ill, and ask him to send for a doctor.'

Ruth looked at her, as if she did not understand the meaning of her words. No more she did at first. But by-and-by the dulled brain began to think most vividly and rapidly, and she spoke in a sharp way which deceived the girls into a belief that nothing had been the matter.

'Yes! I was tired. I am tired. Those sands – oh! those sands, those weary, dreadful sands! But that is all over now. Only my heart aches still. Feel how it flutters and beats,' said she, taking Elizabeth's hand, and holding it to her side. 'I am quite well, though,' she continued, reading pity in the child's looks, as she felt the trembling, quivering beat. 'We will go straight to the dressing-room, and read a chapter; that will still my heart; and then I'll go to bed, and Mr Bradshaw will excuse me, I know, this one night. I only ask for one night. Put on your right frocks, dears, and do all you ought to do. But I know you will,' said she, bending down to kiss Elizabeth, and then, before she had done so, raising her head abruptly. 'You are good and dear girls – God keep you so!'

By a strong effort at self-command, she went onwards at an even pace, neither rushing nor pausing to sob and think. The very regularity of motion calmed her. The front and back doors of the house were on two sides, at right angles with each other. They all shrunk a little from the idea of going in at the front door, now that the strange gentlemen were about, and, accordingly, they went through the quiet farm-yard right into the bright, ruddy kitchen, where the servants were dashing about with the dinner things. It was a contrast in more than colour to the lonely dusky field, which even the little girls perceived; and the noise, the warmth, the very bustle of the servants, were a positive relief to Ruth, and for the time lifted off the heavy press of pent-up passion. A silent house, with moonlit rooms, or with a faint gloom brooding over the apartments, would have been more to be dreaded. Then, she must have given way, and cried out. As it was, she went up the old awkward back stairs, and into the room they were to sit in. There was no candle. Mary volunteered to go down for one; and when she returned she was full of the wonders of preparation in the drawing-room, and ready and eager to dress, so as to take her place there before the gentlemen had finished dinner. But she was struck by the strange paleness of Ruth's face, now that the light fell upon it.

'Stay up here, dear Mrs Denbigh! We'll tell papa you are tired, and are gone to bed.'

Another time Ruth would have dreaded Mr Bradshaw's displeasure; for it was an understood thing that no one was to be ill or tired in his household without leave asked, and cause given and assigned. But she never thought of that now. Her great desire was to hold quiet till she was alone. Quietness it was not – it was rigidity; but she succeeded in being rigid in look and movement, and went through her duties to Elizabeth (who preferred remaining with her up-stairs) with wooden precision. But her heart felt at times like ice, at times like burning fire; always a heavy, heavy weight within her. At last Elizabeth went to bed. Still Ruth dared not think. Mary would come up-stairs soon; and with a strange, sick, shrinking yearning, Ruth awaited her – and the crumbs of intelligence she might drop out about *him*. Ruth's sense of hearing was quickened to miserable intensity as she stood before the chimney-piece, grasping it tight with both hands – gazing into the dying fire, but seeing – not the dead grey embers, or the little sparks of vivid light that ran hither and thither among the wood-ashes – but an old farm-house, and climbing winding road, and a little golden breezy common, with a rural inn on the hill-top, far, far away. And through the thoughts of the past came the sharp sounds of the present – of three voices, one of which was almost silence, it was so hushed. Indifferent people would only have guessed that Mr Donne was speaking by the quietness in which the others listened; but Ruth heard the voice and many of the words, though they conveyed no idea to her mind. She was too much stunned even to feel curious to know to what they related. *He* spoke. That was her one fact.

Presently up came Mary, bounding, exultant. Papa had let her stay up one quarter of an hour longer, because Mr Hickson had asked. Mr Hickson was so clever! She did not know what to make of Mr Donne, he seemed such a dawdle. But he was very handsome. Had Ruth seen him? Oh, no! She could not, it was so dark on those stupid sands. Well, never mind, she would see him to-morrow. She *must* be well to-morrow. Papa seemed a good deal put out that neither she nor Elizabeth were in the drawing-room to-night; and his last words were, 'Tell Mrs Denbigh I hope' (and papa's 'hopes' always meant 'expect') 'she will be able to make breakfast at nine o'clock;' and then she would see Mr Donne.

That was all Ruth heard about him. She went with Mary into her bedroom, helped her to undress, and put the candle out. At length she was alone in her own room! At length!

But the tension did not give way immediately. She fastened her door, and threw open the window, cold and threatening as was the night. She tore off her gown; she put her hair back from her heated face. It seemed now as if she could not think – as if thought and emotion had been repressed so sternly that they would not come to relieve her stupified brain. Till all at once, like a flash of lightning, her life, past and present, was revealed to her to its minutest detail. And when she saw her very present 'Now,' the strange confusion of agony was too great to be borne, and she cried aloud. Then she was quite dead, and listened as to the sound of galloping armies.

'If I might see him! If I might see him! If I might just ask him why he left me; if I had vexed him in any way; it was so strange – so cruel! It was not him, it was his mother,' said she, almost fiercely, as if answering herself. 'Oh, God! but he might have found me out before this,' she continued, sadly. 'He did not care for me, as I did for him. He did not care for me at all,' she went on, wildly and sharply. 'He did me cruel harm. I can never again lift up my face in innocence. They think I have forgotten all, because I do not speak. Oh, darling love! am I talking against you?' asked she, tenderly. 'I am so torn and perplexed! You, who are the father of my child!'

But that very circumstance, full of such tender meaning in many cases, threw a new light into her mind. It changed her from the woman into the mother – the stern guardian of her child. She was still for a time, thinking. Then she began again, but in a low, deep voice.

'He left me. He might have been hurried off, but he might have inquired – he might have learnt and explained. He left me to bear the burden and the shame; and never cared to learn, as he might have done, of Leonard's birth. He has no love for his child, and I will have no love for him.'

She raised her voice while uttering this determination, and then, feeling her own weakness, she moaned out, 'Alas! alas!'

And then she started up, for all this time she had been rocking herself backwards and forwards as she sat on the ground, and began to pace the room with hurried steps.

'What am I thinking of? Where am I? I who have been praying these years and years to be worthy to be Leonard's mother. My God! What a depth of sin is in my heart! Why, the old time would be as white as snow to what it would be now, if I sought him out, and prayed for the explanation, which would re-establish him in my heart. I who have striven (or made a mock of trying) to learn God's holy will, in order to bring up Leonard into the full strength of a Christian – I who have taught his sweet innocent lips to pray, "Lead us not into temptation, but deliver us from evil;"[2] and yet, somehow, I've been longing to give him to his father, who is – who is –' she almost choked, till at last she cried sharp out, 'Oh, my God! I do believe Leonard's father is a bad man, and yet, oh! pitiful God, I love him; I cannot forget – I cannot!'

She threw her body half out of the window into the cold night air. The wind was rising, and came in great gusts. The rain beat down on her. It did her good. A still, calm night would not have soothed her as this did. The wild tattered clouds, hurrying past the moon, gave her a foolish kind of pleasure that almost made her smile a vacant smile. The blast-driven rain came on her again, and drenched her hair through and through. The words 'stormy wind fulfilling His word'[3] came into her mind.

She sat down on the floor. This time her hands were clasped round her knees. The uneasy rocking motion was stilled.

'I wonder if my darling is frightened with this blustering, noisy wind. I wonder if he is awake.'

And then her thoughts went back to the various times of old, when, affrighted by the weather – sounds so mysterious in the night – he had crept into her bed and clung to her, and she had soothed him, and sweetly awed him into stillness and childlike faith, by telling him of the goodness and power of God.

Of a sudden she crept to a chair, and there knelt as in the very presence of God, hiding her face, at first not speaking a word (for did He not know her heart), but by-and-by moaning out, amid her sobs and tears (and now for the first time she wept):

'Oh, my God, help me, for I am very weak. My God! I pray Thee be my rock and my strong fortress, for I of myself am nothing. If I ask in His name,[4] Thou wilt give it me. In the name of Jesus Christ I pray for strength to do Thy will!'

She could not think, or, indeed, remember anything but that she was weak, and God was strong, and 'a very present help in time of trouble';[5] and the wind rose yet higher, and the house shook and vibrated as, in measured time, the great and terrible gusts came from the four quarters of the heavens and blew around it, dying away in the distance with loud and unearthly wails, which were not utterly still before the sound of the coming blast was heard like the trumpets of the vanguard of the Prince of Air.[6]

There was a knock at the bedroom door – a little gentle knock, and a soft child's voice.

'Mrs Denbigh, may I come in, please? I am so frightened!'

It was Elizabeth. Ruth calmed her passionate breathing by one hasty draught of water, and opened the door to the timid girl.

'Oh, Mrs Denbigh! did you ever hear such a night? I am so frightened! and Mary sleeps so sound.'

Ruth was too much shaken to be able to speak all at once; but she took Elizabeth in her arms to reassure her. Elizabeth stood back.

'Why, how wet you are, Mrs Denbigh! and there's the window open, I do believe! Oh, how cold it is!' said she, shivering.

'Get into my bed, dear!' said Ruth.

'But do come too! The candle gives such a strange light with that long wick,⁷ and, somehow, your face does not look like you. Please, put the candle out, and come to bed. I am so frightened, and it seems as if I should be safer if you were by me.'

Ruth shut the window, and went to bed. Elizabeth was all shivering and quaking. To soothe her, Ruth made a great effort; and spoke of Leonard and his fears, and, in a low hesitating voice, she spoke of God's tender mercy, but very humbly, for she feared lest Elizabeth should think her better and holier than she was. The little girl was soon asleep, her fears forgotten; and Ruth, worn out by passionate emotion, and obliged to be still for fear of awaking her bedfellow, went off into a short slumber, through the depths of which the echoes of her waking sobs quivered up.

When she awoke, the grey light of autumnal dawn was in the room. Elizabeth slept on; but Ruth heard the servants about, and the early farm-yard sounds. After she had recovered from the shock of conscious-ness and recollection, she collected her thoughts with a stern calmness. He was here. In a few hours she must meet him. There was no escape, except through subterfuges and contrivances that were both false and cowardly. How it would all turn out she could not say, or even guess. But of one thing she was clear, and to one thing she would hold fast: that was, that, come what might, she would obey God's law, and, be the end of all what it might, she would say, 'Thy will be done!'⁸ She only asked for strength enough to do this when the time came. How the time would come – what speech or action would be requisite on her part, she did not know – she did not even try to conjecture. She left that in His hands.

She was icy cold, but very calm when the breakfast-bell rang. She went down immediately; because she felt that there was less chance of a recognition, if she were already at her place behind the tea-urn, and busied with the cups, than if she came in after all were settled. Her heart seemed to stand still, but she felt almost a strange exultant sense of power over herself. She felt, rather than saw, that he was not there. Mr Bradshaw and Mr Hickson were, and so busy talking election-politics that they did not interrupt their conversation even when they bowed to her. Her pupils sat one on each side of her. Before they were quite settled, and while the other two gentlemen yet hung over the fire, Mr

Donne came in. Ruth felt as if that moment was like death. She had a kind of desire to make some sharp sound, to relieve a choking sensation, but it was over in an instant, and she sat on very composed and silent – to all outward appearance, the very model of a governess who knew her place. And by-and-by she felt strangely at ease in her sense of power. She could even listen to what was being said. She had never dared as yet to look at Mr Donne, though her heart burnt to see him once again. He sounded changed. The voice had lost its fresh and youthful eagerness of tone, though in peculiarity of modulation it was the same. It could never be mistaken for the voice of another person. There was a good deal said at that breakfast, for none seemed inclined to hurry, although it was Sunday morning. Ruth was compelled to sit there, and it was good for her that she did. That half hour seemed to separate the present Mr Donne very effectively, from her imagination of what Mr Bellingham had been. She was no analyser; she hardly even had learnt to notice character; but she felt there was some strange difference between the people she had lived with lately and the man who now leant back in his chair, listening in a careless manner to the conversation, but never joining in, or expressing any interest in it, unless it somewhere, or somehow, touched him himself. Now, Mr Bradshaw always threw himself into a subject; it might be in a pompous, dogmatic sort of way, but he did do it, whether it related to himself or not; and it was part of Mr Hickson's trade to assume an interest if he felt it not.[9] But Mr Donne did neither the one nor the other. When the other two were talking of many of the topics of the day, he put his glass in his eye the better to examine into the exact nature of a cold game-pie at the other side of the table. Suddenly Ruth felt that his attention was caught by her. Until now, seeing his short-sightedness, she had believed herself safe; now her face flushed with a painful, miserable blush. But, in an instant, she was strong and quiet. She looked up straight at his face; and, as if this action took him aback, he dropped his glass, and began eating away with great diligence. She had seen him. He was changed, she knew not how. In fact, the expression, which had been only occasional formerly, when his worse self predominated, had become permanent. He looked restless and dissatisfied. But he was very handsome still; and her quick eye had recognised, with a sort of strange pride, that the eyes and mouth were like Leonard's. Although perplexed by the straightforward brave look she had sent right at him, he was not entirely baffled. He thought this

Mrs Denbigh was certainly like poor Ruth; but this woman was far handsomer. Her face was positively Greek; and then such a proud, superb turn of her head; quite queenly! A governess in Mr Bradshaw's family! Why, she might be a Percy or a Howard[10] for the grandeur of her grace! Poor Ruth! This woman's hair was darker, though; and she had less colour; altogether a more refined-looking person. Poor Ruth! and, for the first time for several years, he wondered what had become of her; though, of course, there was but one thing that could have happened, and perhaps it was as well he did not know her end, for most likely it would have made him very uncomfortable. He leant back in his chair, and, unobserved (for he would not have thought it gentlemanly to look so fixedly at her, if she or any one noticed him), he put up his glass again. She was speaking to one of her pupils, and did not see him.

By Jove! it must be she, though! There were little dimples came out about the mouth as she spoke, just like those he used to admire so much in Ruth, and which he had never seen in any one else – the sunshine without the positive movement of a smile. The longer he looked the more he was convinced; and it was with a jerk that he recovered himself enough to answer Mr Bradshaw's question, whether he wished to go to church or not.

'Church? How far – a mile? No, I think I shall perform my devotions at home to-day.'

He absolutely felt jealous when Mr Hickson sprang up to open the door, as Ruth and her pupils left the room. He was pleased to feel jealous again. He had been really afraid he was too much 'used-up'[11] for such sensations. But Hickson must keep his place. What he was paid for, was doing the talking to the electors, not paying attention to the ladies in their families. Mr Donne had noticed that Mr Hickson had tried to be gallant to Miss Bradshaw; let him, if he liked; but let him beware how he behaved to this fair creature, Ruth or no Ruth. It certainly was Ruth; only how the devil had she played her cards so well as to be the governess – the respected governess, in such a family as Mr Bradshaw's?

Mr Donne's movements were evidently to be the guide of Mr Hickson's. Mr Bradshaw always disliked going to church, partly from principle, partly because he never could find the places in the Prayer-book.[12] Mr Donne was in the drawing-room as Mary came down ready equipped; he was turning over the leaves of the large and handsome Bible. Seeing Mary, he was struck with a new idea.

'How singular it is,' said he, 'that the name of Ruth is so seldom chosen by those good people who go to the Bible before they christen their children. It is a very pretty name, I think.'

Mr Bradshaw looked up. 'Why, Mary!' said he, 'is not that Mrs Denbigh's name?'

'Yes, papa,' replied Mary, eagerly; 'and I know two other Ruths; there's Ruth Brown here, and Ruth Macartney at Eccleston.'

'And I have an aunt called Ruth, Mr Donne! I don't think your observation holds good. Besides my daughters' governess, I know three other Ruths.'

'Oh! I have no doubt I was wrong. It was just a speech of which one perceives the folly the moment it is made.'

But, secretly, he rejoiced with a fierce joy over the success of his device.

Elizabeth came to summon Mary.

Ruth was glad when she got into the open air, and away from the house. Two hours were gone and over. Two out of a day, a day and a half – for it might be late on Monday morning before the Eccleston party returned.

She felt weak and trembling in body, but strong in power over herself. They had left the house in good time for church, so they needed not to hurry; and they went leisurely along the road, now and then passing some country person whom they knew, and with whom they exchanged a kindly placid greeting. But presently, to Ruth's dismay, she heard a step behind, coming at a rapid pace, a peculiar clank of rather high-heeled boots, which gave a springy sound to the walk, that she had known well long ago. It was like a nightmare, where the Evil dreaded is never avoided, never completely shunned, but is by one's side at the very moment of triumph in escape. There he was by her side; and there was still a quarter of a mile intervening between her and the church; but even yet she trusted that he had not recognised her.

'I have changed my mind, you see,' said he, quietly. 'I have some curiosity to see the architecture of the church; some of these old country churches have singular bits about them. Mr Bradshaw kindly directed me part of the way, but I was so much puzzled by "turns to the right", and "turns to the left", that I was quite glad to espy your party.'

That speech required no positive answer of any kind; and no answer did it receive. He had not expected a reply. He knew, if she were Ruth, she could not answer any indifferent words of his; and her silence made him more certain of her identity with the lady by his side.

'The scenery here is of a kind new to me; neither grand, wild, nor yet marked by high cultivation; and yet it has great charms. It reminds me of some part of Wales.' He breathed deeply, and then added, 'You have been in Wales, I believe?'

He spoke low; almost in a whisper. The little church-bell began to call the lagging people with its quick sharp summons. Ruth writhed in body and spirit, but struggled on. The church-door would be gained at last; and in that holy place she would find peace.

He repeated in a louder tone, so as to compel an answer in order to conceal her agitation from the girls:

'Have you never been in Wales?' He used 'never', instead of 'ever', and laid the emphasis on that word, in order to mark his meaning to Ruth, and Ruth only. But he drove her to bay.

'I have been in Wales, sir,' she replied, in a calm, grave tone. 'I was there many years ago. Events took place there, which contribute to make the recollections of that time most miserable to me. I shall be obliged to you, sir, if you will make no further reference to it.'

The little girls wondered how Mrs Denbigh could speak in such a tone of quiet authority to Mr Donne, who was almost a member of Parliament. But they settled that her husband must have died in Wales, and, of course, that would make the recollection of the country 'most miserable', as she said.

Mr Donne did not dislike the answer, and he positively admired the dignity with which she spoke. His leaving her as he did, must have made her very miserable; and he liked the pride that made her retain her indignation, until he could speak to her in private, and explain away a good deal of what she might complain of with some justice.

The church was reached. They all went up the middle aisle into the Eagle's Crag pew. He followed them in, entered himself, and shut the door. Ruth's heart sank as she saw him there; just opposite to her; coming between her and the clergyman who was to read out the word of God. It was merciless – it was cruel to haunt her there. She durst not lift her eyes to the bright eastern light – she could not see how peacefully the marble images of the dead lay on their tombs, for he was between her and all Light and Peace.[13] She knew that his look was on her; that he never turned his glance away. She could not join in the prayer for the remission of sins[14] while he was there, for his very presence seemed as a sign that their stain would never be washed out of her life. But, although goaded and chafed by her thoughts and recollections, she kept very still. No sign of emotion, no flush of colour was on her face, as he looked at her. Elizabeth could not find her place, and then Ruth breathed once, long and deeply, as she moved up the pew, and out of the straight burning glance of those eyes of evil meaning. When they sat down for the reading of the first lesson,[15] Ruth turned the corner of the seat so as no longer to be opposite to him. She could not listen. The words seemed to be uttered in some world far away, from which she was exiled and cast out; their sound, and yet more their meaning, was dim and distant. But in this extreme tension of mind to hold in her bewildered agony, it so happened that one of her senses was preternaturally acute. While all the church and the people swam in misty haze, one point in a dark corner grew clearer and clearer till she saw (what, at another time she could not have discerned at all) a face – a gargoyle I think they call it – at the end of the arch next to the narrowing of the nave into the chancel, and in the shadow of that contraction. The face was beautiful in feature (the next to it was a grinning monkey), but it was not the features that were the most striking part. There was a half-open mouth, not in any way distorted out of its exquisite beauty by the intense expression of suffering it conveyed. Any distortion of the face by mental agony, implies that a struggle with circumstance is going on. But in this face, if such struggle had been, it was over now. Circumstance had conquered; and there was no hope from mortal endeavour, or help from mortal creature to be had. But the eyes looked onward and upward to the 'Hills from whence cometh our help.'[16] And though the parted lips seemed ready to quiver with agony, yet the expression of the whole face, owing to these strange, stony, and yet spiritual eyes, was high and consoling. If mortal gaze had never sought its meaning before, in the deep shadow where it had been placed long centuries ago, yet Ruth's did now. Who could have imagined such a look? Who could have witnessed – perhaps felt – such infinite sorrow, and yet dared to lift it up by Faith into a peace so pure? Or was it a mere conception? If so, what a soul the unknown carver must have had! for creator and handicraftsman must have been one; no two minds could have been in such perfect harmony. Whatever it was – however it came there – imaginer, carver, sufferer, all were long passed away. Human art was ended – human life done – human suffering over; but this remained; it stilled Ruth's beating heart to look on it. She grew still enough to hear words, which have come to many in their time of need, and awed them in the presence of the extremest suffering that the hushed world has ever heard of.

The second lesson for the morning of the 25th of September, is the 26th chapter of St Matthew's Gospel.[17]

And when they prayed again, Ruth's tongue was unloosed, and she also could pray, in His name who underwent the agony in the garden.

As they came out of church, there was a little pause and gathering at the door. It had begun to rain; those who had umbrellas were putting them up; those who had not were regretting, and wondering how long it would last. Standing for a moment, impeded by the people who were thus collected under the porch, Ruth heard a voice close to her say, very low, but very distinctly:

'I have much to say to you – much to explain. I entreat you to give me the opportunity.'

Ruth did not reply. She would not acknowledge that she heard; but she trembled nevertheless, for the well-remembered voice was low and soft, and had yet its power to thrill. She earnestly desired to know why and how he had left her. It appeared to her, as if that knowledge could alone give her a relief from the restless wondering that distracted her mind, and that one explanation could do no harm.

'*No!*' the higher spirit made answer; '*it must not be.*'

Ruth and the girls had each an umbrella. She turned to Mary, and said:

'Mary, give your umbrella to Mr Donne, and come under mine.' Her way of speaking was short and decided; she was compressing her meaning into as few words as possible. The little girl obeyed in silence. As they went first through the churchyard stile, Mr Donne spoke again.

'You are unforgiving,' said he. 'I only ask you to hear me. I have a right to be heard, Ruth! I won't believe you are so much changed, as not to listen to me when I entreat.'

He spoke in a tone of soft complaint. But he himself had done much to destroy the illusion which had hung about his memory for years, whenever Ruth had allowed herself to think of it. Besides which, during the time of her residence in the Benson family, her feeling of what people ought to be had been unconsciously raised and refined; and Mr Donne, even while she had to struggle against the force past of recollections, repelled her so much by what he was at present, that every speech of his, every minute they were together, served to make her path more and more easy to follow. His voice retained something of its former influence. When he spoke, without her seeing him, she could not help remembering former days.

She did not answer this last speech any more than the first. She saw clearly, that, putting aside all thought as to the character of their former relationship, it had been dissolved by his will – his act and deed; and that, therefore, the power to refuse any further intercourse whatsoever remained with her.

It sometimes seems a little strange how, after having earnestly prayed to be delivered from temptation, and having given ourselves with shut eyes into God's hand, from that time every thought, every outward influence, every acknowledged law of life, seems to lead us on from strength to strength.[18] It seems strange sometimes, because we notice the coincidence; but it is the natural, unavoidable consequence of all, truth and goodness being one and the same, and therefore carried out in every circumstance, external and internal, of God's creation.

When Mr Donne saw that Ruth would not answer him, he became only the more determined that she should hear what he had to say. What that was he did not exactly know. The whole affair was most mysterious and piquant.

The umbrella protected Ruth from more than the rain on that walk homewards, for under its shelter she could not be spoken to unheard. She had not rightly understood at what time she and the girls were to dine. From the gathering at meal-times she must not shrink. She must show no sign of weakness. But, oh! the relief, after that walk, to sit in her own room, locked up, so that neither Mary nor Elizabeth could come by surprise, and to let her weary frame (weary with being so long braced up to rigidity and stiff quiet) fall into a chair anyhow – all helpless, nerveless, motionless, as if the very bones had melted out of her!

The peaceful rest which her mind took was in thinking of Leonard. She dared not look before or behind, but she could see him well at present. She brooded over the thought of him, till she dreaded his father more and more. By the light of her child's purity and innocence, she saw evil clearly, and yet more clearly. She thought that, if Leonard ever came to know the nature of his birth, she had nothing for it but to die out of his sight. He could never know – human heart could never know, her ignorant innocence, and all the small circumstances which had impelled her onwards. But God knew. And if Leonard heard of his mother's error, why nothing remained but death; for she felt, then, as if she had it in her power to die innocently out of such future agony; but that escape is not so easy. Suddenly a fresh thought came, and she prayed that, through whatever suffering, she might be purified. Whatever trials, woes, measureless pangs, God might see fit to chastise her with, she would not shrink, if only at last she might come into His presence in heaven. Alas! the shrinking from suffering we cannot help. That part of her prayer was vain. And as for the rest, was not the sure justice of His law finding her out even now? His laws once broken, His justice and the very nature of those laws bring the immutable retribution; but if we turn penitently to Him, He enables us to bear our punishment with a meek and docile heart, 'for His mercy endureth for ever'.[19]

Mr Bradshaw had felt himself rather wanting in proper attention to his guest, inasmuch as he had been unable, all in a minute, to comprehend Mr Donne's rapid change of purpose; and, before it had entered into his mind that, notwithstanding the distance of the church, Mr Donne was going thither, that gentleman was out of the sight, and far out of the reach, of his burly host. But though the latter had so far neglected the duties of hospitality as to allow his visitor to sit in the Eagle's Crag pew with no other guard of honour than the children and the governess, Mr Bradshaw determined to make up for it by extra attention during the remainder of the day. Accordingly he never left Mr Donne. Whatever wish that gentleman expressed, it was the study of his host to gratify. Did he hint at the pleasure which a walk in such beautiful scenery would give him, Mr Bradshaw was willing to accompany him, although at Eccleston it was a principle with him not to take any walks for pleasure on a Sunday. When Mr Donne turned round, and recollected letters which must be written, and which would compel him to stay at home, Mr Bradshaw instantly gave up the walk, and remained at hand, ready to furnish him with any writing materials which could be wanted, and which were not laid out in the half-furnished house. Nobody knew where Mr Hickson was all this time. He had sauntered out after Mr Donne, when the latter set off for church, and he had never returned.

Mr Donne kept wondering if he could have met Ruth – if, in fact, she had gone out with her pupils, now that the afternoon had cleared up. This uneasy wonder, and a few mental imprecations on his host's polite attention, together with the letter-writing pretence, passed away the afternoon – the longest afternoon he had ever spent; and of weariness he had had his share. Lunch was lingering in the dining-room, left there for the truant Mr Hickson; but of the children or Ruth there was no sign. He ventured on a distant inquiry as to their whereabouts.

'They dine early; they are gone to church again. Mrs Denbigh was a member of the Establishment once; and, though she attends chapel at home, she seems glad to have an opportunity of going to church.'

Mr Donne was on the point of asking some further questions about 'Mrs Denbigh', when Mr Hickson came in, loud-spoken, cheerful, hungry, and as ready to talk about his ramble, and the way in which he had lost and found himself, as he was about everything else. He knew how to dress up the commonest occurrence with a little exaggeration, a few puns, and a happy quotation or two, so as to make it sound very agreeable. He could read faces, and saw that he had been missed; both host and visitor looked moped to death. He determined to devote himself to their amusement during the remainder of the day, for he had really lost himself, and felt that he had been away too long on a dull Sunday, when people were apt to get hypped[20] if not well amused.

'It is really a shame to be in-doors in such a place. Rain? Yes, it rained some hours ago, but now it is splendid weather. I feel myself quite qualified for guide, I assure you. I can show you all the beauties of the neighbourhood, and throw in a bog and a nest of vipers to boot.'

Mr Donne languidly assented to this proposal of going out, and then he became restless until Mr Hickson had eaten a hasty lunch, for he hoped to meet Ruth on the way from church, to be near her, and watch her, though he might not be able to speak to her. To have the slow hours roll away – to know he must leave the next day – and yet, so close to her, not to be seeing her – was more than he could bear. In an impetuous kind of way, he disregarded all Mr Hickson's offers of guidance to lovely views, and turned a deaf ear to Mr Bradshaw's expressed wish of showing him the land belonging to the house ('very little for fourteen thousand pounds'), and set off wilfully on the road leading to the church, from which, he averred, he had seen a view which nothing else about the place could equal.

They met the country people dropping homewards.[21] No Ruth was there. She and her pupils had returned by the field-way, as Mr Bradshaw informed his guests at dinner-time. Mr Donne was very captious all through dinner. He thought it never would be over, and cursed Hickson's interminable stories, which were told on purpose to amuse him. His heart gave a fierce bound when he saw her in the drawing-room with the little girls.

She was reading to them – with how sick and trembling a heart, no words can tell. But she could master and keep down outward signs of her emotion. An hour more to-night (part of which was to be spent in family prayer, and all in the safety of company), another hour in the morning (when all would be engaged in the bustle of departure) – if, during this short space of time, she could not avoid speaking to him, she could at least keep him at such a distance as to make him feel that henceforward her world and his belonged to separate systems, wide as the heavens apart.

By degrees she felt that he was drawing near to where she stood. He was by the table examining the books that lay upon it. Mary and Elizabeth drew off a little space, awe-stricken by the future member for Eccleston. As he bent his head over a book, he said, 'I implore you; five minutes alone.'

The little girls could not hear; but Ruth, hemmed in so that no escape was possible, did hear.

She took sudden courage, and said, in a clear voice:

'Will you read the whole passage aloud? I do not remember it.'

Mr Hickson, hovering at no great distance, heard these words, and drew near to second Mrs Denbigh's request. Mr Bradshaw, who was very sleepy after his unusually late dinner, and longing for bedtime, joined in the request, for it would save the necessity for making talk, and he might, perhaps, get in a nap, undisturbed and unnoticed, before the servants came in to prayers.

Mr Donne was caught; he was obliged to read aloud, although he did not know what he was reading. In the middle of some sentence, the door opened, a rush of servants came in, and Mr Bradshaw became particularly wide awake in an instant, and read them a long sermon with great emphasis and unction, winding up with a prayer almost as long.

Ruth sat with her head drooping, more from exhaustion after a season of effort than because she shunned Mr Donne's looks. He had so lost his power over her – his power, which had stirred her so deeply the night before – that, except as one knowing her error and her shame, and making a cruel use of such knowledge, she had quite separated him from the idol of her youth. And yet, for the sake of that first and only love, she would gladly have known what explanation he could offer to account for leaving her. It would have been something gained to her own self-respect, if she had learnt that he was not then, as she felt him to be now, cold and egotistical, caring for no one and nothing but what related to himself.

Home, and Leonard – how strangely peaceful the two seemed! Oh, for the rest that a dream about Leonard would bring!

Mary and Elizabeth went to bed immediately after prayers, and Ruth accompanied them. It was planned that the gentlemen should leave early the next morning. They were to breakfast half an hour sooner, to catch the railway train; and this by Mr Donne's own arrangement, who had been as eager about his canvassing, the week before, as it was possible for him to be, but who now wished Eccleston and the Dissenting interest therein very fervently at the devil.

Just as the carriage came round, Mr Bradshaw turned to Ruth: 'Any message for Leonard beyond love, which is a matter of course?'

Ruth gasped – for she saw Mr Donne catch at the name; she did not guess the sudden sharp jealousy called out by the idea that Leonard was a grown-up man.

'Who is Leonard?' said he, to the little girl standing by him; he did not know which she was.

'Mrs Denbigh's little boy,' answered Mary.

Under some pretence or other, he drew near to Ruth; and in that low voice which she had learnt to loathe he said:

'Our child?'

By the white misery that turned her face to stone – by the wild terror in her imploring eyes – by the gasping breath, which came out as the carriage drove away – he knew that he had seized the spell to make her listen at last.

CHAPTER XXIV

'He will take him away from me. He will take the child from me.'

These words rang like a tolling bell through Ruth's head. It seemed to her that her doom was certain. Leonard would be taken from her! She had a firm conviction – not the less firm because she knew not on what it was based – that a child, whether legitimate or not, belonged of legal right to the father. And Leonard, of all children, was the prince and monarch. Every man's heart would long to call Leonard 'Child'! She had been too strongly taxed to have much power left her to reason coolly and dispassionately, just then, even if she had been with any one who could furnish her with information from which to draw correct conclusions. The one thought haunted her night and day. 'He will take my child away from me!' In her dreams she saw Leonard borne away into some dim land, to which she could not follow. Sometimes he sat in a swiftly-moving carriage, at his father's side, and smiled on her as he passed by, as if going to promised pleasure. At another time, he was struggling to return to her; stretching out his little arms, and crying to her for the help she could not give. How she got through the days, she did not know; her body moved about and habitually acted, but her spirit was with her child. She thought often of writing and warning Mr Benson of Leonard's danger; but then she shrank from recurring to circumstances, all mention of which had ceased years ago; the very recollection of which seemed buried deep for ever. Besides, she feared occasioning discord or commotion in the quiet circle in which she lived. Mr Benson's deep anger against her betrayer had been shown too clearly in the old time to allow her to think that he would keep it down without expression now. He would cease to do anything to forward his election: he would oppose him as much as he could; and Mr Bradshaw would be angry, and a storm would arise, from the bare thought of which Ruth shrank with the cowardliness of a person thoroughly worn out with late contest. She was bodily wearied with her spiritual buffeting.

One morning, three or four days after their departure, she received a letter from Miss Benson. She could not open it at first, and put it on one side, clenching her hands over it all the time. At last she tore it open. Leonard was safe as yet. There were a few lines in his great round hand, speaking of events no larger than the loss of a beautiful 'alley'.[1] There was a sheet from Miss Benson. She always wrote letters in the manner of a diary. 'Monday we did so-and-so; Tuesday, so-and-so, &c.' Ruth glanced rapidly down the pages. Yes, here it was! Sick, fluttering heart, be still!

'In the middle of the damsons, when they were just on the fire, there was a knock at the door. My brother was out, and Sally was washing up, and I was stirring the preserve with my great apron and bib on; so I bade Leonard come in from the garden, and open the door. But I would have washed his face first, if I had known who it was! It was Mr Bradshaw, and the Mr Donne that they hope to send up to the House of Commons, as member of Parliament for Eccleston, and another gentleman, whose name I never heard. They had come canvassing; and when they found my brother was out, they asked Leonard if they could see me. The child said, "Yes! if I could leave the damsons;" and straightway came to call me, leaving them standing in the passage. I whipped off my apron, and took Leonard by the hand, for I fancied I should feel less awkward if he was with me, and then I went and asked them all into the study, for I thought I should like them to see how many books Thurstan had got. Then they began talking politics at me in a very polite manner, only I could not make head or tail of what they meant; and Mr Donne took a deal of notice of Leonard, and called him to him; and I am sure he noticed what a noble, handsome boy he was, though his face was very brown and red, and hot with digging, and his curls all tangled. Leonard talked back as if he had known him all his life, till, I think, Mr Bradshaw thought he was making too much noise, and bid him remember he ought to be seen, not heard. So he stood as still and stiff as a soldier, close to Mr Donne; and as I could not help looking at the two, and thinking how handsome they both were in their different ways, I could not tell Thurstan half the messages the gentlemen left for him. But there was one thing more I must tell you, though I said I would not. When Mr Donne was talking to Leonard, he took off his watch and chain and put it round the boy's neck, who was pleased enough, you may be sure. I bade him give it back to the gentleman, when they were all going away; and I was quite surprised, and very uncomfortable, when Mr Donne said he had given it to Leonard, and that he was to keep it for his own. I could see Mr Bradshaw was annoyed, and he and the other gentleman spoke to Mr Donne, and I heard them say, "too barefaced"; and I shall never forget Mr Donne's proud, stubborn look back at them, nor his way of saying, "I allow no one to interfere with what I choose to do with my own." And he looked so haughty and displeased, I durst say nothing at the time. But when I told Thurstan, he was very grieved and angry; and said he had heard that our party were bribing, but that he never could have thought they would have tried to do it at his house. Thurstan is very much out of spirits about this election altogether; and, indeed, it does make sad work up and down the town. However, he sent back the watch with a letter to Mr Bradshaw; and Leonard was very good about it, so I gave him a taste of the new damson-preserve on his bread for supper.'

Although a stranger might have considered this letter wearisome, from the multiplicity of the details, Ruth craved greedily after more. What had Mr Donne said to Leonard? Had Leonard liked his new acquaintance? Were they likely to meet again? After wondering and wondering over these points, Ruth composed herself by the hope that in a day or two she should hear again; and, to secure this end, she answered the letters by return of post. That was on Thursday. On Friday she had another letter, in a strange hand. It was from Mr Donne. No name, no initials were given. If it had fallen into another person's hands, they could not have recognised the writer, nor guessed to whom it was sent. It contained simply these words:

'For our child's sake, and in his name, I summon you to appoint a place where I can speak, and you can listen, undisturbed. The time must be on Sunday; the limit of distance may be the circumference of your power of walking. My words may be commands, but my fond heart entreats. More I shall not say now, but, remember! your boy's welfare depends on your acceding to this request. Address B. D., Post-Office, Eccleston.'

Ruth did not attempt to answer this letter till the last five minutes before the post went out. She could not decide until forced to it. Either way she dreaded. She was very nearly leaving the letter altogether unanswered. But suddenly she resolved she would know all, the best, the worst. No cowardly dread of herself, or of others, should make her neglect aught that came to her in her child's name. She took up a pen and wrote:

'The sands below the rocks, where we met you the other night. Time, afternoon church.'

Sunday came.

'I shall not go to church this afternoon. You know the way, of course; and I can trust you to go steadily by yourselves.'

When they came to kiss her before leaving her, according to their fond wont, they were struck by the coldness of her face and lips.

'Are you not well, dear Mrs Denbigh? How cold you are!'

'Yes, darling! I am well;' and tears sprang into her eyes as she looked at their anxious little faces. 'Go now, dears. Five o'clock will soon be here, and then we will have tea.'

'And that will warm you!' said they, leaving the room.

'And then it will be over,' she murmured – 'over.'

It never came into her head to watch the girls, as they disappeared down the lane on their way to church. She knew them too well to distrust their doing what they were told. She sat still, her head bowed on her arms for a few minutes, and then rose up and went to put on her walking things. Some thoughts impelled her to sudden haste. She crossed the field by the side of the house, ran down the steep and rocky path, and was carried by the impetus of her descent far out on the level sands – but not far enough for her intent. Without looking to the right hand or to the left, where comers might be seen, she went forwards to the black posts, which, rising above the heaving waters, marked where the fishermen's nets were laid. She went straight towards this place, and hardly stinted her pace even where the wet sands were glittering with the receding waves. Once there, she turned round, and in a darting glance, saw that as yet no one was near. She was perhaps half a mile or more from the grey silvery rocks, which sloped away into brown moorland, interspersed with a field here and there of golden waving corn. Behind were purple hills, with sharp clear outlines, touching the sky. A little on one side from where she stood, she saw the white cottages and houses which formed the village of Abermouth, scattered up and down; and, on a windy hill, about a mile inland, she saw the little grey church, where even now many were worshipping in peace.

'Pray for me!' she sighed out, as this object caught her eye.

And now, close under the heathery fields, where they fell softly down and touched the sands, she saw a figure moving in the direction of the great shadow made by the rocks – going towards the very point where the path from Eagle's Crag came down to the shore.

'It is he!' said she to herself. And she turned round and looked seaward. The tide had turned; the waves were slowly receding, as if loth to lose the hold they had, so lately, and with such swift bounds, gained on the yellow sands. The eternal moan they have made since the world began filled the ear, broken only by the skirl of the grey sea-birds as they alighted in groups on the edge of the waters, or as they rose up with their measured, balancing motion, and the sun-light caught their white breasts. There was no sign of human life to be seen; no boat, or distant sail, or near shrimper. The black posts there were all that spoke of men's work or labour. Beyond a stretch of the waters, a few pale grey hills showed like films; their summits clear, though faint, their bases lost in a vapoury mist.

On the hard, echoing sands, and distinct from the ceaseless murmur of the salt sea waves, came footsteps – nearer – nearer. Very near they were when Ruth, unwilling to show the fear that rioted in her heart, turned round, and faced Mr Donne.

He came forward, with both hands extended.

'This is kind! my own Ruth,' said he. Ruth's arms hung down motionless at her sides.

'What! Ruth, have you no word for me?'

'I have nothing to say,' said Ruth.

'Why, you little revengeful creature! And so I am to explain all before you will even treat me with decent civility.'

'I do not want explanations,' said Ruth, in a trembling tone. 'We must not speak of the past. You asked me to come in Leonard's – in my child's name, and to hear what you had to say about him.'

'But what I have to say about him relates to you even more. And how can we talk about him without recurring to the past? That past, which you try to ignore – I know you cannot do it in your heart – is full of happy recollections to me. Were you not happy in Wales?' he said, in his tenderest tone.

But there was no answer; not even one faint sigh, though he listened intently.

'You dare not speak; you dare not answer me. Your heart will not allow you to prevaricate, and you know you were happy.'

Suddenly Ruth's beautiful eyes were raised to him, full of lucid splendour, but grave and serious in their expression; and her cheeks, heretofore so faintly tinged with the tenderest blush, flashed into a ruddy glow.

'I was happy. I do not deny it. Whatever comes, I will not blench from the truth. I have answered you.'

'And yet,' replied he, secretly exulting in her admission, and not perceiving the inner strength of which she must have been conscious before she would have dared to make it – 'and yet, Ruth, we are not to recur to the past! Why not? If it was happy at the time, is the recollection of it so miserable to you?'

He tried once more to take her hand, but she quietly stepped back.

'I came to hear what you had to say about my child,' said she, beginning to feel very weary.

'*Our* child, Ruth.'

She drew herself up, and her face went very pale.

'What have you to say about him?' asked she, coldly.

'Much,' exclaimed he – 'much that may affect his whole life. But it all depends upon whether you will hear me or not.'

'I listen.'

'Good Heavens! Ruth, you will drive me mad. Oh! what a changed person you are from the sweet, loving creature you were! I wish you were not so beautiful.'

She did not reply, but he caught a deep, involuntary sigh.

'Will you hear me if I speak, though I may not begin all at once to talk of this boy – a boy of whom any mother – any parent, might be proud? I could see that, Ruth. I have seen him; he looked like a prince in that cramped miserable house, and with no earthly advantages. It is a shame he should not have every kind of opportunity laid open before him.'

There was no sign of maternal ambition on the motionless face, though there might be some little spring in her heart, as it beat quick and strong at the idea of the proposal she imagined he was going to make of taking her boy away to give him the careful education she had often craved for him. She should refuse it, as she would everything else which seemed to imply that she acknowledged a claim over Leonard; but yet sometimes, for her boy's sake, she had longed for a larger opening – a more extended sphere.

'Ruth! you acknowledge we were happy once; – there were circumstances which, if I could tell you them all in detail, would show you how in my weak, convalescent state I was almost passive in the hands of others. Ah, Ruth! I have not forgotten the tender nurse who soothed me in my delirium. When I am feverish, I dream that I am again at Llan-dhu, in the little old bedchamber, and you, in white – which you always wore then, you know – flitting about me.'

The tears dropped, large and round from Ruth's eyes – she could not help it – how could she?

'We were happy then,' continued he, gaining confidence from the sight of her melted mood, and recurring once more to the admission which he considered so much in his favour. 'Can such happiness never return?' Thus he went on, quickly, anxious to lay before her all he had to offer, before she should fully understand his meaning.

'If you would consent, Leonard should be always with you – educated where and how you liked – money to any amount you might choose to name should be secured to you and him – if only, Ruth – if only those happy days might return.'

Ruth spoke:

'I said that I was happy, because I had asked God to protect and help me – and I dared not tell a lie. I was happy. Oh! what is happiness or misery that we should talk about them now?'

Mr Donne looked at her, as she uttered these words, to see if she was wandering in her mind, they seemed to him so utterly strange and incoherent.

'I dare not think of happiness – I must not look forward to sorrow. God did not put me here to consider either of these things.'

'My dear Ruth, compose yourself! There is no hurry in answering the question I asked.'

'What was it?' said Ruth.

'I love you so, I cannot live without you. I offer you my heart, my life – I offer to place Leonard wherever you would have him placed. I have the power and the means to advance him in any path of life you choose. All who have shown kindness to you shall be rewarded by me, with a gratitude even surpassing your own. If there is anything else I can do that you can suggest, I will do it.'

'Listen to me!' said Ruth, now that the idea of what he proposed had entered her mind. 'When I said that I was happy with you long ago, I was choked with shame as I said it. And yet it may be a vain, false excuse that I make for myself. I was very young; I did not know how such a life was against God's pure and holy will – at least, not as I know it now; and I tell you truth – all the days of my years since I have gone about with a stain on my hidden soul – a stain which made me loathe myself, and envy those who stood spotless and undefiled; which made me shrink from my child – from Mr Benson, from his sister, from the innocent girls whom I teach – nay, even I have cowered away from God Himself; and what I did wrong then, I did blindly to what I should do now if I listened to you.'

She was so strongly agitated that she put her hands over her face, and sobbed without restraint. Then, taking them away, she looked at him with a glowing face, and beautiful, honest, wet eyes, and tried to speak calmly, as she asked if she needed to stay longer (she would have gone away at once but that she thought of Leonard, and wished to hear all that his father might have to say). He was so struck anew by her beauty, and understood her so little, that he believed that she only required a little more urging to consent to what he wished; for in all she had said there was no trace of the anger and resentment for his desertion of her, which he had expected would be a prominent feature – the greatest obstacle he had to encounter. The deep sense of penitence she expressed, he mistook for earthly shame; which he imagined he could soon soothe away.

'Yes, I have much more to say. I have not said half. I cannot tell you how fondly I will – how fondly I do love you – how my life shall be spent in ministering to your wishes. Money, I see – I know, you despise —'

'Mr Bellingham! I will not stay to hear you speak to me so again. I have been sinful, but it is not you who should—' She could not speak, she was so choking with passionate sorrow.

He wanted to calm her, as he saw her shaken with repressed sobs. He put his hand on her arm. She shook it off impatiently, and moved away in an instant.

'Ruth!' said he, nettled by her action of repugnance, 'I begin to think you never loved me.'

'I! – I never loved you! Do you dare to say so?'

Her eyes flamed on him as she spoke. Her red, round lip curled into beautiful contempt.

'Why do you shrink so from me?' said he, in his turn getting impatient.

'I did not come here to be spoken to in this way,' said she. 'I came, if by any chance I could do Leonard good. I would submit to many humiliations for his sake – but to no more from you.'

'Are not you afraid to brave me so?' said he. 'Don't you know how much you are in my power?'

She was silent. She longed to go away, but dreaded lest he should follow her, where she might be less subject to interruption than she was here – near the fisherman's nets, which the receding tide was leaving every moment barer and more bare, and the posts they were fastened to more blackly uprising above the waters.

Mr Donne put his hands on her arms as they hung down before her – her hands tightly clasped together.

'Ask me to let you go,' said he. 'I will, if you will ask me.' He looked very fierce and passionate and determined. The vehemence of his action took Ruth by surprise, and the painful tightness of the grasp almost made her exclaim. But she was quite still and mute.

'Ask me,' said he, giving her a little shake. She did not speak. Her eyes, fixed on the distant shore, were slowly filling with tears. Suddenly a light came through the mist that obscured them, and the shut lips parted. She saw some distant object that gave her hope.

'It is Stephen Bromley,' said she. 'He is coming to his nets. They say he is a very desperate, violent man, but he will protect me.'

'You obstinate, wilful creature!' said Mr Donne, releasing his grasp. 'You forget that one word of mine could undeceive all these good people at Eccleston; and that if I spoke out ever so little, they would throw you off in an instant. Now!' he continued, 'do you understand how much you are in my power?'

'Mr and Miss Benson know all – they have not thrown me off,' Ruth gasped out. 'Oh! for Leonard's sake! you would not be so cruel.'

'Then do not you be cruel to him – to me. Think once more!'

'I think once more;' she spoke solemnly. 'To save Leonard from the shame and agony of knowing my disgrace, I would lie down and die. Oh! perhaps it would be best for him – for me, if I might; my death would be a stingless grief – but to go back into sin would be the real cruelty to him. The errors of my youth may be washed away by my tears – it was so once when the gentle, blessed Christ was upon earth,[2] but now, if I went into wilful guilt, as you would have me, how could I teach Leonard God's holy will? I should not mind his knowing my past sin, compared to the awful corruption it would be if he knew me living now, as you would have me, lost to all fear of God—' Her speech was broken by sobs. 'Whatever may be my doom – God is just[3] – I leave myself in His hands. I will save Leonard from evil. Evil would it be for him if I lived with you. I will let him die first!' She lifted her eyes to heaven, and clasped and wreathed her hands together tight. Then she said: 'You have humbled me enough, sir. I shall leave you now.'

She turned away resolutely. The dark, grey fisherman was at hand. Mr Donne folded his arms and set his teeth, and looked after her.

'What a stately step she has! How majestic and graceful all her attitudes were! She thinks she has baffled me now. We will try something more, and bid a higher price.' He unfolded his arms, and began to follow her. He gained upon her, for her beautiful walk was now wavering and unsteady. The works which had kept her in motion were running down fast.

'Ruth!' said he, overtaking her. 'You shall hear me once more. Ay, look round! Your fisherman is near. He may hear me, if he chooses – hear your triumph. I am come to offer to marry you, Ruth; come what may, I will have you. Nay – I will make you hear me. I will hold this hand till you have heard me. To-morrow I will speak to any one in Eccleston you like – to Mr Bradshaw; Mr —, the little minister I mean. We can make it worth while for him to keep our secret, and no one else need know but what you are really Mrs Denbigh. Leonard shall still bear this name, but in all things else he shall be treated as my son. He and you would grace any situation. I will take care the highest paths are open to him!'

He looked to see the lovely face brighten into sudden joy; on the contrary, the head was still hung down with a heavy droop.

'I cannot,' said she; her voice was very faint and low.

'It is sudden for you, my dearest. But be calm. It will all be easily managed. Leave it to me.'

'I cannot,' repeated she, more distinct and clear, though still very low.

'Why! what on earth makes you say that?' asked he, in a mood to be irritated by any repetition of such words.

'I do not love you. I did once. Don't say I did not love you then; but I do not now. I could never love you again. All you have said and done since you came with Mr Bradshaw to Abermouth first, has only made me wonder how I ever could have loved you. We are very far apart.

The time that has pressed down my life like brands of hot iron, and scarred me for ever, has been nothing to you. You have talked of it with no sound of moaning in your voice – no shadow over the brightness of your face; it has left no sense of sin on your conscience, while me it haunts and haunts; and yet I might plead that I was an ignorant child – only I will not plead anything, for God knows all— But this is only one piece of our great difference—'

'You mean that I am no saint,' he said, impatient at her speech. 'Granted. But people who are no saints have made very good husbands before now. Come, don't let any morbid overstrained conscientiousness interfere with substantial happiness – happiness both to you and to me – for I am sure I can make you happy – ay! and make you love me, too, in spite of your pretty defiance. I love you so dearly I must win love back. And here are advantages for Leonard, to be gained by you quite in a holy and legitimate way.'

She stood very erect.

'If there was one thing needed to confirm me, you have named it. You shall have nothing to do with my boy, by my consent, much less by my agency. I would rather see him working on the roadside than leading such a life – being such a one as you are. You have heard my mind now, Mr Bellingham. You have humbled me – you have baited me; and if at last I have spoken out too harshly, and too much in a spirit of judgment, the fault is yours. If there were no other reason to prevent our marriage but the one fact that it would bring Leonard into contact with you, that would be enough.'

'It is enough!' said he, making her a low bow. 'Neither you nor your child shall ever more be annoyed by me. I wish you a good evening.'

They walked apart – he back to the inn, to set off instantly, while the blood was hot in him, from the place where he had been so mortified – she to steady herself along till she reached the little path, more like a rude staircase than anything else, by which she had to climb to the house.

She did not turn round for some time after she was fairly lost to the sight of any one on the shore; she clambered on, almost stunned by the rapid beating of her heart. Her eyes were hot and dry; and at last became as if she were suddenly blind. Unable to go on, she tottered into the tangled underwood which grew among the stones, filling every niche and crevice, and little shelving space, with green and delicate tracery. She sank down behind a great overhanging rock, which hid her from any one coming up the path. An ash-tree was rooted in this rock, slanting away from the sea-breezes that were prevalent in most weathers; but this was a still, autumnal Sabbath evening. As Ruth's limbs fell, so they lay. She had no strength, no power of volition to move a finger. She could not think or remember. She was literally stunned. The first sharp sensation which roused her from her torpor was a quick desire to see him once more; up she sprang, and climbed to an out-jutting dizzy point of rock, but a little above her sheltered nook, yet commanding a wide view over the bare naked sands; – far away below, touching the rippling water-line, was Stephen Bromley, busily gathering in his nets; besides him there was no living creature visible. Ruth shaded her eyes, as if she thought they might have deceived her; but no, there was no one there. She went slowly down to her old place, crying sadly as she went.

'Oh! if I had not spoken so angrily to him – the last things I said were so bitter – so reproachful! – and I shall never, never see him again!'

She could not take in the general view and scope of their conversation – the event was too near her for that; but her heart felt sore at the echo of her last words, just and true as their severity was. Her struggle, her constant flowing tears, which fell from very weakness, made her experience a sensation of intense bodily fatigue; and her soul had lost the power of throwing itself forward, or contemplating anything beyond the dreary present, when the expanse of grey, wild, bleak moors, stretching wide away below a sunless sky, seemed only an outward sign of the waste world within her heart, for which she could claim no sympathy; – for she could not even define what its woes were; and if she could, no one would understand how the present time was haunted by the terrible ghost of the former love.

'I am so weary! I am so weary!' she moaned aloud at last. 'I wonder if I might stop here, and just die away.'

She shut her eyes, until through the closed lids came a ruddy blaze of light. The clouds had parted away, and the sun was going down in the crimson glory behind the distant purple hills. The whole western sky was one flame of fire. Ruth forgot herself in looking at the gorgeous sight. She sat up gazing, and, as she gazed, the tears dried on her cheeks; and, somehow, all human care and sorrow were swallowed up in the unconscious sense of God's infinity. The sunset calmed her more than any words, however wise and tender, could have done. It even seemed to give her strength and courage; she did not know how or why, but so it was.

She rose, and went slowly towards home. Her limbs were very stiff, and every now and then she had to choke down an unbidden sob. Her pupils had been long returned from church, and had busied themselves in preparing tea – an occupation which had probably made them feel the time less long.

If they had ever seen a sleep-walker, they might have likened Ruth to one for the next few days, so slow and measured did her movements seem – so far away was her intelligence from all that was passing around her – so hushed and strange were the tones of her voice! They had letters from home announcing the triumphant return of Mr Donne as M.P. for Eccleston. Mrs Denbigh heard the news without a word, and was too languid to join in the search after purple and yellow flowers[4] with which to deck the sitting-room at Eagle's Crag.

A letter from Jemima came the next day, summoning them home. Mr Donne and his friends had left the place, and quiet was restored in the Bradshaw household; so it was time that Mary's and Elizabeth's holiday should cease. Mrs Denbigh had also a letter – a letter from Miss Benson, saying that Leonard was not quite well. There was so much pains taken to disguise anxiety, that it was very evident much anxiety was felt; and the girls were almost alarmed by Ruth's sudden change from taciturn languor to eager, vehement energy. Body and mind seemed strained to exertion. Every plan that could facilitate packing and winding-up affairs at Abermouth, every errand and arrangement that could expedite their departure by one minute, was done by Ruth with stern promptitude. She spared herself in nothing. She made them rest, made them lie down, while she herself lifted weights and transacted business with feverish power, never resting, and trying never to have time to think.

For in remembrance of the Past there was Remorse, – how had she forgotten Leonard these last few days! – how had she repined and been dull of heart to her blessing! And in anticipation of the Future there was one sharp point of red light in the darkness which pierced her brain with agony, and which she would not see or recognise – and saw and recognised all the more for such mad determination – which is not the true shield against the bitterness of the arrows of Death.[5]

When the sea-side party arrived in Eccleston, they were met by Mrs and Miss Bradshaw and Mr Benson. By a firm resolution, Ruth kept from shaping the question, 'Is he alive?' as if by giving shape to her fears she made their realisation more imminent. She said merely, 'How is he?' but she said it with drawn, tight, bloodless lips, and in her eyes Mr Benson read her anguish of anxiety.

'He is very ill, but we hope he will soon be better. It is what every child has to go through.'

END OF VOL. II

VOLUME III

CHAPTER XXV

Mr Bradshaw had been successful in carrying his point. His member had been returned; his proud opponents mortified. So the public thought he ought to be well pleased; but the public were disappointed to see that he did not show any of the gratification they supposed him to feel.

The truth was, that he met with so many small mortifications during the progress of the election, that the pleasure which he would otherwise have felt in the final success of his scheme was much diminished.

He had more than tacitly sanctioned bribery; and now that the excitement was over, he regretted it: not entirely from conscientious motives, though he was uneasy from a slight sense of wrong-doing; but he was more pained, after all, to think that, in the eyes of some of his townsmen, his hitherto spotless character had received a blemish. He, who had been so stern and severe a censor on the undue influence exercised by the opposite party in all preceding elections, could not expect to be spared by their adherents now, when there were rumours that the hands of the scrupulous Dissenters were not clean. Before, it had been his boast that neither friend nor enemy could say one word against him; now, he was constantly afraid of an indictment for bribery, and of being compelled to appear before a Committee to swear to his own share in the business.

His uneasy, fearful consciousness made him stricter and sterner than ever; as if he would quench all wondering slanderous talk about him in the town by a renewed austerity of uprightness; that the slack-principled Mr Bradshaw of one month of ferment and excitement, might not be confounded with the highly-conscientious and deeply-religious Mr Bradshaw, who went to chapel twice a day, and gave a hundred pounds a-piece to every charity in the town, as a sort of thank-offering that his end was gained.

But he was secretly dissatisfied with Mr Donne. In general, that gentleman had been rather too willing to act in accordance with any one's advice, no matter whose; as if he had thought it too much trouble to weigh the wisdom of his friends, in which case Mr Bradshaw's would have, doubtless, proved the most valuable. But now and then he unexpectedly, and utterly without reason, took the conduct of affairs into his own hands, as when he had been absent without leave only just before the day of nomination. No one guessed whither he had gone; but the fact of his being gone was enough to chagrin Mr Bradshaw, who was quite ready to have picked a quarrel on this very head, if the election had not terminated favourably. As it was, he had a feeling of proprietorship in Mr Donne which was not disagreeable. He had given the new M.P. his seat; his resolution, his promptitude, his energy, had made Mr Donne 'our member'; and Mr Bradshaw began to feel proud of him accordingly. But there had been no one circumstance during this period to bind Jemima and Mr Farquhar together. They were still misunderstanding each other with all their power. The difference in the result was this. Jemima loved him all the more, in spite of quarrels and coolness. He was growing utterly weary of the petulant temper of which he was never certain; of the reception which varied day after day, according to the mood she was in and the thoughts that were uppermost; and he was almost startled to find how very glad he was that the little girls and Mrs Denbigh were coming home. His was a character to bask in peace; and lovely, quiet Ruth, with her low tones and soft replies, her delicate waving movements, appeared to him the very type of what a woman should be – a calm, serene soul, fashioning the body to angelic grace.

It was, therefore, with no slight interest that Mr Farquhar inquired daily after the health of little Leonard. He asked at the Bensons' house; and Sally answered him, with swollen and tearful eyes, that the child was very bad – very bad indeed. He asked at the doctor's; and the doctor told him, in a few short words, that 'it was only a bad kind of measles, and that the lad might have a struggle for it, but he thought he would get through. Vigorous children carried their force into everything; never did things by halves; if they were ill, they were sure to be in a high fever directly; if they were well, there was no peace in the house for their rioting. For his part,' continued the doctor, 'he thought he was glad he had had no children; as far as he could judge, they were pretty much all plague and no profit.' But as he ended his speech he sighed;

and Mr Farquhar was none the less convinced that common report was true, which represented the clever, prosperous surgeon of Eccleston as bitterly disappointed at his failure of offspring.

While these various interests and feelings had their course outside the Chapel-house, within there was but one thought which possessed all the inmates. When Sally was not cooking for the little invalid, she was crying; for she had had a dream about green rushes, not three months ago, which, by some queer process of oneiromancy,[1] she interpreted to mean the death of a child; and all Miss Benson's endeavours were directed to making her keep silence to Ruth about this dream. Sally thought that the mother ought to be told; what were dreams sent for but for warnings? But it was just like a pack of Dissenters, who would not believe anything like other folks. Miss Benson was too much accustomed to Sally's contempt for Dissenters, as viewed from the pinnacle of the Establishment, to pay much attention to all this grumbling; especially as Sally was willing to take as much trouble about Leonard as if she believed he was going to live, and that his recovery depended upon her care. Miss Benson's great object was to keep her from having any confidential talks with Ruth; as if any repetition of the dream could have deepened the conviction in Ruth's mind that the child would die.

It seemed to her that his death would only be the fitting punishment for the state of indifference towards him – towards life and death – towards all things earthly or divine, into which she had suffered herself to fall since her last interview with Mr Donne. She did not understand that such exhaustion is but the natural consequence of violent agitation and severe tension of feeling. The only relief she experienced was in constantly serving Leonard; she had almost an animal's jealousy lest any one should come between her and her young. Mr Benson saw this jealous suspicion, although he could hardly understand it; but he calmed his sister's wonder and officious kindness, so that the two patiently and quietly provided all that Ruth might want, but did not interfere with her right to nurse Leonard. But when he was recovering, Mr Benson, with the slight tone of authority he knew how to assume when need was, bade Ruth lie down and take some rest, while his sister watched. Ruth did not answer, but obeyed in a dull, weary kind of surprise at being so commanded. She lay down by her child, gazing her fill at his calm slumber, and as she gazed, her large white eyelids were softly pressed down as with a gentle irresistible weight, and she fell asleep.

She dreamed that she was once more on the lonely shore, striving to carry Leonard away from some pursuer – some human pursuer – she knew he was human, and she knew who he was, although she dared not say his name even to herself, he seemed so close and present, gaining on her flying footsteps, rushing after her as with the sound of the roaring tide. Her feet seemed heavy weights fixed to the ground; they would not move. All at once, just near the shore, a great black whirlwind of waves clutched her back to her pursuer; she threw Leonard on to land, which was safety; but whether he reached it or no, or was swept back like her into a mysterious something too dreadful to be borne, she did not know, for the terror awakened her. At first the dream seemed yet a reality, and she thought that the pursuer was couched even there, in that very room, and the great boom of the sea was still in her ears. But as full consciousness returned, she saw herself safe in the dear old room – the haven of rest – the shelter from storms. A bright fire was glowing in the little old-fashioned, cup-shaped grate, niched into a corner of the wall, and guarded on either side by whitewashed bricks, which served for hobs. On one of these the kettle hummed and buzzed, within two points of boiling whenever she or Leonard required tea. In her dream that home-like sound had been the roar of the relentless sea, creeping swiftly on to seize its prey. Miss Benson sat by the fire, motionless and still; it was too dark to read any longer without a candle; but yet on the ceiling and upper part of the walls the golden light of the setting sun was slowly moving – so slow, and yet a motion gives the feeling of rest to the weary yet more than perfect stillness. The old clock on the staircase told its monotonous click-clack, in that soothing way which more marked the quiet of the house than disturbed with any sense of sound. Leonard still slept that renovating slumber, almost in her arms, far from that fatal pursuing sea, with its human form of cruelty. The dream was a vision; the reality which prompted the dream was over and past – Leonard was safe – she was safe; all this loosened the frozen springs, and they gushed forth in her heart, and her lips moved in accordance with her thoughts.

'What were you saying, my darling?' said Miss Benson, who caught sight of the motion, and fancied she was asking for something. Miss Benson bent over the side of the bed on which Ruth lay, to catch the low tones of her voice.

'I only said,' replied Ruth, timidly, 'thank God! I have so much to thank Him for, you don't know.'

'My dear, I am sure we have all of us cause to be thankful that our boy is spared. See! he is wakening up; and we will have a cup of tea together.'

Leonard strode on to perfect health; but he was made older in character and looks by his severe illness. He grew tall and thin, and the lovely child was lost in the handsome boy. He began to wonder, and to question. Ruth mourned a little over the vanished babyhood, when she was all in all, and over the childhood, whose petals had fallen away; it seemed as though two of her children were gone – the one an infant, the other a bright thoughtless darling; and she wished that they could have remained quick in her memory for ever, instead of being absorbed in loving pride for the present boy. But these were only fanciful regrets, flitting like shadows across a mirror. Peace and thankfulness were once more the atmosphere of her mind; nor was her unconsciousness disturbed by any suspicion of Mr Farquhar's increasing approbation and admiration, which he was diligently nursing up into love for her. She knew that he had sent – she did not know how often he had brought – fruit for the convalescent Leonard. She heard, on her return from her daily employment, that Mr Farquhar had brought a little gentle pony on which Leonard, weak as he was, might ride. To confess the truth, her maternal pride was such that she thought that all kindness shown to such a boy as Leonard was but natural; she believed him to be

A child whom all that looked on, loved.[2]

As in truth he was; and the proof of this was daily shown in many kind inquiries, and many thoughtful little offerings, besides Mr Farquhar's. The poor (warm and kind of heart to all sorrow common to humanity) were touched with pity for the young widow, whose only child lay ill, and nigh unto death.[3] They brought what they could – a fresh egg, when eggs were scarce – a few ripe pears that grew on the sunniest side of the humble cottage, where the fruit was regarded as a source of income – a call of inquiry, and a prayer that God would spare the child, from an old crippled woman, who could scarcely drag herself so far as the Chapel-house, yet felt her worn and weary heart stirred with a sharp pang of sympathy, and a very present remembrance of the time when she too was young, and saw the life-breath quiver out of her child, now an angel in that heaven, which felt more like home to the desolate old creature than this empty earth. To all such, when Leonard was better, Ruth went, and thanked them from her heart. She and the old cripple sat hand in hand over the scanty fire on the hearth of the latter, while she told in solemn, broken, homely words, how her child sickened and died. Tears fell like rain down Ruth's cheeks; but those of the old woman were dry. All tears had been wept out of her long ago, and now she sat patient and quiet, waiting for death. But after this Ruth 'clave unto her',[4] and the two were henceforward a pair of friends. Mr Farquhar was only included in the general gratitude which she felt towards all who had been kind to her boy.

The winter passed away in deep peace after the storms of the autumn, yet every now and then a feeling of insecurity made Ruth shake for an instant. Those wild autumnal storms had torn aside the quiet flowers and herbage that had gathered over the wreck of her early life, and shown her that all deeds, however hidden and long passed by, have their eternal consequences. She turned sick and faint whenever Mr Donne's name was casually mentioned. No one saw it; but she felt the miserable stop in her heart's beating, and wished that she could prevent it by any exercise of self-command. She had never named his identity with Mr Bellingham, nor had she spoken about the sea-side interview. Deep shame made her silent and reserved on all her life before Leonard's birth; from that time she rose again in her self-respect, and spoke as openly as a child (when need was) of all occurrences which had taken place since then; except that she could not, and would not, tell of this mocking echo, this haunting phantom, this past, that would not rest in its grave.[5] The very circumstance that it was stalking abroad in the world, and might re-appear at any moment, made her a coward: she trembled away from contemplating what the reality had been; only she clung more faithfully than before to the thought of the great God, who was a rock in the dreary land, where no shadow was.[6]

Autumn and winter, with their lowering skies, were less dreary than the woeful, desolate feelings that shed a gloom on Jemima. She found too late that she had considered Mr Farquhar so securely her own for so long a time, that her heart refused to recognise him as lost to her, unless her reason went through the same weary, convincing, miserable evidence day after day, and hour after hour. He never spoke to her now, except from common civility. He never cared for her contradictions;

he never tried, with patient perseverance, to bring her over to his opinions; he never used the wonted wiles (so tenderly remembered now they had no existence but in memory) to bring her round out of some wilful mood – and such moods were common enough now! Frequently she was sullenly indifferent to the feelings of others – not from any unkindness, but because her heart seemed numb and stony, and incapable of sympathy. Then afterwards her self-reproach was terrible – in the dead of night, when no one saw it. With a strange perversity, the only intelligence she cared to hear, the only sights she cared to see, were the circumstances which gave confirmation to the idea that Mr Farquhar was thinking of Ruth for a wife. She craved with stinging curiosity to hear something of their affairs every day; partly because the torture which such intelligence gave was almost a relief from the deadness of her heart to all other interests.

And so spring (*gioventù dell'anno*)[7] came back to her, bringing all the contrasts which spring alone can bring to add to the heaviness of the soul. The little winged creatures filled the air with bursts of joy; the vegetation came bright and hopefully onwards, without any check of nipping frost. The ash-trees in the Bradshaws' garden were out in leaf by the middle of May, which that year wore more the aspect of summer than most Junes do. The sunny weather mocked Jemima, and the unusual warmth oppressed her physical powers. She felt very weak and languid; she was acutely sensible that no one else noticed her want of strength; father, mother, all seemed too full of other things to care if, as she believed, her life was waning. She herself felt glad that it was so. But her delicacy was not unnoticed by all. Her mother often anxiously asked her husband if he did not think Jemima was looking ill; nor did his affirmation to the contrary satisfy her, as most of his affirmations did. She thought every morning, before she got up, how she could tempt Jemima to eat, by ordering some favourite dainty for dinner; in many other little ways she tried to minister to her child; but the poor girl's own abrupt irritability of temper had made her mother afraid of openly speaking to her about her health.

Ruth, too, saw that Jemima was not looking well. How she had become an object of dislike to her former friend she did not know; but she was sensible that Miss Bradshaw disliked her now. She was not aware that this feeling was growing and strengthening almost into repugnance, for she seldom saw Jemima out of school-hours, and then only for a minute or two. But the evil element of a fellow-creature's dislike oppressed the atmosphere of her life. That fellow-creature was one who had once loved her so fondly, and whom she still loved, although she had learnt to fear her, as we fear those whose faces cloud over when we come in sight – who cast unloving glances at us, of which we, though not seeing, are conscious, as of some occult influence; and the cause of whose dislike is unknown to us, though every word and action seems to increase it. I believe that this sort of dislike is only shown by the jealous, and that it renders the disliker even more miserable, because more continually conscious than the object; but the growing evidences of Jemima's feeling made Ruth very unhappy at times. This very May, too, an idea had come into her mind, which she had tried to repress – namely, that Mr Farquhar was in love with her. It annoyed her extremely; it made her reproach herself that she ever should think such a thing possible. She tried to strangle the notion, to drown it, to starve it out by neglect – its existence caused her such pain and distress.

The worst was, he had won Leonard's heart, who was constantly seeking him out; or, when absent, talking about him. The best was some journey connected with business, which would take him to the continent for several weeks; and, during that time, surely this disagreeable fancy of his would die away, if untrue; and if true, some way would be opened by which she might put a stop to all increase of predilection on his part, and yet retain him as a friend for Leonard – that darling for whom she was far-seeing and covetous, and miserly of every scrap of love and kindly regard.

Mr Farquhar would not have been flattered if he had known how much his departure contributed to Ruth's rest of mind on the Saturday afternoon on which he set out on his journey. It was a beautiful day; the sky of that intense quivering blue which seemed as though you could look through it for ever, yet not reach the black, infinite space which is suggested as lying beyond. Now and then a thin, torn, vaporous cloud floated slowly within the vaulted depth; but the soft air that gently wafted it was not perceptible among the leaves on the trees, which did not even tremble. Ruth sat at her work in the shadow formed by the old grey garden wall; Miss Benson and Sally – the one in the parlour window-seat mending stockings, the other hard at work in her kitchen – were both within talking distance, for it was weather for open doors and windows; but none of the three kept up any continued conversation; and in the intervals Ruth sang low a brooding song, such as she remembered her mother singing long ago. Now and then she stopped to look at Leonard, who was labouring away with vehement energy at digging over a small plot of ground, where he meant to prick out some celery plants that had been given to him. Ruth's heart warmed at the earnest, spirited way in which he thrust his large spade deep down into the brown soil, his ruddy face glowing, his curly hair wet with the exertion; and yet she sighed to think that the days were over when her deeds of skill could give him pleasure. Now, his delight was in acting himself; last year, not fourteen months ago, he had watched her making a daisy-chain for him, as if he could not admire her cleverness enough; this year – this week, when she had been devoting every spare hour to the simple tailoring which she performed for her boy (she had always made every article he wore, and felt almost jealous of the employment), he had come to her with a wistful look, and asked when he might begin to have clothes made by a man?

Ever since the Wednesday when she had accompanied Mary and Elizabeth, at Mrs Bradshaw's desire, to be measured for spring clothes by the new Eccleston dressmaker, she had been looking forward to this Saturday afternoon's pleasure of making summer trousers for Leonard; but the satisfaction of the employment was a little taken away by Leonard's speech. It was a sign, however, that her life was very quiet and peaceful that she had leisure to think upon the thing at all; and often she forgot it entirely in her low, chanting song, or in listening to the thrush warbling out his afternoon ditty to his patient mate in the holly-bush below.

The distant rumble of carts through the busy streets (it was market-day) not only formed a low rolling bass to the nearer and pleasanter sounds, but enhanced the sense of peace by the suggestion of the contrast afforded to the repose of the garden by the bustle not far off.

But besides physical din and bustle there is mental strife and turmoil.

That afternoon, as Jemima was restlessly wandering about the house, her mother desired her to go on an errand to Mrs Pearson's, the new dressmaker, in order to give some directions about her sisters' new frocks. Jemima went, rather than have the trouble of resisting; or else she would have preferred staying at home, moving or being outwardly quiet according to her own fitful will. Mrs Bradshaw, who, as I have said, had been aware for some time that something was wrong with her daughter, and was very anxious to set it to rights if she only knew how, had rather planned this errand with a view to dispel Jemima's melancholy.

'And Mimie dear,' said her mother, 'when you are there, look out for a new bonnet for yourself; she has got some very pretty ones, and your old one is so shabby.'

'It does for me, mother,' said Jemima, heavily. 'I don't want a new bonnet.'

'But I want you to have one, my lassie. I want my girl to look well and nice.'

There was something of homely tenderness in Mrs Bradshaw's tone that touched Jemima's heart. She went to her mother, and kissed her with more of affection than she had shown to any one for weeks before; and the kiss was returned with warm fondness.

'I think you love me, mother,' said Jemima.

'We all love you, dear, if you would but think so. And if you want anything, or wish for anything, only tell me, and with a little patience I can get your father to give it you, I know. Only be happy, there's a good girl.'

'Be happy! as if one could by an effort of will!' thought Jemima, as she went along the street, too absorbed in herself to notice the bows of acquaintances and friends, but instinctively guiding herself right among the throng and press of carts, and gigs, and market people in High-street.

But her mother's tones and looks, with their comforting power, remained longer in her recollection than the inconsistency of any words spoken. When she had completed her errand about the frocks, she asked to look at some bonnets, in order to show her recognition of her mother's kind thought.

Mrs Pearson was a smart, clever-looking woman of five or six and thirty. She had all the variety of small-talk at her finger ends that was formerly needed by barbers to amuse the people who came to be shaved. She had admired the town till Jemima was weary of its praises, sick and oppressed by its sameness, as she had been these many weeks.

'Here are some bonnets, ma'am, that will be just the thing for you – elegant and tasty, yet quite of the simple style, suitable to young ladies. Oblige me by trying on this white silk!'

Jemima looked at herself in the glass; she was obliged to own it was very becoming, and perhaps not the less so for the flush of modest shame which came into her cheeks as she heard Mrs Pearson's open praises of the 'rich beautiful hair', and the 'Oriental eyes' of the wearer.

'I induced the young lady who accompanied your sisters the other day – the governess, is she, ma'am?'

'Yes – Mrs Denbigh is her name,' said Jemima, clouding over.

'Thank you, ma'am. Well, I persuaded Mrs Denbigh to try on that bonnet, and you can't think how charming she looked in it; and yet I don't think it became her as much as it does you.'

'Mrs Denbigh is very beautiful,' said Jemima, taking off the bonnet, and not much inclined to try on any other.

'Very, ma'am. Quite a peculiar style of beauty. If I might be allowed, I should say that hers was a Grecian style of loveliness, while yours was Oriental. She reminded me of a young person I once knew in Fordham.' Mrs Pearson sighed an audible sigh.

'In Fordham!' said Jemima, remembering that Ruth had once spoken of the place as one in which she had spent some time, while the county in which it was situated was the same in which Ruth was born. 'In Fordham! Why, I think Mrs Denbigh comes from that neighbourhood.'

'Oh, ma'am! she cannot be the young person I mean – I am sure, ma'am – holding the position she does in your establishment. I should hardly say I knew her myself; for I only saw her two or three times at my sister's house; but she was so remarked for her beauty, that I remember her face quite well – the more so, on account of her vicious conduct afterwards.'

'Her vicious conduct!' repeated Jemima, convinced by these words that there could be no identity between Ruth and the 'young person' alluded to. 'Then it could not have been our Mrs Denbigh.'

'Oh, no, ma'am! I am sure I should be sorry to be understood to have suggested anything of the kind. I beg your pardon if I did so. All I meant to say – and perhaps that was a liberty I ought not to have taken, considering what Ruth Hilton was—'

'Ruth Hilton!' said Jemima, turning suddenly round, and facing Mrs Pearson.

'Yes, ma'am, that was the name of the young person I allude to.'

'Tell me about her – what did she do?' asked Jemima, subduing her eagerness of tone and look as best she might, but trembling as on the verge of some strange discovery.

'I don't know whether I ought to tell you, ma'am – it is hardly a fit story for a young lady; but this Ruth Hilton was an apprentice to my sister-in-law, who had a first-rate business in Fordham, which brought her a good deal of patronage from the county families; and this young creature was very artful and bold, and thought sadly too much of her beauty; and, somehow, she beguiled a young gentleman, who took her into keeping[8] (I am sure, ma'am, I ought to apologise for polluting your ears—)'

'Go on,' said Jemima, breathlessly.

'I don't know much more. His mother followed him into Wales. She was a lady of a great deal of religion, and of a very old family, and was much shocked at her son's misfortune in being captivated by such a person; but she led him to repentance, and took him to Paris, where, I think, she died; but I am not sure; for, owing to family differences, I have not been on terms for some years with my sister-in-law, who was my informant.'

'Who died?' interrupted Jemima – 'the young man's mother, or – or Ruth Hilton?'

'Oh dear, ma'am! pray don't confuse the two. It was the mother, Mrs — I forget the name – something like Billington. It was the lady who died.'

'And what became of the other?' asked Jemima, unable, as her dark suspicion seemed thickening, to speak the name.

'The girl? Why, ma'am, what could become of her? Not that I know exactly – only one knows they can but go from bad to worse, poor creatures! God forgive me, if I am speaking too transiently of such degraded women, who, after all, are a disgrace to our sex.'

'Then you know nothing more about her?' asked Jemima.

'I did hear that she had gone off with another gentleman that she met with in Wales, but I'm sure I can't tell who told me.'

There was a little pause. Jemima was pondering on all she had heard. Suddenly she felt that Mrs Pearson's eyes were upon her, watching her; not with curiosity, but with a newly-awakened intelligence; – and yet she must ask one more question; but she tried to ask it in an indifferent, careless tone, handling the bonnet while she spoke.

'How long is it since all this – all you have been telling me about – happened?' (Leonard was eight years old.)

'Why – let me see. It was before I was married, and I was married three years, and poor dear Pearson has been deceased five – I should say, going on for nine years this summer. Blush roses would become your complexion, perhaps, better than these lilacs,' said she, as with superficial observation she watched Jemima, turning the bonnet round and round on her hand – the bonnet that her dizzy eyes did not see.

'Thank you. It is very pretty. But I don't want a bonnet. I beg your pardon for taking up your time.' And with an abrupt bow to the discomfited Mrs Pearson, she was out and away in the open air, threading her way with instinctive energy along the crowded street. Suddenly she turned round, and went back to Mrs Pearson's, with even more rapidity than she had been walking away from the house.

'I have changed my mind,' said she, as she came, breathless, up into the show-room. 'I will take the bonnet. How much is it?'

'Allow me to change the flowers; it can be done in an instant, and then you can see if you would not prefer the roses; but with either foliage it is a lovely little bonnet,' said Mrs Pearson, holding it up admiringly on her hand.

'Oh! never mind the flowers – yes! change them to roses.' And she stood by, agitated (Mrs Pearson thought with impatience) all the time the milliner was making the alteration with skilful, busy haste.

'By the way,' said Jemima, when she saw the last touches were being given, and that she must not delay executing the purpose which was the real cause of her return – 'Papa, I am sure, would not like your connecting Mrs Denbigh's name with such a – story as you have been telling me.'

'Oh dear! ma'am, I have too much respect for you all to think of doing such a thing! Of course I know, ma'am, that it is not to be cast up to any lady that she is like anybody disreputable.'

'But I would rather you did not name the likeness to any one,' said Jemima; 'not to any one. Don't tell any one the story you have told me this morning.'

'Indeed, ma'am, I should never think of such a thing! My poor husband could have borne witness that I am as close as the grave where there is anything to conceal.'

'Oh dear!' said Jemima, 'Mrs Pearson, there is nothing to conceal; only you must not speak about it.'

'I certainly shall not do it, ma'am; you may rest assured of me.'

This time Jemima did not go towards home, but in the direction of the outskirts of the town, on the hilly side. She had some dim recollection of hearing her sisters ask if they might not go and invite Leonard and his mother to tea; and how could she face Ruth, after the conviction had taken possession of her heart that she, and the sinful creature she had just heard of, were one and the same?

It was yet only the middle of the afternoon; the hours were early in the old-fashioned town of Eccleston. Soft white clouds had come slowly sailing up out of the west; the plain was flecked with thin floating shadows, gently borne along by the westerly wind that was waving the long grass in the hay-fields into alternate light and shade. Jemima went into one of these fields, lying by the side of the upland road. She was stunned by the shock she had received. The diver, leaving the green sward, smooth and known, where his friends stand with their familiar smiling faces, admiring his glad bravery – the diver, down in an instant in the horrid depths of the sea, close to some strange, ghastly, lidless-eyed monster, can hardly more feel his blood curdle at the near terror than did Jemima now. Two hours ago – but a point of time on her mind's dial – she had never imagined that she should ever come in contact with any one who had committed open sin; she had never shaped her conviction into words and sentences, but still it was *there*, that all the respectable, all the family and religious circumstances of her life, would hedge her in, and guard her from ever encountering the great shock of coming face to face with Vice. Without being pharisaical in her estimation of herself, she had all a Pharisee's dread of publicans and sinners,[9] and all a child's cowardliness – that cowardliness which prompts it to shut its eyes against the object of terror, rather than acknowledge its existence with brave faith. Her father's often reiterated speeches had not been without their effect. He drew a clear line of partition, which separated mankind into two great groups, to one of which, by the grace of God, he and his belonged; while the other was composed of those whom it was his duty to try and reform, and bring the whole force of his morality to bear upon, with lectures, admonitions, and exhortations – a duty to be performed, because it was a duty – but with very little of that Hope and Faith which is the Spirit that maketh alive. Jemima had rebelled against these hard doctrines of her father's, but their frequent repetition had had its effect, and led her to look upon those who had gone astray with shrinking, shuddering recoil, instead of with a pity, so Christ-like as to have both wisdom and tenderness in it.

And now she saw among her own familiar associates one, almost her house-fellow, who had been stained with that evil most repugnant to her womanly modesty, that would fain have ignored its existence altogether. She loathed the thought of meeting Ruth again. She wished that she could take her up, and put her down at a distance somewhere – anywhere – where she might never see or hear of her more; never be reminded, as she must be whenever she saw her, that such things were, in this sunny, bright, lark-singing earth, over which the blue dome of heaven bent softly down as Jemima sat in the hay-field that June afternoon; her cheeks flushed and red, but her lips pale and compressed, and her eyes full of a heavy, angry sorrow. It was Saturday, and the people in that part of the country left their work an hour earlier on that day. By this, Jemima knew it must be growing time for her to be at home. She had had so much of conflict in her own mind of late, that she had grown to dislike struggle, or speech, or explanation; and so strove to conform to times and hours much more than she had done in happier days. But oh! how full of hate her heart was growing against the world! And oh! how she sickened at the thought of seeing Ruth! Who was to be trusted more, if Ruth – calm, modest, delicate, dignified Ruth – had a memory blackened by sin?

As she went heavily along, the thought of Mr Farquhar came into her mind. It showed how terrible had been the stun, that he had been forgotten until now. With the thought of him came in her first merciful feeling towards Ruth. This would never have been, had there been the least latent suspicion in Jemima's jealous mind that Ruth had purposely done aught – looked a look – uttered a word – modulated a tone – for the sake of attracting. As Jemima recalled all the passages of their intercourse, she slowly confessed to herself how pure and simple had been all Ruth's ways in relation to Mr Farquhar. It was not merely that there had been no coquetting, but there had been simple unconsciousness on Ruth's part, for so long a time after Jemima had discovered Mr Farquhar's inclination for her; and when at length she had slowly awakened to some perception of the state of his feelings, there had been a modest, shrinking dignity of manner, not startled, or emotional, or even timid, but pure, grave, and quiet; and this conduct of Ruth's, Jemima instinctively acknowledged to be of necessity transparent and sincere. Now, and here, there was no hypocrisy; but some time, some-where, on the part of somebody, what hypocrisy, what lies must have been acted, if not absolutely spoken, before Ruth could have been received by them all as the sweet, gentle, girlish widow, which she remembered they had all believed Mrs Denbigh to be when first she came among them. Could Mr and Miss Benson know? Could they be a party to the deceit? Not sufficiently acquainted with the world to understand how strong had been the temptation to play the part they did, if they wished to give Ruth a chance, Jemima could not believe them guilty of such deceit as the knowledge of Mrs Denbigh's previous conduct would imply; and yet how it darkened the latter into a treacherous hypocrite, with a black secret shut up in her soul for years – living in apparent confidence, and daily household familiarity with the Bensons for years, yet never telling the remorse that ought to be corroding her heart! Who was true? Who was not? Who was good and pure? Who was not? The very foundations of Jemima's belief in her mind were shaken.

Could it be false? Could there be two Ruth Hiltons? She went over every morsel of evidence. It could not be. She knew that Mrs Denbigh's former name had been Hilton. She had heard her speak casually, but charily, of having lived in Fordham. She knew she had been in Wales but a short time before she made her appearance in Eccleston. There was no doubt of the identity. Into the middle of Jemima's pain and horror at the afternoon's discovery, there came a sense of the power which the knowledge of this secret gave her over Ruth; but this was no relief, only an aggravation of the regret with which Jemima looked back on her state of ignorance. It was no wonder that when she arrived at home, she was so oppressed with headache that she had to go to bed directly.

'Quiet, mother! quiet, dear, dear mother' (for she clung to the known and tried goodness of her mother more than ever now), 'that is all I want.' And she was left to the stillness of her darkened room, the blinds idly flapping to and fro in the soft evening breeze, and letting in the rustling sound of the branches which waved close to her window, and the thrush's gurgling warble, and the distant hum of the busy town.

Her jealousy was gone – she knew not how or where. She might shun and recoil from Ruth, but she now thought that she could never more be jealous of her. In her pride of innocence, she felt almost ashamed that such a feeling could have had existence. Could Mr Farquhar hesitate between her own self and one who— No! she could not name what Ruth had been, even in thought. And yet he might never know, so fair a seeming did her rival wear. Oh! for one ray of God's holy light to know what was seeming, and what was truth in this traitorous hollow earth! It might be – she used to think such things possible, before sorrow had embittered her – that Ruth had worked her way through the deep purgatory of repentance up to something like purity again; God only knew! If her present goodness was real – if, after having striven back thus far on the heights, a fellow-woman was to throw her down into some terrible depth with her unkind, incontinent tongue, that would be too cruel! And yet, if – there was such woeful uncertainty and deceit somewhere – if Ruth— No! that Jemima with noble candour, admitted was impossible. Whatever Ruth had been, she was good, and to be respected as such, now. It did not follow that Jemima was to preserve the secret always; she doubted her own power to do so, if Mr Farquhar came home again, and were still constant in his admiration of Mrs Denbigh, and if Mrs Denbigh gave him any – the least encouragement. But this last she thought, from what she knew of Ruth's character, was impossible. Only, what was impossible after this afternoon's discovery? At any rate, she would watch, and wait. Come what might, Ruth was in her power. And, strange to say, this last certainty gave Jemima a kind of protecting, almost pitying, feeling for Ruth. Her horror at the wrong was not diminished; but the more she thought of the struggles that the wrong-doer must have made to extricate herself, the more she felt how cruel it would be to baffle all by revealing what had been. But for her sisters' sake she had a duty to perform; she must watch Ruth. For her love's sake she could not have helped watching; but she was too much stunned to recognise the force of her love, while duty seemed the only stable thing to cling to. For the present she would neither meddle nor mar in Ruth's course of life.

CHAPTER XXVI

So it was that Jemima no longer avoided Ruth, nor manifested by word or look the dislike which for a long time she had been scarce concealing. Ruth could not help noticing that Jemima always sought to be in her presence while she was at Mr Bradshaw's house; either when daily teaching Mary and Elizabeth, or when she came as an occasional visitor with Mr and Miss Benson, or by herself. Up to this time Jemima had used no gentle skill to conceal the abruptness with which she would leave the room rather than that Ruth and she should be brought into contact – rather than that it should fall to her lot to entertain Ruth during any part of the evening. It was months since Jemima had left off sitting in the school-room, as had been her wont during the first few years of Ruth's governess-ship. Now, each morning, Miss Bradshaw seated herself at a little round table in the window, at her work, or at her writing; but whether she sewed, or wrote, or read, Ruth felt that she was always watching – watching. At first, Ruth had welcomed all these changes in habit and behaviour, as giving her a chance, she thought, by some patient waiting or some opportune show of enduring constant love, to regain her lost friend's regard; but by-and-by, the icy chillness, immovable and grey, struck more to her heart than many sudden words of unkindness could have done. They might be attributed to the hot impulses of a hasty temper – to the vehement anger of an accuser; but this measured manner was the conscious result of some deep-seated feeling; this cold sternness befitted the calm implacability of some severe judge. The watching, which Ruth felt was ever upon her, made her unconsciously shiver, as you would if you saw that the passionless eyes of the dead were visibly gazing upon you. Her very being shrivelled and parched up in Jemima's presence, as if blown upon by a bitter, keen, east wind.

Jemima bent every power she possessed upon the one object of ascertaining what Ruth really was. Sometimes the strain was very painful; the constant tension made her soul weary; and she moaned aloud, and upbraided circumstance (she dared not go higher – to the maker of circumstance) for having deprived her of her unsuspicious happy ignorance.

Things were in this state when Mr Richard Bradshaw came on his annual home visit. He was to remain another year in London, and then to return and be admitted into the firm. After he had been a week at home he grew tired of the monotonous regularity of his father's household, and began to complain of it to Jemima.

'I wish Farquhar were at home. Though he is such a stiff, quiet old fellow, his coming in in the evenings makes a change. What has become of the Millses? They used to drink tea with us sometimes, formerly.'

'Oh! papa and Mr Mills took opposite sides at the election, and we have never visited since. I don't think they are any great loss.'

'Anybody is a loss – the stupidest bore that ever was would be a blessing, if he only would come in sometimes.'

'Mr and Miss Benson have drank tea here twice since you came.'

'Come, that's capital! Apropos of stupid bores, you talk of the Bensons. I did not think you had so much discrimination, my little sister.'

Jemima looked up in surprise; and then reddened angrily.

'I never meant to say a word against Mr or Miss Benson, and that you know quite well, Dick.'

'Never mind! I won't tell tales. They are stupid old fogeys, but they are better than nobody, especially as that handsome governess of the girls always comes with them to be looked at.'

There was a little pause; Richard broke it by saying:

'Do you know, Mimie, I've a notion, if she plays her cards well, she may hook Farquhar!'

'Who?' asked Jemima, shortly, though she knew quite well.

'Mrs Denbigh, to be sure. We were talking of her, you know. Farquhar asked me to dine with him at his hotel as he passed through town, and – I'd my own reasons for going and trying to creep up his sleeve[1] – I wanted him to tip me, as he used to do.'

'For shame! Dick,' burst in Jemima.

'Well, well! not tip me exactly, but lend me some money. The governor keeps me so deucedly short.'

'Why! it was only yesterday, when my father was speaking about your expenses, and your allowance, I heard you say that you'd more than you knew how to spend.'

'Don't you see that was the perfection of art. If my father had thought me extravagant, he would have kept me in with a tight rein; as it is, I'm in great hopes of a handsome addition, and I can tell you it's needed. If my father had given me what I ought to have had at first, I should not have been driven to the speculations and messes I've got into.'

'What speculations? What messes?' asked Jemima, with anxious eagerness.

'Oh! messes was not the right word. Speculations hardly was; for they are sure to turn out well, and then I shall surprise my father with my riches.' He saw that he had gone a little too far in his confidence, and was trying to draw in.

'But, what do you mean? Do explain it to me.'

'Never you trouble your head about my business, my dear. Women can't understand the share-market, and such things. Don't think I've forgotten the awful blunders you made when you tried to read the state of the money-market aloud to my father, that night when he had lost his spectacles. What were we talking of? Oh! of Farquhar and pretty Mrs Denbigh. Yes! I soon found out that was the subject my gentleman liked me to dwell on. He did not talk about her much himself, but his eyes sparkled when I told him what enthusiastic letters Polly and Elizabeth wrote about her. How old d'ye think she is?'

'I know!' said Jemima. 'At least, I heard her age spoken about, amongst other things, when first she came. She will be five-and-twenty this autumn.'

'And Farquhar is forty, if he is a day. She's young, too, to have such a boy as Leonard; younger-looking, or full as young-looking as she is! I tell you what, Mimie, she looks younger than you. How old are you? Three-and-twenty, ain't it?'

'Last March,' replied Jemima.

'You'll have to make haste and pick up somebody, if you're losing your good looks at this rate. Why, Jemima, I thought you had a good chance of Farquhar a year or two ago. How come you to have lost him? I'd far rather you'd had him than that proud, haughty Mrs Denbigh, who flashes her great grey eyes upon me if ever I dare to pay her a compliment. She ought to think it an honour that I take that much notice of her. Besides, Farquhar is rich, and it's keeping the business of the firm in one's own family; and if he marries Mrs Denbigh she will be sure to be wanting Leonard in when he's of age, and I won't have that. Have a try for Farquhar, Mimie! Ten to one it's not too late. I wish I'd brought you a pink bonnet down. You go about so dowdy – so careless of how you look.'

'If Mr Farquhar has not liked me as I am,' said Jemima, choking, 'I don't want to owe him to a pink bonnet.'

'Nonsense! I don't like to have my sisters' governess stealing a march on my sister. I tell you Farquhar is worth trying for. If you'll wear the pink bonnet I'll give it you, and I'll back you against Mrs Denbigh. I think you might have done something with "our member", as my father calls him, when you had him so long in the house. But, altogether, I should like Farquhar best for a brother-in-law. By the way, have you heard down here that Donne is going to be married? I heard of it in town, just before I left, from a man that was good authority. Some Sir Thomas Campbell's seventh daughter: a girl without a penny; father ruined himself by gambling, and obliged to live abroad. But Donne is not a man to care for any obstacle, from all accounts, when once he has taken a fancy. It was love at first sight, they say. I believe he did not know of her existence a month ago.'

'No! we have not heard of it,' replied Jemima. 'My father will like to know; tell it him;' continued she, as she was leaving the room, to be alone, in order to still her habitual agitation whenever she heard Mr Farquhar and Ruth coupled together.

Mr Farquhar came home the day before Richard Bradshaw left for town. He dropped in after tea at the Bradshaws'; he was evidently disappointed to see none but the family there, and looked round whenever the door opened.

'Look! look!' said Dick to his sister. 'I wanted to make sure of his coming in to-night, to save me my father's parting exhortations against the temptations of the world (as if I did not know much more of the world than he does!), so I used a spell I thought would prove efficacious; I told him that we should be by ourselves, with the exception of Mrs Denbigh, and look how he is expecting her to come in!'

Jemima did see; did understand. She understood, too, why certain packets were put carefully on one side, apart from the rest of the purchases of Swiss toys and jewellery, by which Mr Farquhar proved that none of Mr Bradshaw's family had been forgotten by him during his absence. Before the end of the evening, she was very conscious that her sore heart had not forgotten how to be jealous. Her brother did not allow a word, a look, or an incident, which might be supposed on Mr Farquhar's side to refer to Ruth, to pass unnoticed; he pointed out all to his sister, never dreaming of the torture he was inflicting, only anxious to prove his own extreme penetration. At length Jemima could stand it no longer, and left the room. She went into the school-room, where the shutters were not closed, as it only looked into the garden. She opened the window, to let the cool night air blow in on her hot cheeks. The clouds were hurrying over the moon's face in a tempestuous and unstable manner, making all things seem unreal; now clear out in its bright light, now trembling and quivering in shadow. The pain at her heart seemed to make Jemima's brain grow dull; she laid her head on her arms, which rested on the window-sill, and grew dizzy with the sick weary notion that the earth was wandering lawless and aimless through the heavens, where all seemed one tossed and whirling wrack of clouds. It was a waking nightmare, from the uneasy heaviness of which she was thankful to be roused by Dick's entrance.

'What, you are here, are you? I have been looking everywhere for you. I wanted to ask you if you have any spare money you could lend me for a few weeks?'

'How much do you want?' asked Jemima, in a dull, hopeless voice.

'Oh! the more the better. But I should be glad of any trifle, I am kept so confoundedly short.'

When Jemima returned with her little store, even her careless, selfish brother was struck by the wanness of her face, lighted by the bed-candle she carried.

'Come, Mimie, don't give it up. If I were you, I would have a good try against Mrs Denbigh. I'll send you the bonnet as soon as ever I get back to town, and you pluck up a spirit, and I'll back you against her even yet.'

It seemed to Jemima strange – and yet only a fitting part of this strange, chaotic world – to find that her brother, who was the last person to whom she could have given her confidence in her own family, and almost the last person of her acquaintance to whom she could look for real help and sympathy, should have been the only one to hit upon the secret of her love. And the idea passed away from his mind as quickly as all ideas not bearing upon his own self-interests did.

The night, the sleepless night, was so crowded and haunted by miserable images, that she longed for day; and when day came, with its stinging realities, she wearied and grew sick for the solitude of night. For the next week, she seemed to see and hear nothing but what confirmed the idea of Mr Farquhar's decided attachment to Ruth. Even her mother spoke of it as a thing which was impending, and which she wondered how Mr Bradshaw would like; for his approval or disapproval was the standard by which she measured all things.

'Oh! merciful God,' prayed Jemima, in the dead silence of the night, 'the strain is too great – I cannot bear it longer – my life – my love – the very essence of me, which is myself through time and eternity; and on the other side there is all-pitying Charity. If she had not been what she is – if she had shown any sign of triumph – any knowledge of her prize – if she had made any effort to gain his dear heart, I must have given way long ago, and taunted her, even if I did not tell others – taunted her, even though I sank down to the pit the next moment.

'The temptation is too strong for me. Oh, Lord! where is Thy peace that I believed in, in my childhood? – that I hear people speaking of now, as if it hushed up the troubles of life, and had not to be sought for – sought for, as with tears of blood!'

There was no sound nor sight in answer to this wild imploring cry, which Jemima half thought must force out a sign from Heaven. But there was a dawn stealing on through the darkness of her night.

It was glorious weather for the end of August. The nights were as full of light as the days – everywhere, save in the low dusky meadows by the river side, where the mists rose and blended the pale sky with the lands below. Unknowing of the care and trouble around them, Mary and Elizabeth exulted in the weather, and saw some new glory in every touch of the year's decay. They were clamorous for an expedition to the hills, before the calm stillness of the autumn should be disturbed by storms. They gained permission to go on the next Wednesday – the next half-holiday. They had won their mother over to consent to a full holiday, but their father would not hear of it. Mrs Bradshaw had proposed an early dinner, but the idea was scouted at[2] by the girls. What would the expedition be worth if they did not carry their dinners with them in baskets? Anything out of a basket, and eaten in the open air, was worth twenty times as much as the most sumptuous meal in the house. So the baskets were packed up, while Mrs Bradshaw wailed over probable colds to be caught from sitting on the damp ground. Ruth and Leonard were to go; they four. Jemima had refused all invitations to make one of the party; and yet she had a half sympathy with her sisters' joy – a sort of longing, lingering look back[3] to the time when she too would have revelled in the prospect that lay before them. They too would grow up, and suffer; though now they played, regardless of their doom.

The morning was bright and glorious; just cloud enough, as some one said, to make the distant plain look beautiful from the hills, with its floating shadows passing over the golden corn-fields. Leonard was to join them at twelve, when his lessons with Mr Benson, and the girls' with their masters, should be over. Ruth took off her bonnet, and folded her shawl with her usual dainty, careful neatness, and laid them aside in a corner of the room to be in readiness. She tried to forget the pleasure she always anticipated from a long walk towards the hills, while the morning's work went on; but she showed enough of sympathy to make the girls cling round her with many a caress of joyous love. Everything was beautiful in their eyes; from the shadows of the quivering leaves on the wall to the glittering beads of dew, not yet absorbed by the sun, which decked the gossamer web in the vine outside the window. Eleven o'clock struck. The Latin master went away, wondering much at the radiant faces of his pupils, and thinking that it was only very young people who could take such pleasure in the 'Delectus'.[4] Ruth said, 'Now, do let us try to be very steady this next hour,' and Mary pulled back Ruth's head, and gave the pretty budding mouth a kiss. They sat down to work, while Mrs Denbigh read aloud. A fresh sun-gleam burst into the room, and they looked at each other with glad anticipating eyes.

Jemima came in, ostensibly to seek for a book, but really from that sort of restless weariness of any one place or employment, which had taken possession of her since Mr Farquhar's return. She stood before the bookcase in the recess, languidly passing over the titles in search of the one she wanted. Ruth's voice lost a tone or two of its peacefulness, and her eyes looked more dim and anxious at Jemima's presence. She wondered in her heart if she dared to ask Miss Bradshaw to accompany them in their expedition. Eighteen months ago she would have urged it on her friend with soft loving entreaty; now she was afraid even to propose it as a hard possibility, everything she did or said was taken so wrongly – seemed to add to the old dislike, or the later stony contempt with which Miss Bradshaw had regarded her. While they were in this way Mr Bradshaw came into the room. His entrance – his being at home at all at this time – was so unusual a thing, that the reading was instantly stopped; and all four involuntarily looked at him, as if expecting some explanation of his unusual proceeding.

His face was almost purple with suppressed agitation.

'Mary and Elizabeth, leave the room. Don't stay to pack up your books. Leave the room, I say!' He spoke with trembling anger, and the frightened girls obeyed without a word. A cloud passing over the sun, cast a cold gloom into the room which was late so bright and beaming; but, by equalising the light, it took away the dark shadow from the place where Jemima had been standing, and her figure caught her father's eye.

'Leave the room, Jemima,' said he.

'Why, father?' replied she, in an opposition that was strange even to herself, but which was prompted by the sullen passion which seethed below the stagnant surface of her life, and which sought a vent in defiance. She maintained her ground, facing round upon her father, and Ruth – Ruth, who had risen, and stood trembling, shaking, a lightning-fear having shown her the precipice on which she stood. It was of no use; no quiet, innocent life – no profound silence, even to her own heart, as to the Past; the old offence could never be drowned in the Deep; but thus, when all was calm on the great, broad, sunny sea, it rose to the surface, and faced her with its unclosed eyes, and its ghastly countenance. The blood bubbled up to her brain, and made such a sound there, as of boiling waters, that she did not hear the words which Mr Bradshaw first spoke; indeed, his speech was broken and disjointed by intense passion. But she needed not to hear; she knew. As she rose up at first, so she stood now – numb and helpless. When her ears heard again (as if the sounds were drawing nearer, and becoming more distinct, from some faint, vague distance of space), Mr Bradshaw was saying, 'If there be one sin I hate – I utterly loathe – more than all others, it is wantonness.[5] It includes all other sins. It is but of a piece that you should have come with your sickly hypocritical face, imposing upon us all. I trust Benson did not know of it – for his own sake, I trust not. Before God, if he got you into my house on false pretences, he shall find his charity at other men's expense shall cost him dear – you – the common talk of Eccleston for your profligacy—' He was absolutely choked by his boiling indignation. Ruth stood speechless, motionless. Her head drooped a little forward, her eyes were more than half veiled by the large quivering lids, her arms hung down straight and heavy. At last she heaved the weight off her heart enough to say, in a faint, moaning voice, speaking with infinite difficulty:

'I was so young.'

'The more depraved, the more disgusting you,' Mr Bradshaw exclaimed, almost glad that the woman, unresisting so long, should now begin to resist. But to his surprise (for in his anger he had forgotten her presence), Jemima moved forwards, and said, 'Father!'

'You hold your tongue, Jemima. You have grown more and more insolent – more and more disobedient every day. I now know who to thank for it. When such a woman came into my family there is no wonder at any corruption – any evil – any defilement—'

'Father!'

'Not a word! If, in your disobedience, you choose to stay and hear what no modest young woman would put herself in the way of hearing, you shall be silent when I bid you. The only good you can gain is in the way of warning. Look at that woman' (indicating Ruth, who moved her drooping head a little on one side, as if by such motion she could avert the pitiless pointing – her face growing whiter and whiter still every instant) – 'look at that woman, I say – corrupt long before she was your age – hypocrite for years! If ever you, or any child of mine, cared for her, shake her off from you, as St Paul shook off the viper – even into the fire.'[6] He stopped for very want of breath. Jemima, all flushed and panting, went up and stood side by side with wan Ruth. She took the cold, dead hand which hung next to her in her warm convulsive grasp, and, holding it so tight, that it was blue and discoloured for days, she spoke out beyond all power of restraint from her father.

'Father! I will speak. I will not keep silence. I will bear witness to Ruth. I have hated her – so keenly, may God forgive me! but you may know, from that, that my witness is true. I have hated her, and my hatred was only quenched into contempt – not contempt now, dear Ruth – dear Ruth' – (this was spoken with infinite softness and tenderness, and in spite of her father's fierce eyes and passionate gesture) – 'I heard what you have learnt now, father, weeks and weeks ago – a year it may be, all time of late has been so long; and I shuddered up from her and from her sin; and I might have spoken of it, and told it there and then, if I had not been afraid that it was from no good motive I should act in so doing, but to gain a way to the desire of my own jealous heart. Yes, father, to show you what a witness I am for Ruth, I will own that I was stabbed to the heart with jealousy; some one – some one cared for Ruth that – oh, father! spare me saying all.' Her face was double-dyed with crimson blushes, and she paused for one moment – no more.

'I watched her, and I watched her with my wild-beast eyes. If I had seen one paltering with duty – if I had witnessed one flickering shadow of untruth in word or action – if, more than all things, my woman's instinct had ever been conscious of the faintest speck of impurity in thought, or word, or look, my old hate would have flamed out with the flame of hell! my contempt would have turned to loathing disgust, instead of my being full of pity, and the stirrings of new-awakened love, and most true respect. Father, I have borne my witness!'

'And I will tell you how much your witness is worth,' said her father, beginning low, that his pent-up wrath might have room to swell out. 'It only convinces me more and more how deep is the corruption this wanton has spread in my family. She has come amongst us with her innocent seeming, and spread her nets well and skilfully. She has turned right into wrong, and wrong into right, and taught you all to be uncertain whether there be any such thing as Vice in the world, or whether it ought not to be looked upon as Virtue. She has led you to the brink of the deep pit, ready for the first chance circumstance to push you in. And I trusted – I trusted her – I welcomed her.'

'I have done very wrong,' murmured Ruth, but so low, that perhaps he did not hear her, for he went on lashing himself up.

'I welcomed her. I was duped into allowing her bastard – (I sicken at the thought of it)—'

At the mention of Leonard, Ruth lifted up her eyes for the first time since the conversation began, the pupils dilating, as if she were just becoming aware of some new agony in store for her. I have seen such a look of terror on a poor dumb animal's countenance, and once or twice on human faces. I pray I may never see it again on either! Jemima felt the hand she held in her strong grasp writhe itself free. Ruth spread her arms before her, clasping and lacing her fingers together, her head thrown a little back, as if in intensest suffering.

Mr Bradshaw went on:

'That very child and heir of shame to associate with my own innocent children! I trust they are not contaminated.'

'I cannot bear it – I cannot bear it,' were the words wrung out of Ruth.

'Cannot bear it! cannot bear it!' he repeated. 'You must bear it, madam. Do you suppose your child is to be exempt from the penalties of his birth? Do you suppose that he alone is to be saved from the upbraiding scoff? Do you suppose that he is ever to rank with other boys, who are not stained and marked with sin from their birth? Every creature in Eccleston may know what he is; do you think they will spare him their scorn? "Cannot bear it," indeed! Before you went into your sin, you should have thought whether you could bear the consequences or not – have had some idea how far your offspring would be degraded and scouted, till the best thing that could happen to him would be for him to be lost to all sense of shame, dead to all knowledge of guilt, for his mother's sake.'

Ruth spoke out. She stood like a wild creature at bay, past fear now. 'I appeal to God against such a doom for my child. I appeal to God to help me. I am a mother, and as such I cry to God for help – for help to keep my boy in His pitying sight, and to bring him up in His holy fear. Let the shame fall on me! I have deserved it, but he – he is so innocent and good.'

Ruth had caught up her shawl, and was tying on her bonnet with her trembling hands. What if Leonard was hearing of her shame from common report? What would be the mysterious shock of the intelligence? She must face him, and see the look in his eyes, before she knew whether he recoiled from her; he might have his heart turned to hate her, by their cruel jeers.

Jemima stood by, dumb and pitying. Her sorrow was past her power. She helped in arranging the dress, with one or two gentle touches, which were hardly felt by Ruth, but which called out all Mr Bradshaw's ire afresh; he absolutely took her by the shoulders and turned her by force out of the room. In the hall, and along the stairs, her passionate woeful crying was heard. The sound only concentrated Mr Bradshaw's anger on Ruth. He held the street door open wide and said, between his teeth, 'If ever you, or your bastard, darken this door again, I will have you both turned out by the police!'

He needed not have added this if he had seen Ruth's face.

CHAPTER XXVII

As Ruth went along the accustomed streets, every sight and every sound seemed to bear a new meaning, and each and all to have some reference to her boy's disgrace. She held her head down, and scudded along dizzy with fear, lest some word should have told him what she had been, and what he was, before she could reach him. It was a wild unreasoning fear, but it took hold of her as strongly as if it had been well founded. And, indeed, the secret whispered by Mrs Pearson, whose curiosity and suspicion had been excited by Jemima's manner, and confirmed since by many a little corroborating circumstance, had spread abroad, and was known to most of the gossips in Eccleston before it reached Mr Bradshaw's ears.

As Ruth came up to the door of the Chapel-house, it was opened, and Leonard came out, bright and hopeful as the morning, his face radiant at the prospect of the happy day before him. He was dressed in the clothes it had been such a pleasant pride to her to make for him. He had the dark blue ribbon tied round his neck that she had left out for him that very morning, with a smiling thought of how it would set off his brown handsome face. She caught him by the hand as they met, and turned him, with his face homewards, without a word. Her looks, her rushing movement, her silence, awed him; and although he wondered, he did not stay to ask why she did so. The door was on the latch; she opened it, and only said, 'Up-stairs,' in a hoarse whisper. Up they went into her own room. She drew him in, and bolted the door; and then, sitting down, she placed him (she had never let go of him) before her, holding him with her hands on each of his shoulders, and gazing into his face with a woeful look of the agony that could not find vent in words. At last she tried to speak; she tried with strong bodily effort, almost amounting to convulsion. But the words would not come; it was not till she saw the absolute terror depicted on his face that she found utterance; and then the sight of that terror changed the words from what she meant them to have been. She drew him to her, and laid her head upon his shoulder; hiding her face even there.

'My poor, poor boy! my poor, poor darling! Oh! would that I had died – I had died, in my innocent girlhood!'

'Mother! mother!' sobbed Leonard. 'What is the matter? Why do you look so wild and ill? Why do you call me your "poor boy"? Are we not going to Scaurside Hill? I don't much mind it, mother; only please don't gasp and quiver so. Dearest mother, are you ill? Let me call Aunt Faith!'

Ruth lifted herself up, and put away the hair that had fallen over and was blinding her eyes. She looked at him with intense wistfulness.

'Kiss me, Leonard!' said she – 'kiss me, my darling, once more in the old way!' Leonard threw himself into her arms, and hugged her with all his force, and their lips clung together as in the kiss given to the dying.

'Leonard!' said she at length, holding him away from her, and nerving herself up to tell him all by one spasmodic effort – 'Listen to me.' The boy stood breathless and still, gazing at her. On her impetuous transit from Mr Bradshaw's to the Chapel-house, her wild desperate thought had been that she would call herself by every violent, coarse name which the world might give her – that Leonard should hear those words applied to his mother first from her own lips; but the influence of his presence – for he was a holy and sacred creature in her eyes, and this point remained steadfast, though all the rest were upheaved – subdued her; and now it seemed as if she could not find words fine enough, and pure enough, to convey the truth that he must learn, and should learn from no tongue but hers.

'Leonard – when I was very young I did very wrong. I think God, who knows all, will judge me more tenderly than men – but I did wrong in a way which you cannot understand yet' (she saw the red flush come into his cheek, and it stung her as the first token of that shame which was to be his portion through life) – 'in a way people never forget, never forgive. You will hear me called the hardest names that ever can be thrown at women – I have been, to-day; and, my child, you must bear it patiently, because they will be partly true. Never get confused, by your love for me, into thinking that what I did was right. – Where was I?' said she, suddenly faltering, and forgetting all she had said and all she had got to say; and then, seeing Leonard's face of wonder, and burning shame and indignation, she went on more rapidly, as fearing lest her strength should fail before she had ended.

'And, Leonard,' continued she, in a trembling, sad voice, 'this is not all. The punishment of punishments lies awaiting me still. It is to see you suffer from my wrongdoing. Yes, darling! they will speak shameful things of you, poor innocent child! as well as of me, who am guilty. They will throw it in your teeth through life, that your mother was never married – was not married when you were born—'

'Were not you married? Are not you a widow?' asked he abruptly, for the first time getting anything like a clear idea of the real state of the case.

'No! May God forgive me, and help me!' exclaimed she, as she saw a strange look of repugnance cloud over the boy's face, and felt a slight motion on his part to extricate himself from her hold. It was as slight, as transient as it could be – over in an instant. But she had taken her hands away, and covered up her face with them as quickly – covered up her face in shame before her child; and in the bitterness of her heart she was wailing out, 'Oh! would to God I had died – that I had died as a baby – that I had died as a little baby hanging at my mother's breast!'

'Mother,' said Leonard, timidly putting his hand on her arm; but she shrank from him, and continued her low, passionate wailing. 'Mother,' said he, after a pause, coming nearer, though she saw it not – 'mammy darling,' said he, using the caressing name, which he had been trying to drop as not sufficiently manly, 'mammy, my own, own dear, dear, darling mother, I don't believe them – I don't, I don't, I don't, I don't!' He broke out into a wild burst of crying, as he said this. In a moment her arms were round the poor boy, and she was hushing him up like a baby on her bosom. 'Hush, Leonard! Leonard, be still, my child! I have been too sudden with you! – I have done you harm – oh! I have done you nothing but harm,' cried she, in a tone of bitter self-reproach.

'No, mother!' said he, stopping his tears, and his eyes blazing out with earnestness; 'there never was such a mother as you have been to me, and I won't believe any one who says it. I won't; and I'll knock them down if they say it again, I will!' He clenched his fist, with a fierce defiant look on his face.

'You forget, my child,' said Ruth, in the sweetest, saddest tone that ever was heard, 'I said it of myself; I said it because it was true.' Leonard threw his arms tight round her, and hid his face against her bosom. She felt him pant there like some hunted creature. She had no soothing comfort to give him. 'Oh, that she and he lay dead!'

At last, exhausted, he lay so still and motionless, that she feared to look. She wanted him to speak, yet dreaded his first words. She kissed his hair, his head, his very clothes; murmuring low, inarticulate, moaning sounds.

'Leonard,' said she, 'Leonard, look up at me! Leonard, look up!' But he only clung the closer, and hid his face the more.

'My boy!' said she, 'what can I do or say? If I tell you never to mind it – that it is nothing – I tell you false. It is a bitter shame and a sorrow that I have drawn down upon you. A shame, Leonard, because of me, your mother; but, Leonard, it is no disgrace or lowering of you in the eyes of God.' She spoke now as if she had found the clue which might lead him to rest and strength at last. 'Remember that, always. Remember that, when the time of trial comes – and it seems a hard and cruel thing that you should be called reproachful names by men,[1] and all for what was no fault of yours – remember God's pity and God's justice; and though my sin shall have made you an outcast in the world – oh, my child, my child!' – (she felt him kiss her, as if mutually trying to comfort her – it gave her strength to go on) – 'remember, darling of my heart, it is only your own sin that can make you an outcast from God.'

She grew so faint that her hold of him relaxed. He looked up affrighted. He brought her water – he threw it over her; in his terror at the notion that she was going to die and leave him, he called her by every fond name, imploring her to open her eyes.

When she partially recovered, he helped her to the bed, on which she lay still, wan and death-like. She almost hoped the swoon that hung around her might be Death, and in that imagination she opened her eyes to take a last look at her boy. She saw him pale and terror-stricken; and pity for his affright roused her, and made her forget herself in the wish that he should not see her death, if she were indeed dying.

'Go to Aunt Faith!' whispered she; 'I am weary, and want sleep.'

Leonard arose slowly and reluctantly. She tried to smile upon him, that what she thought would be her last look might dwell in his remembrance as tender and strong; she watched him to the door, she saw him hesitate, and return to her. He came back to her, and said in a timid, apprehensive tone, 'Mother – will *they* speak to me about—it?'

Ruth closed her eyes, that they might not express the agony she felt, like a sharp knife, at this question. Leonard had asked it with a child's desire of avoiding painful and mysterious topics, – from no personal sense of shame as she understood it, shame beginning thus early, thus instantaneously.

'No,' she replied. 'You may be sure they will not.'

So he went. But now she would have been thankful for the unconsciousness of fainting; that one little speech bore so much meaning to her hot, irritable brain. Mr and Miss Benson, all in their house, would never speak to the boy – but in his home alone would he be safe from what he had already learned to dread. Every form in which shame and opprobrium could overwhelm her darling, haunted her. She had been exercising strong self-control for his sake ever since she had met him at the house-door; there was now a re-action. His presence had kept her mind on its perfect balance. When that was withdrawn, the effect of the strain of power was felt. And athwart the fever-mists that arose to obscure her judgment, all sorts of will-o'-the-wisp plans flittered before her; tempting her to this and that course of action – to anything rather than patient endurance – to relieve her present state of misery by some sudden spasmodic effort, that took the semblance of being wise and right. Gradually all her desires, all her longing, settled themselves on one point. What had she done – what could she do, to Leonard, but evil? If she were away, and gone no one knew where – lost in mystery, as if she were dead – perhaps the cruel hearts might relent, and show pity on Leonard; while her perpetual presence would but call up the remembrance of his birth. Thus she reasoned in her hot dull brain; and shaped her plans in accordance.

Leonard stole down-stairs noiselessly. He listened to find some quiet place where he could hide himself. The house was very still. Miss Benson thought the purposed expedition had taken place, and never dreamed but that Ruth and Leonard were on distant sunny Scaurside Hill; and after a very early dinner, she had set out to drink tea with a farmer's wife who lived in the country two or three miles off. Mr Benson meant to have gone with her; but while they were at dinner, he had received an unusually authoritative note from Mr Bradshaw desiring to speak with him, so he went to that gentleman's house instead. Sally was busy in her kitchen, making a great noise (not unlike a groom rubbing down a horse) over her cleaning. Leonard stole into the sitting-room, and crouched behind the large old-fashioned sofa to ease his sore, aching heart, by crying with all the prodigal waste and abandonment of childhood.

Mr Benson was shown into Mr Bradshaw's own particular room. The latter gentleman was walking up and down, and it was easy to perceive that something had occurred to chafe him to great anger.

'Sit down, sir!' said he to Mr Benson, nodding to a chair.

Mr Benson sat down. But Mr Bradshaw continued his walk for a few minutes longer without speaking. Then he stopped abruptly, right in front of Mr Benson; and in a voice which he tried to render calm, but which trembled with passion – with a face glowing purple as he thought of his wrongs (and real wrongs they were) he began:

'Mr Benson, I have sent for you to ask – I am almost too indignant at the bare suspicion to speak as becomes me – but did you – I really shall be obliged to beg your pardon, if you are as much in the dark as I was yesterday, as to the character of that woman who lives under your roof?'

There was no answer from Mr Benson. Mr Bradshaw looked at him very earnestly. His eyes were fixed on the ground – he made no inquiry – he uttered no expression of wonder or dismay. Mr Bradshaw ground his foot on the floor with gathering rage; but, just as he was about to speak, Mr Benson rose up – a poor deformed old man – before the stern and portly figure that was swelling and panting with passion.

'Hear me, sir!' (stretching out his hand as if to avert the words which were impending). 'Nothing you can say, can upbraid me like my own conscience; no degradation you can inflict, by word or deed, can come up to the degradation I have suffered for years, at being a party to a deceit, even for a good end—'

'For a good end! – Nay! what next?'

The taunting contempt with which Mr Bradshaw spoke these words, almost surprised himself by what he imagined must be its successful power of withering; but in spite of it, Mr Benson lifted his grave eyes to Mr Bradshaw's countenance, and repeated:

'For a good end. The end was not, as perhaps you consider it to have been, to obtain her admission into your family – nor yet to put her in the way of gaining her livelihood; my sister and I would willingly have shared what we have with her; it was our intention to do so at first, if not for any length of time, at least as long as her health might require it. Why I advised (perhaps I only yielded to advice) a change of name – an assumption of a false state of widowhood – was because I earnestly desired to place her in circumstances in which she might work out her self-redemption; and you, sir, know how terribly the world goes against all such as have sinned as Ruth did. She was so young, too.'

'You mistake, sir; my acquaintance has not lain so much among that class of sinners as to give me much experience of the way in which they are treated. But, judging from what I have seen, I should say they meet with full as much leniency as they deserve; and supposing they do not – I know there are plenty of sickly sentimentalists just now who reserve all their interest and regard for criminals – why not pick out one of these to help you in your task of washing the blackamoor white? Why choose me to be imposed upon – my household into which to intrude your *protégée*? Why were my innocent children to be exposed to corruption? I say,' said Mr Bradshaw, stamping his foot, 'how dared you come into this house, where you were looked upon as a minister of religion, with a lie in your mouth? How dared you single me out, of all people, to be gulled and deceived, and pointed at through the town as the person who had taken an abandoned woman into his house to teach his daughters?'

'I own my deceit was wrong and faithless.'

'Yes! you can own it, now it is found out! There is small merit in that, I think!'

'Sir! I claim no merit. I take shame to myself. I did not single you out. You applied to me with your proposal that Ruth should be your children's governess.'

'Pah!'

'And the temptation was too great – No! I will not say that – but the temptation was greater than I could stand – it seemed to open out a path of usefulness.'

'Now, don't let me hear you speak so,' said Mr Bradshaw, blazing up. 'I can't stand it. It is too much to talk in that way when the usefulness was to consist in contaminating my innocent girls.'

'God knows that if I had believed there had been any danger of such contamination – God knows how I would have died sooner than have allowed her to enter your family. Mr Bradshaw, you believe me, don't you?' asked Mr Benson, earnestly.

'I really must be allowed the privilege of doubting what you say in future,' said Mr Bradshaw, in a cold contemptuous manner.

'I have deserved this,' Mr Benson replied. 'But,' continued he, after a moment's pause, 'I will not speak of myself, but of Ruth. Surely, sir, the end I aimed at (the means I took to obtain it were wrong, you cannot feel that more than I do) was a right one; and you will not – you cannot say, that your children have suffered from associating with her. I had her in my family, under the watchful eyes of three anxious persons for a year or more; we saw faults – no human being is without them – and poor Ruth's were but slight venial errors; but we saw no sign of a corrupt mind – no glimpse of boldness or forwardness – no token of want of conscientiousness; she seemed, and was, a young and gentle girl, who had been led astray before she fairly knew what life was.'

'I suppose most depraved women have been innocent in their time,' said Mr Bradshaw, with bitter contempt.

'Oh, Mr Bradshaw! Ruth was not depraved, and you know it. You cannot have seen her – have known her daily, all these years, without acknowledging that!' Mr Benson was almost breathless, awaiting Mr

Bradshaw's answer. The quiet self-control which he had maintained so long, was gone now.

'I saw her daily – I did *not* know her. If I had known her, I should have known she was fallen and depraved, and consequently not fit to come into my house, nor to associate with my pure children.'

'Now I wish God would give me power to speak out convincingly what I believe to be His truth, that not every woman who has fallen is depraved; that many – how many the Great Judgment Day will reveal to those who have shaken off the poor, sore, penitent hearts on earth – many, many crave and hunger after a chance for virtue – the help which no man gives to them – help – that gentle tender help which Jesus gave once to Mary Magdalen.'[2] Mr Benson was almost choked by his own feelings.

'Come, come, Mr Benson, let us have no more of this morbid way of talking. The world has decided how such women are to be treated; and, you may depend upon it, there is so much practical wisdom in the world that its way of acting is right in the long run, and that no one can fly in its face with impunity, unless, indeed, they stoop to deceit and imposition.'

'I take my stand with Christ against the world,' said Mr Benson, solemnly, disregarding the covert allusion to himself. 'What have the world's ways ended in? Can we be much worse than we are?'

'Speak for yourself, if you please.'

'Is it not time to change some of our ways of thinking and acting? I declare before God, that if I believe in any one human truth, it is this – that to every woman, who, like Ruth, has sinned, should be given a chance of self-redemption – and that such a chance should be given in no supercilious or contemptuous manner, but in the spirit of the holy Christ.'

'Such as getting her into a friend's house under false colours.'

'I do not argue on Ruth's case. In that I have acknowledged my error. I do not argue on any case. I state my firm belief, that it is God's will that we should not dare to trample any of His creatures down to the hopeless dust; that it is God's will that the women who have fallen should be numbered among those who have broken hearts to be bound up, not cast aside as lost beyond recall. If this be God's will, as a thing of God it will stand; and He will open a way.'

'I should have attached much more importance to all your exhortation on this point, if I could have respected your conduct in other matters. As it is, when I see a man who has deluded himself into considering falsehood right, I am disinclined to take his opinion on subjects connected with morality; and I can no longer regard him as a fitting exponent of the will of God. You perhaps understand what I mean, Mr Benson. I can no longer attend your chapel.'

If Mr Benson had felt any hope of making Mr Bradshaw's obstinate mind receive the truth, that he acknowledged and repented of his connivance at the falsehood by means of which Ruth had been received into the Bradshaw family, this last sentence prevented his making the attempt. He simply bowed and took his leave – Mr Bradshaw attending him to the door with formal ceremony.

He felt acutely the severance of the tie which Mr Bradshaw had just announced to him. He had experienced many mortifications in his intercourse with that gentleman, but they had fallen off from his meek spirit like drops of water from a bird's plumage; and now he only remembered the acts of substantial kindness rendered (the ostentation all forgotten) – many happy hours and pleasant evenings – the children whom he had loved dearer than he thought till now – the young people about whom he had cared, and whom he had striven to lead aright. He was but a young man when Mr Bradshaw first came to his chapel; they had grown old together; he had never recognised Mr Bradshaw as an old familiar friend so completely, as now when they were severed.

It was with a heavy heart that he opened his own door. He went to his study immediately; he sat down to steady himself into his position.

How long he was there – silent and alone – reviewing his life – confessing his sins – he did not know; but he heard some unusual sound in the house that disturbed him – roused him to present life. A slow, languid step came along the passage to the front door – the breathing was broken by many sighs.

Ruth's hand was on the latch when Mr Benson came out. Her face was very white, except two red spots on each cheek – her eyes were deep sunk and hollow, but glittered with feverish lustre. 'Ruth!' exclaimed he. She moved her lips, but her throat and mouth were too dry for her to speak.

'Where are you going?' asked he; for she had all her walking things on, yet trembled so, even as she stood, that it was evident she could not walk far without falling.

She hesitated – she looked up at him, still with the same dry glittering eyes. At last she whispered (for she could only speak in a whisper), 'To Helmsby – I am going to Helmsby.'

'Helmsby! my poor girl – may God have mercy upon you!' for he saw she hardly knew what she was saying. 'Where is Helmsby?'

'I don't know. In Lincolnshire, I think.'

'But why are you going there?'

'Hush! he's asleep,' said she, as Mr Benson had unconsciously raised his voice.

'Who is asleep?' asked Mr Benson.

'That poor little boy,' said she, beginning to quiver and cry.

'Come here!' said he, authoritatively, drawing her into the study. 'Sit down in that chair. I will come back directly.'

He went in search of his sister, but she had not returned. Then he had recourse to Sally, who was as busy as ever about her cleaning.

'How long has Ruth been at home?' asked he.

'Ruth! She has never been at home sin' morning. She and Leonard were to be off for the day somewhere or other with them Bradshaw girls.'

'Then she has had no dinner?'

'Not here, any rate. I can't answer for what she may have done at other places.'

'And Leonard – where is he?'

'How should I know? With his mother, I suppose. Leastways, that was what was fixed on. I've enough to do of my own, without routing after³ other folks.'

She went on scouring in no very good temper. Mr Benson stood silent for a moment.

'Sally,' he said, 'I want a cup of tea. Will you make it as soon as you can; and some dry toast too. I'll come for it in ten minutes.'

Struck by something in his voice, she looked up at him for the first time.

'What ha' ye been doing to yourself, to look so grim and grey? Tiring yourself all to tatters, looking after some naught,⁴ I'll be bound! Well! well! I mun make ye your tea, I reckon; but I did hope as you grew older you'd ha' grown wiser.'

Mr Benson made no reply, but went to look for Leonard, hoping that the child's presence might bring back to his mother the power of self-control. He opened the parlour door, and looked in, but saw no one. Just as he was shutting it, however, he heard a deep, broken, sobbing sigh; and, guided by the sound, he found the boy lying on the floor, fast asleep, but with his features all swollen and disfigured by passionate crying.

'Poor child! This was what she meant, then,' thought Mr Benson. 'He has begun his share of the sorrows too,' he continued, pitifully. 'No! I will not waken him back to consciousness.' So he returned alone into the study. Ruth sat where he had placed her, her head bent back, and her eyes shut. But when he came in she started up.

'I must be going,' she said, in a hurried way.

'Nay, Ruth, you must not go. You must not leave us. We cannot do without you. We love you too much.'

'Love me!' said she, looking at him wistfully. As she looked, her eyes filled slowly with tears. It was a good sign, and Mr Benson took heart to go on.

'Yes! Ruth. You know we do. You may have other things to fill up your mind just now, but you know we love you; and nothing can alter our love for you. You ought not to have thought of leaving us. You would not, if you had been quite well.'

'Do you know what has happened?' she asked, in a low, hoarse voice.

'Yes. I know all,' he answered. 'It makes no difference to us. Why should it?'

'Oh! Mr Benson, don't you know that my shame is discovered?' she replied, bursting into tears – 'and I must leave you, and leave Leonard, that you may not share in my disgrace.'

'You must do no such thing. Leave Leonard! You have no right to leave Leonard. Where could you go to?'

'To Helmsby,' she said, humbly. 'It would break my heart to go, but I think I ought, for Leonard's sake. I know I ought.' She was crying sadly by this time, but Mr Benson knew the flow of tears would ease her brain. 'It will break my heart to go, but I know I must.'

'Sit still here at present,' said he, in a decided tone of command. He went for the cup of tea. He brought it to her without Sally's being aware for whom it was intended.

'Drink this!' He spoke as you would do to a child, if desiring it to take medicine. 'Eat some toast.' She took the tea, and drank it feverishly;

but when she tried to eat, the food seemed to choke her. Still she was docile, and she tried.

'I cannot,' said she at last, putting down the piece of toast. There was a return of something of her usual tone in the words. She spoke gently and softly; no longer in the shrill, hoarse voice she had used at first. Mr Benson sat down by her.

'Now, Ruth, we must talk a little together. I want to understand what your plan was. Where is Helmsby? Why did you fix to go there?'

'It is where my mother lived,' she answered. 'Before she was married she lived there; and wherever she lived, the people all loved her dearly; and I thought – I think, that for her sake some one would give me work. I meant to tell them the truth,' said she, dropping her eyes; 'but still they would, perhaps, give me some employment – I don't care what – for her sake. I could do many things,' said she, suddenly looking up. 'I am sure I could weed – I could in gardens – if they did not like to have me in their houses. But perhaps some one, for my mother's sake – oh! my dear, dear mother! – do you know where and what I am?' she cried out, sobbing afresh.

Mr Benson's heart was very sore, though he spoke authoritatively, and almost sternly:

'Ruth! you must be still and quiet. I cannot have this. I want you to listen to me. Your thought of Helmsby would be a good one, if it was right for you to leave Eccleston; but I do not think it is. I am certain of this, that it would be a great sin in you to separate yourself from Leonard. You have no right to sever the tie by which God has bound you together.'

'But if I am here they will all know and remember the shame of his birth; and if I go away they may forget—'

'And they may not. And if you go away, he may be unhappy or ill; and you, who above all others have – and have from God – remember *that*, Ruth! – the power to comfort him, the tender patience to nurse him, have left him to the care of strangers. Yes; I know! But we ourselves are as strangers, dearly as we love him, compared to a mother. He may turn to sin, and want the long forbearance, the serene authority of a parent; and where are you? No dread of shame, either for yourself, or even for him, can ever make it right for you to shake off your responsibility.' All this time he was watching her narrowly, and saw her slowly yield herself up to the force of what he was saying.

'Besides, Ruth,' he continued, 'we have gone on falsely, hitherto. It has been my doing, my mistake, my sin. I ought to have known better. Now, let us stand firm on the truth. You have no new fault to repent of. Be brave and faithful. It is to God you answer, not to men. The shame of having your sin known to the world, should be as nothing to the shame you felt at having sinned. We have dreaded men too much, and God too little, in the course we have taken. But now be of good cheer. Perhaps you will have to find your work in the world very low – not quite working in the fields,' said he, with a gentle smile, to which she, downcast and miserable, could give no response. 'Nay, perhaps, Ruth,' he went on, 'you may have to stand and wait[5] for some time; no one may be willing to use the services you would gladly render; all may turn aside from you, and may speak very harshly of you. Can you accept all this treatment meekly, as but the reasonable and just penance God has laid upon you – feeling no anger against those who slight you, no impatience for the time to come (and come it surely will – I speak as having the word of God for what I say) when He, having purified you, even as by fire, will make a straight path for your feet?[6] My child, it is Christ the Lord who has told us of this infinite mercy of God. Have you faith enough in it to be brave, and bear on, and do rightly in patience and in tribulation?'

Ruth had been hushed and very still until now, when the pleading earnestness of his question urged her to answer.

'Yes!' said she. 'I hope – I believe I can be faithful for myself, for I have sinned and done wrong. But Leonard—' She looked up at him.

'But Leonard,' he echoed. 'Ah! there it is hard, Ruth. I own the world is hard and persecuting to such as he.' He paused to think of the true comfort for this sting. He went on. 'The world is not everything, Ruth; nor is the want of men's good opinion and esteem the highest need which man has. Teach Leonard this. You would not wish his life to be one summer's day. You dared not make it so, if you had the power. Teach him to bid a noble Christian welcome, to the trials which God sends – and this is one of them. Teach him not to look on a life of struggle, and perhaps of disappointment and incompleteness, as a sad and mournful end, but as the means permitted to the heroes and warriors in the army of Christ, by which to show their faithful following. Tell him of the hard and thorny path which was trodden once by the bleeding feet of One. Ruth! think of the Saviour's life and cruel death, and of His divine faithfulness. Oh, Ruth!' exclaimed he, 'when I look and see what you may be – what you *must* be to that boy, I cannot think how you could be coward enough, for a moment, to shrink from your work! But we have all been cowards hitherto,' he added, in bitter self-accusation. 'God help us to be so no longer!'

Ruth sat very quiet. Her eyes were fixed on the ground, and she seemed lost in thought. At length she rose up.

'Mr Benson!' said she, standing before him, and propping herself by the table, as she was trembling sadly from weakness, 'I mean to try very, very hard, to do my duty to Leonard – and to God,' she added, reverently. 'I am only afraid my faith may sometimes fail about Leonard—'

'Ask, and it shall be given unto you.[7] That is no vain or untried promise, Ruth!'

She sat down again, unable longer to stand. There was another long silence.

'I must never go to Mr Bradshaw's again,' she said at last, as if thinking aloud.

'No, Ruth, you shall not,' he answered.

'But I shall earn no money!' added she, quickly, for she thought that he did not perceive the difficulty that was troubling her.

'You surely know, Ruth, that while Faith and I have a roof to shelter us, or bread to eat, you and Leonard share it with us.'

'I know – I know your most tender goodness,' said she, 'but it ought not to be.'

'It must be at present,' he said, in a decided manner. 'Perhaps, before long you may have some employment; perhaps it may be some time before an opportunity occurs.'

'Hush,' said Ruth; 'Leonard is moving about in the parlour. I must go to him.'

But when she stood up, she turned so dizzy, and tottered so much, that she was glad to sit down again immediately.

'You must rest here. I will go to him,' said Mr Benson. He left her; and when he was gone, she leaned her head on the back of the chair, and cried quietly and incessantly; but there was a more patient, hopeful, resolved feeling in her heart, which all along, through all the tears she shed, bore her onwards to higher thoughts, until at last she rose to prayers.

Mr Benson caught the new look of shrinking shame in Leonard's eye, as it first sought, then shunned, meeting his. He was pained, too, by the sight of the little sorrowful, anxious face, on which, until now, hope and joy had been predominant. The constrained voice, the few words the boy spoke, when formerly there would have been a glad and free utterance – all this grieved Mr Benson inexpressibly, as but the beginning of an unwonted mortification, which must last for years. He himself made no allusion to any unusual occurrence; he spoke of Ruth as sitting, overcome by headache, in the study for quietness: he hurried on the preparations for tea, while Leonard sat by in the great armchair, and looked on with sad dreamy eyes. He strove to lessen the shock which he knew Leonard had received, by every mixture of tenderness and cheerfulness that Mr Benson's gentle heart prompted; and now and then a languid smile stole over the boy's face. When his bed-time came, Mr Benson told him of the hour, although he feared that Leonard would have but another sorrowful crying of himself to sleep; but he was anxious to accustom the boy to cheerful movement within the limits of domestic law, and by no disobedience to it to weaken the power of glad submission to the Supreme; to begin the new life that lay before him, where strength to look up to God as the Law-giver and Ruler of events would be pre-eminently required. When Leonard had gone up-stairs, Mr Benson went immediately to Ruth, and said:

'Ruth! Leonard is just gone up to bed,' secure in the instinct which made her silently rise, and go up to the boy – certain, too, that they would each be the other's best comforter, and that God would strengthen each through the other.

Now, for the first time, he had leisure to think of himself; and to go over all the events of the day. The half hour of solitude in his study, that he had before his sister's return, was of inestimable value; he had leisure to put events in their true places, as to importance and eternal significance.

Miss Faith came in laden with farm produce. Her kind entertainers had brought her in their shandry[8] to the opening of the court in which the Chapel-house stood; but she was so heavily burdened with eggs, mushrooms, and plums, that when her brother opened the door she was almost breathless.

'Oh, Thurstan! take this basket – it is such a weight! Oh, Sally, is that you? Here are some magnum-bonums[9] which we must preserve to-morrow. There are guinea-fowl eggs in that basket.'

Mr Benson let her unburden her body, and her mind too, by giving charges to Sally respecting her housekeeping treasures, before he said a word; but when she returned into the study, to tell him the small pieces of intelligence respecting her day at the farm, she stood aghast.

'Why, Thurstan, dear! What's the matter? Is your back hurting you?'

He smiled to reassure her; but it was a sickly and forced smile.

'No, Faith! I am quite well, only rather out of spirits, and wanting to talk to you to cheer me.'

Miss Faith sat down, straight, sitting bolt-upright to listen the better.

'I don't know how, but the real story about Ruth is found out.'

'Oh, Thurstan!' exclaimed Miss Benson, turning quite white.

For a moment, neither of them said another word. Then she went on:

'Does Mr Bradshaw know?'

'Yes! He sent for me, and told me.'

'Does Ruth know that it has all come out?'

'Yes. And Leonard knows.'

'How? Who told him?'

'I do not know. I have asked no questions. But of course it was his mother.'

'She was very foolish and cruel, then,' said Miss Benson, her eyes blazing, and her lips trembling, at the thought of the suffering her darling boy must have gone through.

'I think she was wise. I am sure it was not cruel. He must have soon known that there was some mystery, and it was better that it should be told him openly and quietly by his mother than by a stranger.'

'How could she tell him quietly?' asked Miss Benson, still indignant.

'Well! perhaps I used the wrong word – of course no one was by – and I don't suppose even they themselves could now tell how it was told, or in what spirit it was borne.'

Miss Benson was silent again.

'Was Mr Bradshaw very angry?'

'Yes, very; and justly so. I did very wrong in making that false statement at first.'

'No! I am sure you did not,' said Miss Faith. 'Ruth has had some years of peace, in which to grow stronger and wiser, so that she can bear her shame now in a way she never could have done at first.'

'All the same it was wrong in me to do what I did.'

'I did it too, as much or more than you. And I don't think it wrong.

I'm certain it was quite right, and I would do just the same again.'

'Perhaps it has not done you the harm it has done me.'

'Nonsense! Thurstan. Don't be morbid. I'm sure you are as good – and better than ever you were.'

'No, I am not. I have got what you call morbid just in consequence of the sophistry by which I persuaded myself that wrong could be right. I torment myself. I have lost my clear instincts of conscience. Formerly, if I believed that such or such an action was according to the will of God, I went and did it, or at least I tried to do it, without thinking of consequences. Now, I reason and weigh what will happen if I do so and so – I grope where formerly I saw. Oh, Faith! it is such a relief to me to have the truth known, that I am afraid I have not been sufficiently sympathising with Ruth.'

'Poor Ruth!' said Miss Benson. 'But at any rate our telling a lie has been the saving of her. There is no fear of her going wrong now.'

'God's omnipotence did not need our sin.'

They did not speak for some time.

'You have not told me what Mr Bradshaw said.'

'One can't remember the exact words that are spoken on either side in moments of such strong excitement. He was very angry, and said some things about me that were very just, and some about Ruth that were very hard. His last words were that he should give up coming to chapel.'

'Oh, Thurstan! did it come to that?'

'Yes.'

'Does Ruth know all he said?'

'No! Why should she? I don't know if she knows he has spoken to me at all. Poor creature! she had enough to craze her almost without that! She was for going away and leaving us that we might not share in her disgrace. I was afraid of her being quite delirious. I did so want you, Faith! However, I did the best I could, I spoke to her very coldly, and almost sternly, all the while my heart was bleeding for her. I dared not give her sympathy; I tried to give her strength. But I did so want you, Faith.'

'And I was so full of enjoyment, I am ashamed to think of it. But the Dawsons are so kind – and the day was so fine— Where is Ruth now?'

'With Leonard. He is her great earthly motive – I thought that being with him would be best. But he must be in bed and asleep now.'

'I will go up to her,' said Miss Faith.

She found Ruth keeping watch by Leonard's troubled sleep; but when she saw Miss Faith she rose up, and threw herself on her neck and clung to her, without speaking. After a while Miss Benson said:

'You must go to bed, Ruth!' So, after she had kissed the sleeping boy, Miss Benson led her away, and helped to undress her, and brought her up a cup of soothing violet-tea – not so soothing as tender actions and soft loving tones.

CHAPTER XXVIII

It was well they had so early and so truly strengthened the spirit to bear, for the events which had to be endured soon came thick and threefold.

Every evening Mr and Miss Benson thought the worst must be over; and every day brought some fresh occurrence to touch upon the raw place. They could not be certain, until they had seen all their acquaintances, what difference it would make in the cordiality of their reception: in some cases it made much; and Miss Benson was proportionably indignant. She felt this change in behaviour more than her brother. His great pain arose from the coolness of the Bradshaws. With all the faults which had at times grated on his sensitive nature (but which he now forgot, and remembered only their kindness), they were his old familiar friends – his kind, if ostentatious, patrons – his great personal interest, out of his own family; and he could not get over the suffering he experienced from seeing their large square pew empty on Sundays – from perceiving how Mr Bradshaw, though he bowed in a distant manner when he and Mr Benson met face to face, shunned him as often as he possibly could. All that happened in the household, which once was as patent to him as his own, was now a sealed book; he heard of its doings by chance, if he heard at all. Just at the time when he was feeling the most depressed from this cause, he met Jemima at a sudden turn of the street. He was uncertain for a moment how to accost her, but she saved him all doubt; in an instant she had his hand in both of hers, her face flushed with honest delight.

'Oh, Mr Benson, I am so glad to see you! I have so wanted to know all about you. How is poor Ruth? dear Ruth! I wonder if she has forgiven me my cruelty to her? And I may not go to her now, when I should be so glad and thankful to make up for it.'

'I never heard you had been cruel to her. I am sure she does not think so.'

'She ought, she must. What is she doing? Oh! I have so much to ask, I can never hear enough; and papa says' – she hesitated a moment, afraid of giving pain, and then, believing that they would understand the state of affairs, and the reason for her behaviour better if she told the truth, she went on: 'Papa says I must not go to your house – I suppose it's right to obey him?'

'Certainly, my dear. It is your clear duty. We know how you feel towards us.'

'Oh! but if I could do any good – if I could be of any use or comfort to any of you – especially to Ruth, I should come, duty or not. I believe it would be my duty,' said she, hurrying on to try and stop any decided prohibition from Mr Benson. 'No! don't be afraid; I won't come till I know I can do some good. I hear bits about you through Sally every now and then, or I could not have waited so long. Mr Benson,' continued she, reddening very much, 'I think you did quite right about poor Ruth.'

'Not in the falsehood, my dear.'

'No! not perhaps in that. I was not thinking of that. But I have been thinking a great deal about poor Ruth's—you know I could not help it when everybody was talking about it – and it made me think of myself, and what I am. With a father and mother, and home and careful friends, I am not likely to be tempted like Ruth; but oh! Mr Benson,' said she, lifting her eyes, which were full of tears, to his face, for the first time since she began to speak, 'if you knew all I have been thinking and feeling this last year, you would see how I have yielded to every temptation that was able to come to me; and, seeing how I have no goodness or strength in me, and how I might just have been like Ruth, or rather worse than she ever was, because I am more headstrong and passionate by nature, I do so thank you and love you for what you did for her! And will you tell me really and truly now if I can ever do anything for Ruth? If you'll promise me that, I won't rebel unnecessarily against papa; but if you don't, I will, and come and see you all this very afternoon. Remember! I trust you!' said she, breaking away. Then turning back, she came to ask after Leonard.

'He must know something of it,' said she. 'Does he feel it much?'

'Very much,' said Mr Benson. Jemima shook her head sadly.

'It is hard upon him,' said she.

'It is,' Mr Benson replied.

For in truth, Leonard was their greatest anxiety in-doors. His health seemed shaken, he spoke half sentences in his sleep, which showed that in his dreams he was battling on his mother's behalf against an unkind and angry world. And then he would wail to himself, and utter sad words of shame, which they never thought had reached his ears. By day, he was in general grave and quiet; but his appetite varied, and he was evidently afraid of going into the streets, dreading to be pointed at as an object of remark. Each separately in their hearts longed to give him change of scene, but they were all silent, for where was the requisite money to come from?

His temper became fitful and variable. At times he would be most sullen against his mother; and then give way to a passionate remorse. When Mr Benson caught Ruth's look of agony at her child's rebuffs, his patience failed; or rather, I should say, he believed that a stronger, severer hand than hers was required for the management of the lad. But, when she heard Mr Benson say so, she pleaded with him.

'Have patience with Leonard,' she said. 'I have deserved the anger that is fretting in his heart. It is only I who can reinstate myself in his love and respect. I have no fear. When he sees me really striving hard and long to do what is right, he must love me. I am not afraid.'

Even while she spoke, her lips quivered, and her colour went and came with eager anxiety. So Mr Benson held his peace, and let her take her course. It was beautiful to see the intuition by which she divined what was passing in every fold of her child's heart, so as to be always ready with the right words to soothe or to strengthen him. Her watchfulness was unwearied, and with no thought of self tainting in it, or else she might have often paused to turn aside and weep at the clouds of shame which came over Leonard's love for her, and hid it from all but her faithful heart; she believed and knew that he was yet her own affectionate boy, although he might be gloomily silent, or apparently hard and cold. And in all this, Mr Benson could not choose but admire the way in which she was insensibly teaching Leonard to conform to the law of right, to recognise Duty in the mode in which every action was performed. When Mr Benson saw this, he knew that all goodness would follow, and that the claims which his mother's infinite love had on the boy's heart would be acknowledged at last, and all the more fully because she herself never urged them, but silently admitted the force of the reason that caused them to be for a time forgotten. By-and-by Leonard's remorse at his ungracious and sullen ways to his mother – ways that alternated with passionate, fitful bursts of clinging love – assumed more the character of repentance; he tried to do so no more. But still his health was delicate; he was averse to going out of doors; he was much graver and sadder than became his age. It was what must be; an inevitable consequence of what had been; and Ruth had to be patient, and pray in secret, and with many tears, for the strength she needed.

She knew what it was to dread the going out into the streets after her story had become known. For days and days she had silently shrunk from this effort. But one evening towards dusk, Miss Benson was busy, and asked her to go an errand for her; and Ruth got up and silently obeyed her. That silence as to inward suffering was only one part of her peculiar and exquisite sweetness of nature; part of the patience with which she 'accepted her penance'.[1] Her true instincts told her that it was not right to disturb others with many expressions of her remorse; that the holiest repentance consisted in a quiet and daily sacrifice. Still there were times when she wearied pitifully of her inaction. She was so willing to serve and work, and every one despised her services. Her mind, as I have said before, had been well cultivated during these last few years; so now she used all the knowledge she had gained in teaching Leonard, which was an employment that Mr Benson relinquished willingly, because he felt that it would give her some of the occupation that she needed. She endeavoured to make herself useful in the house in every way she could; but the waters of house keeping had closed over her place[2] during the time of her absence at Mr Bradshaw's – and, besides, now that they were trying to restrict every unnecessary expense, it was sometimes difficult to find work for three women. Many and many a time Ruth turned over in her mind every possible chance of obtaining employment for her leisure hours, and nowhere could she find it. Now and then Sally, who was her confidante in this wish, procured her some needlework, but it was of a coarse and common kind, soon done, lightly paid for. But whatever it was, Ruth took it, and was thankful, although it added but a few pence to the household purse. I do not mean that there was any great need of money; but a new adjustment of expenditure was required – a reduction of wants which had never been very extravagant.

Ruth's salary of forty pounds was gone, while more of her 'keep', as Sally called it, was thrown upon the Bensons. Mr Benson received about eighty pounds a year for his salary as minister. Of this, he knew that twenty pounds came from Mr Bradshaw; and when the old man appointed to collect the pew-rents brought him the quarterly amount, and he found no diminution in them, he inquired how it was, and learnt that, although Mr Bradshaw had expressed to the collector his determination never to come to chapel again, he had added, that of course his pew-rent should be paid all the same. But this Mr Benson could not suffer; and the old man was commissioned to return the money to Mr Bradshaw, as being what his deserted minister could not receive.

Mr and Miss Benson had about thirty or forty pounds coming in annually from a sum which, in happier days, Mr Bradshaw had invested in Canal shares for them. Altogether their income did not fall much short of a hundred a-year, and they lived in the Chapel-house free of rent. So Ruth's small earnings were but very little in actual hard commercial account, though in another sense they were much; and Miss Benson always received them with quiet simplicity. By degrees, Mr Benson absorbed some of Ruth's time in a gracious and natural way. He employed her mind in all the kind offices he was accustomed to render to the poor around him. And as much of the peace and ornament of life as they gained now, was gained on a firm basis of truth. If Ruth began low down to find her place in the world, at any rate there was no flaw in the foundation.

Leonard was still their great anxiety. At times the question seemed to be, could he live through all this trial of the elasticity of childhood? And then they knew how precious a blessing – how true a pillar of fire,[3] he was to his mother: and how black the night, and how dreary the wilderness would be, when he was not. The child and the mother were each messengers of God – angels to each other.

They had long gaps between the pieces of intelligence respecting the Bradshaws. Mr Bradshaw had at length purchased the house at

Abermouth, and they were much there. The way in which the Bensons heard most frequently of the family of their former friends, was through Mr Farquhar. He called on Mr Benson about a month after the latter had met Jemima in the street. Mr Farquhar was not in the habit of paying calls on any one; and though he had always entertained and evinced the most kind and friendly feeling towards Mr Benson, he had rarely been in the Chapel-house. Mr Benson received him courteously, but he rather expected that there would be some especial reason alleged, before the conclusion of the visit, for its occurrence; more particularly as Mr Farquhar sat talking on the topics of the day in a somewhat absent manner, as if they were not the subjects most present to his mind. The truth was, he could not help recurring to the last time when he was in that room, waiting to take Leonard a ride, and his heart beating rather more quickly than usual at the idea that Ruth might bring the boy in when he was equipped. He was very full now of the remembrance of Ruth; and yet he was also most thankful, most self-gratulatory, that he had gone no further in his admiration of her – that he had never expressed his regard in words – that no one, as he believed, was cognisant of the incipient love which had grown partly out of his admiration, and partly out of his reason. He was thankful to be spared any implication in the nine-days' wonder which her story had made in Eccleston. And yet his feeling for her had been of so strong a character, that he winced, as with extreme pain, at every application of censure to her name. These censures were often exaggerated, it is true; but when they were just in their judgment of the outward circumstances of the case, they were not the less painful and distressing to him. His first rebound to Jemima was occasioned by Mrs Bradshaw's account of how severely her husband was displeased at her daughter's having taken part with Ruth; and he could have thanked and almost blessed Jemima when she dropped in (she dared do no more) her pleading excuses and charitable explanations on Ruth's behalf. Jemima had learnt some humility from the discovery which had been to her so great a shock; standing, she had learnt to take heed lest she fell; and when she had once been aroused to a perception of the violence of the hatred which she had indulged against Ruth, she was more reticent and measured in the expression of all her opinions. It showed how much her character had been purified from pride, that now she felt aware that what in her was again attracting Mr Farquhar was her faithful advocacy of her rival, wherever such advocacy was wise or practicable. He was quite unaware that Jemima had been conscious of his great admiration for Ruth; he did not know that she had ever cared enough for him to be jealous. But the unacknowledged bond between them now was their grief, and sympathy, and pity for Ruth; only in Jemima these feelings were ardent, and would fain have become active; while in Mr Farquhar they were strongly mingled with thankfulness that he had escaped a disagreeable position, and a painful notoriety. His natural caution induced him to make a resolution never to think of any woman as a wife until he had ascertained all her antecedents, from her birth upwards; and the same spirit of caution, directed inwardly, made him afraid of giving too much pity to Ruth, for fear of the conclusions to which such a feeling might lead him. But still his old regard for her, for Leonard, and his esteem and respect for the Bensons, induced him to lend a willing ear to Jemima's earnest entreaty that he would go and call on Mr Benson, in order that she might learn something about the family in general, and Ruth in particular. It was thus that he came to sit by Mr Benson's study fire, and to talk, in an absent way, to that gentleman. How they got on the subject he did not know, more than one-half of his attention being distracted, but they were speaking about politics, when Mr Farquhar learned that Mr Benson took in no newspaper.

'Will you allow me to send you over my *Times*? I have generally done with it before twelve o'clock, and after that it is really waste-paper in my house. You will oblige me by making use of it.'

'I am sure I am very much obliged to you for thinking of it. But do not trouble yourself to send it; Leonard can fetch it.'

'How is Leonard now?' asked Mr Farquhar, and he tried to speak indifferently; but a grave look of intelligence clouded his eyes as he looked for Mr Benson's answer. 'I have not met him lately.'

'No!' said Mr Benson, with an expression of pain in his countenance, though he, too, strove to speak in his usual tone.

'Leonard is not strong, and we find it difficult to induce him to go much out of doors.'

There was a little silence for a minute or two, during which Mr Farquhar had to check an unbidden sigh. But, suddenly rousing himself into a determination to change the subject, he said:

'You will find rather a lengthened account of the exposure of Sir Thomas Campbell's conduct at Baden.[4] He seems to be a complete blackleg,[5] in spite of his baronetcy. I fancy the papers are glad to get hold of anything just now.'

'Who is Sir Thomas Campbell?' asked Mr Benson.

'Oh, I thought you might have heard the report – a true one, I believe – of Mr Donne's engagement to his daughter. He must be glad she jilted him now, I fancy, after this public exposure of her father's conduct.' (That was an awkward speech, as Mr Farquhar felt; and he hastened to cover it, by going on without much connexion:)

'Dick Bradshaw is my informant about all these projected marriages in high life – they are not much in my way; but since he has come down from London to take his share in the business, I think I have heard more of the news and the scandal of what, I suppose, would be considered high life, than ever I did before; and Mr Donne's proceedings seem to be an especial object of interest to him.'

'And Mr Donne is engaged to a Miss Campbell, is he?'

'Was engaged; if I understood right, she broke off the engagement to marry some Russian prince or other – a better match, Dick Bradshaw told me. I assure you,' continued Mr Farquhar, smiling, 'I am a very passive recipient of all such intelligence, and might very probably have forgotten all about it, if the *Times* of this morning had not been so full of the disgrace of the young lady's father.'

'Richard Bradshaw has quite left London, has he?' asked Mr Benson, who felt far more interest in his old patron's family than in all the Campbells that ever were or ever would be.

'Yes. He has come to settle down here. I hope he may do well, and not disappoint his father, who has formed very high expectations from him; I am not sure if they are not too high for any young man to realise.' Mr Farquhar could have said more, but Dick Bradshaw was Jemima's brother, and an object of anxiety to her.

'I am sure, I trust such a mortification – such a grief as any disappoint- ment in Richard, may not befall his father,' replied Mr Benson.

'Jemima – Miss Bradshaw,' said Mr Farquhar, hesitating, 'was most anxious to hear of you all. I hope I may tell her you are all well' (with an emphasis on *all*); 'that—'

'Thank you. Thank her for us. We are all well; all except Leonard, who is not strong, as I said before. But we must be patient. Time, and such devoted, tender love as he has from his mother, must do much.'

Mr Farquhar was silent.

'Send him to my house for the papers. It will be a little necessity for him to have some regular exercise, and to face the world. He must do it, sooner or later.'

The two gentlemen shook hands with each other warmly on parting; but no further allusion was made to either Ruth or Leonard.

So Leonard went for the papers. Stealing along by back streets – running with his head bent down – his little heart panting with dread of being pointed out as his mother's child – so he used to come back, and run trembling to Sally, who would hush him up to her breast with many a rough-spoken word of pity and sympathy.

Mr Farquhar tried to catch him to speak to him, and tame him as it were; and, by-and-by, he contrived to interest him sufficiently to induce the boy to stay a little while in the house, or stables, or garden. But the race through the streets was always to be dreaded as the end of ever so pleasant a visit.

Mr Farquhar kept up the intercourse with the Bensons which he had thus begun. He persevered in paying calls – quiet visits, where not much was said, political or local news talked about, and the same inquiries always made and answered as to the welfare of the two families, who were estranged from each other. Mr Farquhar's reports were so little varied that Jemima grew anxious to know more particulars.

'Oh, Mr Farquhar!' said she; 'do you think they tell you the truth? I wonder what Ruth can be doing to support herself and Leonard? Nothing that you can hear of, you say; and, of course, one must not ask the downright question. And yet I am sure they must be pinched in some way. Do you think Leonard is stronger?'

'I am not sure. He is growing fast; and such a blow as he has had will be certain to make him more thoughtful and full of care than most boys of his age; both these circumstances may make him thin and pale, which he certainly is.'

'Oh! how I wish I might go and see them all! I could tell in a twinkling the real state of things.' She spoke with a tinge of her old impatience.

'I will go again, and pay particular attention to anything you wish me to observe. You see, of course, I feel a delicacy about asking any direct questions, or even alluding in any way to these late occurrences.'

'And you never see Ruth by any chance?'

'Never!'

They did not look at each other while this last question was asked and answered.

'I will take the paper to-morrow myself; it will be an excuse for calling again, and I will try to be very penetrating; but I have not much hope of success.'

'Oh, thank you. It is giving you a great deal of trouble; but you are very kind.'

'Kind, Jemima!' he repeated, in a tone which made her go very red and hot; 'must I tell you how you can reward me? – Will you call me Walter? – say, thank you, Walter – just for once.'

Jemima felt herself yielding to the voice and tone in which this was spoken; but her very consciousness of the depth of her love made her afraid of giving way, and anxious to be wooed, that she might be reinstated in her self-esteem.

'No!' said she, 'I don't think I can call you so. You are too old. It would not be respectful.' She meant it half in joke, and had no idea he would take the allusion to his age so seriously as he did. He rose up, and coldly, as a matter of form, in a changed voice, wished her 'Good-by.' Her heart sank; yet the old pride was there. But, as he was at the very door, some sudden impulse made her speak:

'I have not vexed you, have I, Walter?'

He turned round, glowing with a thrill of delight. She was as red as any rose; her looks dropped down to the ground.

They were not raised when, half an hour afterwards, she said, 'You won't forbid my going to see Ruth, will you? because if you do, I give you notice I shall disobey you.' The arm around her waist clasped her yet more fondly at the idea suggested by this speech, of the control which he should have a right to exercise over her actions at some future day.

'Tell me,' said he, 'how much of your goodness to me, this last happy hour, has been owing to the desire of having more freedom as a wife than as a daughter?'

She was almost glad that he should think she needed any additional motive to her love for him before she could have accepted him. She was afraid that she had betrayed the deep, passionate regard with which she had long looked upon him. She was lost in delight at her own happiness. She was silent for a time. At length she said:

'I don't think you know how faithful I have been to you ever since the days when you first brought me pistachio-candy from London – when I was quite a little girl.'

'Not more faithful than I have been to you,' for in truth, the recollection of his love for Ruth had utterly faded away, and he thought himself a model of constancy; 'and you have tried me pretty well. What a vixen you have been!'

Jemima sighed; smitten with the consciousness of how little she had deserved her present happiness; humble with the recollection of the evil thoughts that had raged in her heart during the time (which she remembered well, though he might have forgotten it) when Ruth had had the affection which her jealous rival coveted.

'I may speak to your father, may not I, Jemima?'

No! for some reason or fancy which she could not define, and could not be persuaded out of, she wished to keep their mutual understanding a secret. She had a natural desire to avoid the congratulations she expected from her family. She dreaded her father's consideration of the whole affair as a satisfactory disposal of his daughter to a worthy man, who, being his partner, would not require any abstraction of capital from the concern; and Richard's more noisy delight at his sister's having 'hooked' so good a match. It was only her simple-hearted mother that she longed to tell. She knew that her mother's congratulations would not jar upon her, though they might not sound the full organ-peal of her love. But all that her mother knew passed onwards to her father; so for the present, at any rate, she determined to realise her secret position alone. Somehow, the sympathy of all others that she most longed for was Ruth's; but the first communication of such an event was due to her parents. She imposed very strict regulations on Mr Farquhar's behaviour; and quarrelled and differed from him more than ever, but with a secret joyful understanding with him in her heart, even while they disagreed with each other – for similarity of opinion is not always – I think not often – needed for fulness and perfection of love.

After Ruth's 'detection', as Mr Bradshaw used to call it, he said he could never trust another governess again; so Mary and Elizabeth had been sent to school the following Christmas, and their place in the family was but poorly supplied by the return of Mr Richard Bradshaw, who had left London, and been received as a partner.

CHAPTER XXIX

The conversation narrated in the last chapter as taking place between Mr Farquhar and Jemima, occurred about a year after Ruth's dismissal from her situation. That year, full of small events, and change of place to the Bradshaws, had been monotonous and long in its course to the other household. There had been no want of peace and tranquillity; there had, perhaps, been more of them than in the preceding years, when, though unacknowledged by any, all must have occasionally felt the oppression of the falsehood – and a slight glancing dread must have flashed across their most prosperous state, lest, somehow or another, the mystery should be disclosed. But now, as the shepherd-boy in John Bunyan sweetly sang, 'He that is low need fear no fall.'[1]

Still their peace was as the stillness of a grey autumnal day, when no sun is to be seen above, and when a quiet film seems drawn before both sky and earth, as if to rest the wearied eyes after the summer's glare. Few events broke the monotony of their lives, and those events were of a depressing kind. They consisted in Ruth's futile endeavours to obtain some employment, however humble; in Leonard's fluctuations of spirits and health; in Sally's increasing deafness; in the final and unmendable wearing-out of the parlour carpet, which there was no spare money to replace, and so they cheerfully supplied its want by a large hearthrug that Ruth made out of ends of list;[2] and, what was more a subject of unceasing regret to Mr Benson than all, the defection of some of the members of his congregation, who followed Mr Bradshaw's lead. Their places, to be sure, were more than filled up by the poor, who thronged to his chapel; but still it was a disappointment to find that people about whom he had been earnestly thinking – to whom he had laboured to do good – should dissolve the connexion without a word of farewell or explanation. Mr Benson did not wonder that they should go; nay, he even felt it right that they should seek that spiritual help from another, which he, by his error, had forfeited his power to offer; he only wished they had spoken of their intention to him in an open and manly way. But not the less did he labour on among those to whom God permitted him to be of use. He felt age stealing upon him apace, although he said nothing about it, and no one seemed to be aware of it; and he worked the more diligently while 'it was yet day'.[3] It was not the number of his years that made him feel old, for he was only sixty, and many men are hale and strong at that time of life; in all probability, it was that early injury to his spine which affected the constitution of his mind as well as his body, and predisposed him, in the opinion of some at least, to a feminine morbidness of conscience. He had shaken off somewhat of this since the affair with Mr Bradshaw; he was simpler and more dignified than he had been for several years before, during which time he had been anxious and uncertain in his manner, and more given to thought than to action.

The one happy bright spot in this grey year, was owing to Sally. As she said of herself, she believed she grew more 'nattered'[4] as she grew older; but that she was conscious of her 'natteredness' was a new thing, and a great gain to the comfort of the house, for it made her very grateful for forbearance, and more aware of kindness than she had ever been before. She had become very deaf; yet she was uneasy and jealous if she were not informed of all the family thoughts, plans, and proceedings, which often had (however private in their details) to be shouted to her at the full pitch of the voice. But she always heard Leonard perfectly. His clear and bell-like voice, which was similar to his mother's, till sorrow had taken the ring out of it, was sure to be heard by the old servant, though every one else had failed. Sometimes, however, she 'got her hearing sudden', as she phrased it, and was alive to every word and noise, more particularly when they did not want her to hear, and at such times she resented their continuance of the habit of speaking loud as a mortal offence. One day, her indignation at being thought deaf called out one of the rare smiles on Leonard's face; she saw it, and said, 'Bless thee, lad! if it but amuses thee, they may shout through a ram's horn to me, and I'll never let on I'm not deaf. It's as good a use as I can be of,' she continued to herself, 'if I can make that poor lad smile a bit.'

If she expected to be everybody's confidante, she made Leonard hers. 'There!' said she, when she came home from her marketing one Saturday night, 'look here, lad! Here's forty-two pound, seven shillings, and twopence! It's a mint of money, isn't it? I took it all in sovereigns for fear of fire.'

'What is it all for, Sally?' said he.

'Ay, lad! that's asking. It's Mr Benson's money,' said she, mysteriously, 'that I've been keeping for him. Is he in the study, think ye?'

'Yes! I think so. Where have you been keeping it?'

'Never you mind!' She went towards the study, but thinking she might have been hard on her darling in refusing to gratify his curiosity, she turned back, and said:

'I say – if thou wilt, thou mayest do me a job of work some day. I'm wanting a frame made for a piece of writing.'

And then she returned to go into the study, carrying her sovereigns in her apron.

'Here, Master Thurstan,' said she, pouring them out on the table before her astonished master. 'Take it, it's all yours.'

'All mine! What can you mean?' asked he, bewildered.

She did not hear him, and went on:

'Lock it up safe, out o' the way. Dunnot go and leave it about to tempt folks. I'll not answer for myself if money's left about. I may be cribbing a sovereign.'[5]

'But where does it come from?' said he.

'Come from!' she replied. 'Where does all money come from, but the Bank, to be sure. I thought any one could tell that.'

'I have no money in the Bank!' said he, more and more perplexed.

'No, I knowed that; but I had. Dunnot ye remember how ye would raise my wage, last Martinmas[6] eighteen year? You and Faith were very headstrong, but I was too deep for you. See thee! I went and put it i' th' Bank. I was never going to touch it; and if I had died it would have been all right, for I'd a will made, all regular and tight – made by a lawyer (leastways he would have been a lawyer, if he hadn't got transported first). And now, thinks I, I think I'll just go and get it out and give it 'em. Banks is not always safe.'

'I'll take care of it for you with the greatest pleasure. Still, you know, banks allow interest.'

'D'ye suppose I don't know all about interest and compound interest too, by this time? I tell ye I want ye to spend it. It's your own. It's not mine. It always was yours. Now you're not going to fret me by saying you think it mine.'

Mr Benson held out his hand to her, for he could not speak. She bent forward to him as he sat there, and kissed him.

'Eh, bless ye, lad! It's the first kiss I've had of ye sin' ye were a little lad, and it's a great refreshment. Now don't you and Faith go and bother me with talking about it. It's just yours, and make no more ado.'

She went back into the kitchen, and brought out her will, and gave Leonard directions how to make a frame for it; for the boy was a very tolerable joiner, and had a box of tools which Mr Bradshaw had given him some years ago.

'It's a pity to lose such fine writing,' said she; 'though I can't say as I can read it. Perhaps you'd just read it for me, Leonard.' She sat open-mouthed with admiration at all the long words.

The frame was made, and the will hung up opposite to her bed, unknown to any one but Leonard; and, by dint of his repeated reading it over to her, she learnt all the words, except 'testatrix', which she would always call 'testy tricks'. Mr Benson had been too much gratified and touched, by her unconditional gift of all she had in the world, to reject it; but he only held it in his hands as a deposit until he could find a safe investment befitting so small a sum. The little re-arrangements of the household expenditure had not touched him as they had done the women. He was aware that meat dinners were not now every-day occurrences; but he preferred puddings and vegetables, and was glad of the exchange. He observed, too, that they all sat together in the kitchen in the evenings; but the kitchen, with the well-scoured dresser, the shining saucepans, the well-blacked grate and whitened hearth, and the warmth which seemed to rise up from the very flags, and ruddily cheer the most distant corners, appeared a very cosy and charming sitting-room; and, besides, it appeared but right that Sally, in her old age, should have the companionship of those with whom she had lived in love and faithfulness so many years. He only wished he could more frequently leave the solitary comfort of his study, and join the kitchen party; where Sally sat as mistress in the chimney-corner, knitting by firelight, and Miss Benson and Ruth, with the candle between them, stitched away at their work; while Leonard strewed the ample dresser with his slate and books. He did not mope and pine over his lessons; they were the one thing that took him out of himself. As yet his mother could teach him, though in some respects it was becoming a strain upon her acquirements and powers. Mr Benson saw this, but reserved his offers of help as long as he could, hoping that before his assistance became absolutely necessary, some mode of employment beyond that of occasional plain-work might be laid open to Ruth.

In spite of the communication they occasionally had with Mr Far-quhar, when he gave them the intelligence of his engagement to Jemima, it seemed like a glimpse into a world from which they were shut out. They wondered – Miss Benson and Ruth did at least – much about the details. Ruth sat over her sewing, fancying how all had taken place; and, as soon as she had arranged the events which were going on among people and places once so familiar to her, she found some descrepancy, and set-to afresh to picture the declaration of love, and the yielding, blushing acceptance; for Mr Farquhar had told little beyond the mere fact that there was an engagement between himself and Jemima which had existed for some time, but which had been kept secret until now, when it was acknowledged, sanctioned, and to be fulfilled as soon as he returned from an arrangement of family affairs in Scotland. This intelligence had been enough for Mr Benson, who was the only person Mr Farquhar saw; as Ruth always shrank from the post of opening the door, and Mr Benson was apt at recognising individual knocks, and always prompt to welcome Mr Farquhar.

Miss Benson occasionally thought – and what she thought she was in the habit of saying – that Jemima might have come herself to announce such an event to old friends; but Mr Benson decidedly vindicated her from any charge of neglect, by expressing his strong conviction that to her they owed Mr Farquhar's calls – his all but out-spoken offers of service – his quiet, steady interest in Leonard; and, moreover (repeating the conversation he had had with her in the street, the first time they met after the disclosure), Mr Benson told his sister how glad he was to find that, with all the warmth of her impetuous disposition hurrying her on to rebellion against her father, she was now attaining to that just self-control which can distinguish between mere wishes and true reasons – that she could abstain from coming to see Ruth while she could do but little good, reserving herself for some great occasion or strong emergency.

Ruth said nothing, but she yearned all the more in silence to see Jemima. In her recollection of that fearful interview with Mr Bradshaw, which haunted her yet, sleeping or waking, she was painfully conscious that she had not thanked Jemima for her generous, loving advocacy; it had passed unregarded at the time in intensity of agony – but now she recollected that by no word, or tone, or touch, had she given any sign of gratitude. Mr Benson had never told her of his meeting with Jemima;

so it seemed as if there were no hope of any future opportunity: for it is strange how two households, rent apart by some dissension, can go through life, their parallel existences running side by side, yet never touching each other, near neighbours as they are, habitual and familiar guests as they may have been.

Ruth's only point of hope was Leonard. She was weary of looking for work and employment, which everywhere seemed held above her reach. She was not impatient of this, but she was very, very sorry. She felt within her such capability, and all ignored her, and passed her by on the other side.[7] But she saw some progress in Leonard. Not that he could continue to have the happy development, and genial ripening, which other boys have; leaping from childhood to boyhood, and thence to youth, with glad bounds, and unconsciously enjoying every age. At present there was no harmony in Leonard's character; he was as full of thought and self-consciousness as many men, planning his actions long beforehand, so as to avoid what he dreaded, and what she could not yet give him strength to face, coward as she was herself, and shrinking from hard remarks. Yet Leonard was regaining some of his lost tenderness towards his mother; when they were alone he would throw himself on her neck and smother her with kisses, without any apparent cause for such a passionate impulse. If any one was by, his manner was cold and reserved. The hopeful parts of his character were the determination evident in him to be a 'law unto himself', and the serious thought which he gave to the formation of this law. There was an inclination in him to reason, especially and principally with Mr Benson, on the great questions of ethics which the majority of the world have settled long ago. But I do not think he ever so argued with his mother. Her lovely patience, and her humility, was earning its reward; and from her quiet piety, bearing sweetly the denial of her wishes – the refusal of her begging – the disgrace in which she lay, while others, less worthy were employed – this, which perplexed him, and almost angered him at first, called out his reverence at last, and what she said he took for his law with proud humility; and thus, softly, she was leading him up to God. His health was not strong; it was not likely to be. He moaned and talked in his sleep, and his appetite was still variable, part of which might be owing to his preference of the hardest lessons to any out-door exercise. But this last unnatural symptom was vanishing before the assiduous kindness of Mr Farquhar, and the quiet but firm desire of his mother.

Next to Ruth, Sally had perhaps the most influence over him; but he dearly loved both Mr and Miss Benson; although he was reserved on this, as on every point not purely intellectual. His was a hard childhood, and his mother felt that it was so. Children bear any moderate degree of poverty and privation cheerfully; but, in addition to a good deal of this, Leonard had to bear a sense of disgrace attaching to him and to the creature he loved best; this it was that took out of him the buoyancy and natural gladness of youth, in a way which no scantiness of food or clothing, or want of any outward comfort, could ever have done.

Two years had passed away – two long, eventless years. Something was now going to happen, which touched their hearts very nearly, though out of their sight and hearing. Jemima was going to be married this August, and by-and-by the very day was fixed. It was to be on the 14th. On the evening of the 13th, Ruth was sitting alone in the parlour, idly gazing out on the darkening shadows in the little garden; her eyes kept filling with quiet tears, that rose, not for her own isolation from all that was going on of bustle and preparation for the morrow's event, but because she had seen how Miss Benson had felt that she and her brother were left out from the gathering of old friends in the Bradshaw family. As Ruth sat, suddenly she was aware of a figure by her; she started up, and in the gloom of the apartment she recognised Jemima. In an instant they were in each other's arms – a long, fast embrace.

'Can you forgive me?' whispered Jemima in Ruth's ear.

'Forgive you! What do you mean? What have I to forgive? The question is, can I ever thank you as I long to do, if I could find words?'

'Oh, Ruth, how I hated you once!'

'It was all the more noble in you to stand by me as you did. You must have hated me when you knew how I was deceiving you all!'

'No, that was not it that made me hate you. It was before that. Oh, Ruth, I did hate you!'

They were silent for some time, still holding each other's hands. Ruth spoke first:

'And you are going to be married to-morrow!'

'Yes,' said Jemima. 'To-morrow, at nine o'clock. But I don't think I could have been married without coming to wish Mr Benson and Miss Faith good-by.'

'I will go for them,' said Ruth.

'No, not just yet. I want to ask you one or two questions first. Nothing very particular; only it seems as if there had been such a strange, long separation between us. Ruth,' said she, dropping her voice, 'is Leonard stronger than he was? I was so sorry to hear about him from Walter. But he is better?' asked she, anxiously.

'Yes, he is better. Not what a boy of his age should be,' replied his mother, in a tone of quiet but deep mournfulness. 'Oh, Jemima!' continued she, 'my sharpest punishment comes through him. To think what he might have been, and what he is!'

'But Walter says he is both stronger in health, and not so – nervous and shy.' Jemima added the last words in a hesitating and doubtful manner, as if she did not know how to express her full meaning without hurting Ruth.

'He does not show that he feels his disgrace so much. I cannot talk about it, Jemima, my heart aches so about him. But he is better,' she continued, feeling that Jemima's kind anxiety required an answer at any cost of pain to herself. 'He is only studying too closely now; he takes to his lessons evidently as a relief from thought. He is very clever, and I hope and trust, yet I tremble to say it, I believe he is very good.'

'You must let him come and see us very often when we come back. We shall be two months away. We are going to Germany, partly on Walter's business. Ruth, I have been talking to papa to-night, very seriously and quietly, and it has made me love him so much more, and understand him so much better.'

'Does he know of your coming here? I hope he does,' said Ruth.

'Yes. Not that he liked my doing it at all. But, somehow, I can always do things against a person's wishes more easily when I am on good terms with them – that's not exactly what I meant; but now to-night, after papa had been showing me that he really loved me more than I ever thought he had done (for I always fancied he was so absorbed in Dick, he did not care much for us girls), I felt brave enough to say that I intended to come here and bid you all good-by. He was silent for a minute, and then said I might do it, but I must remember he did not approve of it, and was not to be compromised by my coming; still I can tell that, at the bottom of his heart, there is some of the old kindly feeling to Mr and Miss Benson, and I don't despair of its all being made up, though, perhaps, I ought to say that mamma does.'

'Mr and Miss Benson won't hear of my going away,' said Ruth, sadly.

'They are quite right.'

'But I am earning nothing. I cannot get any employment. I am only a burden and an expense.'

'Are you not also a pleasure? And Leonard, is he not a dear object of love? It is easy for me to talk, I know, who am so impatient. Oh, I never deserved to be so happy as I am! You don't know how good Walter is. I used to think him so cold and cautious. But now, Ruth, will you tell Mr and Miss Benson that I am here? There is signing of papers, and I don't know what to be done at home. And when I come back, I hope to see you often, if you'll let me.'

Mr and Miss Benson gave her a warm greeting. Sally was called in, and would bring a candle with her, to have a close inspection of her, in order to see if she was changed – she had not seen her for so long a time, she said; and Jemima stood laughing and blushing in the middle of the room, while Sally studied her all over, and would not be convinced that the old gown which she was wearing for the last time was not one of the new wedding ones. The consequence of which misunderstanding was, that Sally, in her short petticoats and bedgown, turned up her nose at the old-fashioned way in which Miss Bradshaw's gown was made. But Jemima knew the old woman, and rather enjoyed the contempt for her dress. At last she kissed them all, and ran away to her impatient Mr Farquhar, who was awaiting her.

Not many weeks after this, the poor old woman whom I have named as having become a friend of Ruth's, during Leonard's illness three years ago, fell down and broke her hip-bone. It was a serious – probably a fatal injury, for one so old; and as soon as Ruth heard of it she devoted all her leisure time to old Ann Fleming. Leonard had now outstript his mother's powers of teaching, and Mr Benson gave him his lessons; so Ruth was a great deal at the cottage both night and day.

There Jemima found her one November evening, the second after their return from their prolonged stay on the Continent. She and Mr Farquhar had been to the Bensons, and had sat there some time; and now Jemima had come on just to see Ruth for five minutes, before the evening was too dark for her to return alone. She found Ruth sitting on a stool before the fire, which was composed of a few sticks on the hearth. The blaze they gave was, however, enough to enable her to read; and she was deep in study of the Bible, in which she had read aloud to the poor old woman, until the latter had fallen asleep. Jemima beckoned her out, and they stood on the green just before the open door, so that Ruth could see if Ann awoke.

'I have not many minutes to stay, only I felt as if I must see you. And we want Leonard to come to us to see all our German purchases, and hear all our German adventures. May he come to-morrow?'

'Yes; thank you. Oh! Jemima, I have heard something – I have got a plan that makes me so happy! I have not told any one yet. But Mr Wynne (the parish doctor, you know) has asked me if I would go out as a sick nurse – he thinks he could find me employment.'

'You, a sick nurse!' said Jemima, involuntarily glancing over the beautiful lithe figure, and the lovely refinement of Ruth's face, as the light of the rising moon fell upon it. 'My dear Ruth, I don't think you are fitted for it!'

'Don't you?' said Ruth, a little disappointed. 'I think I am; at least, that I should be very soon. I like being about sick and helpless people; I always feel so sorry for them; and then I think I have the gift of a very delicate touch, which is such a comfort in many cases. And I should try to be very watchful and patient. Mr Wynne proposed it himself.'

'It was not in that way I meant you were not fitted for it. I meant that you were fitted for something better. Why, Ruth, you are better educated than I am!'

'But if nobody will allow me to teach? – for that is what I suppose you mean. Besides, I feel as if all my education would be needed to make me a good sick nurse.'

'Your knowledge of Latin, for instance,' said Jemima, hitting, in her vexation at the plan, on the first acquirement of Ruth she could think of.

'Well!' said Ruth, 'that won't come amiss; I can read the prescriptions.'

'Which the doctors would rather you did not do.'

'Still, you can't say that any knowledge of any kind will be in my way, or will unfit me for my work.'

'Perhaps not. But all your taste and refinement will be in your way, and will unfit you.'

'You have not thought about this so much as I have, or you would not say so. Any fastidiousness I shall have to get rid of, and I shall be better without; but any true refinement I am sure I shall find of use; for don't you think that every power we have may be made to help us in any right work, whatever that is? Would you not rather be nursed by a person who spoke gently and moved quietly about than by a loud bustling woman?'

'Yes, to be sure; but a person unfit for anything else may move quietly, and speak gently, and give medicine when the doctor orders it, and keep awake at night; and those are the best qualities I ever heard of in a sick nurse.'

Ruth was quite silent for some time. At last she said: 'At any rate it is work, and as such I am thankful for it. You cannot discourage me – and perhaps you know too little of what my life has been – how set apart in idleness I have been – to sympathise with me fully.'

'And I wanted you to come to see us – me in my new home. Walter and I had planned that we would persuade you to come to us very often' (she had planned, and Mr Farquhar had consented); 'and now you will have to be fastened up in a sick room.'

'I could not have come,' said Ruth, quickly. 'Dear Jemima! it is like you to have thought of it – but I could not come to your house. It is not a thing to reason about. It is just feeling. But I do feel as if I could not go. Dear Jemima! if you are ill or sorrowful, and want me, I will come—'

'So you would and must to any one, if you take up that calling.'

'But I should come to you, love, in quite a different way; I should go to you with my heart full of love – so full that I am afraid I should be too anxious.'

'I almost wish I were ill, that I might make you come at once.'

'And I am almost ashamed to think how I should like you to be in some position in which I could show you how well I remember that day – that terrible day in the schoolroom. God bless you for it, Jemima!'

CHAPTER XXX

Mr Wynne, the parish surgeon, was right. He could and did obtain employment for Ruth as a sick nurse. Her home was with the Bensons; every spare moment was given to Leonard and to them; but she was at the call of all the invalids in the town. At first her work lay exclusively

among the paupers. At first, too, there was a recoil from many circumstances, which impressed upon her the most fully the physical sufferings
of those whom she tended. But she tried to lose the sense of these – or
rather to lessen them, and make them take their appointed places – in
thinking of the individuals themselves, as separate from their decaying
frames; and all along she had enough self-command to control herself
from expressing any sign of repugnance. She allowed herself no nervous
haste of movement or touch that should hurt the feelings of the poorest,
most friendless creature, who ever lay a victim to disease. There was
no rough getting over of all the disagreeable and painful work of her
employment. When it was a lessening of pain to have the touch careful
and delicate, and the ministration performed with gradual skill, Ruth
thought of her charge and not of herself. As she had foretold, she found
a use for all her powers. The poor patients themselves were unconsciously
gratified and soothed by her harmony and refinement of manner, voice,
and gesture. If this harmony and refinement had been merely superficial,
it would not have had this balmy effect. That arose from its being the
true expression of a kind, modest, and humble spirit. By degrees her
reputation as a nurse spread upwards, and many sought her good offices
who could well afford to pay for them. Whatever remuneration was
offered to her, she took it simply and without comment; for she felt that
it was not hers to refuse; that it was, in fact, owing to the Bensons for
her and her child's subsistence. She went wherever her services were
first called for. If the poor bricklayer who broke both his legs in a fall
from the scaffolding sent for her when she was disengaged, she went
and remained with him until he could spare her, let who would be the
next claimant. From the happy and prosperous in all but health, she
would occasionally beg off, when some one less happy and more friendless
wished for her; and sometimes she would ask for a little money from
Mr Benson to give to such in their time of need. But it was astonishing
how much she was able to do without money.

Her ways were very quiet; she never spoke much. Any one who has
been oppressed with the weight of a vital secret for years, and much
more any one the character of whose life has been stamped by one
event, and that producing sorrow and shame, is naturally reserved. And
yet Ruth's silence was not like reserve; it was too gentle and tender for
that. It had more the effect of a hush of all loud or disturbing emotions,
and out of the deep calm the words that came forth had a beautiful

power. She did not talk much about religion; but those who noticed her knew that it was the unseen banner which she was following. The low-breathed sentences which she spoke into the ear of the sufferer and the dying carried them upwards to God.

She gradually became known and respected among the roughest boys of the rough populace of the town. They would make way for her when she passed along the streets with more deference than they used to most; for all knew something of the tender care with which she had attended this or that sick person, and, besides, she was so often in connexion with Death that something of the superstitious awe with which the dead were regarded by those rough boys in the midst of their strong life, surrounded her.

She herself did not feel changed. She felt just as faulty – as far from being what she wanted to be, as ever. She best knew how many of her good actions were incomplete, and marred with evil. She did not feel much changed from the earliest Ruth she could remember. Everything seemed to change but herself. Mr and Miss Benson grew old, and Sally grew deaf, and Leonard was shooting up, and Jemima was a mother. She and the distant hills that she saw from her chamber window, seemed the only things which were the same as when she first came to Eccleston. As she sat looking out, and taking her fill of solitude, which sometimes was her most thorough rest – as she sat at the attic window looking abroad – she saw their next-door neighbour carried out to sun himself in his garden. When she first came to Eccleston, this neighbour and his daughter were often seen taking long and regular walks; by-and-by, his walks became shorter, and the attentive daughter would convoy him home, and set out afresh to finish her own. Of late years he had only gone out in the garden behind his house; but at first he had walked pretty briskly there by his daughter's help – now he was carried, and placed in a large, cushioned, easy-chair, his head remaining where it was placed against the pillow, and hardly moving when his kind daughter, who was now middle-aged, brought him the first roses of the summer. This told Ruth of the lapse of life and time.

Mr and Mrs Farquhar were constant in their attentions; but there was no sign of Mr Bradshaw ever forgiving the imposition which had been practised upon him, and Mr Benson ceased to hope for any renewal of their intercourse. Still, he thought that he must know of all the kind attentions which Jemima paid to them, and of the fond regard which both she and her husband bestowed on Leonard. This latter feeling even went so far that Mr Farquhar called one day, and with much diffidence begged Mr Benson to urge Ruth to let him be sent to school at his (Mr Farquhar's) expense.

Mr Benson was taken by surprise, and hesitated. 'I do not know. It would be a great advantage in some respects; and yet I doubt whether it would in others. His mother's influence over him is thoroughly good, and I should fear that any thoughtless allusions to his peculiar position might touch the raw spot in his mind.'

'But he is so unusually clever, it seems a shame not to give him all the advantages he can have. Besides, does he see much of his mother now?'

'Hardly a day passes without her coming home to be an hour or so with him, even at her busiest times; she says it is her best refreshment. And often, you know, she is disengaged for a week or two, except the occasional services which she is always rendering to those who need her. Your offer is very tempting, but there is so decidedly another view of the question to be considered, that I believe we must refer it to her.'

'With all my heart. Don't hurry her to a decision. Let her weigh it well. I think she will find the advantages preponderate.'

'I wonder if I might trouble you with a little business, Mr Farquhar, as you are here?'

'Certainly; I am only too glad to be of any use to you.'

'Why, I see from the report of the Star Life Assurance Company in the *Times*, which you are so good as to send me, that they have declared a bonus on the shares; now it seems strange that I have received no notification of it, and I thought that perhaps it might be lying at your office, as Mr Bradshaw was the purchaser of the shares, and I have always received the dividends through your firm.'

Mr Farquhar took the newspaper, and ran his eye over the report.

'I have no doubt that's the way of it,' said he. 'Some of our clerks have been careless about it; or it may be Richard himself. He is not always the most punctual and exact of mortals; but I'll see about it. Perhaps after all it mayn't come for a day or two; they have always such numbers of these circulars to send out.'

'Oh! I'm in no hurry about it. I only want to receive it some time before I incur any expenses, which the promise of this bonus may tempt me to indulge in.'

Mr Farquhar took his leave. That evening there was a long conference, for, as it happened, Ruth was at home. She was strenuously against the school plan. She could see no advantages that would counterbalance the evil which she dreaded from any school for Leonard; namely, that the good opinion and regard of the world would assume too high an importance in his eyes. The very idea seemed to produce in her so much shrinking affright, that by mutual consent the subject was dropped; to be taken up again, or not, according to circumstances.

Mr Farquhar wrote the next morning, on Mr Benson's behalf, to the Insurance Company, to inquire about the bonus. Although he wrote in the usual formal way, he did not think it necessary to tell Mr Bradshaw what he had done; for Mr Benson's name was rarely mentioned between the partners; each had been made fully aware of the views which the other entertained on the subject that had caused the estrangement; and Mr Farquhar felt that no external argument could affect Mr Bradshaw's resolved disapproval and avoidance of his former minister.

As it happened, the answer from the Insurance Company (directed to the firm) was given to Mr Bradshaw along with the other business letters. It was to the effect that Mr Benson's shares had been sold and transferred above a twelvemonth ago, which sufficiently accounted for the circumstance that no notification of the bonus had been sent to him.

Mr Bradshaw tossed the letter on one side, not displeased to have a good reason for feeling a little contempt at the unbusiness-like forgetfulness of Mr Benson, at whose instance some one had evidently been writing to the Insurance Company. On Mr Farquhar's entrance he expressed this feeling to him.

'Really,' he said, 'these Dissenting ministers have no more notion of exactitude in their affairs than a child! The idea of forgetting that he has sold his shares, and applying for the bonus, when it seems he had transferred them only a year ago!'

Mr Farquhar was reading the letter while Mr Bradshaw spoke.

'I don't quite understand it,' said he. 'Mr Benson was quite clear about it. He could not have received his half-yearly dividends unless he had been possessed of these shares; and I don't suppose Dissenting ministers, with all their ignorance of business, are unlike other men in knowing whether or not they receive the money that they believe to be owing to them.'

'I should not wonder if they were – if Benson was, at any rate. Why,

I never knew his watch to be right in all my life – it was always too fast or too slow; it must have been a daily discomfort to him. It ought to have been. Depend upon it, his money matters are just in the same irregular state; no accounts kept, I'll be bound.'

'I don't see that that follows,' said Mr Farquhar, half amused. 'That watch of his is a very curious one – belonged to his father and grand-father, I don't know how far back.'

'And the sentimental feelings which he is guided by prompt him to keep it, to the inconvenience of himself and every one else.'

Mr Farquhar gave up the subject of the watch as hopeless.

'But about this letter. I wrote, at Mr Benson's desire, to the Insurance Office, and I am not satisfied with this answer. All the transaction has passed through our hands. I do not think it is likely Mr Benson would write and sell the shares without, at any rate, informing us at the time, even though he forgot all about it afterwards.'

'Probably he told Richard, or Mr Watson.'

'We can ask Mr Watson at once. I am afraid we must wait till Richard comes home, for I don't know where a letter would catch him.'

Mr Bradshaw pulled the bell that rang into the head clerk's room, saying as he did so:

'You may depend upon it, Farquhar, the blunder lies with Benson himself. He is just the man to muddle away his money in indiscriminate charity, and then to wonder what has become of it.'

Mr Farquhar was discreet enough to hold his tongue.

'Mr Watson,' said Mr Bradshaw, as the old clerk made his appearance, 'here is some mistake about those Insurance shares we purchased for Benson, ten or a dozen years ago. He spoke to Mr Farquhar about some bonus they are paying to the shareholders, it seems; and, in reply to Mr Farquhar's letter, the Insurance Company say the shares were sold twelve months since. Have you any knowledge of the transaction? Has the transfer passed through your hands? By the way' (turning to Mr Farquhar), 'who kept the certificates? Did Benson or we?'

'I really don't know,' said Mr Farquhar. 'Perhaps Mr Watson can tell us.'

Mr Watson meanwhile was studying the letter. When he had ended it, he took off his spectacles, wiped them, and replacing them, he read it again.

'It seems very strange, sir,' he said at length, with his trembling, aged voice, 'for I paid Mr Benson the account of the dividends myself last June, and got a receipt in form, and that is since the date of the alleged transfer.'

'Pretty nearly twelve months after it took place,' said Mr Farquhar.

'How did you receive the dividends? An order on the Bank, along with old Mrs Cranmer's?' asked Mr Bradshaw, sharply.

'I don't know how they came. Mr Richard gave me the money, and desired me to get the receipt.'

'It's unlucky Richard is from home,' said Mr Bradshaw. 'He could have cleared up this mystery for us.'

Mr Farquhar was silent.

'Do you know where the certificates were kept, Mr Watson?' said he.

'I'll not be sure, but I think they were with Mrs Cranmer's papers and deeds in box A, 24.'

'I wish old Cranmer would have made any other man his executor. She, too, is always coming with some unreasonable request or other.'

'Mr Benson's inquiry about his bonus is perfectly reasonable, at any rate.'

Mr Watson, who was dwelling in the slow fashion of age on what had been said before, now spoke:

'I'll not be sure, but I am almost certain, Mr Benson said, when I paid him last June, that he thought he ought to give the receipt on a stamp,[1] and had spoken about it to Mr Richard the time before, but that Mr Richard said it was of no consequence. Yes,' continued he, gathering up his memory as he went on, 'he did – I remember now – and I thought to myself that Mr Richard was but a young man. Mr Richard will know all about it.'

'Yes,' said Mr Farquhar, gravely.

'I sha'n't wait till Richard's return,' said Mr Bradshaw. 'We can soon see if the certificates are in the box Watson points out; if they are there, the Insurance people are no more fit to manage their concern than that cat, and I shall tell them so. If they are not there (as I suspect will prove to be the case), it is just forgetfulness on Benson's part, as I have said from the first.'

'You forget the payment of the dividends,' said Mr Farquhar, in a low voice.

'Well, sir! what then?' said Mr Bradshaw, abruptly. While he spoke

– while his eye met Mr Farquhar's – the hinted meaning of the latter flashed through his mind; but he was only made angry to find that such a suspicion could pass through any one's imagination.

'I suppose I may go, sir,' said Watson, respectfully, an uneasy consciousness of what was in Mr Farquhar's thoughts troubling the faithful old clerk.

'Yes. Go. What do you mean about the dividends?' asked Mr Bradshaw, impetuously of Mr Farquhar.

'Simply, that I think there can have been no forgetfulness – no mistake on Mr Benson's part,' said Mr Farquhar, unwilling to put his dim suspicion into words.

'Then, of course, it is some blunder of that confounded Insurance Company. I will write to them to-day, and make them a little brisker and more correct in their statements.'

'Don't you think it would be better to wait till Richard's return? He may be able to explain it.'

'No, sir!' said Mr Bradshaw, sharply. 'I do not think it would be better. It has not been my way of doing business to spare any one, or any company, the consequences of their own carelessness; nor to obtain information second-hand when I could have it direct from the source. I shall write to the Insurance Office by the next post.'

Mr Farquhar saw that any further remonstrance on his part would only aggravate his partner's obstinacy; and, besides, it was but a suspicion, an uncomfortable suspicion. It was possible that some of the clerks at the Insurance Office might have made a mistake. Watson was not sure, after all, that the certificates had been deposited in box A, 24; and when he and Mr Farquhar could not find them there, the old man drew more and yet more back from his first assertion of belief that they had been placed there.

Mr Bradshaw wrote an angry and indignant reproach of carelessness to the Insurance Company. By the next mail one of their clerks came down to Eccleston; and having leisurely refreshed himself at the inn, and ordered his dinner with care, he walked up to the great warehouse of Bradshaw and Co., and sent in his card, with a pencil notification, 'On the part of the Star Insurance Company,' to Mr Bradshaw himself.

Mr Bradshaw held the card in his hand for a minute or two without raising his eyes. Then he spoke out loud and firm:

'Desire the gentleman to walk up. Stay! I will ring my bell in a minute or two, and then show him up-stairs.'

When the errand-boy had closed the door, Mr Bradshaw went to a cupboard where he usually kept a glass, and a bottle of wine (of which he very seldom partook, for he was an abstemious man). He intended now to take a glass, but the bottle was empty; and though there was plenty more to be had for ringing, or even simply going into another room, he would not allow himself to do this. He stood and lectured himself in thought.

'After all, I am a fool for once in my life. If the certificates are in no box which I have yet examined, that does not imply they may not be in some one which I have not had time to search. Farquhar would stay so late last night! And even if they are in none of the boxes here, that does not prove——' He gave the bell a jerking ring, and it was yet sounding when Mr Smith, the insurance clerk, entered.

The manager of the Insurance Company had been considerably nettled at the tone of Mr Bradshaw's letter; and had instructed the clerk to assume some dignity at first in vindicating (as it was well in his power to do) the character of the proceedings of the Company, but at the same time he was not to go too far, for the firm of Bradshaw and Co. was daily looming larger in the commercial world, and if any reasonable explanation could be given it was to be received, and bygones be bygones.

'Sit down, sir!' said Mr Bradshaw.

'You are aware, sir, I presume, that I come on the part of Mr Dennison, the manager of the Star Insurance Company, to reply in person to a letter of yours, of the 29th, addressed to him?'

Mr Bradshaw bowed. 'A very careless piece of business,' he said, stiffly.

'Mr Dennison does not think you will consider it as such when you have seen the deed of transfer, which I am commissioned to show you.'

Mr Bradshaw took the deed with a steady hand. He wiped his spectacles quietly, without delay, and without hurry, and adjusted them on his nose. It is possible that he was rather long in looking over the document – at least, the clerk had just begun to wonder if he was reading through the whole of it, instead of merely looking at the signature, when Mr Bradshaw said: 'It is possible that it may be——of course, you will allow me to take this paper to Mr Benson, to – to inquire if this be his signature?'

'There can be no doubt of it, I think, sir,' said the clerk, calmly smiling, for he knew Mr Benson's signature well.

'I don't know, sir – I don't know.' (He was speaking as if the pronunciation of every word required a separate effort of will, like a man who has received a slight paralytic stroke.)

'You have heard, sir, of such a thing as forgery – forgery, sir?' said he, repeating the last word very distinctly; for he feared that the first time he had said it, it was rather slurred over.

'Oh, sir, there is no room for imagining such a thing, I assure you. In our affairs we become aware of curious forgetfulness on the part of those who are not of business habits.'

'Still I should like to show it Mr Benson, to prove to him his forgetfulness, you know. I believe on my soul it is some of his careless forgetfulness – I do, sir,' said he. Now he spoke very quickly. 'It must have been. Allow me to convince myself. You shall have it back to-night, or the first thing in the morning.'

The clerk did not quite like to relinquish the deed, nor yet did he like to refuse Mr Bradshaw. If that very uncomfortable idea of forgery should have any foundation in truth – and he had given up the writing! There were a thousand chances to one against its being anything but a stupid blunder; the risk was more imminent of offending one of the directors.

As he hesitated, Mr Bradshaw spoke, very calmly, and almost with a smile on his face. He had regained his self-command. 'You are afraid, I see. I assure you, you may trust me. If there has been any fraud – if I have the slightest suspicion of the truth of the surmise I threw out just now' – he could not quite speak the bare naked word that was chilling his heart – 'I will not fail to aid the ends of justice, even though the culprit should be my own son.'

He ended, as he began, with a smile – such a smile! – the stiff lips refused to relax and cover the teeth. But all the time he kept saying to himself:

'I don't believe it – I don't believe it. I'm convinced it's a blunder of that old fool Benson.'

But when he had dismissed the clerk, and secured the piece of paper, he went and locked the door, and laid his head on his desk, and moaned aloud.

He had lingered in the office for the two previous nights; at first, occupying himself in searching for the certificates of the Insurance shares; but, when all the boxes and other repositories for papers had been ransacked, the thought took hold of him that they might be in Richard's private desk; and, with the determination which over-looks the means to get at the end, he had first tried all his own keys on the complicated lock, and then broken it open with two decided blows of a poker, the instrument nearest at hand. He did not find the certificates. Richard had always considered himself careful in destroying any dangerous or tell-tale papers; but the stern father found enough, in what remained, to convince him that his pattern son – more even than his pattern son, his beloved pride – was far other than what he seemed.

Mr Bradshaw did not skip or miss a word. He did not shrink while he read. He folded up letter by letter; he snuffed the candle just when its light began to wane, and no sooner; but he did not miss or omit one paper – he read every word. Then, leaving the letters in a heap upon the table, and the broken desk to tell its own tale, he locked the door of the room which was appropriated to his son as junior partner, and carried the key away with him.

There was a faint hope, even after this discovery of many circum-stances of Richard's life which shocked and dismayed his father – there was still a faint hope that he might not be guilty of forgery – that it be no forgery after all – only a blunder – an omission – a stupendous piece of forgetfulness. That hope was the one straw that Mr Bradshaw clung to.

Late that night Mr Benson sat in his study. Everyone else in the house had gone to bed; but he was expecting a summons to some one who was dangerously ill. He was not startled, therefore, at the knock which came to the front door about twelve; but he was rather surprised at the character of the knock, so slow and loud, with a pause between each rap. His study-door was but a step from that which led into the street. He opened it, and there stood – Mr Bradshaw; his large, portly figure not to be mistaken even in the dusky night.

He said, 'That is right. It was you I wanted to see.' And he walked straight into the study. Mr Benson followed, and shut the door. Mr Bradshaw was standing by the table, fumbling in his pocket. He pulled out the deed; and, opening it, after a pause, in which you might have counted five, he held it out to Mr Benson.

'Read it!' said he. He spoke not another word until time had been allowed for its perusal. Then he added:

'That is your signature?' The words were an assertion, but the tone was that of question.

'No, it is not,' said Mr Benson, decidedly. 'It is very like my writing. I could almost say it was mine, but I know it is not.'

'Recollect yourself a little. The date is August the third, of last year, fourteen months ago. You may have forgotten it.' The tone of the voice had a kind of eager entreaty in it, which Mr Benson did not notice – he was so startled at the fetch[2] of his own writing.

'It is most singularly like mine; but I could not have signed away these shares – all the property I have – without the slightest remembrance of it.'

'Stranger things have happened. For the love of Heaven, think if you did not sign it. It's a deed of transfer for those Insurance shares, you see. You don't remember it? You did not write this name – these words?' He looked at Mr Benson with craving wistfulness for one particular answer. Mr Benson was struck at last by the whole proceeding, and glanced anxiously at Mr Bradshaw, whose manner, gait, and voice, were so different from usual that he might well excite attention. But as soon as the latter was aware of this momentary inspection, he changed his tone all at once.

'Don't imagine, sir, I wish to force any invention upon you as a remembrance. If you did not write this name, I know who did. Once more I ask you, – does no glimmering recollection of – having needed money, we'll say – I never wanted you to refuse my subscription to the chapel, God knows! – of having sold these accursed shares? – Oh! I see by your face you did not write it; you need not to speak to me – I know.'

He sank down into a chair near him. His whole figure drooped. In a moment he was up, and standing straight as an arrow, confronting Mr Benson, who could find no clue to this stern man's agitation.

'You say you did not write these words?' pointing to the signature, with an untrembling finger. 'I believe you; Richard Bradshaw did write them.'

'My dear sir – my dear old friend!' exclaimed Mr Benson, 'you are rushing to a conclusion for which, I am convinced, there is no foundation; there is no reason to suppose that because—'

'There is reason, sir. Do not distress yourself – I am perfectly calm.'
His stony eyes and immovable face did indeed look rigid. 'What we
have now to do is to punish the offence. I have not one standard for
myself and those I love – (and Mr Benson, I did love him) – and another
for the rest of the world. If a stranger had forged my name, I should
have known it was my duty to prosecute him. You must prosecute
Richard.'[3]

'I will not,' said Mr Benson.

'You think, perhaps, that I shall feel it acutely. You are mistaken.
He is no longer as my son to me. I have always resolved to disown any
child of mine who was guilty of sin. I disown Richard. He is as a stranger
to me.[4] I shall feel no more at his exposure – his punishment—' He
could not go on, for his voice was choking. 'Of course, you understand
that I must feel shame at our connexion; it is that that is troubling me;
that is but consistent with a man who has always prided himself on the
integrity of his name; but as for that boy, who has been brought up all
his life as I have brought up my children, it must be some innate
wickedness! Sir, I can cut him off, though he has been as my right-hand
– beloved. Let me be no hindrance to the course of justice, I beg. He
has forged your name – he has defrauded you of money – of your all,
I think you said.'

'Some one has forged my name. I am not convinced that it was your
son. Until I know all the circumstances, I decline to prosecute.'

'What circumstances?' asked Mr Bradshaw, in an authoritative
manner, which would have shown irritation but for his self-command.

'The force of the temptation – the previous habits of the person—'

'Of Richard. He is the person,' Mr Bradshaw put in.

Mr Benson went on, without taking any notice. 'I should think it
right to prosecute, if I found out that this offence against me was only
one of a series committed, with premeditation, against society. I should
then feel, as a protector of others more helpless than myself—'

'It was your all,' said Mr Bradshaw.

'It was all my money; it was not my all,' replied Mr Benson; and
then he went on as if the interruption had never been: 'Against an
habitual offender. I shall not prosecute Richard. Not because he is your
son – do not imagine that! I should decline taking such a step against
any young man without first ascertaining the particulars about him,
which I know already about Richard, and which determine me against

doing what would blast his character for life – would destroy every good quality he has.'

'What good quality remains to him?' asked Mr Bradshaw. 'He has deceived me – he has offended God.'

'Have we not all offended Him?' Mr Benson said, in a low tone.

'Not consciously. I never do wrong consciously. But Richard – Richard.' The remembrance of the undeceiving letters – the forgery – filled up his heart so completely that he could not speak for a minute or two. Yet when he saw Mr Benson on the point of saying something, he broke in:

'It is no use talking, sir. You and I cannot agree on these subjects. Once more, I desire you to prosecute that boy, who is no longer a child of mine.'

'Mr Bradshaw, I shall not prosecute him. I have said it once for all. To-morrow you will be glad that I do not listen to you. I should only do harm by saying more at present.'

There is always something aggravating in being told, that the mood in which we are now viewing things strongly will not be our mood at some other time. It implies that our present feelings are blinding us, and that some more clear-sighted spectator is able to distinguish our future better than we do ourselves. The most shallow person dislikes to be told that any one can gauge his depth. Mr Bradshaw was not soothed by this last remark of Mr Benson's. He stooped down to take up his hat and be gone. Mr Benson saw his dizzy way of groping, and gave him what he sought for; but he received no word of thanks. Mr Bradshaw went silently towards the door, but, just as he got there, he turned round, and said:

'If there were more people like me, and fewer like you, there would be less evil in the world, sir. It's your sentimentalists that nurse up sin.'

Although Mr Benson had been very calm during this interview, he had been much shocked by what had been let out respecting Richard's forgery; not by the fact itself so much as by what it was a sign of. Still, he had known the young man from childhood, and had seen, and often regretted, that his want of moral courage had rendered him peculiarly liable to all the bad effects arising from his father's severe and arbitrary mode of treatment. Dick would never have had 'pluck' enough to be a hardened villain, under any circumstances; but, unless some good influence, some strength, was brought to bear upon him, he might easily sink into the sneaking scoundrel. Mr Benson determined to go to Mr Farquhar's the first thing in the morning, and consult him as a calm, clear-headed family friend – partner in the business, as well as son- and brother-in-law to the people concerned.

CHAPTER XXXI

While Mr Benson lay awake for fear of oversleeping himself, and so being late at Mr Farquhar's (it was somewhere about six o'clock – dark as an October morning is at that time), Sally came to his door and knocked. She was always an early riser; and if she had not been gone to bed long before Mr Bradshaw's visit last night, Mr Benson might safely have trusted to her calling him.

'Here's a woman down below as must see you directly. She'll be up-stairs after me if you're not down quick.'

'Is it any one from Clarke's?'

'No, no! not it, master,' said she, through the keyhole; 'I reckon it's Mrs Bradshaw, for all she's muffled up.'

He needed no other word. When he went down, Mrs Bradshaw sat in his easy-chair, swaying her body to and fro, and crying without restraint. Mr Benson came up to her, before she was aware that he was there.

'Oh! sir,' said she, getting up and taking hold of both his hands, 'you won't be so cruel, will you? I have got some money somewhere – some money my father settled on me, sir; I don't know how much, but I think it's more than two thousand pounds, and you shall have it all. If I can't give it you now, I'll make a will, sir. Only be merciful to poor Dick – don't go and prosecute him, sir.'

'My dear Mrs Bradshaw, don't you agitate yourself in this way. I never meant to prosecute him.'

'But Mr Bradshaw says that you must.'

'I shall not, indeed. I have told Mr Bradshaw so.'

'Has he been here? Oh! is not he cruel? I don't care. I have been a good wife till now. I know I have. I have done all he bid me, ever since we were married. But now I will speak my mind, and say to everybody how cruel he is – how hard to his own flesh and blood! If he puts poor Dick in prison, I will go too. If I'm to choose between my husband and my son, I choose my son; for he will have no friends, unless I am with him.'

'Mr Bradshaw will think better of it. You will see, that, when his first anger and disappointment are over, he will not be hard or cruel.'

'You don't know Mr Bradshaw,' said she, mournfully, 'if you think he'll change. I might beg and beg – I have done many a time, when we had little children, and I wanted to save them a whipping – but no begging ever did any good. At last I left it off. He'll not change.'

'Perhaps not for human entreaty. Mrs Bradshaw, is there nothing more powerful?'

The tone of his voice suggested what he did not say.

'If you mean that God may soften his heart,' replied she, humbly, 'I'm not going to deny God's power – I have need to think of Him,' she continued, bursting into fresh tears, 'for I am a very miserable woman. Only think! he cast it up against me last night, and said, if I had not spoilt Dick this never would have happened.'

'He hardly knew what he was saying, last night. I will go to Mr Farquhar's directly, and see him; and you had better go home, my dear Mrs Bradshaw; you may rely upon our doing all that we can.'

With some difficulty he persuaded her not to accompany him to Mr Farquhar's; but he had, indeed, to take her to her own door before he could convince her that, at present, she could do nothing but wait the result of the consultations of others.

It was before breakfast, and Mr Farquhar was alone; so Mr Benson had a quiet opportunity of telling the whole story to the husband before the wife came down. Mr Farquhar was not much surprised, though greatly distressed. The general opinion he had always entertained of Richard's character had predisposed him to fear, even before the inquiry respecting the Insurance shares. But it was still a shock when it came, however much it might have been anticipated.

'What can we do?' said Mr Benson, as Mr Farquhar sat gloomily silent.

'That is just what I was asking myself. I think I must see Mr Bradshaw, and try and bring him a little out of this unmerciful frame of mind.

That must be the first thing. Will you object to accompany me at once? It seems of particular consequence that we should subdue its obduracy before the affair gets wind.'

'I will go with you willingly. But I believe I rather serve to irritate Mr Bradshaw; he is reminded of things he has said to me formerly, and which he thinks he is bound to act up to. However, I can walk with you to the door, and wait for you (if you'll allow me) in the street. I want to know how he is to-day, both bodily and mentally; for indeed, Mr Farquhar, I should not have been surprised last night if he had dropped down dead, so terrible was his strain upon himself.'

Mr Benson was left at the door as he had desired, while Mr Farquhar went in.

'Oh, Mr Farquhar, what is the matter?' exclaimed the girls, running to him. 'Mamma sits crying in the old nursery. We believe she has been there all night. She will not tell us what it is, nor let us be with her; and papa is locked up in his room, and won't even answer us when we speak, though we know he is up and awake, for we heard him tramping about all night.'

'Let me go up to him!' said Mr Farquhar.

'He won't let you in. It will be of no use.' But in spite of what they said, he went up; and, to their surprise, after hearing who it was, their father opened the door, and admitted their brother-in-law. He remained with Mr Bradshaw about half an hour, and then came into the dining-room, where the two girls stood huddled over the fire, regardless of the untasted breakfast behind them; and, writing a few lines, he desired them to take his note up to their mother, saying that it would comfort her a little, and that he should send Jemima, in two or three hours, with the baby – perhaps to remain some days with them. He had no time to tell them more; Jemima would.

He left them, and rejoined Mr Benson. 'Come home and breakfast with me. I am off to London in an hour or two, and must speak with you first.'

On reaching his house, he ran up-stairs to ask Jemima to breakfast alone in her dressing-room, and returned in five minutes or less.

'Now I can tell you about it,' said he. 'I see my way clearly to a certain point. We must prevent Dick and his father meeting just now, or all hope of Dick's reformation is gone for ever. His father is as hard as the nether mill-stone.[1] He has forbidden me his house.'

'Forbidden you!'

'Yes; because I would not give up Dick as utterly lost and bad; and because I said I should return to London with the clerk, and fairly tell Dennison (he's a Scotchman, and a man of sense and feeling) the real state of the case. By the way, we must not say a word to the clerk; otherwise he will expect an answer, and make out all sorts of inferences for himself, from the unsatisfactory reply he must have. Dennison will be upon honour – will see every side of the case – will know you refuse to prosecute; the company of which he is manager are no losers. Well! when I said what I thought wise, of all this – when I spoke as if my course were a settled and decided thing, the grim old man asked me if he was to be an automaton in his own house. He assured me he had no feeling for Dick – all the time he was shaking like an aspen; in short, repeated much the same things he must have said to you last night. However, I defied him; and the consequence is, I'm forbidden the house, and, what is more, he says he will not come to the office while I remain a partner.'

'What shall you do?'

'Send Jemima and the baby. There's nothing like a young child for bringing people round to a healthy state of feeling; and you don't know what Jemima is, Mr Benson! No! though you've known her from her birth. If she can't comfort her mother, and if the baby can't steal into her grandfather's heart, why – I don't know what you may do to me. I shall tell Jemima all, and trust to her wit and wisdom to work at this end, while I do my best at the other.'

'Richard is abroad, is not he?'

'He will be in England to-morrow. I must catch him somewhere; but that I can easily do. The difficult point will be, what to do with him – what to say to him, when I find him. He must give up his partnership, that's clear. I did not tell his father so, but I am resolved upon it. There shall be no tampering with the honour of the firm to which I belong.'

'But what will become of him?' asked Mr Benson, anxiously.

'I do not yet know. But, for Jemima's sake – for his dour old father's sake – I will not leave him adrift. I will find him some occupation as clear from temptation as I can. I will do all in my power. And he will do much better, if he has any good in him, as a freer agent, not cowed by his father into a want of individuality and self-respect. I believe I must dismiss you, Mr Benson,' said he, looking at his watch; 'I have to explain all to my wife, and to go to that clerk. You shall hear from me in a day or two.'

Mr Benson half envied the younger man's elasticity of mind, and power of acting promptly. He himself felt as if he wanted to sit down in his quiet study, and think over the revelations and events of the last twenty-four hours. It made him dizzy even to follow Mr Farquhar's plans, as he had briefly detailed them; and some solitude and consideration would be required before Mr Benson could decide upon their justice and wisdom. He had been much shocked by the discovery of the overt act of guilt which Richard had perpetrated, low as his opinion of that young man had been for some time; and the consequence was, that he felt depressed, and unable to rally for the next few days. He had not even the comfort of his sister's sympathy, as he felt bound in honour not to tell her anything; and she was luckily so much absorbed in some household contest with Sally that she did not notice her brother's quiet languor.

Mr Benson felt that he had no right at this time to intrude into the house which he had been once tacitly forbidden. If he went now to Mr Bradshaw's without being asked, or sent for, he thought it would seem like presuming on his knowledge of the hidden disgrace of one of the family. Yet he longed to go: he knew that Mr Farquhar must be writing almost daily to Jemima, and he wanted to hear what he was doing. The fourth day after her husband's departure she came, within half an hour after the post-delivery, and asked to speak to Mr Benson alone.

She was in a state of great agitation, and had evidently been crying very much.

'Oh, Mr Benson!' said she, 'will you come with me, and tell papa this sad news about Dick? Walter has written me a letter at last, to say he has found him – he could not at first; but now it seems that, the day before yesterday, he heard of an accident which had happened to the Dover coach; it was overturned – two passengers killed, and several badly hurt. Walter says we ought to be thankful, as he is, that Dick was not killed. He says it was such a relief to him on going to the place – the little inn nearest to where the coach was overturned – to find that Dick was only severely injured; not one of those who was killed. But it is a terrible shock to us all. We had had no more dreadful fear to lessen the shock; mamma is quite unfit for anything, and we none of us dare to tell papa.' Jemima had hard work to keep down her sobs thus far, and now they over-mastered her.

'How is your father? I have wanted to hear every day,' asked Mr Benson, tenderly.

'It was careless of me not to come and tell you; but, indeed, I have had so much to do. Mamma would not go near him. He has said something which she seems as if she could not forgive. Because he came to meals, she would not. She has almost lived in the nursery; taking out all Dick's old playthings, and what clothes of his were left, and turning them over, and crying over them.'

'Then Mr Bradshaw has joined you again; I was afraid, from what Mr Farquhar said, he was going to isolate himself from you all?'

'I wish he had,' said Jemima, crying afresh. 'It would have been more natural than the way he has gone on; the only difference from his usual habit is, that he has never gone near the office, or else he has come to meals just as usual, and talked just as usual; and even done what I never knew him do before, tried to make jokes – all in order to show us how little he cares.'

'Does he not go out at all?'

'Only in the garden. I am sure he does care after all; he must care; he cannot shake off a child in this way, though he thinks he can; and that makes me so afraid of telling him of this accident. Will you come, Mr Benson?'

He needed no other word. He went with her, as she rapidly threaded her way through the by-streets. When they reached the house, she went in without knocking, and putting her husband's letter into Mr Benson's hand, she opened the door of her father's room, and saying – 'Papa, here is Mr Benson,' left them alone.

Mr Benson felt nervously incapable of knowing what to do, or to say. He had surprised Mr Bradshaw sitting idly over the fire – gazing dreamily into the embers. But he had started up, and drawn his chair to the table, on seeing his visitor; and, after the first necessary words of politeness were over, he seemed to expect him to open the conversation.

'Mrs Farquhar has asked me,' said Mr Benson, plunging into the subject with a trembling heart, 'to tell you about a letter she has received from her husband;' he stopped for an instant, for he felt that he did not get nearer the real difficulty, and yet could not tell the best way of approaching it.

'She need not have given you that trouble. I am aware of the reason of Mr Farquhar's absence. I entirely disapprove of his conduct. He is regardless of my wishes; and disobedient to the commands which, as my son-in-law, I thought he would have felt bound to respect. If there is any more agreeable subject that you can introduce, I shall be glad to hear you, sir.'

'Neither you, nor I, must think of what we like to hear or to say. You must hear what concerns your son.'

'I have disowned the young man who was my son,' replied he, coldly.

'The Dover coach has been overturned,' said Mr Benson, stimulated into abruptness by the icy sternness of the father. But, in a flash, he saw what lay below that terrible assumption of indifference. Mr Bradshaw glanced up, in his face one look of agony – and then went grey-pale; so livid that Mr Benson got up to ring the bell in affright, but Mr Bradshaw motioned to him to sit still.

'Oh! I have been too sudden, sir – he is alive, he is alive!' he exclaimed, as he saw the ashy face working in a vain attempt to speak; but the poor lips (so wooden, not a minute ago) went working on and on, as if Mr Benson's words did not sink down into the mind, or reach the understanding. Mr Benson went hastily for Mrs Farquhar.

'Oh, Jemima!' said he, 'I have done it so badly – I have been so cruel – he is very ill, I fear – bring water, brandy—' and he returned with all speed into the room. Mr Bradshaw – the great, strong, iron man – lay back in his chair in a swoon, a fit.

'Fetch my mother, Mary. Send for the doctor, Elizabeth,' said Jemima, rushing to her father. She and Mr Benson did all in their power to restore him. Mrs Bradshaw forgot all her vows of estrangement from the dead-like husband, who might never speak to her, or hear her again, and bitterly accused herself for every angry word she had spoken against him during these last few miserable days.

Before the doctor came, Mr Bradshaw had opened his eyes and partially rallied, although he either did not, or could not speak. He looked struck down into old age. His eyes were sensible in their expression, but had the dim glaze of many years of life upon them. His lower jaw fell from his upper one, giving a look of melancholy depression to the face, although the lips hid the unclosed teeth. But he answered correctly (in monosyllables, it is true) all the questions which the doctor chose to ask. And the medical man was not so much impressed with the serious character of the seizure as the family, who knew all the hidden mystery behind, and had seen their father lie for the first time with the precursor aspect of death upon his face. Rest, watching, and a little medicine were what the doctor prescribed; it was so slight a prescription, for what had appeared to Mr Benson so serious an attack, that he wished to follow the medical man out of the room to make further inquiries, and learn the real opinion which he thought must lurk behind. But as he was following the doctor, he – they all – were aware of the effort Mr Bradshaw was making to rise, in order to arrest Mr Benson's departure. He did stand up, supporting himself with one hand on the table, for his legs shook under him. Mr Benson came back instantly to the spot where he was. For a moment, it seemed as if he had not the right command of his voice: but at last he said, with a tone of humble, wistful entreaty, which was very touching:

'He is alive, sir, is he not?'

'Yes, sir – indeed he is; he is only hurt. He is sure to do well. Mr Farquhar is with him,' said Mr Benson, almost unable to speak for tears.

Mr Bradshaw did not remove his eyes from Mr Benson's face for more than a minute after his question had been answered. He seemed as though he would read his very soul, and there see if he spoke the truth. Satisfied at last, he sank slowly into his chair; and they were silent for a little space, waiting to perceive if he would wish for any further information just then. At length he put his hands slowly together in the clasped attitude of prayer, and said – 'Thank God!'

CHAPTER XXXII

If Jemima allowed herself now and then to imagine that one good would result from the discovery of Richard's delinquency, in the return of her father and Mr Benson to something of their old understanding and their old intercourse – if this hope fluttered through her mind, it was doomed to disappointment. Mr Benson would have been most happy to go, if Mr Bradshaw had sent for him; he was on the watch for what might be even the shadow of such an invitation – but none came. Mr Bradshaw, on his part, would have been thoroughly glad if the wilful seclusion of his present life could have been broken by the occasional visits of the old friend whom he had once forbidden the house; but this prohibition having passed his lips, he stubbornly refused to do anything which might be construed into unsaying it. Jemima was for some time in despair of his ever returning to the office, or resuming his old habits of business. He had evidently threatened as much to her husband. All that Jemima could do was to turn a deaf ear to every allusion to this menace, which he threw out from time to time, evidently with a view to see if it had struck deep enough into her husband's mind for him to have repeated it to his wife. If Mr Farquhar had named it – if it was known only to two or three to have been, but for one half hour even, his resolution – Mr Bradshaw could have adhered to it, without any other reason than the maintenance of what he called consistency, but which was in fact doggedness. Jemima was often thankful that her mother was absent, and gone to nurse her son. If she had been at home, she would have entreated and implored her husband to fall back into his usual habits, and would have shown such a dread of his being as good as his word, that he would have been compelled to adhere to it by the very consequence affixed to it. Mr Farquhar had hard work, as it was, in passing rapidly enough between the two places – attending to his business at Eccleston; and deciding, comforting, and earnestly talking, in Richard's sick-room. During an absence of his, it was necessary to apply to one of the partners on some matter of importance; and accordingly, to Jemima's secret joy, Mr Watson came up and asked if her father was well enough to see him on business? Jemima carried in this inquiry literally; and the hesitating answer which her father gave was in the affirmative. It was not long before she saw him leave the house, accompanied by the faithful old clerk; and when he met her at dinner, he made no allusion to his morning visitor, or to his subsequent going out. But from that time forwards he went regularly to the office. He received all the information about Dick's accident, and his progress towards recovery, in perfect silence, and in as indifferent a manner as he could assume; but yet he lingered about the family sitting-room every morning until the post had come in which brought all letters from the south.

When Mr Farquhar at last returned to bring the news of Dick's perfect convalescence, he resolved to tell Mr Bradshaw all that he had done and arranged, for his son's future career; but, as Mr Farquhar told Mr Benson afterwards, he could not really say if Mr Bradshaw had attended to one word that he said.

'Rely upon it,' said Mr Benson, 'he has not only attended to it, but treasured up every expression you have used.'

'Well, I tried to get some opinion, or sign of emotion, out of him. I had not much hope of the latter, I must own; but I thought he would have said whether I had done wisely or not in procuring that Glasgow situation for Dick – that he would, perhaps, have been indignant at my ousting him from the partnership so entirely on my own responsibility.'

'How did Richard take it?'

'Oh, nothing could exceed his penitence. If one had never heard of the proverb, "When the devil was sick, the devil a monk would be,"[1] I should have had greater faith in him; or if he had had more strength of character to begin with, or more reality and less outward appearance of good principle instilled into him. However, this Glasgow situation is the very thing; clear, defined duties, no great trust reposed in him, a kind and watchful head, and introductions to a better class of associates than I fancy he has ever been thrown amongst before. For, you know, Mr Bradshaw dreaded all intimacies for his son, and wanted him to eschew all society beyond his own family – would never allow him to ask a friend home. Really, when I think of the unnatural life Mr Bradshaw expected him to lead, I get into charity with him, and have hopes. By the way, have you ever succeeded in persuading his mother to send Leonard to school? He may run the same risk from isolation as Dick: not be able to choose his companions wisely when he grows up, but be too much overcome by the excitement of society to be very discreet as to who are his associates. Have you spoken to her about my plan?'

'Yes! but to no purpose. I cannot say that she would even admit an argument on the subject. She seemed to have an invincible repugnance to the idea of exposing him to the remarks of other boys on his peculiar position.'

'They need never know of it. Besides, sooner or later, he must step out of his narrow circle, and encounter remark and scorn.'

'True,' said Mr Benson, mournfully. 'And you may depend upon it, if it really is the best for Leonard, she will come round to it by-and-by. It is almost extraordinary to see the way in which her earnest and most unselfish devotion to this boy's real welfare leads her to right and wise conclusions.'

'I wish I could tame her so as to let me meet her as a friend. Since the baby was born, she comes to see Jemima. My wife tells me, that she sits and holds it soft in her arms, and talks to it as if her whole soul went out to the little infant. But if she hears a strange footstep on the stair, what Jemima calls the "wild-animal look" comes back into her eyes, and she steals away like some frightened creature. With all that she has done to redeem her character, she should not be so timid of observation.'

'You may well say "with all that she has done"! We of her own household hear little or nothing of what she does. If she wants help, she simply tells us how and why; but if not – perhaps because it is some relief to her to forget for a time the scenes of suffering in which she has been acting the part of comforter, and perhaps because there always was a shy, sweet reticence about her – we never should know what she is and what she does, except from the poor people themselves, who would bless her in words if the very thought of her did not choke them with tears. Yet, I do assure you, she passes out of all this gloom, and makes sunlight in our house. We are never so cheerful as when she is at home. She always had the art of diffusing peace, but now it is positive cheerfulness. And about Leonard; I doubt if the wisest and most thoughtful schoolmaster could teach half as much directly, as his mother does unconsciously and indirectly every hour that he is with her. Her noble, humble, pious endurance of the consequences of what was wrong in her early life, seems expressly fitted to act upon him, whose position is (unjustly, for he has done no harm) so similar to hers.'

'Well! I suppose we must leave it alone for the present. You will think me a hard practical man when I own to you, that all I expect from Leonard's remaining a home-bird is that, with such a mother, it will do him no harm. At any rate, remember my offer is the same for a year – two years hence, as now. What does she look forward to making him into, finally?'

'I don't know. The wonder comes into my mind sometimes; but never into hers, I think. It is part of her character – part perhaps of that which made her what she was – that she never looks forward, and seldom back. The present is enough for her.'

And so the conversation ended. When Mr Benson repeated the substance of it to his sister, she mused awhile, breaking out into an occasional whistle (although she had cured herself of this habit in a great measure), and at last she said:

'Now, do you know, I never liked poor Dick; and yet I'm angry with Mr Farquhar for getting him out of the partnership in such a summary way. I can't get over it, even though he has offered to send Leonard to school. And here he's reigning lord-paramount at the office! As if you, Thurstan, weren't as well able to teach him as any schoolmaster in England! But I should not mind that affront, if I were not sorry to think of Dick (though I never could abide him) labouring away in Glasgow for a petty salary of nobody knows how little, while Mr Farquhar is taking halves, instead of thirds, of the profits here!'

But her brother could not tell her – and even Jemima did not know, till long afterwards – that the portion of income which would have been Dick's as a junior partner, if he had remained in the business, was carefully laid aside for him by Mr Farquhar; to be delivered up, with all its accumulated interest, when the prodigal should have proved his penitence by his conduct.

When Ruth had no call upon her time, it was indeed a holiday at Chapel-house. She threw off as much as she could of the care and sadness in which she had been sharing; and returned fresh and helpful, ready to go about in her soft, quiet way, and fill up every measure of service, and heap it with the fragrance of her own sweet nature. The delicate mending, that the elder women could no longer see to do, was put by for Ruth's swift and nimble fingers. The occasional copying, or patient writing to dictation, that gave rest to Mr Benson's weary spine, was done by her with sunny alacrity. But, most of all, Leonard's heart rejoiced when his mother came home. Then came the quiet confidences, the tender exchange of love, the happy walks from which he returned stronger and stronger – going from strength to strength as his mother led the way. It was well, as they saw now, that the great shock of the disclosure had taken place when it did. She, for her part, wondered at her own cowardliness in having even striven to keep back the truth from her child – the truth that was so certain to be made clear, sooner or later, and which it was only owing to God's mercy that she was alive to encounter with him, and, by so encountering, shield and give him good courage. Moreover, in her secret heart, she was thankful that all occurred while he was yet too young to have much curiosity as to his father. If an unsatisfied feeling of this kind occasionally stole into his mind, at any rate she never heard any expression of it; for the past was a sealed book between them. And so, in the bright strength of good endeavour, the days went on, and grew again to months and years.

Perhaps one little circumstance which occurred during this time had scarcely external importance enough to be called an event; but in Mr Benson's mind it took rank as such. One day, about a year after Richard Bradshaw had ceased to be a partner in his father's house, Mr Benson encountered Mr Farquhar in the street, and heard from him of the creditable and respectable manner in which Richard was conducting himself in Glasgow, where Mr Farquhar had lately been on business.

'I am determined to tell his father of this,' said he; 'I think his family are far too obedient to his tacit prohibition of all mention of Richard's name.'

'Tacit prohibition?' inquired Mr Benson.

'Oh! I dare say I use the words in a wrong sense for the correctness of a scholar; but what I mean is, that he made a point of immediately leaving the room if Richard's name was mentioned; and did it in so marked a manner, that by degrees they understood that it was their father's desire that he should never be alluded to; which was all very well as long as there was nothing pleasant to be said about him; but to-night I am going there, and shall take good care he does not escape me before I have told him all I have heard and observed about Richard. He will never be a hero of virtue, for his education has drained him of all moral courage; but with care, and the absence of all strong temptation for a time, he will do very well; nothing to gratify paternal pride, but certainly nothing to be ashamed of.'

It was on the Sunday after this that the little circumstance to which I have alluded took place.

During the afternoon service, Mr Benson became aware that the large Bradshaw pew was no longer unoccupied. In a dark corner Mr Bradshaw's white head was to be seen, bowed down low in prayer. When last he had worshipped there, the hair on that head was iron-grey, and even in prayer he had stood erect, with an air of conscious righteousness sufficient for all his wants, and even some to spare with which to judge others. Now, that white and hoary head was never uplifted; part of his unobtrusiveness might, it is true, be attributed to the uncomfortable feeling which was sure to attend any open withdrawal of the declaration he had once made, never to enter the chapel in which Mr Benson was minister again; and, as such a feeling was natural to all men, and especially to such a one as Mr Bradshaw, Mr Benson instinctively respected it, and passed out of the chapel with his household, without ever directing his regards to the obscure place where Mr Bradshaw still remained immovable.

From this day Mr Benson felt sure that the old friendly feeling existed once more between them, although some time might elapse before any circumstance gave the signal for a renewal of their intercourse.

CHAPTER XXXIII

Old people tell of certain years when typhus fever[1] swept over the country like a pestilence; years that bring back the remembrance of deep sorrow – refusing to be comforted – to many a household; and which those whose beloved passed through the fiery time[2] unscathed, shrink from recalling: for great and tremulous was the anxiety – miserable the constant watching for evil symptoms; and beyond the threshold of home a dense cloud of depression hung over society at large. It seemed as if the alarm was proportionate to the previous light-heartedness of fancied security – and indeed it was so; for, since the days of King Belshazzar, the solemn decrees of Doom have ever seemed most terrible when they awe into silence the merry revellers of life. So it was this year to which I come in the progress of my story.

The summer had been unusually gorgeous. Some had complained of the steaming heat, but others had pointed to the lush vegetation, which was profuse and luxuriant. The early autumn was wet and cold, but people did not regard it, in contemplation of some proud rejoicing of the nation,[3] which filled every newspaper and gave food to every tongue. In Eccleston these rejoicings were greater than in most places; for, by the national triumph of arms, it was supposed that a new market for the staple manufacture of the place would be opened; and so the trade, which had for a year or two been languishing, would now revive with redoubled vigour. Besides these legitimate causes of good spirits, there was the rank excitement of a coming election, in consequence of Mr Donne having accepted a Government office,[4] procured for him by one of his influential relations. This time, the Cranworths roused themselves from their magnificent torpor of security in good season, and were going through a series of pompous and ponderous hospitalities, in order to bring back the Eccleston voters to their allegiance.

While the town was full of these subjects by turns – now thinking and speaking of the great revival of trade – now of the chances of the election, as yet some weeks distant – now of the balls at Cranworth Court, in which Mr Cranworth Cranworth had danced with all the belles of the shopocracy of Eccleston – there came creeping, creeping, in hidden, slimy courses, the terrible fever – that fever which is never utterly banished from the sad haunts of vice and misery, but lives in such darkness, like a wild beast in the recesses of his den. It had begun in the low Irish lodging-houses;[5] but there it was so common it excited little attention. The poor creatures died almost without the attendance of the unwarned medical men, who received their first notice of the spreading plague from the Roman Catholic priests.

Before the medical men of Eccleston had had time to meet together and consult, and compare the knowledge of the fever which they had severally gained, it had, like the blaze of a fire which had long smouldered, burst forth in many places at once – not merely among the loose-living and vicious, but among the decently poor – nay, even among the well-to-do and respectable. And, to add to the horror, like all similar pestilences, its course was most rapid at first, and was fatal in the great majority of cases – hopeless from the beginning. There was a cry, and then a deep silence, and then rose the long wail of the survivors.

A portion of the Infirmary of the town was added to that already set apart for a fever-ward; the smitten were carried thither at once, whenever it was possible, in order to prevent the spread of infection; and on that lazar-house[6] was concentrated all the medical skill and force of the place.

But when one of the physicians had died, in consequence of his attendance – when the customary staff of matrons and nurses had been swept off in two days – and the nurses belonging to the Infirmary had shrunk from being drafted into the pestilential fever-ward – when high wages had failed to tempt any to what, in their panic, they considered as certain death – when the doctors stood aghast at the swift mortality among the untended sufferers, who were dependent only on the care of the most ignorant hirelings, too brutal to recognise the solemnity of Death (all this had happened within a week from the first acknowledgment of the presence of the plague) – Ruth came one day, with a quieter step than usual, into Mr Benson's study, and told him she wanted to speak to him for a few minutes.

'To be sure, my dear! Sit down!' said he; for she was standing and leaning her head against the chimney-piece, idly gazing into the fire. She went on standing there, as if she had not heard his words; and it was a few moments before she began to speak. Then she said:

'I want to tell you, that I have been this morning and offered myself as matron to the fever-ward while it is so full. They have accepted me; and I am going this evening.'

'Oh, Ruth! I feared this; I saw your look this morning as we spoke of this terrible illness.'

'Why do you say "fear", Mr Benson? You yourself have been with John Harrison, and old Betty, and many others, I dare say, of whom we have not heard.'

'But this is so different! in such poisoned air! among such malignant cases! Have you thought and weighed it enough, Ruth?'

She was quite still for a moment, but her eyes grew full of tears. At last she said, very softly, with a kind of still solemnity:

'Yes! I have thought, and I have weighed. But through the very midst of all my fears and thoughts I have felt that I must go.'

The remembrance of Leonard was present in both their minds; but for a few moments longer they neither of them spoke. Then Ruth said:

'I believe I have no fear. That is a great preservative, they say. At any rate, if I have a little natural shrinking, it is quite gone when I remember that I am in God's hands! Oh, Mr Benson,' continued she, breaking out into the irrepressible tears – 'Leonard, Leonard!'

And now it was his turn to speak out the brave words of faith.

'Poor, poor mother!' said he. 'But be of good heart. He, too, is in God's hands. Think what a flash of time only will separate you from him, if you should die in this work!'

'But he – but he – it will be long to him, Mr Benson! He will be alone!'

'No, Ruth, he will not. God and all good men will watch over him.

But if you cannot still this agony of fear as to what will become of him, you ought not to go. Such tremulous passion will predispose you to take the fever.'

'I will not be afraid,' she replied, lifting up her face, over which a bright light shone, as of God's radiance. 'I am not afraid for myself. I will not be so for my darling.'

After a little pause, they began to arrange the manner of her going, and to speak about the length of time that she might be absent on her temporary duties. In talking of her return, they assumed it to be certain, although the exact time when was to them unknown, and would be dependent entirely on the duration of the fever; but not the less, in their secret hearts, did they feel where alone the issue lay. Ruth was to communicate with Leonard and Miss Faith through Mr Benson alone, who insisted on his determination to go every evening to the hospital to learn the proceedings of the day, and the state of Ruth's health.

'It is not alone on your account, my dear! There may be many sick people of whom, if I can give no other comfort, I can take intelligence to their friends.'

All was settled with grave composure; yet still Ruth lingered, as if nerving herself up for some effort. At length she said, with a faint smile upon her pale face:

'I believe I am a great coward. I stand here talking because I dread to tell Leonard.'

'You must not think of it,' exclaimed he. 'Leave it to me. It is sure to unnerve you.'

'I must think of it. I shall have self-control enough in a minute to do it calmly – to speak hopefully. For only think,' continued she, smiling through the tears that would gather in her eyes, 'what a comfort the remembrance of the last few words may be to the poor fellow, if—' The words were choked, but she smiled bravely on. 'No!' said she, 'that must be done; but perhaps you will spare me one thing – will you tell Aunt Faith? I suppose I am very weak, but, knowing that I must go, and not knowing what may be the end, I feel as if I could not bear to resist her entreaties just at last. Will you tell her, sir, while I go to Leonard?'

Silently he consented, and the two rose up and came forth, calm and serene. And calmly and gently did Ruth tell her boy of her purpose; not daring even to use any unaccustomed tenderness of voice or gesture, lest, by so doing, she should alarm him unnecessarily as to the result. She spoke hopefully, and bade him be of good courage; and he caught her bravery, though his, poor boy! had root rather in his ignorance of the actual imminent danger than in her deep faith.

When he had gone down, Ruth began to arrange her dress. When she came down-stairs she went into the old familiar garden and gathered a nosegay of the last lingering autumn flowers – a few roses and the like.

Mr Benson had tutored his sister well; and although Miss Faith's face was swollen with crying, she spoke with almost exaggerated cheerfulness to Ruth. Indeed, as they all stood at the front door, making-believe to have careless nothings to say, just as at an ordinary leave-taking, you would not have guessed the strained chords of feeling there were in each heart. They lingered on, the last rays of the setting sun falling on the group. Ruth once or twice had roused herself to the pitch of saying 'Good-by,' but when her eye fell on Leonard she was forced to hide the quivering of her lips, and conceal her trembling mouth amid the bunch of roses.

'They won't let you have your flowers, I'm afraid,' said Miss Benson. 'Doctors so often object to the smell.'[7]

'No; perhaps not,' said Ruth, hurriedly. 'I did not think of it. I will only keep this one rose. Here, Leonard, darling!' She gave the rest to him. It was her farewell; for having now no veil to hide her emotion, she summoned all her bravery for one parting smile, and, smiling, turned away. But she gave one look back from the street, just from the last point at which the door could be seen, and catching a glimpse of Leonard standing foremost on the step, she ran back, and he met her half-way, and mother and child spoke never a word in that close embrace.

'Now, Leonard,' said Miss Faith, 'be a brave boy. I feel sure she will come back to us before very long.'

But she was very near crying herself; and she would have given way, I believe, if she had not found the wholesome outlet of scolding Sally, for expressing just the same opinion respecting Ruth's proceedings as she herself had done not two hours before. Taking what her brother had said to her as a text, she delivered such a lecture to Sally on want of faith that she was astonished at herself, and so much affected by what she had said that she had to shut the door of communication between the kitchen and the parlour pretty hastily, in order to prevent Sally's threatened reply from weakening her belief in the righteousness of what Ruth had done. Her words had gone beyond her conviction.

Evening after evening Mr Benson went forth to gain news of Ruth; and night after night he returned with good tidings. The fever, it is true, raged; but no plague came nigh her. He said her face was ever calm and bright, except when clouded by sorrow as she gave the accounts of the deaths which occurred in spite of every care. He said that he had never seen her face so fair and gentle as it was now, when she was living in the midst of disease and woe.

One evening Leonard (for they had grown bolder as to the infection) accompanied him to the street on which the hospital abutted. Mr Benson left him there, and told him to return home; but the boy lingered, attracted by the crowd that had gathered, and were gazing up intently towards the lighted windows of the hospital. There was nothing beyond that to be seen; but the greater part of these poor people had friends or relations in that palace of Death.

Leonard stood and listened. At first their talk consisted of vague and exaggerated accounts (if such could be exaggerated) of the horrors of the fever. Then they spoke of Ruth – of his mother; and Leonard held his breath to hear.

'They say she has been a great sinner, and that this is her penance,' quoth one. And as Leonard gasped, before rushing forward to give the speaker straight the lie, an old man spoke:

'Such a one as her has never been a great sinner; nor does she do her work as a penance, but for the love of God, and of the blessed Jesus. She will be in the light of God's countenance when you and I will be standing afar off. I tell you, man, when my poor wench died, as no one would come near, her head lay at that hour on this woman's sweet breast. I could fell you,' the old man went on, lifting his shaking arm, 'for calling that woman a great sinner. The blessing of them who were ready to perish is upon her.'

Immediately there arose a clamour of tongues, each with some tale of his mother's gentle doings, till Leonard grew dizzy with the beatings of his glad, proud heart. Few were aware how much Ruth had done; she never spoke of it, shrinking with sweet shyness from over-much allusion to her own work at all times. Her left hand truly knew not what her right hand did;[8] and Leonard was overwhelmed now to hear of the love and the reverence with which the poor and outcast had surrounded her. It was irrepressible. He stepped forward with a proud bearing, and touching the old man's arm, who had first spoken, Leonard tried to speak; but for an instant he could not, his heart was too full: tears came before words, but at length he managed to say:

'Sir, I am her son!'

'Thou! thou her bairn! God bless you, lad,' said an old woman, pushing through the crowd. 'It was but last night she kept my child quiet with singing psalms the night through. Low and sweet, low and sweet, they tell me – till many poor things were hushed, though they were out of their minds, and had not heard psalms this many a year. God in heaven bless you, lad!'

Many other wild, woe-begone creatures pressed forward with blessings on Ruth's son, while he could only repeat:

'She is my mother.'

From that day forward Leonard walked erect in the streets of Eccleston, where 'many arose and called her blessed.'[9]

After some weeks the virulence of the fever abated; and the general panic subsided – indeed, a kind of fool-hardiness succeeded. To be sure, in some instances the panic still held possession of individuals to an exaggerated extent. But the number of patients in the hospital was rapidly diminishing, and, for money, those were to be found who could supply Ruth's place. But to her it was owing that the overwrought fear of the town was subdued; it was she who had gone voluntarily, and, with no thought of greed or gain, right into the very jaws of the fierce disease. She bade the inmates of the hospital farewell, and after carefully submitting herself to the purification recommended by Mr Davis, the principal surgeon of the place, who had always attended Leonard, she returned to Mr Benson's just at gloaming time.

They each vied with the other in the tenderest cares. They hastened tea; they wheeled the sofa to the fire; they made her lie down; and to all she submitted with the docility of a child; and when the candles came, even Mr Benson's anxious eye could see no change in her looks, but that she seemed a little paler. The eyes were as full of spiritual light, the gently parted lips as rosy, and the smile, if more rare, yet as sweet as ever.

CHAPTER XXXIV

The next morning, Miss Benson would insist upon making Ruth lie down on the sofa. Ruth longed to do many things; to be much more active; but she submitted, when she found that it would gratify Miss Faith if she remained as quiet as if she were really an invalid.

Leonard sat by her holding her hand. Every now and then he looked up from his book, as if to make sure that she indeed was restored to him. He had brought her down the flowers which she had given him the day of her departure, and which he had kept in water as long as they had any greenness or fragrance, and then had carefully dried and put by. She too, smiling, had produced the one rose which she had carried away to the hospital. Never had the bond between her and her boy been drawn so firm and strong.

Many visitors came this day to the quiet Chapel-house. First of all Mrs Farquhar appeared. She looked very different from the Jemima Bradshaw of three years ago. Happiness had called out beauty; the colouring of her face was lovely, and vivid as that of an autumn day; her berry-red lips scarce closed over the short white teeth for her smiles; and her large dark eyes glowed and sparkled with daily happiness. They were softened by a mist of tears as she looked upon Ruth.

'Lie still! Don't move! You must be content to-day to be waited upon, and nursed! I have just seen Miss Benson in the lobby,[1] and had charge upon charge not to fatigue you. Oh, Ruth! how we all love you, now we have you back again! Do you know, I taught Rosa to say her prayers as soon as ever you were gone to that horrid place, just on purpose that her little innocent lips might pray for you – I wish you could hear her say it – "Please, dear God, keep Ruth safe." Oh, Leonard! are not you proud of your mother?'

Leonard said 'Yes,' rather shortly, as if he were annoyed that any one else should know, or even have a right to imagine, how proud he was. Jemima went on:

'Now, Ruth! I have got a plan for you. Walter and I have partly made it; and partly it's papa's doing. Yes, dear! papa has been quite anxious to show his respect for you. We all want you to go to the dear

Eagle's Crag for this next month, and get strong, and have some change in that fine air at Abermouth. I am going to take little Rosa there. Papa has lent it to us. And the weather is often very beautiful in November.'

'Thank you very much. It is very tempting; for I have been almost longing for some such change. I cannot tell all at once whether I can go; but I will see about it, if you will let me leave it open a little.'

'Oh! as long as you like, so that you will but go at last. And, Master Leonard! you are to come too. Now, I know I have you on my side.'

Ruth thought of the place. Her only reluctance arose from the remembrance of that one interview on the sands. That walk she could never go again; but how much remained! How much that would be a charming balm and refreshment to her!

'What happy evenings we shall have together! Do you know, I think Mary and Elizabeth may perhaps come.'

A bright gleam of sunshine came into the room. 'Look! how bright and propitious for our plans. Dear Ruth, it seems like an omen for the future!'

Almost while she spoke, Miss Benson entered, bringing with her Mr Grey, the rector of Eccleston. He was an elderly man, short and stoutly built, with something very formal in his manner; but any one might feel sure of his steady benevolence who noticed the expression of his face, and especially of the kindly black eyes that gleamed beneath his grey and shaggy eyebrows. Ruth had seen him at the hospital once or twice, and Mrs Farquhar had met him pretty frequently in general society.

'Go and tell your uncle,' said Miss Benson to Leonard.

'Stop, my boy! I have just met Mr Benson in the street, and my errand now is to your mother. I should like you to remain and hear what it is; and I am sure that my business will give these ladies' – bowing to Miss Benson and Jemima – 'so much pleasure, that I need not apologise for entering upon it in their presence.'

He pulled out his double eye-glass, saying, with a grave smile:

'You ran away from us yesterday so quietly and cunningly, Mrs Denbigh, that you were, perhaps, not aware that the Board was sitting at that very time, and trying to form a vote sufficiently expressive of our gratitude to you. As Chairman, they requested me to present you with this letter, which I shall have the pleasure of reading.'

With all due emphasis he read aloud a formal letter from the Secretary to the Infirmary, conveying a vote of thanks to Ruth.

The good rector did not spare her one word, from date to signature; and then, folding the letter up, he gave it to Leonard, saying:

'There, sir! when you are an old man, you may read that testimony to your mother's noble conduct with pride and pleasure. For, indeed,' continued he, turning to Jemima, 'no words can express the relief it was to us. I speak of the gentlemen composing the Board of the Infirmary. When Mrs Denbigh came forward, the panic was at its height, and the alarm of course aggravated the disorder. The poor creatures died rapidly; there was hardly time to remove the dead bodies before others were brought in to occupy the beds, so little help was to be procured on account of the universal terror; and the morning when Mrs Denbigh offered us her services, we seemed at the very worst. I shall never forget the sensation of relief in my mind when she told us what she proposed to do; but we thought it right to warn her to the full extent—

'Nay, madam,' said he, catching a glimpse of Ruth's changing colour, 'I will spare you any more praises. I will only say, if I can be a friend to you, or a friend to your child, you may command my poor powers to the utmost.'

He got up, and bowing formally, he took his leave. Jemima came and kissed Ruth. Leonard went up-stairs to put the precious letter away. Miss Benson sat crying heartily in a corner of the room. Ruth went to her, and threw her arms round her neck, and said:

'I could not tell him just then. I durst not speak for fear of breaking down; but if I have done right, it was all owing to you and Mr Benson. Oh! I wish I had said how the thought first came into my head from seeing the things Mr Benson has done so quietly ever since the fever first came amongst us. I could not speak; and it seemed as if I was taking those praises to myself, when all the time I was feeling how little I deserved them – how it was all owing to you.'

'Under God, Ruth,' said Miss Benson, speaking through her tears.

'Oh! I think there is nothing humbles one so much as undue praise. While he was reading that letter, I could not help feeling how many things I have done wrong! Could he know of – of what I have been?' asked she, dropping her voice very low.

'Yes!' said Jemima, 'he knew – everybody in Eccleston did know – but the remembrance of those days is swept away. Miss Benson,' she continued, for she was anxious to turn the subject, 'you must be on my side, and persuade Ruth to come to Abermouth for a few weeks. I want her and Leonard both to come.'

'I'm afraid my brother will think that Leonard is missing his lessons sadly. Just of late we could not wonder that the poor child's heart was so full; but he must make haste, and get on all the more for his idleness.' Miss Benson piqued herself on being a disciplinarian.

'Oh, as for lessons, Walter is so very anxious that you should give way to his superior wisdom, Ruth, and let Leonard go to school. He will send him to any school you fix upon, according to the mode of life you plan for him.'

'I have no plan,' said Ruth. 'I have no means of planning. All I can do is to try and make him ready for anything.'

'Well,' said Jemima, 'we must talk it over at Abermouth; for I am sure you won't refuse to come, dearest, dear Ruth! Think of the quiet, sunny days, and the still evenings, that we shall have together, with little Rosa to tumble about among the fallen leaves; and there's Leonard to have his first sight of the sea.'

'I do think of it,' said Ruth, smiling at the happy picture Jemima drew. And both smiling at the hopeful prospect before them, they parted – never to meet again in life.

No sooner had Mrs Farquhar gone than Sally burst in.

'Oh! dear, dear!' said she, looking around her. 'If I had but known that the rector was coming to call, I'd ha' put on the best covers, and the Sunday tablecloth! You're well enough,' continued she, surveying Ruth from head to foot; 'you're always trim and dainty in your gowns, though I reckon they but tuppence a yard, and you've a face to set 'em off; but as for you' (as she turned to Miss Benson), 'I think you might ha' had something better on than that old stuff, if it had only been to do credit to a parishioner like me, whom he has known ever sin' my father was his clerk.'

'You forget, Sally, I had been making jelly all the morning. How could I tell it was Mr Grey when there was a knock at the door?' Miss Benson replied.

'You might ha' letten me do the jelly; I'se warrant I could ha' pleased Ruth as well as you. If I had but known he was coming, I'd ha' slipped round the corner and bought ye a neck-ribbon, or summut to lighten ye up. I'se loth he should think I'm living with Dissenters, that don't know how to keep themselves trig² and smart.'

'Never mind, Sally; he never thought of me. What he came for, was to see Ruth; and, as you say, she's always neat and dainty.'

'Well! I reckon it cannot be helped now; but if I buy ye a ribbon, will you promise to wear it when church-folks come? for I cannot abide the way they have of scoffing at the Dissenters about their dress.'

'Very well! we'll make that bargain,' said Miss Benson; 'and now, Ruth, I'll go and fetch you a cup of warm jelly.'

'Oh! indeed, Aunt Faith,' said Ruth, 'I am very sorry to balk you; but, if you're going to treat me as an invalid, I am afraid I shall rebel.'

But when she found that Aunt Faith's heart was set upon it, she submitted very graciously: only dimpling up a little, as she found that she must consent to lie on the sofa, and be fed, when, in truth, she felt full of health, with a luxurious sensation of languor stealing over her now and then, just enough to make it very pleasant to think of the salt breezes, and the sea beauty which awaited her at Abermouth.

Mr Davis called in the afternoon, and his visit was also to Ruth. Mr and Miss Benson were sitting with her in the parlour, and watching her with contented love, as she employed herself in household sewing, and hopefully spoke about the Abermouth plan.

'Well! so you had our worthy rector here to-day; I am come on something of the same kind of errand; only I shall spare you the reading of my letter, which, I'll answer for it, he did not. Please to take notice,' said he, putting down a sealed letter, 'that I have delivered you a vote of thanks from my medical brothers; and open and read it at your leisure; only rest now, for I want to have a little talk with you on my own behoof. I want to ask you a favour, Mrs Denbigh.'

'A favour!' exclaimed Ruth; 'what can I do for you? I think I may say I will do it, without hearing what it is.'

'Then you're a very imprudent woman,' replied he; 'however, I'll take you at your word. I want you to give me your boy.'

'Leonard?'

'Ay! there it is, you see, Mr Benson. One minute she is as ready as can be, and the next, she looks at me as if I was an ogre!'

'Perhaps we don't understand what you mean,' said Mr Benson.

'The thing is this. You know I've no children; and I can't say I've ever fretted over it much; but my wife has; and whether it is that she has infected me, or that I grieve over my good practice going to a stranger, when I ought to have had a son to take it after me, I don't know; but, of late, I've got to look with covetous eyes on all healthy boys, and at last I've settled down my wishes on this Leonard of yours, Mrs Denbigh.'

Ruth could not speak; for, even yet, she did not understand what he meant. He went on:

'Now, how old is the lad?' He asked Ruth, but Miss Benson replied:

'He'll be twelve next February.'

'Umph! only twelve! He's tall and old looking for his age. You look young enough, it is true.' He said this last sentence as if to himself, but seeing Ruth crimson up, he abruptly changed his tone.

'Twelve, is he! Well, I take him from now. I don't mean that I really take him away from you,' said he, softening all at once, and becoming grave and considerate. 'His being your son – the son of one whom I have seen – as I have seen you, Mrs Denbigh (out and out the best nurse I ever met with, Miss Benson; and good nurses are things we doctors know how to value) – his being your son is his great recommendation to me; not but what the lad himself is a noble boy. I shall be glad to leave him with you as long and as much as we can; he could not be tied to your apron-string all his life, you know. Only I provide for his education, subject to your consent and good pleasure, and he is bound apprentice to me. I, his guardian, bind him to myself, the first surgeon in Eccleston, be the other who he may; and in process of time he becomes partner, and some day or other succeeds me. Now, Mrs Denbigh, what have you got to say against this plan? My wife is just as full of it as me. Come! begin with your objections. You're not a woman if you have not a whole bag-full of them ready to turn out against any reasonable proposal.'

'I don't know,' faltered Ruth. 'It is so sudden—'

'It is very, very kind of you, Mr Davis,' said Miss Benson, a little scandalised at Ruth's non-expression of gratitude.

'Pooh! pooh! I'll answer for it, in the long run, I am taking good care of my own interests. Come, Mrs Denbigh, is it a bargain?'

Now Mr Benson spoke.

'Mr Davis, it is rather sudden, as she says. As far as I can see, it is the best as well as the kindest proposal that could have been made; but I think we must give her a little time to think about it.'

'Well, twenty-four hours! Will that do?'

Ruth lifted up her head. 'Mr Davis, I am not ungrateful because I can't thank you' (she was crying while she spoke); 'let me have a fortnight to consider about it. In a fortnight I will make up my mind. Oh, how good you all are!'

'Very well. Then this day fortnight – Thursday the 28th – you will let me know your decision. Mind! if it's against me, I sha'n't consider it a decision, for I'm determined to carry my point. I'm not going to make Mrs Denbigh blush, Mr Benson, by telling you, in her presence, of all I have observed about her this last three weeks, that has made me sure of the good qualities I shall find in this boy of hers. I was watching her when she little thought of it. Do you remember that night when Hector O'Brien was so furiously delirious, Mrs Denbigh?'

Ruth went very white at the remembrance.

'Why now, look there! how pale she is at the very thought of it. And yet, I assure you, she was the one to go up and take the piece of glass from him which he had broken out of the window for the sole purpose of cutting his throat, or the throat of any one else, for that matter. I wish we had some others as brave as she is.'

'I thought the great panic was passed away!' said Mr Benson.

'Ay! the general feeling of alarm is much weaker; but, here and there, there are as great fools as ever. Why, when I leave here, I am going to see our precious member, Mr Donne—'

'Mr Donne?' said Ruth.

'Mr Donne, who lies ill at the Queen's – came last week, with the intention of canvassing, but was too much alarmed by what he heard of the fever to set to work; and, in spite of all his precautions, he has taken it; and you should see the terror they are in at the hotel; landlord, landlady, waiters, servants – all; there's not a creature will go near him, if they can help it; and there's only his groom – a lad he saved from drowning, I'm told – to do anything for him. I must get him a proper nurse, somehow or somewhere, for all my being a Cranworth-man. Ah, Mr Benson! you don't know the temptations we medical men have. Think, if I allowed your member to die now, as he might very well, if he had no nurse – how famously Mr Cranworth would walk over the course! – Where's Mrs Denbigh gone to? I hope I've not frightened her away by reminding her of Hector O'Brien, and that awful night, when I do assure you she behaved like a heroine!'

As Mr Benson was showing Mr Davis out, Ruth opened the study-door, and said, in a very calm, low voice:

'Mr Benson! will you allow me to speak to Mr Davis alone?'

Mr Benson immediately consented, thinking that, in all probability, she wished to ask some further questions about Leonard; but as Mr Davis came into the room, and shut the door, he was struck by her pale, stern face of determination, and awaited her speaking first.

'Mr Davis! I must go and nurse Mr Bellingham,' said she at last, clenching her hands tight together, but no other part of her body moving from its intense stillness.

'Mr Bellingham?' asked he, astonished at the name.

'Mr Donne, I mean,' said she, hurriedly. 'His name was Bellingham.'

'Oh! I remember hearing he had changed his name for some property. But you must not think of any more such work just now. You are not fit for it. You are looking as white as ashes.'

'I must go,' she repeated.

'Nonsense! Here's a man who can pay for the care of the first hospital nurses in London – and I doubt if his life is worth the risk of one of theirs even, much more of yours.'

'We have no right to weigh human lives against each other.'

'No! I know we have not. But it's a way we doctors are apt to get into; and, at any rate, it's ridiculous of you to think of such a thing. Just listen to reason.'

'I can't! I can't!' cried she, with a sharp pain in her voice. 'You must let me go, dear Mr Davis!' said she, now speaking with soft entreaty.

'No!' said he, shaking his head authoritatively. 'I'll do no such thing.'

'Listen!' said she, dropping her voice, and going all over the deepest scarlet; 'he is Leonard's father! Now! you will let me go!'

Mr Davis was indeed staggered by what she said, and for a moment he did not speak. So she went on:

'You will not tell! You must not tell! No one knows, not even Mr Benson, who it was. And now – it might do him so much harm to have it known. You will not tell!'

'No! I will not tell,' replied he. 'But, Mrs Denbigh, you must answer me this one question, which I ask you in all true respect, but which I must ask, in order to guide both myself and you aright – Of course I knew Leonard was illegitimate – in fact, I will give you secret for secret; it was being so myself that first made me sympathise with him, and desire to adopt him. I knew that much of your history; but tell me, do you now care for this man? Answer me truly – do you love him?'

For a moment or two she did not speak; her head was bent down;

then she raised it up, and looked with clear and honest eyes into his face.

'I have been thinking – but I do not know – I cannot tell – I don't think I should love him, if he were well and happy – but you said he was ill – and alone – how can I help caring for him? – how can I help caring for him?' repeated she, covering her face with her hands, and the quick hot tears stealing through her fingers. 'He is Leonard's father,' continued she, looking up at Mr Davis suddenly. 'He need not know – he shall not – that I have ever been near him. If he is like the others, he must be delirious – I will leave him before he comes to himself – but now let me go – I must go.'

'I wish my tongue had been bitten out before I had named him to you. He would do well enough without you; and, I dare say, if he recognises you, he will only be annoyed.'

'It is very likely,' said Ruth, heavily.

'Annoyed, – why! he may curse you for your unasked-for care of him. I have heard my poor mother – and she was as pretty and delicate a creature as you are – cursed for showing tenderness when it was not wanted. Now, be persuaded by an old man like me, who has seen enough of life to make his heart ache – leave this fine gentleman to his fate. I'll promise you to get him as good a nurse as can be had for money.'

'No!' said Ruth, with dull persistency – as if she had not attended to his dissuasions; 'I must go. I will leave him before he recognises me.'

'Why, then,' said the old surgeon, 'if you're so bent upon it, I suppose I must let you. It is but what my mother would have done – poor, heart-broken thing! However, come along, and let us make the best of it. It saves me a deal of trouble, I know; for, if I have you for a right hand, I need not worry myself continually with wondering how he is taken care of. Go get your bonnet, you tenderhearted fool of a woman! Let us get you out of the house without any more scenes or explanations; I'll make all straight with the Bensons.'

'You will not tell my secret, Mr Davis,' she said, abruptly.

'No! not I! Does the woman think I had never to keep a secret of the kind before? I only hope he'll lose his election, and never come near the place again. After all,' continued he, sighing, 'I suppose it is but human nature!' He began recalling the circumstances of his own early life, and dreamily picturing scenes in the grey dying embers of the fire;

and he was almost startled when she stood before him, ready equipped, grave, pale, and quiet.

'Come along!' said he. 'If you're to do any good at all, it must be in these next three days. After that, I'll ensure his life for this bout; and mind! I shall send you home then; for he might know you, and I'll have no excitement to throw him back again, and no sobbing and crying from you. But now every moment your care is precious to him. I shall tell my own story to the Bensons, as soon as I have installed you.'

Mr Donne lay in the best room of the Queen's Hotel – no one with him but his faithful, ignorant servant, who was as much afraid of the fever as any one else could be, but who, nevertheless, would not leave his master – his master who had saved his life as a child, and afterwards put him in the stables at Bellingham Hall, where he learnt all that he knew. He stood in a farther corner of the room, watching his delirious master with affrighted eyes, not daring to come near him, nor yet willing to leave him.

'Oh! if that doctor would but come! He'll kill himself or me – and them stupid servants won't stir a step over the threshold; how shall I get over the night? Blessings on him – here's the old doctor back again! I hear him creaking and scolding up the stairs!'

The door opened, and Mr Davis entered, followed by Ruth.

'Here's the nurse, my good man – such a nurse as there is not in the three counties.[3] Now, all you'll have to do is to mind what she says.'

'Oh, sir! he's mortal bad! won't you stay with us through the night, sir?'

'Look there!' whispered Mr Davis to the man, 'see how she knows how to manage him! Why, I could not do it better myself!'

She had gone up to the wild, raging figure, and with soft authority had made him lie down: and then, placing a basin of cold water by the bed-side, she had dipped in it her pretty hands, and was laying their cool dampness on his hot brow, speaking in a low soothing voice all the time, in a way that acted like a charm in hushing his mad talk.

'But I will stay!' said the doctor, after he had examined his patient; 'as much on her account as his, and partly to quieten the fears of this poor, faithful fellow.'

CHAPTER XXXV

The third night after this was to be the crisis – the turning point between
Life and Death. Mr Davis came again to pass it by the bed-side of the
sufferer. Ruth was there, constant and still, intent upon watching the
symptoms, and acting according to them, in obedience to Mr Davis's
directions. She had never left the room. Every sense had been strained
in watching – every power of thought or judgment had been kept on
the full stretch. Now that Mr Davis came and took her place, and that
the room was quiet for the night, she became oppressed with heaviness,
which yet did not tend to sleep. She could not remember the present
time, or where she was. All times of her earliest youth – the days of her
childhood – were in her memory with a minuteness and fulness of detail
which was miserable; for all along she felt that she had no real grasp
on the scenes that were passing through her mind – that, somehow,
they were long gone by, and gone by for ever – and yet she could not
remember who she was now, nor where she was, and whether she had
now any interests in life to take the place of those which she was conscious
had passed away, although their remembrance filled her mind with
painful acuteness. Her head lay on her arms, and they rested on the
table. Every now and then she opened her eyes, and saw the large room,
handsomely furnished with articles that were each one incongruous
with the other, as if bought at sales. She saw the flickering night-light
– she heard the ticking of the watch, and the two breathings, each going
on at a separate rate – one hurried, abruptly stopping, and then panting
violently, as if to make up for lost time; and the other slow, steady
and regular, as if the breather was asleep; but this supposition was
contradicted by an occasional repressed sound of yawning. The sky
through the uncurtained window looked dark and black – would this
night never have an end? Had the sun gone down for ever, and would
the world at last awaken to a general sense of everlasting night?

Then she felt as if she ought to get up, and go and see how the
troubled sleeper in yonder bed was struggling through his illness; but
she could not remember who the sleeper was, and she shrunk from
seeing some phantom-face on the pillow, such as now began to haunt

the dark corners of the room, and look at her, jibbering and mowing as they looked. So she covered her face again, and sank into a whirling stupor of sense and feeling. By-and-by she heard her fellow-watcher stirring, and a dull wonder stole over her as to what he was doing; but the heavy languor pressed her down, and kept her still. At last she heard the words, 'Come here,' and listlessly obeyed the command. She had to steady herself in the rocking chamber before she could walk to the bed by which Mr Davis stood; but the effort to do so roused her, and, although conscious of an oppressive headache, she viewed with sudden and clear vision all the circumstances of her present position. Mr Davis was near the head of the bed, holding the night-lamp high, and shading it with his hand, that it might not disturb the sick person, who lay with his face towards them, in feeble exhaustion, but with every sign that the violence of the fever had left him. It so happened that the rays of the lamp fell bright and full upon Ruth's countenance, as she stood with her crimson lips parted with the hurrying breath, and the fever-flush brilliant on her cheeks. Her eyes were wide open, and their pupils distended. She looked on the invalid in silence, and hardly understood why Mr Davis had summoned her there.

'Don't you see the change? He is better! – the crisis is past!'

But she did not speak; her looks were riveted on his softly-unclosing eyes, which met hers as they opened languidly. She could not stir or speak. She was held fast by that gaze of his, in which a faint recognition dawned, and grew to strength.

He murmured some words. They strained their sense to hear. He repeated them even lower than before; but this time they caught what he was saying.

'Where are the water-lilies? Where are the lilies in her hair?'

Mr Davis drew Ruth away.

'He is still rambling,' said he. 'But the fever has left him.'

The grey dawn was now filling the room with its cold light; was it that made Ruth's cheek so deadly pale? Could that call out the wild entreaty of her look, as if imploring help against some cruel foe that held her fast, and was wrestling with her Spirit of Life? She held Mr Davis's arm. If she had let it go, she would have fallen.

'Take me home,' she said, and fainted dead away.

Mr Davis carried her out of the chamber, and sent the groom to keep watch by his master. He ordered a fly to convey her to Mr Benson's, and lifted her in when it came, for she was still half unconscious. It was he who carried her up-stairs to her room, where Miss Benson and Sally undressed and laid her in her bed.

He awaited their proceedings in Mr Benson's study. When Mr Benson came in, Mr Davis said:

'Don't blame me. Don't add to my self-reproach. I have killed her. I was a cruel fool to let her go. Don't speak to me.'

'It may not be so bad,' said Mr Benson, himself needing comfort in that shock. 'She may recover. She surely will recover. I believe she will.'

'No, no! she won't. But by —, she shall, if I can save her.' Mr Davis looked defiantly at Mr Benson, as if he were Fate. 'I tell you she shall recover, or else I am a murderer. What business had I to take her to nurse him—'

He was cut short by Sally's entrance, and announcement that Ruth was now prepared to see him.

From that time forward Mr Davis devoted all his leisure, his skill, his energy to save her. He called on the rival surgeon to beg him to undertake the management of Mr Donne's recovery, saying, with his usual self-mockery, 'I could not answer it to Mr Cranworth if I had brought his opponent round, you know, when I had had such a fine opportunity in my power. Now, with your patients, and general Radical interest, it will be rather a feather in your cap; for he may want a good deal of care yet, though he is getting on famously – so rapidly, in fact, that it's a strong temptation to me to throw him back – a relapse, you know.'

The other surgeon bowed gravely, apparently taking Mr Davis in earnest, but certainly very glad of the job thus opportunely thrown in his way. In spite of Mr Davis's real and deep anxiety about Ruth, he could not help chuckling over his rival's literal interpretation of all he had said.

'To be sure, what fools men are! I don't know why one should watch and strive to keep them in the world. I have given this fellow something to talk about confidentially to all his patients; I wonder how much stronger a dose the man would have swallowed! I must begin to take care of my practice for that lad yonder. Well-a-day! well-a-day! What was this sick fine gentleman sent here for, that she should run a chance of her life for him? or why was he sent into the world at all, for that matter?'

Indeed, however much Mr Davis might labour with all his professional skill – however much they might all watch – and pray[1] – and weep – it was but too evident that Ruth 'home must go, and take her wages.'[2] Poor, poor Ruth!

It might be that, utterly exhausted by watching and nursing, first in the hospital, and then by the bedside of her former lover, the power of her constitution was worn out; or, it might be, her gentle, pliant sweetness, but she displayed no outrage or discord even in her delirium. There she lay in the attic-room in which her baby had been born, her watch over him kept, her confession to him made; and now she was stretched on the bed in utter helplessness, softly gazing at vacancy with her open, unconscious eyes, from which all the depth of their meaning had fled, and all they told was of a sweet, child-like insanity within. The watchers could not touch her with their sympathy, or come near her in her dim world; – so, mutely, but looking at each other from time to time with tearful eyes, they took a poor comfort from the one evident fact that, though lost and gone astray, she was happy and at peace. They had never heard her sing; indeed the simple art which her mother had taught her, had died, with her early joyousness, at that dear mother's death. But now she sang continually, very soft, and low. She went from one old childish ditty to another without let or pause, keeping a strange sort of time with her pretty fingers, as they closed and unclosed themselves upon the counterpane. She never looked at any one with the slightest glimpse of memory or intelligence in her face; no, not even at Leonard.

Her strength faded day by day; but she knew it not. Her sweet lips were parted to sing, even after the breath and the power to do so had left her, and her fingers fell idly on the bed.[3] Two days she lingered thus – all but gone from them, and yet still there.

They stood around her bed-side, not speaking, or sighing, or moaning; they were too much awed by the exquisite peacefulness of her look for that. Suddenly she opened wide her eyes, and gazed intently forwards, as if she saw some happy vision, which called out a lovely, rapturous, breathless smile. They held their very breaths.

'I see the Light coming,' said she. 'The Light is coming,' she said. And, raising herself slowly, she stretched out her arms, and then fell back, very still for evermore.

They did not speak. Mr Davis was the first to utter a word.

'It is over!' said he. 'She is dead!'

Outrang through the room the cry of Leonard:

'Mother! mother! mother! You have not left me alone! You will not leave me alone! You are not dead! Mother! Mother!'

They had pent in his agony of apprehension till then, that no wail of her child might disturb her ineffable calm. But now there was a cry heard through the house, of one refusing to be comforted:[4] 'Mother! Mother!'

But Ruth lay dead.

CHAPTER XXXVI

A stupor of grief succeeded to Leonard's passionate cries. He became so much depressed, physically as well as mentally, before the end of the day, that Mr Davis was seriously alarmed for the consequences. He hailed with gladness a proposal made by the Farquhars, that the boy should be removed to their house, and placed under the fond care of his mother's friend, who sent her own child to Abermouth the better to devote herself to Leonard.

When they told him of this arrangement, he at first refused to go and leave *her*; but when Mr Benson said:

'*She* would have wished it, Leonard! Do it for her sake!' he went away very quietly; not speaking a word, after Mr Benson had made the voluntary promise that he should see her once again. He neither spoke nor cried for many hours; and all Jemima's delicate wiles were called forth, before his heavy heart could find the relief of tears. And then he was so weak, and his pulse so low, that all who loved him feared for his life.

Anxiety about him made a sad distraction from the sorrow for the dead. The three old people who now formed the household in the Chapel-house, went about slowly and dreamily, each with a dull wonder at their hearts why they, the infirm and worn-out, were left, while she was taken in her lovely prime.

The third day after Ruth's death, a gentleman came to the door and asked to speak to Mr Benson. He was very much wrapped up in furs and cloaks, and the upper exposed part of his face was sunk and hollow, like that of one but partially recovered from illness. Mr and Miss Benson were at Mr Farquhar's, gone to see Leonard, and poor old Sally had been having a hearty cry over the kitchen fire before answering the door-knock. Her heart was tenderly inclined just then towards any one who had the aspect of suffering; so, although her master was out, and she was usually chary of admitting strangers, she proposed to Mr Donne (for it was he) that he should come in and await Mr Benson's return in the study. He was glad enough to avail himself of her offer; for he was feeble and nervous, and come on a piece of business which he exceedingly disliked, and about which he felt very awkward. The fire was nearly, if not quite, out; nor did Sally's vigorous blows do much good, although she left the room with an assurance that it would soon burn up. He leant against the chimney-piece, thinking over events, and with a sensation of discomfort, both external and internal, growing and gathering upon him. He almost wondered whether the proposal he meant to make with regard to Leonard could not be better arranged by letter than by an interview. He became very shivery, and impatient of the state of indecision to which his bodily weakness had reduced him.

Sally opened the door and came in. 'Would you like to walk up-stairs, sir?' asked she, in a trembling voice, for she had learnt who the visitor was from the driver of the fly, who had run up to the house to inquire what was detaining the gentleman that he had brought from the Queen's Hotel; and, knowing that Ruth had caught the fatal fever from her attendance on Mr Donne, Sally imagined that it was but a piece of sad civility to invite him up-stairs to see the poor dead body, which she had laid out and decked for the grave, with such fond care that she had grown strangely proud of its marble beauty.

Mr Donne was glad enough of any proposal of a change from the cold and comfortless room where he had thought uneasy, remorseful thoughts. He fancied that a change of place would banish the train of reflection that was troubling him; but the change he anticipated was to a well-warmed, cheerful sitting-room, with signs of life, and a bright fire therein; and he was on the last flight of stairs – at the door of the room where Ruth lay – before he understood whither Sally was conducting him. He shrank back for an instant, and then a strange sting of curiosity impelled him on. He stood in the humble low-roofed attic, the window open, and the tops of the distant snow-covered hills filling up the whiteness of the general aspect. He muffled himself up in his cloak, and shuddered, while Sally reverently drew down the sheet, and showed the beautiful, calm, still face, on which the last rapturous smile still lingered, giving an ineffable look of bright serenity. Her arms were crossed over her breast; the wimple-like cap marked the perfect oval of her face, while two braids of the waving auburn hair peeped out of the narrow border, and lay on the delicate cheeks.

He was awed into admiration by the wonderful beauty of that dead woman.

'How beautiful she is!' said he, beneath his breath. 'Do all dead people look so peaceful – so happy?'

'Not all,' replied Sally, crying. 'Few has been as good and as gentle as she was in their lives.' She quite shook with her sobbing.

Mr Donne was disturbed by her distress.

'Come, my good woman! we must all die—' he did not know what to say, and was becoming infected by her sorrow. 'I am sure you loved her very much, and were very kind to her in her lifetime; you must take this from me to buy yourself some remembrance of her.' He had pulled out a sovereign, and really had a kindly desire to console her, and reward her, in offering it to her.

But she took her apron from her eyes, as soon as she became aware of what he was doing, and, still holding it midway in her hands, she looked at him indignantly, before she burst out:

'And who are you, that think to pay for my kindness to her by money? And I was not kind to you, my darling,' said she, passionately addressing the motionless, serene body – 'I was not kind to you. I frabbed you,[1] and plagued you from the first, my lamb! I came and cut off your pretty locks in this very room – I did – and you said never an angry word to me; – no! not then, nor many a time at after, when I was very sharp and cross to you. – No! I never was kind to you, and I dunnot think the world was kind to you, my darling, – but you are gone where the angels are very tender to such as you – you are, my poor wench!' She bent down and kissed the lips, from whose marble, unyielding touch Mr Donne recoiled, even in thought.

Just then, Mr Benson entered the room. He had returned home before his sister, and came up-stairs in search of Sally, to whom he wanted to speak on some subject relating to the funeral. He bowed in recognition of Mr Donne, whom he knew as the member for the town, and whose presence impressed him painfully, as his illness had been the proximate cause of Ruth's death. But he tried to check this feeling, as it was no fault of Mr Donne's. Sally stole out of the room, to cry at leisure in her kitchen.

'I must apologise for being here,' said Mr Donne. 'I was hardly conscious where your servant was leading me to, when she expressed her wish that I should walk up-stairs.'

'It is a very common idea in this town, that it is a gratification to be asked to take a last look at the dead,' replied Mr Benson.

'And in this case, I am glad to have seen her once more,' said Mr Donne. 'Poor Ruth!'

Mr Benson glanced up at him at the last word. How did he know her name? To him she had only been Mrs Denbigh. But Mr Donne had no idea that he was talking to one unaware of the connexion that had formerly existed between them; and, though he would have preferred carrying on the conversation in a warmer room, yet, as Mr Benson was still gazing at her with sad, lingering love, he went on:

'I did not recognise her when she came to nurse me; I believe I was delirious. My servant, who had known her long ago, in Fordham, told me who she was. I cannot tell you how I regret that she should have died in consequence of her love of me.'

Mr Benson looked up at him again, a stern light filling his eyes as he did so. He waited impatiently to hear more, either to quench or confirm his suspicions. If she had not been lying there, very still and calm, he would have forced the words out of Mr Donne, by some abrupt question. As it was, he listened silently, his heart quick-beating.

'I know that money is but a poor compensation, – is no remedy for this event, or for my youthful folly.'

Mr Benson set his teeth hard together, to keep in words little short of a curse.

'Indeed, I offered her money to almost any amount before; – do me justice, sir,' catching the gleam of indignation on Mr Benson's face: 'I offered to marry her, and provide for the boy as if he had been legitimate. It's of no use recurring to that time,' said he, his voice faltering; 'what is done cannot be undone. But I came now to say, that I should be glad to leave the boy still under your charge, and that every expense you think it right to incur in his education I will gladly defray; – and place a sum of money in trust for him – say, two thousand pounds – or more:

fix what you will. Of course, if you decline retaining him, I must find some one else; but the provision for him shall be the same, for my poor Ruth's sake.'

Mr Benson did not speak. He could not, till he had gathered some peace from looking at the ineffable repose of the Dead.

Then, before he answered, he covered up her face; and in his voice there was the stillness of ice.

'Leonard is not unprovided for. Those that honoured his mother will take care of him. He shall never touch a penny of your money. Every offer of service you have made, I reject in his name, – and in her presence,' said he, bending towards the Dead. 'Men may call such actions as yours, youthful follies! There is another name for them with God. Sir! I will follow you down-stairs.'

All the way down, Mr Benson heard Mr Donne's voice urging and entreating, but the words he could not recognise for the thoughts that filled his brain – the rapid putting together of events that was going on there. And when Mr Donne turned at the door, to speak again, and repeat his offers of service to Leonard, Mr Benson made answer, without well knowing whether the answer fitted the question or not:

'I thank God, you have no right, legal or otherwise, over the child. And for her sake, I will spare him the shame of ever hearing your name as his father.'

He shut the door in Mr Donne's face.

'An ill-bred, puritanical old fellow! He may have the boy, I am sure, for aught I care. I have done my duty, and will get out of this abominable place as soon as I can. I wish my last remembrance of my beautiful Ruth was not mixed up with all these people.'

Mr Benson was bitterly oppressed with this interview; it disturbed the peace with which he was beginning to contemplate events. His anger ruffled him, although such anger had been just, and such indignation well-deserved; and both had been unconsciously present in his heart for years against the unknown seducer, whom he met face to face by the death-bed of Ruth.

It gave him a shock which he did not recover from for many days. He was nervously afraid lest Mr Donne should appear at the funeral; and not all the reasons he alleged to himself against this apprehension, put it utterly away from him. Before then, however, he heard casually (for he would allow himself no inquiries) that he had left the town. No!

Ruth's funeral passed over in calm and simple solemnity. Her child, her own household, her friend, and Mr Farquhar, quietly walked after the bier, which was borne by some of the poor to whom she had been very kind in her lifetime. And many others stood aloof in the little burying-ground, sadly watching that last ceremony.

They slowly dispersed; Mr Benson leading Leonard by the hand, and secretly wondering at his self-restraint. Almost as soon as they had let themselves into the Chapel-house, a messenger brought a note from Mrs Bradshaw, with a pot of quince marmalade, which, she said to Miss Benson, she thought Leonard might fancy, and if he did, they were to be sure and let her know, as she had plenty more; or, was there anything else that he would like? She would gladly make him whatever he fancied.

Poor Leonard! he lay stretched on the sofa, white and tearless, beyond the power of any such comfort, however kindly offered; but this was only one of the many homely, simple attentions, which all came round to offer him, from Mr Grey, the rector, down to the nameless poor who called at the back door to inquire how it fared with *her* child.[2]

Mr Benson was anxious, according to Dissenting custom, to preach an appropriate funeral sermon. It was the last office he could render to her; it should be done well and carefully. Moreover, it was possible that the circumstances of her life, which were known to all, might be made effective in this manner to work conviction of many truths. Accordingly, he made great preparation of thought and paper; he laboured hard, destroying sheet after sheet – his eyes filling with tears between-whiles, as he remembered some fresh proof of the humility and sweetness of her life. Oh, that he could do her justice! but words seemed hard and inflexible, and refused to fit themselves to his ideas. He sat late on Saturday, writing; he watched through the night till Sunday morning was far advanced. He had never taken such pains with any sermon, and he was only half satisfied with it after all.

Mrs Farquhar had comforted the bitterness of Sally's grief by giving her very handsome mourning. At any rate, she felt oddly proud and exulting when she thought of her new black gown; but when she remembered why she wore it, she scolded herself pretty sharply for her satisfaction, and took to crying afresh with redoubled vigour. She spent the Sunday morning in alternately smoothing down her skirts, and adjusting her broad hemmed collar, or bemoaning the occasion with tearful earnestness. But the sorrow overcame the little quaint vanity of her heart, as she saw troop after troop of humbly-dressed mourners pass by into the old chapel. They were very poor – but each had mounted some rusty piece of crape, or some faded black ribbon. The old came halting and slow – the mothers carried their quiet, awe-struck babes.

And not only these were there – but others – equally unaccustomed to nonconformist worship: Mr Davis, for instance, to whom Sally acted as chaperone; for he sat in the minister's pew, as a stranger; and, as she afterwards said, she had a fellow-feeling with him, being a Church-woman herself, and Dissenters had such awkward ways; however, she had been there before, so she could set him to rights about their fashions.

From the pulpit, Mr Benson saw one and all – the well-filled Bradshaw pew – all in deep mourning, Mr Bradshaw conspicuously so (he would have attended the funeral gladly if they would have asked him) – the Farquhars – the many strangers – the still more numerous poor – one or two wild-looking outcasts who stood afar off,[3] but wept silently and continually. Mr Benson's heart grew very full.

His voice trembled as he read and prayed. But he steadied it as he opened his sermon – his great, last effort in her honour – the labour that he had prayed God to bless to the hearts of many. For an instant the old man looked on all the upturned faces, listening, with wet eyes, to hear what he could say to interpret that which was in their hearts, dumb and unshaped, of God's doings as shown in her life. He looked, and, as he gazed, a mist came before him, and he could not see his sermon, nor his hearers, but only Ruth, as she had been – stricken low, and crouching from sight, in the upland field by Llan-dhu – like a woeful, hunted creature. And now her life was over! her struggle ended! Sermon and all was forgotten. He sat down, and hid his face in his hands for a minute or so. Then he arose, pale and serene. He put the sermon away, and opened the Bible, and read the seventh chapter of Revelations, beginning at the ninth verse.[4]

Before it was finished, most of his hearers were in tears. It came home to them as more appropriate than any sermon could have been. Even Sally, though full of anxiety as to what her fellow-Churchman would think of such proceedings, let the sobs come freely as she heard the words:

'And he said to me, These are they which came out of great tribulation, and have washed their robes, and made them white in the blood of the Lamb.

'Therefore are they before the throne of God, and serve him day and night in his temple; and he that sitteth on the throne shall dwell among them.

'They shall hunger no more, neither thirst any more; neither shall the sun light on them, nor any heat.

'For the Lamb which is in the midst of the throne shall feed them, and shall lead them unto living fountains of waters, and God shall wipe away all tears from their eyes.'

———————————

'He preaches sermons sometimes,' said Sally, nudging Mr Davis, as they rose from their knees at last. 'I make no doubt there was as grand a sermon in yon paper-book as ever we hear in church. I've heard him pray uncommon fine – quite beyond any but learned folk.'

Mr Bradshaw had been anxious to do something to testify his respect for the woman, who, if all had entertained his opinions, would have been driven into hopeless sin. Accordingly, he ordered the first stonemason of the town to meet him in the chapel-yard on Monday morning, to take measurement and receive directions for a tombstone. They threaded their way among the grassy heaps to where Ruth was buried, in the south corner, beneath the great Wych-elm. When they got there, Leonard raised himself up from the new-stirred turf. His face was swollen with weeping; but when he saw Mr Bradshaw he calmed himself, and checked his sobs, and, as an explanation of being where he was when thus surprised, he could find nothing to say but the simple words:

'My mother is dead, sir.'

His eyes sought those of Mr Bradshaw with a wild look of agony, as if to find comfort for that great loss in human sympathy; and at the first word – the first touch of Mr Bradshaw's hand on his shoulder – he burst out afresh.

'Come, come! my boy! – Mr Francis, I will see you about this to-morrow – I will call at your house. – Let me take you home, my poor fellow. Come, my lad, come!'

The first time, for years, that he had entered Mr Benson's house, he

came leading and comforting her son – and, for a moment, he could
not speak to his old friend, for the sympathy which choked up his voice,
and filled his eyes with tears.

THE END

NOTES

A Note on the Notes: access to the *Concise Oxford Dictionary* is assumed and words or phrases are only explained if they do not appear there or are used in some special sense. Quotations from the full *Oxford English Dictionary* are indicated by *OED*. In compiling these notes, I have consulted Alan Shelston's edition of *Ruth* (Oxford University Press, 1985) and Michael Wheeler's Ph.D. thesis (London, 1975), *Elizabeth Gaskell's Use of Literary Sources in* Mary Barton *and* Ruth.

1 (Title page) *Phineas Fletcher*: Phineas Fletcher (1582–1650), 'An Hymn' (published 1633). Quoted complete, the poem metaphorically urges the soul's repentance at Christ's feet and literally reflects the tears of Mary Magdalen (see ch. XI, note 7).

VOLUME I

CHAPTER I

1 *an assize-town*: Gaskell deliberately keeps the town anonymous, though she probably had in mind somewhere like Norwich, whose prosperity extended beyond the Tudor period well into the eighteenth century. The action's date is also vague. The action occupies not much over twelve years (Leonard's age at his next birthday, near the end of the story) and references bring its conclusion close to the novel's composition, in the early 1850s. The railway is firmly established, though Ruth's journey from Wales is by stagecoach (the two systems overlapped, but not for long); the election seems to be post-Reform Act (1832); and if the Queen's child (p. 104) is literally Victoria's, then that gives 1840 at the earliest. Yet Gaskell holds off contemporaneity; the novel opens 'now many years ago' and the tone is essentially of romance, implying temporal distance. Later, Eccleston, though a manufacturing town, is scarcely gripped by the industrialization of *Mary Barton* and *North and South*.

2 *Pitt's days of taxation*: in 1784, William Pitt increased (rather than invented, as often claimed) the tax on windows in houses; builders thereafter tended to restrain the number of windows.

3 *Monnoyer*: Jean-Baptiste Monnoyer (1634–99), a Frenchman noted for flower painting, worked in England.

4 *sandal ribbon*: ribbon for fastening a low shoe or slipper of a kind likely to be worn for dancing.

5 *pomps and vanities*: echoing the renunciation of worldly things ('the pomps and vanity of this wicked world') made by a child's godparents at baptism (see the Catechism in the Book of Common Prayer, response to the third question, and compare the Baptism Service). Gaskell uses such allusions lightly but with point to comment on the motives and responses of characters.

6 *the premium*: a payment for training when someone is first apprenticed or articled to a profession, whether law or medicine or a trade.

CHAPTER II

1 *satin pelisse*: a long mantle or cloak, lined with fur.

2 *the blue Persian*: either Persian silk, or Persian cord (a material for women's dresses, made of cotton and wool).

3 *siding away*: 'tidying up', 'putting away' (northern dialect).

4 *a craddy*: a challenge to perform a difficult or dangerous act.

5 *God watches over orphans*: the old woman's indignation seeks authority for her rebuff to Bellingham, rather than a precise quotation, but compare Psalms 10:14, 68:5, and 149:9. Throughout, Gaskell draws on the Bible and the Prayer Book, not least to create the Christian life of the Benson household and to enforce love and forgiveness. Often, Gaskell uses a biblical-sounding phrase or turn of style, though not quoting: such instances commonly underscore crucial points in the narrative and action; she is also capable of humorous allusions to the Bible, as with the Welsh inn's inhabitants crowding 'every window of the ark' (p. 54).

6 *out-goings and in-comings on working-days*: possibly echoing Ezekiel 43:11.

7 *Alnaschar visions*: proverbial for imagined future plans or prospects (usually on a large scale and dashed before they come into being); from Alnaschar, a beggar, in *The Arabian Nights' Entertainment* ('The Barber's Fifth Brother') who day-dreams of acquiring a vast fortune from his little stock-in-trade of glassware and so eventually marrying the Vizier's daughter; imitating how he will then spurn the Vizier, with his foot he overturns his whole stock and his vision collapses with its wreck.

CHAPTER III

1 *agaceries*: 'knowing behaviour', 'coquetry'.

2 *turkeys . . . among the nettles*: turkeys have a simple digestive system, unable to cope with highly fibrous plants like nettles.

3 *mines of Potosi*: South American mines, proverbial for their wealth (particularly in silver).

4 *the sure balm . . . the weary one home*: biblical in tone, though no specific quotations.

The Beautiful Messenger is, of course, death, and the 'weary one' echoes Job 3:17 (a favourite text of Gaskell's).

5 *a Mrs Brownrigg*: Elizabeth Brownrigg, a midwife, murdered her apprentice and was hanged in 1767; her name was proverbial for cruelty.

CHAPTER IV

1 *steeds galloping apace*: *Romeo and Juliet*, III.ii; Gaskell, reversing Juliet's desire for slow-seeming time to move more quickly, here insists on time's inexorable pace.

2 *my countenance, and my God*: Psalms 42:5 or rather, as Thomas is reading the Book of Common Prayer, 42:6–7, the version quoted.

3 *blood of all the Howards*: Alexander Pope (1688–1744), *An Essay on Man*, Epistle iv, 215; the reference, ironically enforcing Bellingham's aristocratic pride, comes when Pope is praising individual worth.

4 *oaken shovel-board*: or 'shove ha'penny' board. A polished board along which tokens or coins (halfpence) are propelled by a blow from the hand, the score depending on how the coins lie on the board.

5 *that is why I cry*: compare Gaskell's similar point in *Mary Barton*, ch. 22 (Penguin Classics, pp. 244–5).

6 *manty-maker's shop*: 'manty' was a colloquial form for mantua, a woman's loose gown; hence a dressmaker's shop.

7 *gigot sleeves*: or 'leg of mutton' sleeves, puffed out at the shoulders; fashionable in the 1830s, and outmoded by the 1840s, they were thought particularly absurd in the 1850s.

8 *whom he may devour*: I Peter 5:8.

9 *as man judgeth*: a proverbial version of I Samuel 16:7; 'wrestling for her soul' alludes to Jacob wrestling with the angel (Genesis 32:24–9).

10 *'the hill' of the hundred*: the hundred was an administrative unit of a county.

11 *dormer-windows*: projecting vertical windows in the sloping roof; presumably more secure against storms than skylights.

12 *such tents the patriarchs loved*: S. T. Coleridge (1772–1834), 'Inscription for a Fountain on a Heath', l. 2; the biblical sycamore is the Egyptian fig-tree.

13 *King Charles in the oak*: after the battle of Worcester (1651), Charles II escaped by hiding in an oak tree; hence the popular inn-sign (the Royal Oak).

CHAPTER V

1 *mountain village of North Wales*: Gaskell was familiar with the area around Snowdonia and the reference below (p. 55) to 'I have seen – but I shall see no more', oddly personal, is a possible memory of a visit in July 1845 to Ffestiniog and Portmadoc, during which her only son, Willie, died of scarlet fever.

2 *a Welsh car*: a wheeled vehicle or conveyance.

3 *whist-players . . . écarté . . . picquet . . . beggar-my-neighbour*: whist, a fashionable game, needs four people (or three and dummy); écarté and piquet, for two, are both games for gamblers; beggar-my-neighbour, regarded by Bellingham as lower class, is played for fun.

4 *There are . . . a holy strain repeat*: 'St Matthew' (stanza 4), from *The Christian Year* (1827) by John Keble (1792–1866); Gaskell quotes from memory.

5 *Riquet-with-the-Tuft*: the hunchbacked prince in the fairytale by Charles Perrault (1628–1703); he has the power of giving wit and the one he loves can give him beauty.

CHAPTER VI

1 *bridal of the earth and sky*: 'Virtue', from *The Temple* by George Herbert (1593–1633).

CHAPTER VII

1 *worn in a sick room*: its rustling sound would constantly disturb the invalid.

2 *the presence of the shadow of God*: perhaps echoing Psalms 91:1.

CHAPTER VIII

1 *dead in trespasses and sins*: Ephesians 2:1. The Fordham penitentiary, possibly linked to the workhouse, would like the Female Penitentiary in Manchester receive women who 'having deviated from the paths of virtue', were 'desirous to abandon their vicious courses, and to become qualified by virtue and industry, for reputable situations' (Edward Baines, *History, Directory and Gazatteer* [sic] *of the County Palatine of Lancaster*, 1825, II, 145).

2 *the shadow of death*: a common biblical phrase; Cruden's Concordance gives nineteen examples.

CHAPTER IX

1 *the syren waters*: the idea is proverbial, from the sirens in Homer's *Odyssey*, whose song tempts sailors to their destruction.

2 *What have I to do with Thee*: the cry to Jesus of the man possessed by a devil: Matthew 8:29 (where it is two demoniacs); Mark 1:24, Luke 4:34. The demons in Matthew enter the Gadarene swine and are destroyed by drowning.

3 *the still small voice*: the voice of God or inspiration, from I Kings 19:12; often taken to be some inner voice, as of conscience.

4 *It blesseth . . . and him that takes*: *The Merchant of Venice*, IV.i.

CHAPTER XI

1 *Facciolati*: Jacopo Facciolati (1682–1769) was an Italian lexicographer; the work referred to is probably his complete Latin lexicon (*Lexicon Totius Latinatus*) of 1771.

2 *Dim Saesoneg*: Benson's Welsh is so incomprehensible that the boy, baffled, declares he has 'No English'.

3 *seraph's powers of representation*: seraphs, six-winged and close to God (Isaiah 6:2), were associated with inspired speech (compare Thomas Gray, 'The Progress of Poety', iii.2, where Milton is imagined as writing *Paradise Lost*, inspired on 'the seraph-wings of Ecstasy').

4 *Doing good, hoping for nothing again*: Luke 6:35.

5 *put a blister on it*: blistering was a common nineteenth-century medical practice. The blister was raised by plasters of various substances, including Spanish fly, in the belief that the blister's fluid drew blood away from inflammation.

6 *sole power and potentate*: possibly echoing I Timothy 6:15.

7 *led the Magdalen aright*: Mary Magdalen is traditionally the sexually sinful woman whose forgiveness by Jesus led to her salvation after a life of penance. Both the tradition and its various threads in the Gospels are crucial to Gaskell's conception of Ruth. Mary Magdalen is named as a woman from whom Jesus had cast out seven devils; she was present at the crucifixion, found the tomb empty, and was the first to meet the risen Jesus (Matthew, 27, 28; Mark, 15, 16; Luke, 8, 24; John, 19, 20). She was later identified with the woman who anointed Jesus (Matthew 26:6ff.; Mark 14:3ff.; Luke 7:36ff.; John 12:1ff.), because John called her Mary, sister of Martha and Lazarus. In Luke's version (the key account for Gaskell), the woman is a sinner, which in later tradition clinched the idea of Mary Magdalen as a redeemed prostitute. The woman in Luke weeps, washes Jesus's feet with her tears, dries them with her hair, then anoints his feet. Jesus says, 'Her sins, which are many, are forgiven; for she loved much', and, to her, 'Thy faith hath saved thee; go in peace' (Luke 7:47, 50). Famous as a weeper ('maudlin' is derived from 'Magdalen'), Mary Magdalen is also the type of the fallen woman, while her forgiveness by Jesus makes her the type of the penitent, saved by love. Gaskell's difficulties over Ruth's guilt, forgiveness, and social restoration lie partly in the original complex figure of the Magdalen.

8 *blink all encounter*: 'to evade', 'to shirk' any encounter; 'blink at' was still grammatically improper in the mid nineteenth century.

9 *Cain-like look*: Cain, after his brother's murder, was marked by God (Genesis 4:13–15); the reference to 'his hand against every man's' properly belongs to Ishmael (Genesis 16:12). It is not clear for what situation Thomas Wilkins needed the baptismal certificate.

CHAPTER XII

1 *as if it were the Queen's*: if Faith is being specific, the reference dates the action at this point at the earliest to 1840, when Queen Victoria's first child was born.
2 *fall to the ground vain and useless*: perhaps echoing Matthew 10:29.
3 *much of her life had passed*: indicating the intensity and significance of Ruth's brief stay in Wales; compare Gaskell's comment in *Mary Barton* (ch. 11): 'For we have every one of us felt how a very few minutes . . . will sometimes suffice to place all time past and future in an entirely new light' (Penguin Classics, p. 131).
4 *amidst which Eccleston lies*: Gaskell seems to have no one place in mind for Eccleston; though apparently in Cheshire, its topographical surroundings are odd. Alan Shelston has argued persuasively for Macclesfield as the original, though it is not itself flat. Whatever else, Eccleston is not a recent industrial development like Manchester or the Milton Northern of *North and South*. Eccleston has its smoke cloud, but this is not specifically industrial (as it is in Milton Northern). There are some factories, but it is not highly industrialized; Benson's congregation has farmers, shop people, and the poor, but no factory hands. Though the labour interest is important later in the parliamentary election, no account is given of it, nor of the Irish population among which the fever is said to have begun.

CHAPTER XIII

1 *'trumpet's lordly blare'* . . . *of Abdallah*: quotation and allusion not traced.
2 *cap . . . the shape of a 'mutch'*: a close-fitting cap, worn by women and children.
3 *them that had gone astray*: biblical, with general reference to strayed sheep (Psalms 119:176 and Isaiah 53:6) and to the Good Shepherd (Matthew 18:12).
4 *a purer ether, a diviner air*: William Wordsworth (1770–1850), 'Laodamia', stanza 18; Gaskell quotes from memory.
5 *Who ask not . . . genial sense of youth*: Wordsworth, 'Ode to Duty', stanza 2. The Ode is echoed below in the reference to the law that governed the Benson household.
6 *God be merciful to me a sinner*: Luke 18:13.
7 *two widow's caps*: close-fitting caps, without ornament or decoration.
8 *Queen Eleanor . . . Fair Rosamond*: in legend Henry II kept his mistress, Fair Rosamond (Rosamond Clifford), hidden at Woodstock, but his wife Eleanor found her way in and presented Rosamond with poison; Thomas Percy, *Reliques of Ancient English Poetry* (1765) includes a ballad on the legend.
9 *mim*: 'proper', 'correct', 'primly silent or quiet'.

VOLUME II

CHAPTER XIV

1 *be farred*: 'be blowed!'

2 *th' overseer*: the parish officer responsible for poor-relief; since abandoned children became a charge on the parish, he was concerned that the parents should if possible be found.

3 *neat-tipped*: a tippet is a cape or muffler, often of fur, covering the shoulders.

4 *The chapel*: the building described by Gaskell closely resembles the Unitarian chapel at Knutsford, Cheshire, which she attended in her childhood. Built in 1689, it still stands in Brook Street (Gaskell and her husband are buried in the graveyard), though it is not obscurely tucked away as is the Eccleston chapel: see Nikolaus Pevsner, *Cheshire* (Buildings of England, 1971), p. 251; plate 56 shows the very similar Unitarian chapel at Wilmslow. Alan Shelston has pointed out that the situation of Benson's chapel fits well with the chapel at Macclesfield. While Benson's religious affiliations are never given, it is usually (and reasonably) assumed he is a Unitarian, a descendant like his chapel and congregation of the seventeenth-century Nonconformists (Puritans), many of whom evolved a more liberal theology from the Calvinism of their predecessors: see Angus Easson, *Elizabeth Gaskell*, pp. 4–12.

5 *the time of Matthew and Philip Henry*: Philip Henry (1631–96) and his son Matthew (1662–1714) were noted Nonconformists (Dissenters), Philip being fined after the Restoration for preaching. Matthew was also a minister and his *Biblical Commentary* was often reprinted. Gaskell indicates a time in the late seventeenth century and early eighteenth when Nonconformists were tolerated but still objects of suspicion to the Established Church of England. They were subject to measures designed to limit participation in public life and to restrict their control of education: see Gerald R. Cragg, *The Church and the Age of Reason 1648–1789* (1960; rev. ed. 1970), 'Restoration and Revolution in England 1660–1714'. In the later eighteenth century (see Gaskell's reference below to George III), with the achievement of full civil rights, many Dissenting chapels were enlarged and rebuilt.

6 *their 'white plains'*: unidentified.

7 *old Scottish paraphrase*: the metrical translation of the Psalms by the Englishmen Thomas Sternhold (d. 1549) and John Hopkins (d. 1570), adopted in Scotland in 1564 and used in England by Nonconformists.

8 *the Good Shepherd, in Poussin's beautiful picture*: Jesus, as the Good Shepherd (Matthew 18:12; John 10:11), carries back in his arms the lost or straying lamb to the fold; a favourite pictorial subject, though never painted by Nicolas Poussin (1594–1665).

9 *the Prodigal Son . . . to be called Thy child*: Luke 15:18–19, in the parable of the Prodigal Son.

CHAPTER XV

1 *as fringes to the garment*: only an incidental part of the main thing; the expression may be influenced by Numbers 15:38.

2 *Do unto others . . . should do unto you*: the answer is Jesus; see Luke 6:31, though the actual form of Faith's words is closer to that of the Catechism, answering the question, 'What is thy duty towards thy Neighbour?'

3 *found favour with him*: echoes a number of biblical passages, the most obvious of which would be Ruth 2:13.

4 *mithering*: 'bothering', 'worrying'.

5 *with innocent snow*: John Milton (1608–74), 'On the Morning of Christ's Nativity', l. 39.

6 *a wilderness of girls*: adapting *The Merchant of Venice*, III.i ('I would not have given it for a wilderness of monkeys').

7 *he was 'tormented in this flame'*: Dives (the rich man) in the parable of Dives and Lazarus, Luke 16:24; 'in his day and generation' is biblical in tone, but not a quotation.

8 *rushlight*: a candle, giving a feeble light, made by dipping the pith of a rush in tallow.

9 *beheld by the angels of little children*: Matthew 18:10.

CHAPTER XVI

1 *to lightly his offer*: 'to make light of', 'disdain', 'despise' his offer (dialect).

2 *leisure night in counting-houses*: though Saturday was a working day for most of the nineteenth century, business offices would finish work for the week early on that evening; household chores might continue into the night.

3 *pipeclaying the kitchen*: applying a paste of clay to give a clean white appearance to the hearthstones around the kitchen grate.

4 *a Methodee*: Sally, being Church of England, regards even former Methodists with suspicion. Only recently established as a separate church in the early nineteenth century, Methodists were noted, as enthusiasts, for extempore preaching and praying. On Methodism, see Gerald R. Cragg, *The Church and the Age of Reason 1648–1789*, 'Methodism and the Evangelical Revival'.

5 *gaupus*: 'silly person', 'simpleton'.

6 *blackleading the kitchen fire*: blacklead, graphite in a liquid base such as turpentine, was applied to the metalwork of grates and stoves to preserve it and give a glossy polish.

7 *song of Barbary Allen*: in the traditional song, beginning 'In Scarlet Town where I was born', Barbara Allen's scorn for Jemmy Gray's love kills him; she then dies of remorse.

8 *croup . . . typhus fever . . . burnt to ashes after*: croup is inflammation of the larynx and windpipe, to which children were liable and which was often fatal; typhus was common in poor sanitary conditions; and Miss Benson does not spare the danger from open fires.

9 *dance, ye merry men every one*: 'Dance, Thumbkin', a nursery song in which the thumb and each finger has a verse: see *The Oxford Dictionary of Nursery Rhymes*, ed. Iona and Peter Opie (1951), pp. 403–4.

10 *thole*: 'endure'.

11 *heavy puddings*: 'indigestible' puddings.

12 *travailing in the new birth*: Sally was in the labour pains of her personal conversion to Christ.

13 *please God to call me*: the last part of the answer to the question, 'What is thy duty towards thy Neighbour?'.

14 *locusts and wild honey*: John the Baptist's food in the desert (Matthew 3:4; Mark 1:6).

15 *that do with all thy might*: Ecclesiastes 9:10.

CHAPTER XVII

1 *to baptise infants*: Gaskell, while remaining ambiguous about Benson's exact sect, yet makes clear he is not a Baptist (who only baptize those who have reached the age of understanding).

2 *utterly schismatic*: all Dissenters can be called schismatic, as having seceded from the Church of England. Gaskell's treatment is lightly humorous, aware as she was that Unitarians, such as herself, by Sally's judgement were schismatic too.

3 *drouthy*: 'thirsty'.

4 *the right hand did*: alluding to Jesus's command; Matthew 6:3.

5 *Thine almighty blessing*: Benson's extempore prayer has strong biblical echoes, particularly of the parallel incident in Matthew 19:13–14, Mark 10:13–14, and Luke 18:15–16, which use both 'rebuked' and 'suffer' ('allow', 'permit').

6 *coucher*: the ceremony of going to bed; Gaskell uses humorously a word usually associated with the court ceremony of kings like Louis XIV.

7 *single knock, just like a beggar's*: while people of social standing or on official business might give a double knock (rat-tat), those whose standing was humble or who looked for favours knocked only once.

8 *Jemima, Kezia, and Keren-Happuch*: see Job 42:14.

9 *figured . . . the French wars*: 'figured away', from going through a set of steps in a dance, means 'played a part in', even 'made some name for himself'. The wars, given the novel's general setting, are likely to be those against Louis XIV, notable for the Duke of Marlborough's victories.

10 *Minerva Press*: run by William Lane in the 1790s and 1800s, the Minerva Press specialized in Gothic and Romantic fiction.

11 *the supper-tray*: an important feature of small evening parties. Supper, vital as a meal when dinner in the eighteenth century and amongst the old-fashioned in the early nineteenth century was taken at one or two in the afternoon, was less important as a substantial meal as dinner got later (five or six in the provinces, seven or eight in London and smart society). The arrival of the tray would also indicate that the evening was drawing to a close. See further Maggie Lane, *Jane Austen and Food* (1995) (on supper, in particular, pp. 51–4).

CHAPTER XVIII

1 *Upon a market-day*: 'The Derby Ram'; see *The Oxford Dictionary of Nursery Rhymes*, ed. Opie, pp. 145–6.

2 *Life let us cherish*: a lyric on life's transience from the German of the Swiss poet Johann Martin Usteri (1763–1827).

3 *southern-wood*: a kind of wormwood with scented leaves. Blackcurrant leaves (below) were put into a pot of India tea to make it taste like China tea.

4 *bees . . . forgot to tell 'em*: the belief that bees must be told of deaths lest they die or fly away is widespread, as is that of clothing the bees in mourning; in an 1837 example, 'a black crape scarf was appended to each hive'. See *A Dictionary of Superstitions*, ed. Iona Opie and Moira Taten (1989), entries 'Bees, news told to' and 'Bees take part in funeral/wedding'.

5 *Chancery*: the Court of Chancery's jurisdiction included disputes over wills and the property of those dying intestate. It was notoriously slow and expensive: Dickens had satirized its proceedings in *Bleak House* (1852–3).

6 *scomfish*: 'injure', 'do for'.

7 *run your rig*: 'go through your rigmarole, your patter'.

8 *I'm clipped of law*: 'deprived of my fair share', 'sold short' of law.

CHAPTER XIX

1 *spoileth the child*: Proverbs (traditionally written by Solomon) 13:24, 'He that spareth his rod hateth his son', from which comes the common saying.

2 *stones at a poor child*: Sally alludes to Jesus's rebuke over the woman taken in adultery: John 8:7.

3 *wait patiently upon God*: Psalms 37:7.

4 *old Bacchanalian carving*: the hop-leaf is similar in shape to that of the vine, the plant of Bacchus, god of wine.

5 *morn or dusky eve*: a version of Milton, *Paradise Lost*, I, 742–3 ('from morn / To noon . . . from noon to dewy eve').

6 *kept watch over Rizpah*: Rizpah's sons were hanged by the Gibeonites, having been handed over by order of King David (II Samuel 21). Rizpah watched by them day and night to keep off birds or beasts of prey (21:10).

7 *Thy will, not mine, be done*: Jesus's words during the Agony in the Garden; Luke 22:42 (compare Matthew 26:39, 42; Mark 14:36).

8 *Oh, mercy . . . Lucy should be dead*: Wordsworth, 'Strange fits of passion', l. 28.

CHAPTER XX

1 *to her desk*: a portable writing-desk or writing-box, which opens to give a writing slope and has space inside for ink-wells, stationery, and for keeping letters: see Leonee Ormond, *Writing* (1981), ch. 4, 'The Writing Desk'.

2 *pro Bradshaw, Farquhar, & Co.*: Elizabeth's idea of Farquhar produces a humorously incongruous mix of love and business formality ('pro' is 'on behalf of ').

3 *martingale*: a restraining strap on a horse's harness.

4 *by rule and line*: 'by precise measure of ruler and plumbline', 'by the book'.

5 *to pull out the mote*: Matthew 7:4; Luke 6:42.

6 *beauty of holiness*: the phrase is in I Chronicles 16:29; II Chronicles 20:21; Psalms 29:2, 96:9.

7 *quill up*: in quilling, a ribbon or strip of lace is 'gathered into cylindrical folds resembling a row of quills' (*OED*).

8 *pair of Limerick ones*: Limerick was a very fine leather, supposedly made from unborn calves.

9 *a rest and a support*: biblical in tone, though not a quotation.

10 *keeping a calm sough*: 'keeping quiet'.

11 *the bed-candle*: candles would be set out in the hall for the household to light and take on their way to bed.

12 *On revient . . . A ses premiers amours*: 'A man returns, always returns, to his first loves', a song from the opera *Joconde* (1814) by the composer Nicolò Isouard (1775–1818) and librettist Charles-Guillaume Étienne (1777–1845).

CHAPTER XXI

1 *get him some hock*: sprinkle the strawberries with sugar, mix them, and then sprinkle hock on them; best slightly chilled. Gaskell enjoyed strawberries when in Germany (*Letters of Mrs Gaskell*, ed. J. A. V. Chapple and Arthur Pollard, 1966, p. 44).

2 *a king's cushion*: a seat made by the crossed and clasped hands of two people.

3 *a portionless widow*: a widow without money or property in her own right or from her husband.

4 *more blessed to love than to be beloved*: adapting Acts 20:35 ('It is more blessed to give than to receive').

5 *Abermouth*: although said to be only 'twenty miles' from Eccleston, Gaskell probably draws on her visits to Silverdale on the Lancashire coast.

6 *electioneering purposes*: while Eccleston had returned a member to Parliament for centuries (Mr Cranworth's 'ancestors' point back that far), the proposed election takes place some time after the 1832 Reform Act; the Act extended the vote in boroughs (towns) to occupants of buildings valued at £10. Corruption, direct and indirect, only began to be checked in the 1850s, by legislation and by improved public standards. Traditionally, the Tory party, especially among landowners, was identified with the Church of England; the Liberal (Whig) party therefore attracted Dissenters and manufacturers.

7 *walked over the course*: 'there was no competition', 'they only needed to walk to win' (the metaphor is from horse-racing).

8 *did not quake prophetically*: 'failed to recognize the significance' (of the growing industrial interest). The priests of the Greek oracles shook when they were possessed by the god.

9 *pew-rent*: to secure one's seating in church or chapel and to guarantee the clergyman income (certainly in Benson's case), individuals or families paid rent, their name being displayed on the bench or pew.

10 *parliamentary agents*: men concerned with managing legislation through Parliament for private interests (e.g. railway companies) and conducting the campaigns of parliamentary candidates.

11 *the right of water*: Cranworth, as landowner, would have the control of water on his property, supplies of which were needed either as a source of power or in processes of washing and dyeing by the manufacturers.

12 *the Long Parliament*: elected in 1640, it opposed Charles I and directed the war against the King; dissolved by Cromwell in 1653, it only dissolved itself in 1660, opening the way to the Restoration. Pilson's invocation of membership in it as guarantee of the proposed candidate's soundness is decidedly tongue in cheek.

13 *member for the county*: it was common for a whole county to be represented by one or two members of Parliament. When a family was as confident of the voters as the Cranworths, they could expect anyone they put up as candidate to be equally ready to stand down when the next family member was of age and wished to take the borough (town) seat.

CHAPTER XXII

1 *since Julius Cæsar's time*: a typical Gaskell joke for 'time out of mind'; compare *Wives and Daughters*, ch. 4: 'I have heard that there were Hamleys of Hamley before the Romans' (Penguin Classics, p. 41).

2 *a briefless barrister*: a lawyer as yet without (or incapable of finding) cases to conduct in court. The sneer implies that Hickson is unable to find employment rather than that he has a sincere 'disgust to the law'.

3 *a high-priest style*: 'from a position of moral purity' (with overtones of being high-flown and pontificating).

4 *a hydra-headed monster*: in classical mythology the hydra had numerous heads; if one were cut off, two grew in its place. The reference that follows, to the rules of duelling by which opponents measure swords to make sure neither has unfair advantage, suggests Hickson's fondness for grandiloquent but mixed metaphors.

5 *administer the screw*: 'put the pressure on'; the metaphor is from torture with the thumbscrew.

6 *through evil to good*: though Farquhar does not support doing evil, his question reminds Benson of his lie to protect Ruth. The phrase is echoed below in Benson's 'aching remembrance of the evil he had done that good might come', itself a version of Romans 3:8.

7 *carte du pays*: 'the lie of the land'; literally, a map.

8 *coaching up*: 'getting up', 'cramming'.

9 *little birds sang west*: Elizabeth Barrett Browning (1806–61), 'Rhyme of the Duchess of May', l. 29.

10 *running waters all abroad*: possibly an echo of Wordsworth, 'Resolution and Independence' (stanzas 1 and 3: 'pleasant noise of waters'; 'distant waters roar').

11 *than a man's hand*: I Kings 18:44.

12 *to be at six*: in line with the fashionable dinner hour for the 1820s and 1830s; probably still rather early for London, if the novel's action is now somewhere in the mid 1830s to late 1840s. The children would have had their main meal about two or three.

13 *packets*: apparently in the modern sense of 'lots' of money (though the usage is not recorded by *OED* before 1922); with also an idea of the act being covert, the money being done up in packets.

14 *cold dinner on the Sundays*: requiring servants to cook would break the fourth commandment to keep holy the sabbath day.

15 *Volscians in Corioli*: *Coriolanus*, V.vi.

16 *cottoned*: 'took to'.

17 *all things under the sun*: alluding to Ecclesiastes; the wording is closest to 9:3, but Bradshaw's doubt matches best with 8:9 – 'All this have I seen, and applied my heart unto every work that is done under the sun.'

18 *had no pinery*: a hothouse for growing pineapples, a considerable luxury. The point nicely brings out Bradshaw's assumptions about his wealth (in affording to buy pineapples) and Donne's about his; it also tellingly reflects on the latter's insensitivity.

CHAPTER XXIII

1 *at the station*: another reminder of the action's date. Railways quickly spread after the 1830 opening of the first passenger line; the 1840s saw a particularly rapid expansion.

2 *deliver us from evil*: from the Lord's Prayer (e.g. Matthew 6:13; Luke 11:4).

3 *stormy wind fulfilling His word*: Psalms 148:8.

4 *my strong fortress . . . ask in His name*: two biblical quotations, the first occurring often: 'my rock and my fortress', Psalms 18:2, 31:3, 71:3 (and II Samuel 22:2); 'Whatsoever ye shall ask of the Father in my name, he may give it you', John 15:16 (compare 14:13–14). 'I of myself am nothing' is biblical in tone, but not a quotation.

5 *help in time of trouble*: Psalms 46:1.

6 *the Prince of Air*: Satan: see Ephesians 2:2.

7 *that long wick*: before the introduction of self-consuming wicks for candles, the wicks needed to be trimmed at intervals.

8 *Thy will be done*: again, from the Lord's Prayer.

9 *if he felt it not*: adapting *Hamlet*, III.iv ('Assume a virtue if you have it not').

10 *a Percy or a Howard*: the families of the Dukes of Northumberland and of Norfolk respectively; Bellingham links appearance with class.

11 *used-up*: 'exhausted of all emotion', 'worn out by previous indulgence in sensation', 'blasé'. Given as a quotation because it is slightly slangy and was the title of a play (1845) by C. J. Mathews.

12 *in the Prayer-book*: Bradshaw finds the Church of England service (as against Benson's dissenting chapel) confusing when he tries to follow the set forms of prayer and the service in the Book of Common Prayer.

13 *Light and Peace*: two key biblical words, often given separately to Jesus (the Light of the World, the Prince of Peace), but never in this collocation.

14 *for the remission of sins*: the General Confession in the Morning Prayer, 'to be said of [i.e. by] the whole Congregation'.

15 *of the first lesson*: a reading from an Epistle.

16 *from whence cometh our help*: Psalms 121:1.

17 *25th of September . . . St Matthew's Gospel*: the Book of Common Prayer provided that the New Testament should be read through three times over the course of the year, at Matins and at Evensong. Matthew 26 came round at Matins on 29 January, 28 May, and 25 September; its account of the Agony in the Garden is crucial to Ruth's spiritual crisis.

18 *from strength to strength*: Psalms 84:7; 'to be delivered from temptation', above, of course echoes the Lord's Prayer.

19 *His mercy endureth for ever*: Psalms 136:1.

20 *apt to get hypped*: 'suffer from hypochondria', 'get depressed'. 'Hypped' was a common (colloquial) term in the nineteenth century.

21 *dropping homewards*: walking casually or sauntering, rather than purposefully.

CHAPTER XXIV

1 *a beautiful 'alley'*: a marble.

2 *Christ was upon earth*: Ruth recalls, at this moment of crisis, Jesus's forgiveness of Mary Magdalen (Luke 7:36ff.); see also ch. XI, note 7.

3 *God is just*: a term commonly used of God: e.g. Deuteronomy 32:4; Isaiah 45:21.

4 *purple and yellow flowers*: appropriate as the colours of the Liberal (Whig) party.

5 *the true shield ... arrows of Death*: conflating a number of biblical references, including Ephesians 6:16 (shield and darts) and I Samuel 15:32 (bitterness of death).

VOLUME III

CHAPTER XXV

1 *green rushes ... process of oneiromancy*: oneiromancy is telling the future by the interpretation of dreams. Green is commonly regarded as an unlucky colour and a harbinger of death.

2 *A child whom all that looked on, loved*: Wordsworth, 'Six months to six years added': Gaskell quotes from memory.

3 *nigh unto death*: a reminiscence of Luke 7:12 (where Jesus brings back to life the widow's only son).

4 *'clave unto her'*: Ruth 1:14.

5 *would not rest in its grave*: an echo of *Macbeth*, III.ii, combined with Banquo's ghost.

6 *a rock ... where no shadow was*: Isaiah 32:2.

7 *gioventù dell'anno*: 'the youthfulness of the year'.

8 *took her into keeping*: 'took her under his protection'; a euphemism for 'made her his mistress'.

9 *Pharisee's dread of publicans and sinners*: the Pharisees were notable for their adherence to strict morality and the letter of God's law; in the New Testament they often express their contempt for publicans (tax-collectors) and sinners. See Jesus's parable of the Pharisee and the publican (Luke 18:10–14), which brings out the New Testament distinction, crucial to *Ruth*, between the letter that killeth and the Spirit that quickeneth. The point is enforced below in the reference to 'the Spirit that maketh alive'.

CHAPTER XXVI

1 *to creep up his sleeve* : 'to get into the good books of', 'to creep into the favour of'.

2 *scouted at* : 'scoffed at', 'rejected by'.

3 *longing, lingering look back* : Thomas Gray, 'Elegy in a Country Churchyard' (1750), l. 88; the idea of loss and parting is picked up below in 'played, regardless of their doom', quoting Gray's 'Ode on a Distant Prospect of Eton College' (1742), ll. 51–2.

4 *the 'Delectus'* : a schoolbook by Richard Valpy (1744–1836), author of classical textbooks and grammars. The reference is either to his Latin grammar of 1816 or his anthology of thoughts and stories (*Delectus Sententiarum et Historiarum*) of 1800.

5 *it is wantonness* : Bradshaw probably has no particular biblical text in mind, but II Peter 2 suggests wantonness as an inclusive sin.

6 *the viper – even into the fire* : in Acts 28:3–5, when Paul was shipwrecked on Melita (Malta).

CHAPTER XXVII

1 *reproachful names by men* : echoing Matthew 5:11.

2 *to Mary Magdalen* : Luke 7:36ff.; see ch. XI, note 7.

3 *without routing after* : 'without running about after'.

4 *some naught* : 'some worthless person'.

5 *to stand and wait* : Milton, Sonnet: 'When I consider how my light is spent'.

6 *as by fire . . . for your feet* : Benson primarily invokes Hebrews 12; in particular, verse 29 declares God to be 'a consuming fire', while verse 13 commands the making of 'straight paths for your feet'.

7 *Ask, and it shall be given unto you* : Matthew 7:7; Luke 11:9.

8 *shandry* : a light cart or trap on springs.

9 *magnum-bonums* : large yellow cooking plums.

CHAPTER XXVIII

1 *accepted her penance* : echoing Leviticus 26:41.

2 *closed over her place* : echoing Job 7:10 and Psalms 103:16.

3 *a pillar of fire* : alluding to God as a pillar of fire by night (Exodus 13:21), leading the Jews out of Egypt; so Leonard leads Ruth through a metaphorical wilderness to a Promised Land.

4 *at Baden* : the fashionable health spa in Germany; the implication might well be that he was cheating at the casino.

5 *a complete blackleg* : a swindler in any form of gambling.

CHAPTER XXIX

1 *He that is low need fear no fall*: *The Pilgrim's Progress*, pt 2, in the Valley of Humiliation.

2 *ends of list*: remnants of cloth.

3 *it was yet day*: John 9:4; i.e. while he was still alive, for 'the night cometh, when no man can work'.

4 *nattered*: 'peevish', 'grumbling'.

5 *cribbing a sovereign*: 'to crib' is 'to steal' or 'to take furtively'.

6 *last Martinmas*: the feast of St Martin, 11 November, the traditional date in England for hiring servants and hence for revising wages.

7 *on the other side*: Luke 10:31, 32; the parable of the Good Samaritan.

CHAPTER XXX

1 *receipt on a stamp*: in the nineteenth century (and later) a tax had to be paid if a receipt was to be legally valid. The tax was paid by a stamp being stuck on the form and cancelled by a signature written across it.

2 *the fetch*: the double or identical form.

3 *must prosecute Richard*: where the injury was personal, the individual had to bring the prosecution: as Byron did in 1806, on discovering a servant had been robbing him (*In My Hot Youth: Byron's Letters and Journals, 1798–1810*, ed. Leslie A. Marchand, 1973, pp. 100, 116).

4 *as a stranger to me*: 'stranger' is commonly used in the Bible to distinguish those who are not Jews. Bradshaw declares his son to be cast off from him; Gaskell would be aware of the irony, in Bradshaw's adherence to the letter rather than the spirit, that many biblical references to strangers urge fellowship between them and Jews.

CHAPTER XXXI

1 *as the nether mill-stone*: Job 41:24.

CHAPTER XXXII

1 *When the devil was sick, the devil a monk would be*: from the medieval Latin; generally known in the couplet: 'The Devil was sick; the Devil a monk would be; / The Devil was well; the devil a monk he'd be.' The sense of penitence in adversity, forgotten in prosperity, is neatly caught in the idiomatic use of 'the devil'.

CHAPTER XXXIII

1 *typhus fever*: a continuous fever, the patient becoming very weak and delirious; breaking out, in later stages, with purple spots. Those weakened by poor diet and hard labour were most liable to it. Typhus was highly contagious, especially where there was poor sanitation and overcrowding. Sudden changes of temperature (see below, in this chapter) were also thought likely to bring it on.

2 *fiery time*: alludes to the miraculous preservation of Shadrach, Meshach, and Abed-nego in the fiery furnace (Daniel 3). Daniel is picked up in the reference below to Belshazzar, who saw at a great feast the writing on the wall, which prophesied his death (Daniel 5).

3 *proud rejoicing of the nation*: the reference is deliberately vague; 'proud rejoicing' may be a further allusion to Belshazzar's feast.

4 *accepted a Government office*: when an MP was appointed to a parliamentary post under the government, he was required to stand for re-election. Normally, such a bye-election would be a formality, the MP being returned unopposed.

5 *Irish lodging-houses*: while the presence of Irish labour in towns predated the 1840s influx of the famine years, the reference seems more appropriate to the date (early 1850s) of the novel's composition.

6 *that lazar-house*: originally, in the Middle Ages, for lepers; by transference, any kind of isolation hospital or ward. Gaskell deliberately uses an archaic term to enforce the sense of plague in Eccleston.

7 *object to the smell*: because the flowers 'greatly injure the purity of the air during the night' by giving out carbon dioxide (Thomas Andrew, *Domestic Medicine*, 1849, 'Ventilation').

8 *her right hand did*: Matthew 6:3.

9 *called her blessed*: Proverbs 31:28.

CHAPTER XXXIV

1 *in the lobby*: in the hallway.

2 *trig*: 'spruce', 'smart'.

3 *the three counties*: a general phrase, for 'all round about'; no specific counties are meant.

CHAPTER XXXV

1 *all watch – and pray*: echoes Matthew 26:41 and Mark 13:33, 14:38.

2 *and take her wages*: *Cymbeline*, IV.ii.

3 *fingers fell idly on the bed*: Ruth's songs and the movement of her fingers suggest Gaskell may be drawing on the pathos of Ophelia's madness and on Falstaff's death (*Henry V*, II.iii).

4 *refusing to be comforted*: Jeremiah 31:15.

CHAPTER XXXVI

1 *frabbed you*: 'to harass', 'to worry'.

2 *Almost as soon as . . . with* her *child*: this passage was omitted by Gaskell from the second edition (1855); presumably because it is repeated, more effectively, in the concluding graveyard scene.

3 *who stood afar off*: Luke 17:12 (the reference is to lepers, who were physically outcasts; by transference, Gaskell refers to moral outcasts).

4 *Revelations . . . at the ninth verse*: the chapter describes the blessed who worship about the Lamb; Gaskell quotes verses 14–17.

READ MORE IN PENGUIN

In every corner of the world, on every subject under the sun, Penguin represents quality and variety – the very best in publishing today.

For complete information about books available from Penguin – including Puffins, Penguin Classics and Arkana – and how to order them, write to us at the appropriate address below. Please note that for copyright reasons the selection of books varies from country to country.

In the United Kingdom: Please write to *Dept. EP, Penguin Books Ltd, Bath Road, Harmondsworth, West Drayton, Middlesex UB7 ODA*

In the United States: Please write to *Consumer Sales, Penguin USA, P.O. Box 999, Dept. 17109, Bergenfield, New Jersey 07621-0120.* VISA and MasterCard holders call 1-800-253-6476 to order Penguin titles

In Canada: Please write to *Penguin Books Canada Ltd, 10 Alcorn Avenue, Suite 300, Toronto, Ontario M4V 3B2*

In Australia: Please write to *Penguin Books Australia Ltd, P.O. Box 257, Ringwood, Victoria 3134*

In New Zealand: Please write to *Penguin Books (NZ) Ltd, Private Bag 102902, North Shore Mail Centre, Auckland 10*

In India: Please write to *Penguin Books India Pvt Ltd, 706 Eros Apartments, 56 Nehru Place, New Delhi 110 019*

In the Netherlands: Please write to *Penguin Books Netherlands bv, Postbus 3507, NL-1001 AH Amsterdam*

In Germany: Please write to *Penguin Books Deutschland GmbH, Metzlerstrasse 26, 60594 Frankfurt am Main*

In Spain: Please write to *Penguin Books S. A., Bravo Murillo 19, 1° B, 28015 Madrid*

In Italy: Please write to *Penguin Italia s.r.l., Via Felice Casati 20, I–20124 Milano*

In France: Please write to *Penguin France S. A., 17 rue Lejeune, F–31000 Toulouse*

In Japan: Please write to *Penguin Books Japan, Ishikiribashi Building, 2–5–4, Suido, Bunkyo-ku, Tokyo 112*

In South Africa: Please write to *Longman Penguin Southern Africa (Pty) Ltd, Private Bag X08, Bertsham 2013*

READ MORE IN PENGUIN

A CHOICE OF CLASSICS

Matthew Arnold	**Selected Prose**
Jane Austen	**Emma**
	Lady Susan/The Watsons/Sanditon
	Mansfield Park
	Northanger Abbey
	Persuasion
	Pride and Prejudice
	Sense and Sensibility
William Barnes	**Selected Poems**
Anne Brontë	**Agnes Grey**
	The Tenant of Wildfell Hall
Charlotte Brontë	**Jane Eyre**
	Shirley
	Villette
Emily Brontë	**Wuthering Heights**
Samuel Butler	**Erewhon**
	The Way of All Flesh
Lord Byron	**Selected Poems**
Thomas Carlyle	**Selected Writings**
Arthur Hugh Clough	**Selected Poems**
Wilkie Collins	**Armadale**
	The Moonstone
	No Name
	The Woman in White
Charles Darwin	**The Origin of Species**
	Voyage of the *Beagle*
Benjamin Disraeli	**Sybil**
George Eliot	**Adam Bede**
	Daniel Deronda
	Felix Holt
	Middlemarch
	The Mill on the Floss
	Romola
	Scenes of Clerical Life
	Silas Marner

READ MORE IN PENGUIN

A CHOICE OF CLASSICS

READ MORE IN PENGUIN

A CHOICE OF CLASSICS

Thomas Hardy	**Desperate Remedies**
	The Distracted Preacher and Other Tales
	Far from the Madding Crowd
	Jude the Obscure
	The Hand of Ethelberta
	A Laodicean
	The Mayor of Casterbridge
	A Pair of Blue Eyes
	The Return of the Native
	Selected Poems
	Tess of the d'Urbervilles
	The Trumpet-Major
	Two on a Tower
	Under the Greenwood Tree
	The Well-Beloved
	The Woodlanders
Lord Macaulay	**The History of England**
Henry Mayhew	**London Labour and the London Poor**
John Stuart Mill	**The Autobiography**
	On Liberty
William Morris	**News from Nowhere** and **Other Writings**
John Henry Newman	**Apologia Pro Vita Sua**
Robert Owen	**A New View of Society and Other Writings**
Walter Pater	**Marius the Epicurean**
John Ruskin	**Unto This Last and Other Writings**
Walter Scott	**Ivanhoe**
	Heart of Mid-Lothian
	Old Mortality
	Rob Roy
	Waverley